It is all-consuming you when you find the person who just fits with you. There is no contemplation. No guessing. No wondering. There is just you and them. Everyone and everything else in your life sits around you like a circle you're in the center of. That other person, your love, your counterpoint, they are always there with you, in the center. Holding you there like gravity, just as a daisy holds onto its petals.

Maddy C. James

Layout & Formatting: Lakehouse WC

Cover Design: Jassa H

Editor Sage Santiago, edit October 2023

ISBN - Paperback: 979-8862276855

Second edition; September 2023

Website: https://authormaddyjames.wixsite.com/authormaddyjames

This story is fictional in nature. All characters and places are made up figments of my imagination, formed while dreaming or drinking chai lattes sitting on my porch.
2023 Maddy James
All rights reserved.

SOMETHING IN THE TEXAS SUN

Book One

HENNESSEY RIDGE RANCH

(VINTAGE SPECIAL EDITION COVER)

Author's note:

This story is for all my country lovers who have always wanted a gritty cowboy. One who can hold his own in the field and the bedroom. He has a heart of gold with blackened edges and a dirty mouth, and he looks at you like you're the only one on the face of the earth. Yee haw.

SOMETHING IN THE TEXAS SUN
Nick & Kate's fireside playlist

1. Help Me Make it Through The Night- Tyler Childers
   Take the ribbon from your hair, shake it loose and let it fall...
2. Last Night- Morgan Wallen
   I can't remember everything we said, but baby we said it all...
3. Vincent Black Lightning 1952- Logan Halstead
   And I've seen you on the corners and cafes it seems...
4. Feeling Whitney Post Malone
   *And I've been looking for someone to put up with all my bullsh*t...*
5. Can't Help Falling In Love -Amber Irish
   Darling so it goes, some things are meant to be....
6. Never was Mine -JR Carroll
   You'd tell me all about Texas, bout the place you've been spending your time...
7. Something In The Orange- Zach Bryan
   I need to hear you say you've been waiting all night....
8. Space and Time-SG Goodman
   I never wanna leave this world, without saying I love you...
9. Only God can Judge me- 2Pac
   Is it a crime to fight for what is mine...?
10. Cowboys and Angels –Jessie Murph
    Like whiskey and fire...bad reputation that you can't deny...
11. All Over Again- Luke Combs
    I'd start going through withdrawals, that's about the time you'd call and we'll be falling all over again.
12. Lady May- Tyler Childers
    But I am baptized in your name...lovely lady may

WARNINGS:

This story is spicy in nature and intended for 18+ with descriptive, open door sexual content and contains discussions of addiction, death, alcohol abuse and the struggle to stay sober. I trust you know what you're comfortable with.

Chapter 1 - The Call
Katie

My grandmother used to say a woman's fate begins on the very day she least expects it... I never imagined she would be right.

"Can anyone tell me the absolute, definitive way to tell the difference between bamboo and double brushed polyester just by feel alone?"

I sketched in my notebook as usual, absorbing nothing from the lecture as my professor droned on about fabrics while I waited for my nine o'clock class to end. My second year was quickly shaping up to be as painful as my first, and I honestly hated it. I just couldn't tell a soul yet, not even my dad.

I would finish what I started and graduate because the alternative meant admitting I was wrong about New York, and I'm not the best at admitting I'm wrong about anything. I'm the one who sticks things out until the painful end, even if it kills me. It wasn't the city's fault. New York is incredible. Overwhelming, but incredible. But I felt like an outsider, like the entire city saw me as a simple, straight-laced—or dull, as my sister Charlotte would call me—rancher's daughter from Hays County, Texas. The fact that I was ready to give it all up told me that maybe the city and Charlotte were both right.

My Aunt Tracey's smiling face flashing across the lock screen of my phone sent my heart into my stomach. I knew. I just *knew* something awful had happened.

"Aunt Trace?" I half whispered the words into my phone as I scrambled up out of my seat, trying to get into the hallway to speak freely. I was clumsy at the best of times, but in an emergency, it really wasn't pretty. I tripped my way out of the aisle, cursing under my breath as my shin smacked the chair beside me. Aunt Tracey's crying carried through the phone, filling my chest with dread.

"Katie... baby, it's your dad. He was... he was hurt today." I stood there, not knowing what to do, frozen and waiting for the details to come.

"What do you mean? Where is he?" I tried to swallow through the dryness of my mouth and thick tears of panic already filled my eyes. Everything was going blurry.

Her words came out jumbled. "I'm so sorry to tell you this, honey, but he's pretty banged up, mostly his leg, I think. I don't know, it was... Well, I'm not exactly sure. They're taking him to Austin."

"What? What *happened?*" My frantic, high-pitched voice sounded foreign in my own head. The seconds seemed endless while I waited for her to gather her thoughts so she could tell me more.

"It was the tractor." She breathed deeply, attempting to escape her sob. "It flipped over on him while he was driving it. I don't know how, but Uncle Roger was there. He called the paramedics."

Nope, no way, not possible. My dad learned how to drive a tractor when he was five years old. There was not a chance in hell he flipped it or lost control of it. He was a fifth generation Hennessey. My dad could operate a tractor in his sleep, blindfolded, and sitting backwards. I started walking with no actual destination in mind, I just knew I had to move my body. As impossible as it seemed, I could feel that it was true, and I had to get to him immediately.

"I'm coming." I moved frantically through the crowded halls, juggling my bag, my iPad, and my water bottle.

"I'll call you back as soon as I get a flight." I hung up and pulled up the airline's website on my phone, trying to concentrate as I searched for available flights and the phone number to call for last-minute seats. The only coherent thought in my mind was *Not again, please...*

Chapter 2 - It all went to shit.
Katie

Two hours and forty-five minutes later, I sat in a standby seat on a flight headed for Austin. I didn't even know what I'd packed in my carry on. The time between leaving the school and boarding the plane was a total blur. My aunt would pick me up at the airport to take me directly to the hospital as soon as I landed. She'd told me my dad was going into surgery immediately. Even with the four-hour flight, if I was lucky, I would be there when he woke up. His right leg had been completely crushed. The repair would be extensive, but it was possible. He also had some broken ribs and had a fractured wrist. There was no internal damage that they could see.

The doctors said he was lucky, and when my aunt called to tell me right before I boarded, I sobbed tears of joy. I couldn't bear the thought of losing more of them. I lost my mom, Vanessa, when I was seven. Killed in a car accident. No drunk driver. No reason. She was simply there one minute and not there the next. Her nightshirt still lay on her bed, her sandals at the front door, but she was gone.

She did the accounting for a neighboring ranch near Austin and had made the drive a thousand times. She hit a median on her way home and died on impact. It wasn't even a long drive. Our family's land, all one hundred and sixty-five thousand acres of it, sits just outside of Reeds Canyon, Texas, southwest of Austin. My dad, Daniel Hennessey, is one of the largest cattle ranchers in central Texas. Our family has raised the same generational cattle lines since 1890 on our ranch, Hennessey Ridge. We had a lot of space for my mom to work at home, but she didn't want to. She wanted her own thing. Working for Tom and Stella Harris on their ranch seemed like a good fit. It took me four years to look at them after she died. In my little mind, they were to blame.

My dad never talked about it. He never re-married, and he talked about *her* often but never her death. It was as if not talking about it made less real. Like she was just gone for a while instead of forever.

As the plane taxied down the runway, I put my headphones over my ears and leaned my head back against the seat, thinking of home. The ranch is my favorite place in the world, even though I've only gone back once since leaving for New York two and a half years ago. *Once.* The weight of that sat heavy on my shoulders as I watched the ascent through my window.

Going home meant I would definitely have to see my other loss, Nick Stratton. I've done a great job of avoiding him for almost five years. It truthfully wasn't even hard. He wasn't around and he wasn't the same person I knew when we were young. My Aunt Tracey said he fell from grace, whatever that means. He didn't fall. He dove, right in to a life I couldn't understand.

When we were kids, Nick was like my best friend. His mom and dad were my parent's closest friends and neighbors. "Closest" being fourteen miles down the road. We were always thrust together, so we grew close over the years. Almost every day after school, he would be there. He'd have my horse saddled and we'd ride through my property, racing, climbing the trees, picking on each other, and getting into as much mischief as humanely possible. Mostly it was Nick creating the mischief and me going along with whatever he said or did. As we got older, we'd sit under the live oaks, sometimes just in silence. He'd read, and I'd sketch outfits while we ate snacks. He made me laugh. He protected me. He knew all my secrets. When my mom died he was there for me, and continued to be long after that. I was younger than him by two years and hung onto his every word. I'd never admit it now, but back then I looked up to him.

Then it all went to shit.

The night his dad told him he had cancer, we went out for a ride. I was fourteen. He was distraught, distant, scared, and not himself. We rode back to the main house. Standing there, on the back porch in the dark, I looked up at him and tried to make him feel better. I told him it would all be okay, somehow. He closed the space between us and kissed me, unexpectedly, incredibly. I had never kissed anyone before, but I knew he had.

He had a different girlfriend every other week. He played football back then and was working his way through the cheerleaders at his high school. For me, that kiss was sheer bliss. I hadn't realized the depth of my feelings for him until it happened. When he pulled away, he told me it was a mistake. I was utterly humiliated.

Things became awkward between us. He stopped coming around the ranch, his dad went into the hospital, and his mom continued her path of self-destruction. I tried to reach out to him, but he just blew me off most of the time, saying he was busy. I never understood why or what I did wrong. Finally, after a year of trying, crying, and self-doubt, I gave up on him and made a plan to get out of there. I chose to go as far as I could, where he wouldn't haunt me. New York City and F.I.T sounded perfect for my creative soul.

My dad shocked me and hired Nick full-time the spring I left for New York. The last I'd heard, he was in no shape to work for anyone, but my dad always said everyone deserves a second chance. He'd always liked Nick. To welcome him, my dad gifted him his own American Quarter named King. Apparently, Nick was ready to give his all to the ranch and start fresh.

I'd thought about reaching out to him, but by then too much time had passed. I didn't understand the person he was anymore, and I was leaving anyway. I watched that horse come off the trailer, though. King was so strong and beautiful, perfect for Nick. At least the Nick I knew in another life.

So that was it. I left without a word to him and he moved onto the ranch. When I was home in the summer, I heard he was doing very well. He moved up in position to first lead under Frank Gibson, our head cowboy or "cow boss" who was second generation on our ranch. He was grooming Nick for when his time came to retire.

For the first time in a long time, in the quiet hum of being in the air, I closed my eyes and let myself think of home, my dad, and all I had missed over the last couple of years. My mind went to Nick when we were young. What his eyes looked when he talked about something he was interested in or knew a lot about. His laugh that was so contagious it always made me laugh with him. How he looked the night he kissed me. His hand on my face and his lips were the last thing I remember thinking about as I drifted to sleep, before I even got through an episode of *Friends*.

Chapter 3 - Leather and Spice
Katie

The pilot announcing our approaching landing woke me out of a dead sleep. I must have been out for most of the flight. I looked at my unresponsive phone, praying silently that my dad's surgery was going well. When the city came into view, my mind was full of the next steps. I was a planner, so I couldn't help it. My dad would need my help to heal, and that was a very good reason for me to take a much-needed break from my New York life. I would talk to my uncle about it first, and then my dad in a couple of days. I needed this for more reasons than one. Time to breathe, collect my thoughts, plan for the future. I just hoped he'd agree.

When I came out of the gate, my phone came alive with two missed phone calls from my aunt and one message.

Aunt Trace: *He's out of surgery, doing great and heading to recovery. It went very well the doctor is pleased.*

I didn't bother to listen to the voicemails. That information was all I needed to know. My eyes filled with tears, blurring my vision for the tenth time that day. I promised myself I'd get to the safety of the truck before I let my tears fall. I didn't want to have a breakdown alone outside of baggage claim. I looked around for my aunt quickly but I didn't see her anywhere. I headed outside before calling, knowing with the day she'd had that it was possible she was just late.

I navigated through the crowd, searching and pulling out my phone. I stepped into the fresh air of a gloomy fall day and sought out my uncle's gray Ford pickup truck. It was nowhere to be found. The door of an older black Dodge Ram shut in front of me.

"Katelyn..." A deep and somewhat familiar voice called my full name. I turned to meet it and my breath hitched. I found myself staring directly into the past that I'd run from.

Nick.

He came quickly to me, but I didn't move. I couldn't. *Holy hotness.*

He'd changed a lot in the last three years. He stood well over a foot taller than me, at least six-foot-four, and he was so gorgeous it stunned me, leaving me frozen in place. He wasn't polished or pretty. He was just...masculine. Solid. Almost rough around the edges. Growing into your looks, that is a real thing, let me tell you.

I took it all in, his chiselled features, his strong cheekbones and jaw. His skin, smooth and slightly tanned from years in the sun. Even though he wasn't smiling, I could see the outline of his dimples that always made an appearance when he did. His dark chestnut hair, thick, wavy, and a little longer than I remembered, poked out slightly from under his Hennessey Ridge baseball hat. He's what a man would look like if a Roman god and a rugged cowboy had a baby. Years of hard physical labor had left his body powerful and defined, with wide shoulders and strong arms. As he pulled my bag from me, I could see every muscle under his skin contract, highlighting a smattering of tattoos covering his entire left arm. He looked like he had been through a particularly tough day. He was dusty and dirty from head to toe, but that didn't take away from his appeal. In fact, it added to it and served to heighten the cowboy aura that surrounded him. Above all else it was his eyes, wide and the color of green tourmaline, that had my attention now as they always had, hovering over me like deep pools. Focused only on my face, taking me in. Unwavering and fervent as he spoke again.

"Let's go."

His words snapped me from my ogling and caused me to flinch. He certainly knew I had been staring at him. All I could do was nod and try to recover with standard questions.

"Why did they send you? Where's my aunt?" I followed him to his truck.

He spoke without breaking stride in a calm, deep voice. "She told me she'd let you know I was coming. She's at the hospital. She had to meet with the doctor after the surgery. Roger had to meet with the labor inspector about your dad's accident. Get in and I'll take you to her." His tone was terse, as if he was annoyed that he had to be the one to pick me up.

He opened the back door of his crew cab and placed my bag on the seat beside his cowboy hat, which I imagined always stayed close. He reached in front of me to open the passenger door, causing me to notice how the veins ripple in his hands as he gripped the handle.

I looked up and realized, looking into the dark tint of his truck window, that I was a mess. I hadn't even looked at myself since heading to class that morning. I wore tights and a t-shirt with a big, gray hoodie tied around my waist. My long, muted blonde hair was piled into a messy, uneven bun on the top of my head, and it was obvious I had been crying, a lot. My eyes were puffy with mascara hiding under them.

I did what he said and got right into his truck, only because his tone told me not to object. The most delicious scent of leather and spices washed over me, momentarily stunning me. I welcomed it, then managed to straighten up before he got in beside me. He said nothing as the truck roared to life. He pulled his hat off, running a hand through his hair, and threw it on the back seat. I knew instantly as his arm sailed past me where the heavenly leather and spice originated from. It was him. He smelled incredible.

"Katelyn?" I looked up into those eyes and felt my stomach drop into my feet. "Your seatbelt…"

I nodded and fumbled to do it up as he pulled out of the loading zone.

The way he said my name differently than anyone else always brought me back to our younger years together. Everyone called me Katie or Pixie. No one called me Katelyn except him, or my dad if I was in trouble.

He turned his playlist up. It offered me Luke Combs and Zach Bryan as we made the short drive to Dell Seton. A few minutes of easy silence passed.

"Have you heard anything else?" I asked, my voice meek and nervous as we turned onto the highway. This was the first time we had been really alone together since *that* night. It was the strangest, most surreal sensation.

"I just know what you know. He's out of surgery and doing well."

His brow was furrowed and his jaw tense as he spoke, like he was tormented by my simple existence. Tears started coming, but I fiercely pushed them down. I would not cry in his truck. I would not cry in front of him. I gulped and focused out the front window.

"He's really strong. He'll be fine."

I nodded instead of speaking, not chancing the sobs trying desperately to escape.

When we pulled up to the hospital, I turned to grab my bag and unbuckle myself. By the time I had it done, he was already at my door, opening it. He stood over me, waiting.

My Aunt Tracey came rushing out. She looked like hell, but so did I. Her wispy blonde hair was tucked behind her ears and she had mascara shadows under her eyes just like me. She hugged Nick. "Thank you, love, for bringing her."

Nick pulled away and patted her hand. "No problem. How's he doing now?"

That should've been my question, not his.

"He's not awake yet, but the doctors are happy with how it went." She sighed. "What a day this has been."

She turned her focus to me, putting both hands on either side of my face. "He'll be glad to see you though, Pixie. I called you. Did you get my message about Nick coming?"

I nodded, no sense in telling her I didn't and that I was totally blindsided.

Nick's eyes bore into me. He knew I wasn't telling her the truth. He backed up to give us some space. Some small compartment of my brain mourned that his delicious scent went with him.

"Okay well, I'll head back to give Roger a hand then. Keep me posted okay, Trace?" He looked to me, stunning me once again with his eyes and what was behind them.

"See ya…" were his only words as he turned to leave. I headed into the hospital with my aunt, but his eyes stayed with me all the way up to my dad's room.

Chapter 4 - Something In The Texas Sun
Katie

Eight days, about a hundred phone calls, too many boxes into storage, three broken nails, and a lot of takeout later, I stepped through the airport doors for the second time that month and into the warm November breeze. The air felt different, buzzing and sweet. There's something in the Texas sun that just pulls you in and makes you never want to leave.

I inhaled deeply. I was heartbroken my dad's injury was the reason I came home, but another more prominent feeling made my guilt resurface. Relief.

I popped my sunglasses on. I'd missed the incessant warmth of home that lingered even through the winter months. I felt very over dressed in my coat and jeans from New York. It was a perfectly sunny seventy-two degrees and everyone around me wandered happily to their destinations in t-shirts.

My dad had just returned home from the hospital. The doctors were pleased to say he would make a full recovery, albeit a slow one. The majority of the damage was done to his knee, so they had managed to provide him with a brand new one. I went back to New York after his surgery and began packing up my life. It went much faster than I expected. Now, I was home to stay. At least for a while.

Fortunately, my Uncle Roger waited to take me home instead of Nick. He was grateful I had agreed to stay for a few months. He and my aunt had their own farm, an extension of our ranch, where they grew pecans, wildflowers, and corn. Aunt Tracey was also an expert beekeeper and her honey graced the shelves of almost every grocer and farmer's market in the surrounding three counties.

They knew that out of all the girls, theirs included, I was the only one that *would* come. Charlotte was too young and a little too self-absorbed to do anything for anyone, unless it benefitted her of course. It had to be me.

My dad already had a great staff in place, so he didn't really *need* my help at all, but he had a knack for understanding my problems before I even did. I wondered if he knew I was ready to come home, or that I needed a break. When he woke up in the hospital and saw me there, I offered and he didn't hesitate, telling me he "could really use my help."

"Hey, Pixie." Uncle Roger smiled, his eyes crinkling in the corners. He looked so much like my dad. He swallowed me up into a giant bear hug. They *all* call me pixie—I'm fairly small as far as physical size goes. I tell people I'm five-foot-two, but I am more like five-foot-one on a good day if I'm being honest. When I was young, it started with my mom calling me the little fairy that lived in her garden. She claimed I was tiny and never inside. Somehow that turned to Pixie and it stuck.

Uncle Roger is a big man, at least three times my size, as all the Hennessey men are. We've always had an easy relationship. I feel as comfortable with him as I do my own dad.

"How is he today?"

He chuckled at my question, pulling up his hat and rubbing his forehead. "Well, you know him, he's as stubborn as a bull and telling everyone what to do. He's frustrated that he can't just jump out of bed yet and head into the field."

I nodded in agreement. *Sounds about right.*

We drove along through the countryside that has my heart. This wasn't how I saw my future when I left for New York, but I forced myself to remember my dad's words. "Life doesn't always give us the option for change, and sometimes we have to just go with it." God, I love him. He's truly my best friend and I have always been his. Of course, he loves Charlotte, but they've never been as close as we are. Losing him was never even on my radar until two weeks ago, and it scared the shit out of me.

We pulled up to the house just before dinnertime. I savored to the familiar sound of gravel crunching under our tires as we made our way down the long driveway. Our house looks like it grew out of the earth it's been there for so long, the bottom three feet is stone and the rest is old, rustic log wall, pitted together with Texas mortar over a hundred years ago and filled as the years went by to modernize it and keep it up to code. It was at that precise moment, watching the live oaks blow in the breeze and listening to the sound of insects buzzing, that I was grateful to be home. I couldn't wait to hug my dad.

Inside was as cozy as always when I came in the door. Soaring ceilings and dark, log cabin walls greeted me, as did tasteful furniture that had been passed down for generations through my family. To the right of the large foyer was a formal parlor, with a massive stone fireplace that still burned real wood and a thick, barn wood mantel.

What hit me most when I came in was the comforting scents of my childhood mixed with fresh muffins or cake. I suddenly became very aware of my aching hunger. The promise of food made my stomach growl. But my dad was my priority.

I threw my coat on the thick banister, climbing the massive oak staircase as Uncle Roger went into the kitchen to see my aunt. My dad's voice reached me before I reached the top step. He was speaking to the day nurse, and judging by his tone of voice, I was sure he would make himself crazy waiting to recover.

I peeked around the corner of his open bedroom door with a smile. It had only been six days since I had seen him, but when he saw me, his face lit up like a kid on Christmas morning. His love for me was almost embarrassing at times but always reliable. He looked youthful still at almost fifty-five, though his dark hair had a hint of gray running through it. His eyes still twinkled when he smiled, the most comforting smile I'd ever known.

"Hello, love. I'd get up, but they're telling me I can't." He shrugged.

He looked well, all things considered, and it almost brought me to tears for the hundredth time since his accident. I sat down carefully next to him and gave him the best hug I could.

"Are you hungry? Aunt Trace is cooking up a feast down there today." He patted my hand.

"Starving, but first, I wanted to check in on you. How are you feeling?

"I'd be just fine if they'd let me try to move." He said his next words with gumption. "But I'll be riding with you before you know it."

I smiled wide, happy he was so positive. "I'm sure you will."

"How about you? Are you ready for all this? I know you like change about as much as you like mustard on your burger."

I laughed at his comparison. I hated mustard and change, he was right.

I had no idea how to answer that question though. I knew a lot when it came to the ranch, but I hadn't been involved in a while, so this was going to take some getting used to for me. I would help him heal and keep myself busy and involved, working where I could on the ranch for Frank in unison with the cowboys. I knew that also meant working with Nick. It was inevitable.

My dad had filled me in at the hospital, giving me the lay of the land. He told me that Nick not only knew the ranch, he knew the contacts and the suppliers, often handling small tasks for him and Frank in those departments. My dad wanted me to help with that too while he healed, and most importantly, act as his eyes and ears for him.

He snapped me out of my running thoughts. "Kate? Did you hear me? Are you still feeling okay about all of this?"

"Yes, sorry. I'm just tired. I'm as ready as I can be." I shrugged. I would fake it until I made it. For him.

"Good, then head down and get something to eat already. New York doesn't feed you properly."

"Yes, they do, just not pecan pie every day," I teased, mentioning our favorite treat.

I could sense that he was ready for a nap. I sat for a few more minutes and we watched Ice Road Truckers as he started dozing off. As strong as he was, he was still human and this had been a major endeavor for his body. I left him snoring softly and closed the door behind me.

I made the short walk to my room, two doors down. It hadn't changed one bit since I had left. Soft yellow curtains over the dark walnut cabin style walls.

My large and very comfortable king-sized bed with a white, pillowy duvet called to me after an already long and emotional day. I pulled out my suitcase, which already sat neatly on my bed. I assumed Uncle Roger brought it up for me when I was with my dad. He was equal parts gruff and thoughtfully sweet.

I went into the little, vintage, jack-and-jill-style bathroom that connected my room to Charlotte's and washed my face. The hot water felt so good after the long flight.

I dug out my coziest pair of tights and one of my dad's old flannels from the closet. To finish the elegant look, I popped slippers onto my feet and headed downstairs to see my Aunt and begin my hunt for food.

Chapter 5 - Just Perfect
Katie

Our large farmhouse kitchen was warm and hectic when I entered, despite the cool breeze blowing through the open windows. Aunt Tracey was a hot mess trying to get dinner out to feed us all. Now that their daughters, Tessa and Remi, were grown and away at school with Charlotte in Dallas, she didn't cook large meals very often. To feed all the bunkhouse boys and our family was a big project for her.

My Dad had a cook employed for the bunk house five days a week, but Aunt Tracey insisted on making a home cooked meal for all of us, probably to keep her hands busy. Everyone agreed because no one dared to argue with her. *Ever*. She's a small woman, but round and warm, with wild, almost white, blonde Marilyn-Monroe-esque hair and big blue eyes. She always looked glamorous, with her nails always perfectly polished. She's strong and opinionated and the best cook I had ever known. Her cinnamon rolls and pies were what my southern foodie dreams were made of.

I smiled at her from the doorway. Her usually tough exterior shaken as she scrambled around the kitchen in her messy apron. She squealed and enveloped me in a strong squeeze the moment she saw me.

"So glad you're home, baby." She got back to her work right away, turning up her music as she did. It was Elvis, as always.

I scanned the large butcher block island and found what my senses told me earlier would be there. Freshly made chocolate chip banana bread. A lot of it. I cut myself a large slice as Aunt Tracey scolded me.

"That isn't for right now girl, dinner will be done in thirty minutes."

I took a large, delicious bite and swallowed it down. Smiling to remind her it would all be okay, even if I ate bread before dinner. "Too late, and so good," I said.

One look at her face told me it might be best to get out of her way all together.

I curled up in my dad's favorite wing-back chair in front of the fireplace in the parlor while I waited, taking in the beautiful view of the sun going down over the valley out the front window.

True to her word, thirty minutes later Aunt Tracey yelled that dinner was ready. I sprung up quickly. If I didn't get in there first, the cowboys would come and demolish the table, leaving me to eat their over-picked scraps.

My aunt and the help had prepared a feast for an army. Grilled steaks, deviled eggs, salad from the gardens, homemade biscuits, baked beans, a mountain of baked potatoes, and all the fixings. It was official. I was starving.

I grabbed a plate and began filling it as the boys started piling in, saying "good evening" and taking off their hats as they entered the kitchen, placing them in a chair of their choosing at the huge harvest table. It seated twenty-eight and tonight it would be close to full.

I didn't see Nick yet. I was both relieved and disappointed.

I couldn't comprehend the feelings he gave me, that he'd always given me. They were foreign yet familiar, something I wasn't used to anymore. Nervous. Energized. Frazzled. All at the same time.

I finished filling my plate as the line started to form. I remembered some of the cowboys, they all still seemed the same. Young, hardworking, sweaty and dusty after a day in the field. Seeing them scramble into line behind me made me happy that I had gotten there first. I turned quickly, wanting to get out of there and let the vultures feast. The chatter was so loud. It was like being in the mess hall at summer camp.

I gazed down at my plate, napkin, and drink, working to balance them and make it to the parlor in once piece. Then I crashed into something, hard. A six-foot, four-inch brick wall. A warm, large hand steadied me with a strong grip on my arm, stopping me dead in my tracks. My gaze remained focused on where my plate had been. Then travelled further inward, to where my plate clung to my flannel. I pulled it off, food narrowly escaping falling to the floor, most of it clinging to my clothing.

I looked up, prepared to read the riot act to the clumsy cowboy that had done this, when leather and spice filled my senses. Of course, it was Nick. His green eyes held me in place from under his backwards ranch ball cap, questioning my very existence in his personal space.

"Jesus, Katelyn, still don't know how to look where you're going I see." He made sure I was steady and then looked down to make sure nothing had landed on his precious boots, inspecting them carefully. It's a cowboy thing, but the irony was rich considering the dust caking him. His black t-shirt clung to his arms, giving me a closer look at his tattoos.

He pulled his hand away that had been holding me up, satisfied, I suppose, that I was alright. His face hovered over mine, and then he smirked.

"Were you just trying to let me know that you're home?" He leaned in slightly, his delicious scent invading me. "That's a little forward for you, trying to jump right into my arms like that, isn't it?"

He waited for my answer. When it didn't come out of my mouth, which probably hanging open, his smirk grew big enough to reveal his dimples and he nodded. "Don't worry, Katelyn, we *all* know you're here."

His voice was deep and smooth, just like it had been just the week before, but this time it was more overwhelming, so close to me and so very southern.

I averted my eyes from his and started cleaning myself up with my one and only napkin. I couldn't think clearly looking at him. I lost my temper sometimes when embarrassed. This was one of those times.

My voice came out shaky. "I wasn't trying to do anything. You should look where *you're* going. This isn't the bunkhouse, you know, people have etiquette, they get in line. Y'all are acting like pigs at a trough."

I gestured to the train of hungry boys forming at the kitchen island in front of him. He didn't seem to mind my annoyance. He towered over me, looking at me like I was entertainment. He grabbed another handful of napkins off the island and handed them to me, then smiled wide. I ignored how glorious it was.

"I'm sorry, Kate, I'm having a hard time taking you seriously looking like that. We should really get you cleaned up, yeah? Or just get you a new shirt all together. You want mine?"

Arrogant, cocky...

He tugged up the bottom of his t-shirt, pulling me from my thoughts and exposing the base of very defined abs that disappeared into his jeans. He still smirked at me, like he was *actually* about to take it off.

My mind wandered away from my angry thoughts to the possibility of how he looked underneath that shirt. The image flashed through my mind quickly before I sobered myself up and looked back to his face. Staring at his body only seemed to fuel him even further. Like he knew he was ridiculously hot and I would want to see that.

"No, I don't want your shirt. Keep your clothes on!" I swatted at him.

He shook his head before turning to dismiss me. The line had opened up in front of him and I was left standing there, feeling awkward. Yet another embarrassing moment for me caused by him. His stupid, beautiful grin reminded me of the same one he wore when he sang the theme song of my youth over and over from the age of five on. It rang in my head. *"We all know Kate, she's just a little lightweight, she can't even open the cattle gate..."* It was always followed by hysterical boyish laughter.

I thought about how to deal with him going forward while I cleaned myself up. I wasn't quite sure how to act around him now. Even though he had smiled, I saw no hint of real warmth in his eyes. Those eyes harbored some kind of darkness that I wasn't privy to anymore. They belonged now to someone else. This man in front of me, whose secrets I no longer knew, was now my dad's go-to cowboy. Physically stunning, particularly cocky, and all mine to deal with every day for the foreseeable future. Just perfect.

Chapter 6 - He was always there.
Katie

I got to my room and quickly stripped my food covered clothes off to take them to the wash. I grabbed another pair of tights and a t-shirt and tossed my hair into a giant bun on top of my head.

I headed down to our pantry, trying to push *him* from my mind. The room was quiet and peaceful. To call it a pantry is an understatement. It's like a second kitchen with floor to ceiling shelving, in addition to produce storage, the space houses ingredients for all the handmade food we could render. Breads, cookies, cakes, we made it all. One didn't just go to the store and buy these types of things. Everything was handmade and fresh. Except cereal, *thank God*. I grabbed a box of Rice Krispies and some milk from the fridge.

Cheers to the first meal of the day.

I thought carefully while I ate. Why did I *always* get sucked back in? I didn't want to be so attracted to him. It was almost too unfair that he was now *that* gorgeous. And arrogant. And condescending. Every time I looked at him, I became that girl he pulled away from. He had changed so much.

When we were young, he did most things for me before I could even ask. He left daisies in my saddles for the first time when I was eight and he was ten or eleven. Come to think of it, he left me daisies a lot through the years, whenever he saw a pretty bunch around the property, he picked them for me. I would always find them waiting around the house. The kitchen island, the mailbox, the porch, the parlor, on the mantel. He used to be sweet. A memory of him yelling for me to help him save a frog that had fallen into a window well when we were even younger, maybe even before my mom died, came to me. We pulled it out with a fishing net and walked that frog the three miles to the creek so he could be safe and comfortable. Nick had said it would find its family there. The memories were fuzzy, but more came as I drained my bowl. The way he spoke so sweetly to the cows when they were being vaccinated or branded.

One thing became clear. He was just *always there*.

I rinsed my bowl in the pantry sink and remembered the bread my aunt made. Craving another slice, I went back into the kitchen in search of it. All the boys had finished eating dinner. Some sat at the table eating dessert, laughing and talking. Others had already thanked my aunt and headed back to the bunkhouse, probably exhausted after a long day and a big meal. The housekeeper and cook that my father hired when I was nine, Melia, my *Tia* for all intents and purposes, worked on clearing plates with the help of Aunt Tracey. Melia came from Mexico fifteen years ago. After spending ten of those years with us, she wasn't an employee, she was simply part of our family. She held me when I cried, cared for me when I was sick, taught me everything she could, and kept this house running like a tight ship for my father. She filled a gap for Charlotte and I when our mother died, and I couldn't imagine my life without her. Melia smiled when she saw me. I immediately sunk into her comforting hug.

"I'm so happy to see you home *cariño*. It's just me and all these men around here without you girls. *Ahora tengo a mi pequeña amiga de vuelta.*" -Now I have my little buddy back.-

"I'm glad to be home too, Tia."

Aunt Tracey turned to me then, hearing me speak to Melia. "Where'd you get to, hun? Did you eat?"

"Yeah, I did." I didn't have the heart to tell her most of my dinner had ended up in the composter. I scanned the room for the bread. There had been four trays of it earlier.

"Where is the bread you made?"

"The boys have it at the table. If you can fight, you might get a piece."

Something she said caught the attention of Nick, who sat ten feet away at the head of the table talking to Zac Gracy, a fellow ranch cowboy.

He leaned back in his chair and looked at me with an "oops, sorry" type of face as he shoved the last bite of the last piece of banana bread into his perfect mouth.

Chapter 7 - I had one job
Nick

I'm not going to say I didn't want to see her. Looking at her was probably the easiest thing I've ever done. There was a time when all I could do was think about her face, her lips, her eyes, her voice. That fucking soft, slightly husky voice. But I had one job now. All I had to do was stay away from her and my future on this ranch was locked in. Solid.

I was convinced she was sent here just to distract me at the precise moment I actually had my shit together and had something that resembled a future in front of me.

Before Daniel's accident, it had been three years since I laid eyes on her. I sat on her front porch, waiting for Frank, and she waltzed out the door to her friend's car. She waved at me from the backseat as they pulled away and even offered me a smile. She should've been pissed at me for dismissing her over and over through the years.

I remember thinking I didn't deserve that smile from her. I had half a mind to ask her to stay, to apologize, to tell her how fucked up I was, to ask her to go for a ride in the hills like we used to, but I didn't. My family had just lost everything, and she was the fucking princess of Hennessey Ridge. I had nothing to offer her.

I was nothing if not a sucker for punishment, so I offered to pick her up from the airport two weeks ago. I talked myself up the whole drive there. I didn't know her anymore, we hadn't seen each other in years. She wouldn't be that beautiful or sweet anymore. She wouldn't be what I remembered.

Then she got into my truck, and I knew I was full of shit the second those blue eyes focused on mine. She has the type of body that deserves to be worshipped. She was a pretty girl three years ago, but now her features were enhanced to perfection. Full hips, small waist, long legs despite her shorter stature. Her long, honey blonde hair just begged me to get my hands lost in it.

It took me three days to stop thinking about her after I left her at the hospital. I wasn't in the habit of looking for random one-nighters anymore, but I was prepared to do anything to rid her face from my mind. Desperate times call for desperate measures, and Reeds Canyon is always full of women looking for a night or two with a cowboy. Which I used to love, but then it just got old and kind of lonely.

I went to the hospital to visit Daniel instead of going to town. That was when he told me Kate was coming home full time to help him while he healed, and that I should work with her and make her feel welcome. I nodded and said all the right things, but the reality that I'd have to see her every day hit me like a fucking truck.

Now, here we were. I tried to focus on Zac's words while I simultaneously watched her talking behind him. Those eyes of hers were the most brilliant shade of blue and always happy, always smiling, unless she looked at me. Whenever those stunning eyes found me, they became full of questions.

I got sucked into those eyes when I looked at her, every damn time. Even as a kid, which is why I'd kissed her in the first place. I needed her in that moment. It was selfish, but at least I had the good sense not to drag her down with me afterwards. Had I been able to see the future and knew then that my dad would eventually recover, maybe I wouldn't have gone down the path I did, but I was a seventeen-year-old kid. Hearing my dad was really fucking sick while watching my mom turn into a raging drunk in response was too much. I cared for him in the day when I could, barely making it to my classes of my last year, and then once he was asleep at night I was gone, sinking into the numb oblivion that Jack Daniels offered me. It wasn't the answer. It was self-sabotage at its finest. Not my proudest moments, but hindsight is a bitch.

I let out an exhausted sigh. I had been up since four and hadn't slept much the night before, knowing she was coming home. I continued pretending to care what Zac said while watching her in my periphery as she talked to Tracey, tucking a piece of hair behind her ear while she laughed. Her enticing, full lips turn up in the best way possible when she smiles. I hadn't been on the receiving end of that smile since she had been back, but I could see it from here and it gutted me. *Fuck.*

I had to be professional. For Daniel. I owed everything to him. Smack in the middle of my 'drink all the whiskey in central Texas, fight everyone, and fuck every woman in town' rampage I woke up at the county jail, not remembering why I was there and not really giving a shit either. They told me that I knocked some guy out cold for looking at the girl I was with. As I sat in that cell, I realized that I didn't even know her first name.

Apparently, after he went down, I fought three of his friends until the owner of the bar pulled me back and called the cops and paramedics. The flow of energy coursing through my veins as I hit them all was all I remembered. Remembering that rush and my bloody knuckles were the only proof I had that it really happened.

Daniel was the one who bailed me out. Bailed me out *and* got them all to drop the charges. I expected him to lecture me, instead, he offered me a job on the ranch. He told me he wanted better for me. It was my chance to choose a different life, but I'd only get one. I was nineteen. I took it because he was the only one that didn't look at me like I was a fuckup. Also, because I wanted it to stop. All of it.

My dad was doing much better by then and I knew I had to be there for him because my mom sure as shit wasn't. The only answer that made sense was working on the ranch because it reminded me of the last good part of my life. The part with her. The part I let go. She left to New York, but I could still feel close to her. Then, the longer I stayed, the more I learned to love the land and discovered a sort of peace in it. I had no other choice now, being a cowboy on this ranch meant everything to me. I would push through her time here, treat her like everyone else, like every other ranch hand that crossed my path. I just had to get past those fucking eyes.

Chapter 8 - Princess Katie

The alarm went off way too early, and for a minute, I forgot where I was. Expecting the familiar surroundings of my New York bedroom, I turned to where my alarm clock usually sat to hit the snooze button. Instead, I crashed my arm into the bedside table. Great start to the day. I shot up, a little disoriented, and managed to hit the snooze button on the other side of the bed. My arm throbbed where I'd smacked it, so I decided five more minutes in bed was warranted. I made the mistake of pulling the warm duvet over my head and settled in.

"Katie..." A soft voice woke me from my sleep. It called again, louder, "Katie...*es tarde cariño*." -it's late honey-

Suddenly, I was quite aware of the alarm singing in the room. My eyes flew open, finding Melia in the doorway. I slept in. How did I not hear that? Thank God for Melia, she always had my back.

"Thank you, Tia, I hear it." My voice croaked out as I shut the alarm off completely. Melia said nothing and softly closed the door.

The next few minutes were a mad rush of me hopping out of bed and rummaging to find the right articles of clothing. All my old ranch clothes hung gracefully in my closet like I never left. They were perfectly washed, pressed, and ready for my return. Of course, my dad had seen to it. I settled on the most worn in, comfortable jeans I had and, of course, the standard soft and warm flannel. I added thick socks and my tried-and-true cowboy boots. The soft leather Lucchese boots looked worn and tattered but they slid on like butter, perfectly molded to my feet. They cost more than most people's first cars, and they were one of my most prized possessions.

I quickly washed my face and brushed my teeth, all while simple braiding my hair in one long, thick braid that hung almost to my waist. Not an easy multitask, but I managed. My worn cowboy hat that used to be my dad's hung on the inside of my door, so I scooped it up and headed downstairs.

The smell of freshly brewed coffee hit me as I entered the hallway. No one slept here. The ranch hands and cooks would have been up at four getting ready for the day. Meals were planned by the week. Feeding a group of hungry boys was no joke. I may have been late, but there was no way I wasn't getting a mug of Melia's coffee. I scolded myself as I poured a huge travel mug full of the steaming and delicious brew. I added a hefty amount of vanilla almond milk to make it actually taste good. I'm pretty convinced that anyone who chooses to drink their coffee black simply doesn't have taste buds.

I checked my phone, I should've been at the barn already. Saddling Buttercup was something I hadn't done in a long time, so I wanted to be there early.

I went through the steps of saddling him in my mind as I stepped out into the cool morning air. The sun wasn't up yet and wouldn't be for a little while. The number of stars in the sky told me the day would dawn sunny and bright, not a cloud in sight.

The walk to the barn took all of ten minutes and I woke more with each crunching step beneath my boots. This land was my happy place. Little golf carts and RZ riders were scattered around the ranch for cowboys to ride quickly between the buildings or to see to an animal that needed help, but I preferred to walk. The ranch was well-lit and as quiet as ever. Never for one second had I ever felt unsafe on this property.

My coffee was almost gone by the time the lights from the barn came into sight, and they were *all* on. I knew then that I was the last one to arrive. Nick must have seen me coming before anyone else. He stared at me with a look of "of course she's the last one. Of course, she's late." The feeling of inadequacy washed over me.

"Did we wake you up, princess?"

His voice was smooth, calm. He was poking fun at me, just like he did when I was younger, but it still pissed me off. He always teetered on the line of being sweet and behaving like a total ass. A sweet ass, that was him. And to make matters worse, he certainly had one.

"We've all been here since quarter to five but we don't mind waiting an extra thirty minutes just for you. Maybe we could get someone to fetch you a Starbucks, yeah?" He clearly was leaning more toward the ass side of things today.

"I'm only technically fifteen minutes late." I heard my Texas drawl coming back strong. "Besides, I'm sure you had some horse shit to shovel or something else useful to do while you waited?"

He tipped his hat and looked at me like he had more of a right to be there than I did.

"Well, yes, ma'am, but all the shit is now clean. We also did that while you were still sleeping." He looked behind me, down the row to my horse, and nodded in that direction.

"Can you can saddle him yourself or do you need someone to do that for you?"

I could feel my cheeks blush pink at his insinuation. I turned my face away. "Of course, I can do it." Fire coated my words. I didn't want him to think he had any effect on me whatsoever.

"And, Katelyn...We're done waiting on you, so be sure to make it quick." Stern authority filled his tone, a boss speaking to their employee.

I moved to the tack wall and easily found the ultralight saddle my father had bought me years before. Breezing past Nick, I headed into the barn to grab my saddle gear and greet Buttercup.

Truth be told, saddling my horse was like riding a bike, and I remembered how to do it precisely. It always amazed me the way the horses responded to me. I hadn't ridden Buttercup in months, but he knew who I was the moment I stepped up to the stall. I patted and nuzzled him, taking a moment to telepathically say *yes, it's me, I'm here, let's ride*.

I almost thought Nick looked genuinely impressed when I came out leading Buttercup, ready for the morning. I turned to him then, feigning shock. I was in the wrong here, I knew it, I shouldn't have been late, but he was so uppity and judgemental I just couldn't help myself and pushed back a little.

"Since saddling him up was so easy, and seeing as you're just standing around anyway, maybe you actually *could* run along and get me a coffee like you offered? Double vanilla almond milk? Thanks. I smiled a "bless your heart" type smile at him, then turned to leave the barn. He shook his head, a small smirk on his lips, like I was the world's biggest pain in his sweet ass, but said nothing more as he mounted King.

I watched him under hooded eyes. He patted that horse like he was his best friend, muttering something to him. I had to admit to myself that it hurt my guts just to look at him. I had never seen him in this way. Early in the day, full cowboy glory, before the day's dust had a chance to settle on him. God, he was gorgeous. I felt a pull to him in the pit of my stomach. *He's only gorgeous if he doesn't open his mouth to antagonize me,* I reminded myself. Besides, I wouldn't get sucked back into that Venus fly trap. I spent enough time when I was young crying and trying to sort out my feelings for him after he humiliated me. Fool me once, shame on you, fool me twice…you know the rest.

"I know you're out of practice, but we're on our own. Zac and Jacob had to go with Frank for a bit and everyone else is tied up." He spoke like he was talking to a child that he was babysitting. "It's only a handful of calves, but we'll be riding fast and far. Hope you're ready."

He turned to me one last time and grinned before taking off into the field ahead of me. "If you get too tired, we can send for someone to come pick you up in a golf cart," he hollered back.

Keep talking. I hadn't ridden in a while, but I was an expert rider, at least I used to be. I could certainly handle it. From what I was told, we were riding to the east pasture. The field on that side was full of the winter grasses, so they had corralled a large herd there two weeks prior. They would stay for a little while until the grasses wore thin and then they would be moved to fuller pastures. It was a constant ebb and flow, feeding from the land, then allowing it to rest.

We rode silently in the dark until we arrived at more rocky and hilly terrain. Secretly, my hands were hurting. I knew blisters were starting, that was inevitable, and I wished I had been home a little more and was used to it. I made a mental note to change my gloves to thicker ones the next day. My legs were killing me. Going over bumps meant I had to sit up just a little off the saddle to support my weight and not bobble around. This was really rough terrain and I simply wasn't used to it. He, on the other hand, seemed like he could do it for ten days straight and not bat an eye. I felt his eyes on me and the same familiar annoyance crept back up as he rode along expertly and looked back as if I was just slowing him down.

"Need that golf cart yet, princess?" His laugh was the only sound for miles as the sun finally started to wake. It was like we were the only two people on earth.

Chapter 9 – War
Katie

Dawn in Texas is something most people that live outside the state never really experience to its fullest. My grandmother used to say that when God designed the world, He made Texas first.

The pinks and purples reached like fingers across the sky. Just like I had suspected, the sunrise that morning was perfection. It took us until the sky was fully lit to reach the herd, and by then, I was ready for a break. Nick looked back at me, baring the same look of pity he wore in the truck two weeks earlier. We rode through some of the roughest terrain I have ever gone through to reach our destination, but I made it. Just barely.

He pulled his horse up to an available post and hopped off with ease, tying King up and getting ready to provide him with some water. It was rough terrain for the horses too, but unlike me, they were built for this. I tried to do the same, determined to appear just as at ease as him. My body unfortunately had other ideas. I pulled one leg off to the side saddle and jumped the short distance to the flat earth. What should've been an easy landing turned into my legs completely giving out. I went down hard and fast.

Fuck. My. Life.

I didn't want to look his way. This only furthered the point he was quite obviously trying to make, that I had no business trying to work in the field with him. I was sure Nick would be glaring at me from his horse.

But he instantly was there. Like, right there in front of me. I still have no idea how he got there so fast. It had seemed like one second flat before he was on his knees in the dusty grass beside me, cursing.

"Fuck, Kate, are you okay?" He lifted my hat off my face, like he was trying to see if I was conscious.

Before I was ready for it, those green eyes stared intensely into mine.

"You shouldn't curse so much," I muttered in my haze.

I had only been this close to him once before, and his eyes looked even more hypnotizing now, just an inch from my face. He laughed at my words.

"I see you are." He pulled slightly away from me, giving me space.

"I'm fine." In truth, I wasn't so sure.

I tried to stand like nothing had happened, but again, I went down. My legs were clearly not prepared for a ride of that magnitude. He caught me with a strong grip, taking action into his own hands. Before I knew what was even happening, he had scooped me up easily into his arms.

"You clearly weren't ready for this ride. I thought you'd be okay. I'm sorry, that was a bad call in judgement."

He seemed completely genuine, but I couldn't be sure if it was just another opportunity to point out how inadequate I was.

"Put me down right now!" I struggled under his strength.

"Why so you can just fall again? No, just simmer down and I'll carry you to the hill. You can sit there and have a drink. Have you eaten anything today?" He moved fast, like I weighed absolutely nothing to him. "You don't set out on a full day without food. That would just be stupidity."

Not helping. "I had some coffee." I managed to eek out.

"Breakfast of fucking champ- You should've eaten," he bit out.

I was feeling a little lightheaded. I stopped fighting and let him carry me to the hill. He was warm and he smelled so good. I could feel the warmth from his chest on my face. It certainly wasn't terrible by any means.

He set me down gently and pulled a water from his bag. He added some electrolyte powder into it, shook it up, and handed it to me. He also grabbed a protein bar that promised me chocolate and peanut butter goodness.

"Eat this." He tore open the wrapper. "Please." He deadpanned, struggling to be polite.

All I had eaten in thirty-six hours was a bowl of Rice Krispies and a slice of bread. I realized maybe I wasn't as prepared for this ride as I thought I was.

After a few sips of the cool, citrusy water and the protein bar, I felt a bit better. The warm morning sun on my face helped too.

"You were pretty pale five minutes ago. You're looking a bit better now. The last thing I need is you dropping dead out here on me."

"I'm feeling better, I think." I said to him.

"I shouldn't have taken you on such a rough ride on your first day back."

He looked so genuine I almost felt bad for yelling at him and protesting, yet somehow, I felt like I was missing something. I decided to give him a moment of honesty.

"It's not your fault, I'm out of practice and I didn't eat much yesterday."

Nick said nothing more. He swallowed the last of his protein bar while I picked away at mine. We sat on the hill for a little while in silence and looked out to the fields below, watching the cattle graze in the morning sun. A distant familiarity hovered between us. We had done this a million times in another life.

"Still beautiful, isn't it?" he asked, like he was reading my thoughts.

I sighed at the beauty of it. "No place like it." I turned and offered him a smile. "Thank you for the bar and the drink. It really helped."

He didn't speak or smile back. He just looked at me, then turned his eyes back out to the field.

"Well, you don't look half dead now. Think we can get started?"

"Of course we can. I'm fine now." I rolled my eyes.

He nodded and stood up, oblivious to my sass.

I rose with ease, definitely feeling stronger and better. Tagging cattle was something I had helped with a lot in my youth, so I knew the practice well. Mama cows could get a little ornery when you went near their babies, so someone had to keep them calm while the babies were tagged. That was my job. Nick's was to catch them and tag them.

Watching Nick work was mesmerizing. Beginning his chase, rope swinging overhead, lassoing the calf from the back of King. It happened very quickly. Once the rope latched around the calf's neck, he signaled to King to stop like he spoke his language. He dismounted and got to the calf so quickly. He was careful to help the baby to the ground with his hands, not the rope.

A true cowboy through and through. Confident, sure of himself, you could just see it in him. I watched him as long as I could before his eyes met mine across the field.

"Katelyn..." His tone was sharp as he looked up from over the calf. "The mama." He pointed to her and snapped me out of my Nick-trance to tend to her. I quickly got my shit together so he wouldn't witness me drooling over him.

It didn't take us long to finish. We headed back through the pastures just before lunch. Nick found an easier ride back for me, and I was so hungry when we arrived at the barn. Some branding of new cattle was happening to the west and another hill full of cattle was being moved by a few of the other cowboys. It was a busy place, always bustling with activity.

The cook set up an enormous table full of sandwiches, cheeses, and fruit inside the bunkhouse. I had always loved coming in here. It was a large, open common room with a commercial grade kitchen just beyond it. Most days, this was where the cooking and eating happened. The eating hall itself, next to the common room, was sparse. Warm cabin walls were on all sides, like the main house and the rest of the bunkhouse. Bright windows lined the east wall with two large harvest tables to seat up to forty filling out the space. The chairs were wood and heavy. Strong. Strong enough to endure years of cowboys. The floors were thick oak and beat up beyond measure. They had been there for seventy-five years, but I always felt they added character. Despite being sanded down and re-stained twice now, the days of worn boots marching across them showed.

Pictures of cowboys lost and memories graced the north wall. At the far end on the west wall hung a huge flag map of the state of Texas from 1948 when the new and "modern" bunkhouse was built. Every cowboy who had ever stayed in the bunkhouse signed it upon arrival. It was tradition, and I always loved reading the notes and signatures on it. Ranch traditions ran deep, and no one messed with them. The state and ranch pride was something lost to a lot of people outside the ranching world, but to these cowboys, it was their way life.

"Are you going to walk or drive back to the main house?" Nick's voice was low, his eyes intense on mine.

"Maybe I'll take a golf cart this time." I sighed, giving in, I was exhausted.

Nick stood over me, and opened my hand gently. I looked down to see him drop keys into it and close my fingers around them. The warmth of his hand overtook me.

"Figured you would say that."

Every cell in me came alive with his touch. So many times, so many nights after he kissed me, I dreamt of being this close to him again. Now, here I was. I couldn't resist him for even a second. I was hopeless. He was my personal kryptonite.

"Thanks."

He said nothing else, nodding, then turning to let me gather lunch.

I filled two plates with sandwiches, fruit, and freshly baked cookies, then placed them in a small box. As I was leaving the bunkhouse, I thought I could feel his eyes on me. My body took over where my mind screamed in protest. I found him easily. He talked to another cowboy while leaning against the back wall, but his gaze focused me, just as I'd suspected. He didn't look away, or pretend he wasn't looking. He smirked and stared right at me like it was his God given right to do so, then tipped his hat to me as I went through the door.

The sun sat high in the sky as I drove back to the house, breathing in the fresh air and listening to the wildlife. The sun felt amazing on my skin. In New York it was probably thirty degrees and raining. I would be tanned in no time. In less than five minutes I was parked and inside the main house, kicking off my muddy boots.

I grabbed some lemonade from the kitchen, it was homemade and heavenly. I turned to go upstairs and enjoy the mini-feast with my dad when my uncle strolled into the kitchen.

"Hey, Pix, you look rough. Strong start to your day?"

"It was just a long ride this morning. I don't remember the terrain being so unbalanced before."

My uncle took a minute to think. "Where did you go?"

"To the southeast pasture, to tag the new calves."

He started laughing. "You went *what* way?" he asked again, still chuckling to himself.

I explained the ride to him in a little more detail and the time it took us to reach it.

"Oh honey…" His laughter boomed through the room. "He has officially initiated you into the crew. That is the worst route to take. Even experienced riders have trouble with it from time to time."

My thoughts flashed back to the very flat and simple ride back, and to him apologizing for taking me that way more than once. It hit me instantly that I knew that easy route with perfect clarity. We could've gone that way to begin with. Suddenly I was angry. He had taken me that way *on purpose?* All of the embarrassment of falling and my sore legs, my blisters? It could've been avoided if he had just chosen to be a decent human being and not been hell bent on making a fool of me? Just when I thought there may have been hope for us to get along.

My thoughts raged. *This means war.*

Chapter 10 - Charlotte Moment
Katie

"Are you not hungry, Katie?"

My dad looked concerned as he enjoyed a large turkey wrap filled with fresh lettuce from the garden.

"Hmm? Oh, yes, I am."

I made a solid effort to take a good-sized bite of my own wrap. My ravenous appetite from the hour before had dissipated and now I truthfully wasn't even hungry.

My mind raced, cataloging the events of the morning again. How he instantly assumed I couldn't saddle my horse, the look of constant annoyance he wore, my brutal trek downhill for two hours, falling, him rushing to help me. Did he have a hero complex? Did he just feel the need to show he was my boss? He was really grating on my nerves and I was sick of thinking about him and the smug look he wore. If Nick had been standing in front of me at that very moment I would have punched him. I made a silent pact with myself to stop dwelling and put him right out of my mind. I couldn't control him or his choosing to be an asshole, but I could avoid him for the rest of my day so I didn't *actually* punch him.

My Dad cut into my thoughts. "How are you and Nick getting along?"

Trying to avoid him here Dad...

"Fine," I replied curtly.

My dad grinned, like after almost twenty years he knew what that kind of "fine" meant. Apparently, I said it just like my mom had back in the day and that always let him know that something was up.

"That doesn't sound fine. He's been through a lot and he is really important to me and to this ranch. I could see him running everything for me at some point if neither of you girls do. I hope you two will get along alright."

My dad's little speech just further annoyed me. As if it was *me* creating the problem?

I felt the frustration fill up my throat. I gulped it back.

"I'm trying. It's fine. We're getting along fine." There was that word again, I hated myself for using it.

My dad smiled. I gave in. "He rode me through some rough terrain this morning. Apparently, everyone thinks this is pretty funny but me. I'm out of practice and I didn't appreciate it."

He chuckled. "You have to toughen up a little if you're going to work with them. It seems about right. He knows the land almost as well as I do. That boy would spend off days riding just to ride and memorizing locations around the property. He would always keep you safe and if he gave you a bit of a hard time today, that is to be expected. They do it to everyone new."

"But I'm not new?"

"Well, you're not new to living here, but you're new to working with the crew. In his eyes, you're a rookie. Another little chuckle escaped him. "I guess that means you're one of them now."

Why was this just okay with everyone? Was this third grade? Clearly my dad wasn't going to give me the sympathy I was looking for. *Men. Particularly, cowboy men.*

I had had just about enough for the day and it was only three o'clock. I wanted to shower before heading down to the grain silos. We needed to start inventorying our supply. My dad had asked me to sit with the supplier and Frank to go over the quantities ordered. It was a simple task I could take care of that he couldn't. It was a learning meeting for me, but I looked forward to something that didn't involve Nick. And it was the last thing on my list for that day.

I looked at my phone. I knew I had a few minutes to spare, and I needed to talk to a girl before my head exploded. Any girl would do. Even Charlotte, who I knew I could vent to without any judgement.

We are very different, but she is still my best friend. I wonder sometimes how we came from the same parents. I would get pictures from her travels and adventures from different places or her friends at school, parties, and boys. She would get back pictures of my Starbucks or the books I was reading. I had never met a boy worth going out with very long, whereas Charlotte seemed to fall in love with everyone. Boys or girls depending on the day. She could never understand why I loved my simple routine. Life was an adventure to her, and the ranch bored her to tears. She was turning eighteen in March and she travelled with our cousins every chance she got. They all attended a very snooty boarding school, kids travelled from all over to attend.

It suited Charlotte perfectly.

She already talked about going to college in California so she could experience west coast life and, of course, the boys there for four years straight. She was pretty and friendly and everyone liked her. She lit up the room when she came into it in a "look at me" kind of way, and no one could resist her.

The phone rang in my ear. I didn't even know if I'd get through to her, she was in Seattle on a week-long trip with her art class. I wondered if she wasn't answering to avoid me, like maybe she thought I needed her for something. She did that sometimes when she couldn't be bothered.

"Hey…what's up?" she asked, answering my call.
Loud beeping and music filled the background, like she was at some sort of arcade with kids yelling and laughing. I knew then that this would be a short conversation.

"I just need to vent…about Nick Stratton. Got a minute?"

Charlotte started laughing. Her tone changed instantly. "Hells yes, I do. One second, I'm just gonna go outside."

"It's not that crucial."

"First off, you called me, so it is, and are you kidding? My sister wants to talk about a *guy*? And that guy is *Nick Stratton*? He is something to look at, isn't he?" Charlotte sounded way too excited, she probably assumed we were hooking up. I had been home for two days.

"I never really got too close to him last summer but from a distance he was a ten."

I had come home last summer, in July, but he had been on a small leave. It was during one of his dad's tough times and he had requested a couple of weeks off to be with him, to which my dad was quick to approve. It had just happened to be the only week I had been home in two years. Charlotte, on the other hand, had seen him from afar every summer for the last couple of years.

"He never really pays much attention to me. He is always so serious and seems so involved in his work. He kind of seems a little scary now, like he would anger fuck me if I let him." I winced at her words and she laughed. "Not that he would, I suppose. He never even looks at me the way the other cowboys do. Even in my prettiest bathing suits."

I put my head in my hand. "He's kind of old to look at you Char, he's almost twenty-two, you're seventeen."

She laughed like I was nuts. "Whatever, he's probably perfect for you. A little dark maybe, but it could work." She continued on, "He seems very serious. Still hot, but serious, too serious, kind of boring. Again, maybe perfect for—"

"Ha Ha Ha," I said slowly, my voice dripping sarcasm.

She cut to the chase. "So...what is happening with him? Wait, do you want him to anger fuck *you?*"

"Oh my God, Char!" Even I laughed then, not even entirely sure what she even meant and wondering how she was younger than me and so familiar with the term "anger-fuck".

Cleary, she was going to focus on the wrong thing but she was all I had, so I proceeded to tell her everything. Every little annoying detail about him since I had arrived, even the short way he spoke to me at the airport like I was wasting his time. Charlotte listened patiently.

"I don't remember the last time I heard you talk this much. About anything. Let alone a guy. He is always learning from Dad. He cares a lot about what he thinks." She confirmed what I already assumed. "Maybe he's afraid you're there to take his place. You know he had nothing, right? You guys used to be friends, I remember. Do you know what happened? His dad was so sick and his mom just drinks now. She's like that drunk everyone knows about, but pretends they don't, ya know? She fell out the door at Ophelia's boutique the last time I saw her, she was so out of it. Jackie from the pet store was with her, holding her up, and they lost *everything* when his dad was in the hospital. Did you know Dad had to bail Nick out of jail for beating the shit out of a bunch of guys at Back Alley?"

I knew my dad had helped him; I didn't know he bailed him out of jail.

She snorted back laughter. "Now he's like, reformed. Dad says he even wants to take over for Frank one day."

I listened to her small-town gossip intently. It all seemed frivolous besides a couple of things she said that stuck out in her ramblings.

Maybe he thinks you're there to take his place and *that he seemed scary.* He scared me a little too. Not in a hurt me kind of way, but just like he was a loose cannon. His home life must have really messed him up over those years we drifted apart.

The conversation quickly went south.

"I saw him working with his shirt off in the summer, outside the north side barn, while I was riding Juniper. It was super-hot that day, but my fucking God, it honestly made me wish that shirts just didn't even exist anymore."

I laughed at her and rolled my eyes. You can take the girl out of Texas, but you can't take Texas out of the girl.

"Okay time to go, Charlotte," I answered.

Of course, her mind would end up in the gutter. Yes, Nick was undoubtedly gorgeous. But thanks to her comment, I was now picturing him without his shirt, wondering where those tattoos on his arm ended. In my mind, it was just as good as she described.

She laughed, knowing the door to that conversation was closed. "Sometimes I wonder if you'll grow up to become a nun."

"Hardly," I replied. "I just don't tell everyone every single detail of my life or visibly drool over every guy I see."

"Whatever…it's the only way to live, darling. Love ya, gotta go!" she quipped happily, hanging up the phone.

Just like that, my one and only lousy consultant was gone. "Better than nothing." I mumbled to myself.

I took a heavenly shower. The extra hot water poured over me, soothing my body and stinging my blistered palms, temporarily pushing him from my mind. I needed to gather myself together. Even if his behaviour was because he was afraid I would take his place, it didn't give him the right to treat me like an outsider. This was my home and my father's business. I had just as much of a right to be here as he did. Even more.

I changed into fresh clothes and dried my hair with the blow dryer, taking an extra-long time until it was like a sheet hanging down my back. Inventory was a simple enough job, and I planned to sink into bed with a book and dinner at the end of the day. I could hardly wait.

I felt the need to check on my dad one more time before heading out to the silos to meet Frank and Amanda Beckett, Dad's grain supplier.

Dad went over the pricing I should expect, and we agreed to go over everything later. I would function as his stand in, taking notes and reporting back to him. I kissed him on the top of his head and made my way downstairs to grab my boots. Feeling my appetite coming back, I stopped in the kitchen for a ginger cookie before heading out the door.

    I made the quick ride over to the silos in a golf cart. The day was already starting to cool at four o'clock, and there was a note of fall in the air. I hopped out of the cart and tossed the key in my bag before heading inside the little building attached to the first of the three large silos. I pulled the heavy door open to head inside and was surprised at the sight that greeted me. Nick, not Frank, sat with Amanda, deeply involved with going over the inventory without me.

Chapter 11 - Maybe check your phone?
Katie

"Hello, Katie, you might not remember me, I'm Amanda." Amanda was a taller woman in her fifties, comfortably dressed in jeans and the standard footwear, a pair of Texas made cowboys boots. Her hair was short and naturally blonde. She wore it spiky and to the side. She had big glasses and a hooded sweater. She reached out her hand to shake mine. I obliged.

"We're pretty much wrapped up here, I'm glad Nick could accommodate my time change when Frank couldn't make it back."

I smiled at her and pretended I knew what she was talking about. "Of course," I said, locking my eyes with Nick's across the room. He gave nothing away.

I was sure the meeting was scheduled for four o'clock.

"That about wraps it up. Nick can fill you in for your dad. I'm glad you guys are on board to order from us this year again. Nick says almost double the supply. They're saying it will be a cold winter."

She turned to Nick. "I have to head to the fairgrounds to set up, Gary has a title to defend." They laughed.

I had no idea what they were talking about. Nick did. He knew everyone in town. He turned to me to explain.

"I'm not sure if you remember Gary, Amanda's husband. He owns the Los Amigos Cantina on Bakersfield. The fall fair and chili fest is this weekend. Gary has won best chili three years running."

He turned to Amanda then. "I'll be there to try it out and so will Katelyn, won't you, Kate?" Nick spoke for me, his eyes boring into mine.

"I'll do my best," I said quietly.

It was annoying that he spoke for me like that. Like he had any say in where I went.

"See y'all there then." Amanda closed the door happily behind her, noticing zero tension whatsoever.

I didn't waste a second before I turned to Nick.

"What the hell? Why did you take my meeting with her and not tell me. I'm perfectly capable, you know." Maybe I should've given him a chance to explain, but I was losing my patience very quickly.

"I—" he started, but I cut him off. I tend to do that when I'm fired up. I'm going to just blame it on my being a Leo.

"I don't care what is up with you, okay? Making me go that tough terrain this morning? What was that? Hero complex? Boss complex? Insecurities? Whatever, not my problem, Nick. I'm here to do a job to help my dad. I'll probably be gone in a few months and you can have it all back. Until then, you need to stop tormenting me on purpose."

Now it was Nick's turn. He put his head down and chuckled for a moment, as if what I had just said was ridiculous.

"Yep, Katelyn. You are exactly right, you will be gone, but right now, you're acting like a self-absorbed little child. I shouldn't have taken you that way this morning, I already apologized more than once." His voice was ice cold water over my hot little tantrum. I hadn't seen him angry since we were kids and this was different. I shrunk a little bit in my boots. He wasn't raising his voice really, but I knew as soon as I heard him talk, I was one hundred percent finished with having a fit. His tone simply commanded it.

"You should be thanking me for taking this meeting on for you. They have a line-up of ranchers wanting to order from them, they're the only organic supplier in Hill Country. Do you know they wait for us? They base their season on us entirely. This has nothing to do with me. It is you. You come waltzing in here after not giving a flying fuck for the last three years…"

He turned from me, pulling his hat off and running his hand through his hair. "You have no idea what it takes to run this place. You haven't been here. You left, remember? But I have." Anger filtered through his calm tone. "I've watched your dad's face of disappointment when he hangs up the phone with you after you've told him you aren't coming home for Thanksgiving or your spring break or any other opportunity you had to come home. I've lived and breathed this ranch for three years. Going to school is one thing, not ever coming home and letting your dad down is just shitty. You think I have a hero complex? Give me a fucking break. The real world, the one outside this ranch, doesn't revolve around you. You are so goddamn lucky to be born into this. If it weren't for your dad, I don't know what I'd be doing. I'd probably be on some barstool or in jail somewhere. You can play house all you want here, I'll pick up the pieces of it and fill your place again when you leave. If you want to be taken seriously, start with being on time."

He turned to exit the building. I opened my mouth to respond, but he cut me off.

"Also, a little rough ride didn't hurt you. It's a reality check, Princess, and maybe have a look at your phone. I tried to get a hold of you when Amanda got here early. It would be a good idea to turn it on since you want to take on important responsibilities." He walked out the door before I could speak another word.

I stood there, stunned, and pulled my phone out. It sure enough was on silent. Four calls from a number I hadn't assigned a contact to yet.

Three text messages from the same number.

I read the texts.

The first one asking me to get down to the silos early to meet with Amanda. Frank was tied up. Second one two minutes later.

Unknown: *"Kate? Do you want me to jump in or can you make it?"*

Finally, the last one.

Unknown: *"Ok I'm going to start with her. She has another meeting so she's in a rush. Meet us when you can."*

He hadn't tried to take over after all. In fact, he had stepped in when I needed him to.

His little speech had affected me more than I cared to admit. Was that how he saw me now? He thought I was like Charlotte? Spoiled and self-absorbed? I ran out the door to explain myself, but he had already taken off on King. Gone, almost out of sight. I watched him ride into the north fields and then disappear into the hills.

Chapter 12 - Really?
Nick

Boss complex? Fucking hero complex?? Really???

I don't know who the fuck she thought she was. I took off, seeing red. My anger wasn't just because of her sassy little attitude. I was angry at myself because I let her get under my skin. I don't know how she brought it out in me. It's something I can't quite pinpoint or control, but I knew one thing, I needed to get a handle on it. I was trying to look after the ranch and make sure it had everything it needed for the colder months, but of course she would make it about her.

I rode fast across five miles, to my sacred spot on the property, as far north as I could ride before some major hills took over the land. At the top of the two largest hills a clearing overlooked a massive valley. Wildflowers grew here in the spring, blue bonnet, poppies, and oleander mostly. Daniel has so much land that much of it is just untouched, like this place. I couldn't tell you one reason why, but I have a special bond with it. It feels like it's mine. I always wished I could put a little cabin on it. Maybe wake up in the mornings and sit on a wide porch in the dark and quiet. I tied up King and pushed those thoughts away quickly.

It would never truly be mine to put a cabin on and I knew it, but I would take it how it was for as long as I could. I had never been here with another soul. It was my thinking place. My place to stress about my dad, to figure out how to control my bat shit crazy mother, to worry about the ranch, to stop myself from heading to the local bar and drinking a bottle of whiskey. It was my place to just be, to not owe a thing to anyone.

I felt a little better after sitting for a while. The feeling that I could use a stiff drink, or three, started to fade. I breathed in the fresh air as my anger settled. Not staring into her face made it easier. I pictured those eyes, wide and surprised by my words, appearing all shocked and innocent after provoking the whole argument. She just knew how to push my buttons, always had. I tried to imagine things from her side, and if I was being honest with myself, I hadn't exactly given her an easy time.

I thought about her responsibilities for her age, the fact that her sister was a total child even though she was only a couple of years younger than her, how she had no one to rely on but her dad, who was badly injured and could've died too. I thought about us and how I ignored her to suit my own needs, never telling her how I felt about her, how much I cared about her, how much I missed her. I sighed.

Asshole Nick: 1, Nice Nick: 0.

I removed my flannel and rolled it up under my neck, laying back in the cool grass in my t-shirt felt great after my long-as-fuck day. I was exhausted. I covered my eyes with my hat to block out the last of the day's sun. As I fell asleep I remembered a vision of her long blonde braid coming apart as a muddy, barefoot Katie dug tadpoles out of Shelby creek with me. A sort of peace filled me, for the first time in a long time.

Chapter 13 - Welcome Little One
Katie

I looked up slowly into his eyes that were so close to mine, his hand grazing my face, tucking hair behind my ear, then drifting down my neck, to my shoulder. He leaned down and kissed my cheek first, then my lips.

"You just can't stop thinking about me, can you, Katelyn?" His lips turned up into an all-knowing grin—he knew he was right.

I shot up in bed as my alarm blared, pulling me from my dream. What was the matter with me? I had been home for two days and he was infiltrating my dreams? I rubbed my eyes, scratching the memory of how his lips felt on mine from my mind, ignoring how hot and flustered I felt. I was determined to be early. I wanted to avoid any looks of disappointment from Nick about being late again.

I went to stand up quickly and instantly regretted it. My *everything* hurt after our ride to the east pastures. This was going to take some getting used to. My jeans from the day before were still slung over my chair. I threw them on and selected a new flannel from my closet and another pair of thick socks.

I went over the day in my mind as I washed my face with steaming water, hoping it would help wake me up. We had two more baby calves to tag that morning. It had been a late calving season of sorts. I began weaving my hair into a long French braid.

It was supposed to be a warm Saturday. The first day of the fall fair and chili fest. I thought about what Nick had said the day before, and as annoyed as I was that he spoke for me, he was right, I should go to the fair. Small town Texas life thrived on community, and our family was a big part of that. We were a large employer and an essential cog in the wheel to many other businesses in the Reeds Canyon area. This fall fair was such a huge tradition for everyone in town.

My dad had taken us every year when I was young. I still had a foggy, flashing memory of my mom on the teacup ride with me. I felt a pang of grief even though my memories of her were so fuzzy now.

I had tried keep a journal in my younger years, writing things down so I would never forget them. How she smelled like roses. The books she had read me as a child. Her favorite bible verses. I hadn't opened it in years. I made a mental note to do that very soon. I always felt closer to her here, even now.

There had been no replacement for my dad. His love had died with my mom, he always said. I always found it sad. I wished he would find someone to share his time with. Every year on her birthday, we ate her favorite meal and had cake. Homemade mac n' cheese, fresh bread, and angel food cake with fresh strawberries and whipped cream. Sadly, the last few years my dad had done it all alone and for that, I felt terrible.

I thought of Nick's words. My dad's "look of disappointment" when I didn't come home. Was I as selfish as Charlotte in some of my ways? I would be there this year, I reminded myself, and that thought comforted me just a little as I put my toothbrush back in its holder. I focused on my first task of the day, talking to Nick.

I applied some lip balm, pleased with myself for actually being on time. Unlike the day before, I even made sure I had time for breakfast. I wasn't going down in the field again. Heading downstairs in our very dark and quiet house was easy. Knowing where every creek in the floorboards was helped me to not wake my father.

Two of the soft kitchen pot lights were already on as I entered. I poured myself some steaming coffee and carried it with some oatmeal to the parlor, sitting in front of the fireplace in my dad's chair.

My uncle came through the door on his cellphone, talking to the night herder. Possible wolves spotted in the south woods. They'd have to keep a watch on them and so on, normal ranch troubles. He filled his mug and waved at me before disappearing back out the front door.

I looked at my phone to check the time, I was determined to apologize to Nick before the day went too far. I was willing to be civil with him and work as best I could with him for my dad, but it was quite apparent at this point we would probably never really be great friends again.

Cowboys were already bustling about when I entered the barn. I looked around but didn't see Nick anywhere. I thought for sure he'd be there with his phone in hand, timing my arrival.

I made my way into the stalls to saddle Buttercup for the morning. I finished quickly and waited around a few more minutes before asking someone where Nick was.

Carter Stevenson was almost twenty-two and had been on the ranch in the summers his whole life. He got brought on full-time three years ago. I had known him since I was a kid. He was quiet and friendly. Very soft spoken and a hard worker. He was tall and thin and always used to be a bit awkward. Now, he had filled out into a good-looking man, his sandy blond hair hung almost to his shoulders, always covered by a cowboy hat. I decided he would be the right person to ask.

"Hey, Carter." I started over to him, giving him a big smile. Carter smiled back.

"Have you seen Nick? We're supposed to go out to the east pastures and tag the new calves this morning."

He pulled me into a big, friendly hug. "Hey, girl, I saw you the other day. I would've said hi then, but you looked so annoyed I didn't want to get in your way."

He was, of course, referring to my first night when I had donned the stunning dinner attire in the kitchen.

He gestured toward the east pasture. "He is out there now. Jacob and Trent were there through the night. I guess a heifer is having trouble calving, Nick rode up to check on her, I just heard they called for the vet. Zac and I were just headed out that way too to relieve them if you want to ride with us?"

"Yeah, I'd like to, thanks."

My conversation with Nick would have to wait. My focus shifted to the mama cow that was having trouble. I hopped up on Buttercup and took off with Carter and Zac into the east pastures, hoping everything was okay.

The sky was still as dark as night and filled with stars when we arrived. We had ridden silently. The heifer's low groan carried through the fields as we approached. Jacob Foster, a big, burly twenty-four-year-old with wild curly hair crouched beside Nick. Jacob came from wealth; his father had played in the NBA for the Miami Heat and he went a little wild in his youth. For some reason, ranch life is where bad boys go to die and his parents had asked my dad if he would hire him. Jacob held a light and Nick craned his neck, trying to spy a tail or a nose with every push. A nose meant the baby was positioned right, a tail meant the calf was breech—trouble for a natural birth. Two hooves were already born unto the world and usually to follow that you would see something of the calf's face, but that hadn't happened, not yet at least. I heard them say the mama had been calving for about twelve hours, and the worry was that she didn't seem to be trying to push anymore. Tensions were high, so I tried to stay in the background as much as I could. I had been at enough births to know Nick wouldn't help pull the baby until he knew for sure the calf wasn't breech. If he could just see an inkling of the baby's face, he could help her while she pushed.

I could hear him talking to her as she labored.

"Come on, Mama, give me something…"

Carter took over for Jacob and sent the two night boys back to the bunkhouse, leaving just the four of us in the field.

Another contraction came and the mama just didn't seem to have it in her. She pushed meagrely, and the two little hooves came a little further into the world.

"Come *on,* Mama," he urged again, his voice full of gravel and kindness. Seeing him speak sweetly to her reminded me of the Nick I knew from our younger years, and right now I was trying not to remember that. I didn't want to be the love-struck rancher's daughter while I was home.

He patted her and spoke to her just a little more. She laid down, seeming exhausted.

"How long 'till the vet gets here?" Nick called to Carter. Somewhere in his turn to Carter, he noticed that I had arrived. He didn't acknowledge I was there other than a slight nod in my direction, swiftly moving his eyes from mine to Carter's, breaking the trance that had held me there.

"Anytime," Carter responded.

"They have a cart ready for him as soon as he gets here."

As if their speaking about him manifested him out of thin air, the vet came bumping over the valley. He was there in less than two minutes, asking Nick how long she had been laying for. "Just a few minutes, but she gave up pushing about fifteen minutes ago," Nick responded quickly.

He was covered in sweat and was like a machine on auto pilot. I wondered briefly if he ever slept. He lifted his hat and pushed his fingers through his wavy hair, throwing his hat to the ground. This was a go with the flow procedure and although C sections were possible, they didn't like to do them if they didn't have to.

The vet gave the heifer a shot of epinephrine, a type of adrenaline to help relax her and give a little more room for the calf to push through the birth canal. I had seen this used before and it almost always worked.

Another contraction started and what seemed like amniotic fluid and blood spilled out in front of us. Carter took a step back. He looked white and really queasy. I acted quickly, running to the group and taking the light from Carter as he went to put his head between his knees.

"Sorry guys. I need a second," he muttered, as he sat down in the grass. Nick took one look at him and pulled off his flannel and his white t-shirt from under it, momentarily leaving him standing shirtless in the field, ten feet from me. I gulped, audibly. He was as perfect under his clothes as I had imagined. Better, actually. He grabbed a fresh water bottle from a cooler bag and poured the cold water all over the t-shirt, ringing it out and handing it to Carter.

"Here, put this on the back of your neck and your forehead. It'll help."

I tried not to stare, I knew I shouldn't, but *my God*, I couldn't help it. His clothes hid strong, muscular arms and so many abs I lost count. He didn't look too muscular, just perfect. I took inventory of the tattoos that I could see. Making mental notes of them quickly. A huge, intricate cross of sorts stretched across his back. Starting near his shoulder blade, what looked like detailed, interwoven bones and greenery extended down, leading to his sleeved left arm. What resembled a whiskey bottle pouring out words ran down his inner arm, surrounded by waves. Intricate skeleton figures facing each other in an embrace with some sort of saying around them, angel's wings and various other sketches I couldn't quite make out. All of it intertwined with blue bonnet and greenery. All colorless and shaded. His right side was free of tattoos except for a long line of written words in a different language running down his side, past his waist, disappearing into his jeans.

He put on his flannel again, doing up each button. My twenty seconds of pleasure were up. When my eyes reached his face, he was looking right at me. He had obviously noticed me staring because he smirked before turning back to his work as I prayed that I could melt into the earth below me. He didn't look back again. He was laser focused, talking to the mama cow while her next contraction began. She stood up again as the little baby life tried to force itself from her. I prayed for that relief for her. The epinephrine magic happened quickly, and mercifully, a little nose appeared. The little calf wasn't breech after all. Satisfied enough with the baby's position, the vet pulled along with the contractions. Gently enough to not hurt the calf, but strong enough to help the mama along.

I stood dutifully holding the light. It was my one and only job, and I was going to do it right. Nick and I locked eyes for a fleeting second.

"Like what you saw, Princess?"

Air. I need air. I opened my mouth but no words came. I'm sure my cheeks were flushed.

"Yeah, you did." He smirked.

I couldn't even argue because hell yes, I liked it. *Damn him and his hotter than hot body, I mean, who looks like that?* Our attention mercifully turned back to the mama with her next contraction. I had seen this before, and I knew he had too. We were close. With each push, he came out a little more, an eye, a little more of his head, until finally the worst was over. The very big baby calf slid gently and perfectly to the earth. We silently cheered so as not to scare the Mama.

"He is a biggun," the vet barked, lifting up his legs to see the sex. "Makes sense why she had some trouble."

We backed away to let Mama cow began the cleaning process. The doctor pulled his gloves off and shook Nick's hand. "Thanks for being here when I couldn't."

I smiled at the mama and her baby, off in my own little world of wonder, avoiding Nick's eyes.

"Welcome to the world, little one," I whispered. All this commotion and the sun hadn't even risen yet.

Chapter 14 - He's just...complicated
Katie

Carter recovered from his queasy spell and Nick decided we all should ride a little further into the east pastures. Zac chatted all the way there. His fiery copper hair is a metaphor for his personality. He's a smaller guy, but what he lacked in size he made up for in personality. I could tell after five minutes of listening to him that he looked up to Nick. He talked his ear off every chance he could, always seeking his approval.

By late morning, I was hot and hungry. I was the weak link, clearly. It was obvious to me so it must have been obvious to Nick, since stopped us to break for an early lunch after we returned from the east to the barn. We would head to the west side next to check for new calves and monitor the grasses, since the herd needed to move soon. And that was a longer ride in the sun.

I always felt like Nick was keeping an eye on me. Like I was some fragile, helpless girl he had to watch. If I hadn't fallen off Buttercup, would he still look at me like that? I had been riding since before I was five, was he going to fear for my safety forever based on one weak moment?

I ignored the eyes I could feel on me and checked out the food before me. Everything was top-notch. Steaks, salads, and fruit. It tasted like heaven after our busy morning. Of course, I hadn't ever eaten this much in New York. I had forgotten how much riding took out of me. It was such a workout. Surprisingly though, I felt after only two days my body was starting to remember.

We sat at a picnic table outside the barn in the mid-day sun slowly soaking it up and eating. I stayed quiet, listening to the boys joke and laugh and talk about things that had happened recently and people I didn't know anymore. It was a simple way of life. Not an easy one. But simple nonetheless.

These boys knew hard work and were proud of it. I could see the beauty in it and was starting to appreciate the heart these cowboys put into my dad's land every day. I watched Nick as they chatted, easily jumping topics between sports, politics, the economy, ranch business, and people from town. He knew a lot, about a lot.

We finished eating eventually, duties on the ranch weren't determined by the clock. Everyone just knew the time of the day by routine, or so it seemed. We rode steadily, talking all the way to the west pastures, hovering between each other while riding and holding different conversations. I swore I could feel Nick's eyes on me still. I glanced at him as he rode past me up ahead. He looked back as he talked to Zac, and when his eyes met mine, it did something odd to my stomach.

I spoke about my dad to Carter, who rode with me for a while. How scary his accident had been, how easy it was for me to come back. I confessed I had been ready for a break from New York. Carter and I had always gotten along well, and he was easy to talk to. I told him that Charlotte had always had a huge crush on him and he had never known it. We laughed about it now. He joked that he would ask her on a date when she came home.

"And when are you actually coming back for good then, Katie?" Carter asked with a grin.

I laughed and shook my head.

"I'm serious. I'm just trying to figure out how we can prove Nick wrong."

"What?" I turned my eyes to him, confused.

"Well, he seems to think you'll go back to New York. I told him maybe you'd stay. It's kind of a joke that he's always right about everything. It would be nice to prove him wrong. Just once."

Nick had been talking about me to Carter or even other guys at the bunkhouse, and I hated that I liked to know that.

"Well, I'm just here for a few months. My dad says he feels more comfortable when I'm home. Like I'm going to spot something someone else might not. Meanwhile, I feel like I have no idea what I'm doing."

He smiled then and nodded as I continued.

"About Nick and me, we haven't gotten off on the right foot. I feel like he doesn't seem to like me or think I belong here. I just want to keep the peace. Has he said anything about why he'd be upset with me?"

"No, never." He thought for a minute. "I think you're looking at it all wrong if you don't mind me sayin'. You remember how he treated you back when we were kids? Pulling your hair, or I don't know, say, making mud pies and leaving them at your back door for you to step on? He was always pulling pranks on you." He snickered. "Ever wonder why that was? We all knew. He always talked about you when we were kids."

"Then what is his deal now? He always looks cryptic or dark or some combination of both."

"He's just...complicated. He's been through a lot of shit. Shit I really didn't know if he'd come back from. He's tough as hell though, and stubborn. He wants to do his best for your dad."

My look of confusion must have been amusing because he smiled.

"You two will figure it out, bud. I have faith in you both. See ya in a bit, I gotta talk to Zac." He pointed and rode ahead to catch him.

My mind filled with questions while I rode along in silence. I had always wished Nick liked me when I was young after we kissed, doodling *Katelyn Stratton* on the inside of my journal became a quest, finding the perfect way to sign my name as a married woman. Thank God those journals were safely located at the bottom of a tote in our attic. He generally looked at me with annoyance most of the time now. I thought back over every conversation we had had in the last few days and decided Carter was wrong. Nothing indicated Nick wanted anything to do with me anymore.

I caught up with the boys and finally we made our way through to the west pasture. It was a beautiful, very large, open space. Full of trees and shade.

A freshwater creek ran through it, where I used to catch tadpoles when I was small while my dad worked. The cattle loved it here. There were no hills to block the wind so they stayed so cool in the summer and the insects weren't as plentiful.

We checked on them and the food supply as we were expected to. All the boys agreed they had maybe a few more weeks yet before they had to move. I tried to remember the last time I had just spent a day out here like this. It felt good for my soul, and by the time we were done and heading back to the barn, I felt relaxed and happy.

We finished up early to shower and change before going to the fair. The cowboys talked about it on the way back. I got the impression by how they spoke that everyone was going in groups together. I piped up to hitch a ride with one of them, I didn't care who, I just didn't want to go alone.

"How are y'all getting there? Could I go with whoever is driving?"

We had reached the barn by then and were finishing cooling down our horses. Carter laughed as Nick came into view from washing his hands.

"Pretty sure Nick was intent on taking you him—" Nick smacked carter in the arm with the small hand towel before he could finish his sentence. He turned to me then, his green eyes stunning me as he handed the towel to Carter.

"I'm going to drive you. Your dad asked me to make sure you got there and got home. He figured you wouldn't want to go on your own. I'll pick you up." He said it, he didn't ask, as if I would never say no to him.

I only nodded. I didn't like how he expected I would say yes, but the thought of being in his truck with him again was too good to pass up. His dark eyes lightened.

"Is an hour enough time? Long enough to clean up and make yourself, you know, fancy nightlife like?" He used air quotes when he said the word fancy. I could hear Carter snorting back laughter from the other side of the stall where he was working with his horse.

I laughed, looking down at my horrid appearance. "Fancy? I'm not fancy enough for you right now?"

My braided hair was messy and sweaty, I was covered in dust and mud from riding though the pastures, and I still wore some blood from the early morning delivery. I was the polar opposite of "fancy".

He laughed, a real laugh, and it was the most beautiful sound. "If you're going like that, I'm going like this..." He was way worse off than me, and we both broke into laughter.

A sort of awkward silence filled the space between us as our laughter tapered off. The other two cowboys were walking out and I realized that we were finally alone.

He started before I could. "Look, Kate, I'm really sorry I got so upset yesterday."

He pulled his hat off and tousled his hair. "You don't know me anymore, but I am very...protective of this place now, and defending my motives to you caused me to lose my temper. Having you back here is taking some getting used to. It's no excuse to talk to you like that though. When I heard you were coming back, I assumed you were just as...entitled as your sister. No offense to her but..."

I nodded, she was entitled, I got it.

"I thought maybe you were just coming home because you were feeling guilty about not seeing your dad over the last couple years, but after working with you the last few days, I can see that you're here for the right reasons and you love this place too." He looked directly into my eyes. "Like you always used to. Assumption is the death of truth, right?" he said, quoting one of my dad's sayings.

He leaned up against the timber door frame of Buttercup's stall, hanging his hat on the hook there as he spoke. His eyes raked over me as he thought, like he was trying to figure out how to proceed.

"Can we just start over? It doesn't make any sense for us to have to work together and not at least try to get along."

I sighed, grateful we were putting this behind us.

"This is a big adjustment for me too. I shouldn't have assumed you were trying to undermine me with Amanda. I'm sorry too. If I'm being honest, I was trying to push your buttons. I always did a good job of that." I smiled wide. He smiled back in response.

"That's sure as shit true, but still no excuse for me to treat you like that, Princess."

I shrugged. "Better than what you used to do when you were pissed off at me. You could always just go back to that I guess, torment me and pull my hair? Seems easier than this, holding in your frustration." I laughed before I realized what those words actually sounded like and then I turned to blush hot fire. I didn't dare look back at him. My stupid big mouth, it always failed me. *Note to self, don't make jokes without saying them in your mind first.*

Oddly enough, the way he raised an eyebrow when I said it and the half-smirk he wore before I turned away was not what I expected, like the idea possibly intrigued him. He ignored my comment though, mercifully, and approached, sticking out his hand for me to shake.

"Okay so in other words, it's settled. We're friends, yeah?"

"Yeah, I'd like that better than bickering." I reached out to accept his hand. It was rough from hard work and very big, molding perfectly with mine. I could almost sense what it would feel like running over my skin. I sucked in a breath, as if it might be my last one. I expected him to pull away, but he didn't. His body moved in closer, his hand sliding slightly up to my elbow, leaving a steady trail of goosebumps in its wake. I definitely stopped breathing, not fully understanding what was happening.

For a fraction of a second he just stood there, looking into my eyes. Conflicted, honest. The darkness dissipating.

I had seen that look on him before—once, years ago and most recently, just that very morning in my dream. I could feel the heat from his body, smell the soap on his freshly washed skin in the air mixed with his signature leather and spice scent. It made me almost dizzy.

Before I could register his movements, he reached a hand up to my face and dragged the pad of his thumb across my cheekbone, letting it linger there. He gripped me possessively with his other at my elbow, pulling me to him.

"And for the record, you always look fucking beautiful Katelyn." He leaned in.

I closed my eyes the instant I felt his lips dust against mine. Not because I was trying to be dramatic, but only because I genuinely thought I might pass out. Every nerve ending in my body turned to fire as his hand on my cheek moved into my hair, cradling my head. The minty sweetness of his breath mixed with mine sent tiny shockwaves through my body.

It was me who moved closer then, parting my lips first. His hand on my elbow slid to my waist and pulled tighter, crushing me to him so our bodies pressed together. I fit into him like the shape of his body was carved out perfectly just for me. A tiny moan escaped from my lips and the sound he offered in return felt like a growl. I could feel the connection between us vibrating in a quiet hum. The innate need to squeeze my thighs together as his tongue danced expertly with mine was overwhelming. Of all he times I imagined kissing Nick, I never imagined my body to react quite like this, turning me into pool of fiery mush.

I wanted him closer. I wanted *more*. But my stupid brain reminded me he worked for my father and I had been home for only two days. I wasn't about to be another one of his friends with benefits, or another buckle bunny from town. I pulled my body back, panting for air. He released his tight grip on my waist and I instantly regretted my reaction. His eyes pulled away from mine, as if I had broken the connection, and icy glaze returned.

He grabbed his hat from the frame. "See you in an hour." He headed out the door to the barn.

"Yep, in an hour," I replied awkwardly, my heart racing. He turned and looked at me one last time before disappearing behind the timber frame. *What the fuck was that?*

I stood there, stunned, trying to decipher his touch. It was like standing on the edge of a high dive, deciding whether or not to jump off into the water below. My body still blazed from his touch and his lips on mine. I took a moment to gather myself, then began walking, knowing my time to get ready was limited. I felt like I was flying.

Nick was so shrouded in mystery. When he was young I knew it all, now all I saw was some sort of conflicted soul that had "been through some shit" as Carter said. His kiss consumed my thoughts, and before I knew it, I mindlessly walked through the front door of the house. It was quiet. The late afternoon sunlight streamed through the front window.

It suddenly hit me. I only had an hour. I hadn't been to a fair in at least five years and after that kiss, this night almost felt like a date. I looked down at my dirty jeans and boots and remembered his words. *You always look fucking beautiful Katelyn.* It dumbfounded me to realize he thought I *ever* looked beautiful, especially like this. My brain wouldn't settle, as if I had taken a few shots of espresso on my walk back.

How was I going to be ready in an hour and what the hell was I going to wear?

Chapter 15 - Best part of being a woman
Katie

I ran up the stairs and hopped into the shower, scrubbing out my long hair vigorously as if it would make the washing go faster. My nails were even dirty after the last couple of days. All the scrubbing to achieve a squeaky clean I-don't-work-in-cow-poo-look took time I didn't have.

I hopped out and threw my hair up in a large, fluffy towel. First things first, I needed an outfit. I pulled open my closet to slim pickings. Jeans, flannels, t-shirts, jeans, repeat. Then a thought occurred to me. Dad still kept some of Mom's old dresses in the very back of the closet in one of the spare rooms. Charlotte and I used to play dress up with them when we were young. Every few months or so he had Melia wash them. She wasn't coming back for them obviously, but my dad said he would keep just a few. He always hoped maybe one of us girls would want them one day. Charlotte was too tall for them now, so that left them to me. At this moment, I was thankful he kept them. My mother's sundresses.

I swung back the door and pulled them out. There were about ten dresses, the ones my dad thought to be her favorites. My mom used to love wearing them. Not only to keep cool in the scorching Texas heat, but because in her words, *"The best part of being a woman was always being able to wear pretty clothes."*

I still remembered her saying that whenever she forced me to wear one against my will. I sorted through them one by one, touching the material and remembering them in my own way. They used to be big on me, but now I was pretty sure they would fit just right.

I easily selected a sky-blue dress in the softest linen I had ever felt. Everyone has a color they feel is *their* color. Blue is mine. Any shade of it. It had a square neckline and large, off the shoulder flutter sleeves. The dress was short, even on me, ending at my mid-thigh. The snug bodice gave way to an A-line skirt. It fit to absolute perfection. I selected a pair of ivory sandals from the bottom of the closet. They were open and strappy. Done, minus the towel on my head.

I headed back to my room with my loot, satisfied with my selection. I glanced at the clock. I had the time to dry it carefully. I added some beachy waves and put it half up, leaving wisps to frame my face. I even opted to apply some mascara, which I didn't do often. It made my eyes seem larger and more dramatic than normal.

Truthfully, the whole ordeal had only taken me only twenty-five minutes. I added some lip gloss and a little bit of my favorite vanilla and citrus perfume. I looked into the tall mirror outside my bathroom to view my overall appearance. I no longer looked like I was up to my knees in dirt all day. I was happy but so nervous and not quite ready for the night ahead. A few minutes with my dad were in order.

The door to his room was open just a few inches and I could hear the TV going as I approached.

On Tuesday, he was able to begin standing in a boot and I knew he was ready to start getting back to normal.

I knocked lightly and entered the room, hoping I wasn't waking him. My dad did the little gasping thing he does when he thinks I look pretty.

"You look just lovely, Pixie, and so much like Mom. You've really gotten some sun these last few days. Being outside agrees with you."

I nodded. I could see the reminders of my standard sun tan coming back.

He seemed a bit choked up. I knew I looked like her, I probably did a lot more so in her dress and shoes.

"Well, after a few days in the dirt it feels nice to put a dress on." I laughed, my stomach was doing nervous flip flops waiting for Nick to arrive.

"Lena is going tonight, her mom called me today to see if you were home yet. She said Lena has been trying to get a hold of you. Have you not answered her?"

Lena Baker had been my absolute best friend all through middle and high school until I left for New York. She was the kind of friend that you always picked up right where you left off when you came home. I had been home for three days almost and hadn't even texted her back.

"Thanks for the heads up, I'll text her."

"Nick will be getting you tonight and bringing you home after?" my dad asked, although he already knew the answer. "Of course, you are capable of driving yourself if you want but I hoped the two of you would spend some time together. Maybe become buddies again. I know you have to re-adjust to life here, maybe having a friendly face from the past will help."

I smiled innocently. If he only knew our past.

"Obviously, since you asked him to do it you know he is taking me. Good thing I've got you planning my social life or I'd be in bed before nine. I'm exhausted."

I sat down beside his bed and talked with him about the new calf and the trouble of the early morning. Though he already knew, Frank had called him afterwards to fill him in, he still acted like he loved hearing about it from my point of view. If the picture of "doting dad" was in the dictionary, my dad's face would be the one you saw.

I checked the time and said goodnight, knowing Nick would arrive any minute.

I grabbed a light ivory sweater wrap from the front closet that was mine from my younger teenage years and I put it over my arm for later, just in case it got chilly out.

I headed downstairs and waited for what seemed like an eternity, fiddling with my keys and my purse strap. I popped some gum into my mouth just as the black Ram pickup truck ambled up the driveway. My stomach flip-flopped. I told myself not to be nervous. It was *Nick*. The same Nick I had known my whole life. He carefully parked in the driveway right near the door.

The moment I saw him get out of the truck, I knew I was lying to myself. My body betrayed me, and I felt the pull to him just from *looking* at him. I remembered his lips on mine, the feeling warming me from the inside out. He wore very faded and worn blue jeans that fit him perfectly, a silver cross around his neck, and a white t-shirt. I could see the underlay of his tattooed arm and shoulder through it and the white did a good job of making him look even more tanned. He pulled his cowboy hat off the front seat and put it on as he approached the door. I felt like I might throw up. He was that goddamn good looking.

Here we go.

Chapter 16 - Hot and Cold
Katie

I waited for a full twenty seconds after he rang the bell before coming to the door. The last thing I wanted him to know was that I was ready for him. I swung open the door and suddenly he stood before of me, sucking the breath out of my lungs.

"Hey," I said, trying to be casual and failing miserably. I gave up and smiled at him.

"Hey, you ready to go?" Nick asked it causally, as if he was talking to another cowboy and in a rush, his eyes not meeting mine entirely.

"Sure…" I wasn't a conceded girl, but I did think I looked nice enough for him to say so. After that kiss, I had hoped something would shift between us. I felt his emotions in it. I was still thinking about the look in his eyes. He interrupted my heated thoughts with business.

"Does your dad have a time he wants you home by?"

I laughed an odd, nervous sounding laugh. "Well, no. I'm okay to have a little fun, I don't have a curfew anymore."

I'm okay to have a little fun? God, I was so awkward. The true definition of face palm.

"Okay, well I'll have you home early anyway. I'm sure you're pretty tired after the last few days." He looked straight ahead as we walked to his truck, distracted.

"Okay then..." I trailed off, not sure what else to say in response to his cool demeanor.

He opened the door to the truck and helped me up. My small size made it necessary to always use the running boards. His hand supported my back. The small touch sent a current racing through my blood. I shoved it down.

I turned to look at him, to say thank you and smile, but he had already started closing the door. He hopped into his side and brought the truck to life. I looked out the window, taking my time to breathe in the intoxicating scent of Nick that saturated his truck. He set the radio to the local country station and we started on our way.

The music and fresh air soothed my nerves and I let myself relax a little on the short twenty-minute drive to the fair grounds. Nick filled the silence, reminding me of what to expect from the fair. As he spoke about local people and life, his tone grew softer.

The fair grounds were full of life, people, and sound when we turned the corner through the gates. Twinkle lights filled the space. There was a Ferris wheel, a full midway of rides, and even a kiddie-land for the smaller children. Pumpkin launching, two funhouses, and a few rows of carnival games were took up a long isle alongside booths where local vendors could sell their handmade items. Different restaurants and participants lined another row with chili to try and each had a little box on their table to vote on your favorite. Whichever restaurant had the highest points at the end of the weekend was the winner and crowned official chili fest king or queen. I loved the festive vibe. Nick came around the truck to meet me and we started our walk in. Again, he placed his hand on my back to guide me.

"Katelyn Daniellllle!!!!!!!" a high-pitched, sing-song voice yelled as we passed through the entrance.

I looked around to see *where* it came from, already knowing *who* it came from. Lena was heading toward me, fast. Nick dropped his hand immediately and gave some room for the bubbly brunette to encase me in a bear hug. Lena was, as always, effortlessly beautiful. Her glowing dark skin was always perfect, her cheeks rosy and highlighted to perfection, her lips glossy pink. She had the most beautiful smile I had ever seen in real life, it was warming in any situation.

Nick said hello to her. He had seen her a million times around my house but the two of them had never really interacted much. She was with her older brother Devon and his girlfriend. He and Nick had gone to school together and played football together in a different life. They talked for a minute while Lena and I caught up a bit.

"Are you free to roam with me? David and Casey are over near the Ferris wheel, you can come and help me talk to Casey...ugh he's so hot, I need back-up."

As if she needed my help. She always had anyone's attention if she wanted it.

She looked from me to Nick and back again. "Oh, or are you two together tonight?" Lena asked, realizing we may be on a date.

I instantly blushed.

"She's free," Nick piped up, shrugging his shoulders. I quickly turned to him to see if he was joking or not. He was so hot and cold. Either I had the wrong impression about the night, or he kissed me and realized I wasn't just going to sleep with him so I was no longer interesting. I had hoped that maybe he just wanted to be the one to bring me. Mistake number one was expecting anything from someone he used to be, not who he was now.

"I'll catch up with Zac and Jacob while you guys do your thing. Kate, I'll find you later? A couple hours?" His tone was as polite as can be but...

What the hell?

I didn't have the time to even respond before he turned to talk to Devon again. Every time I let my guard down in any way with him, he shot me down. He stopped before heading off with the rest of the guys and came closer, looking down at me. His deep green pools burned into mine. I didn't recognize the look he wore. If I didn't know any better, I would think it was worry.

"Text me if you want to leave early, or you need anything, and Katelyn...be safe."

By the time I realized what was happening, he'd joined Zac in making a game plan and I was left there, stunned. Again.

I had no choice, so I left with Lena and vented to her about Nick as we wandered the fair for over an hour. I told her all about the things he had said to me since I arrived, all the history we had brimming to the surface. The fact that I had let him get to me again drove me crazy. Lena laughed and tried to get a word in edgewise, which was unusual for her. Normally she was the one doing all the talking. I knew I was being a conversation hog.

"So, it's obvious you do still have feelings for him, even now after all this time—" Lena started.

I cut her off. "No, I don't."

Lena continued anyway, ignoring my blatant lie. "No one catches Nick Stratton, you know. He changed a lot after you guys stopped talking. Devon says he was with so many different girls, but he never actually dated any of them. I think he kind of dated Kristin Kessel in twelfth grade for a few months before he went right off the deep end of partying, but that's like, it. After that, it's just been a different girl any time I've seen him and *not* the kind that he'd bring home to meet his parents. I hate to tell you, but he's dating your dad's ranch."

She was right. He *was* dating the ranch. That's why he brought me, to make my dad happy. I was so embarrassed and mad at myself for thinking the wrong thing.

Well, no more wishing for anything where he was concerned. It would be strictly business from here on out. I wasn't going to let him get under my skin any more than he already had.

I looked at Lena, who looked very, very bored and patient, bless her soul.

"I'm sorry I've been such a downer. I'm sure you didn't want to spend the night listening to me whine about some stupid guy from my childhood," I said.

"Let's go find Casey," I added, locking arms with her.

"Thank God. My eyes were starting to glaze over." Lena laughed, looking relieved, which made me laugh in turn and swat her for her dramatics. I had missed her. We wandered for another fifteen minutes looking for Casey and David, finally finding them at a row of games.

There was a bow and arrow shoot, and a huge boxing glove that was for punching to see what your high score could be. The two of them were there showing their strength with a couple of other guys I didn't recognize. David Barnell, always the loudest kid in our grade, hobbled around, slurring his words. Clearly drunk. *Great.* Drunk boys were my least favorite.

As we got a little closer, I could smell alcohol on the other two as well. They both seemed pretty out of it. One of them was tall and just a really big guy all around, like he was a football player. He had shaggy brown hair and was actually kind of cute, minus the fact that he looked at me like I was his next shot of whatever he was drinking. The other one was smaller and chubby, he wore a beanie on his head and clothes that were two sizes too big. As we got a little closer, Casey gave up his next punch to come and talk to Lena, the two of them falling into a little love bubble. It was quite obvious that Casey felt the same way about Lena and she did about him.

I stood a few feet away, giving them some space while awkwardly looking at my Pinterest page on my phone. This night had turned out to be so different than I expected. I was starting to feel like a third wheel.

It was eight-thirty, and I prepared to text Nick and tell him I was ready to leave. It meant I'd have to endure the ride home with him, but I didn't have to pretend to enjoy it. What had started out to be possibly a fun night had quickly become a total bust. I was tired. I came, I saw, I was ready to leave.

I opened my phone to find his last text under his newly appointed contact name. Perfectly labeled, in my opinion. *Kryptonite.*

A deep voice interrupted me. "How come you're just standing here all alone, gorgeous?"

I looked up. *Shit.*

Chapter 17 - Fury
Katie

The "football player" stood two feet from me. I backed up to get him out of my personal space. He moved closer, instantly filling the space I created. He smelled strongly of whiskey and pot. Now that he was close to me, he didn't seem cute. He seemed like a sleazebag.

"Hey..." I said carefully. He was leering at me, like he was going to try to kiss me or something. I didn't want to encourage him, so I decided a generic question was best

"How do you know Casey and David?" I backed up again, this time a generous five feet. Again, he filled the space without hesitation. He clearly didn't understand boundaries, probably due to the amount of alcohol flowing through his system. He reached out and touched a strand of my hair dangling in front of my face.

"We go to school together," he slurred. "I like your hair, you got a boyfriend? Can I be your boyfriend?" He chuckled, thinking he was hilarious.

No one had invaded my personal space this uninvited before, so I wasn't sure if I was overreacting in my panic, but I backed up again and pushed his hand away from me. Something about him gave me a bad feeling. I looked at Lena, who was twenty feet away. She was oblivious, encased in her little love bubble.

"I do have a boyfriend, he's just getting me a drink," I answered quickly, trying anything to get the creep away from me. He smiled a crooked smile, devious.

"I think you're lying. How come he left you here all alone? That wasn't very smart of him, maybe you need a better man." He was more aggressive this time, pushing right into my personal space and touching my shoulder. I felt like I might throw up. Again, the only thing I could do was back away. I knew then, in that instant, he wasn't going to leave me alone. I had to just try to get away.

"Lena and I have to go soon, so I'll see you later." I attempted to maneuver around him but he was too big and stepped in front of me to block my path.

"Come on, don't be like that gorgeous, I just thought you were hot. Let's just hang out for a bit, I bet I can make you feel good."

I searched for ways around him and asked myself if I was ready to kick him in the balls, hard, if he didn't let me by.

"I have to go." I said it a little more firmly, even though inside I was scared to death of his size and the quiet, dark area we had drifted into beside a trailer.

I tried the other way around him and was quick enough to get by but not quick enough to fully get away. He grabbed a big handful of my hair, right at the roots, and pulled me toward him. Pain shot through my head as my body slammed into his, hard.

"You're just being a tease, a little bitch. You know what I do with little bitches? I remind them who's really in charge." He laughed wickedly into my ear, droplets of his gross saliva landing on my shoulder. Bile rose in my stomach. I was just about to scream for help, kick him, anything, when someone came from my right and a loud crack sounded over the fair noise. The football player let go of my hair abruptly and I fell to the ground, landing in the gravel.

"Shiiiit dude you broke my nose!" he complained to my savior. Another cracking sound followed and the peripheral vision of the football player's head hitting the earth stopped me from looking.

A deep voice spoke, lethal. It sent a shiver up my spine.

"I'm about to break both of your fucking hands, you piece of shit." *Nick*. I looked up to see him closing his eyes, like he was trying to control himself, and I felt my bones run cold at the sheer fury I saw there. He looked like he was about to burn down the entire fairground around us. The football player looked to me frantically. Nick grabbed his face and turned it back to his.

"Don't fucking look at her, Patterson. If you ever even breathe in her direction again, your body will be at the bottom of the fucking river. Now, you're going to apologize."

The vile boy he called Patterson looked at him in an are-you-serious? type of way. Nick didn't hesitate for one second, he grabbed most of his fingers and bent them backwards, hard. I don't know how they weren't broken.

"You play football, right? Running back? Need these fingers for catching? I'm giving you one more fucking second. Tell her you know that she'd never want a worthless little dick like you that doesn't know how to respect a woman." He twisted Patteron's wrist and bent his fingers even further, beyond their normal realm of movement, and I looked away. I didn't need to see them break. Patterson yelped but chose to speak immediately with a pleading tone.

"I...I'm sorry I'm a worthless dick...that doesn't know how to respect a woman. I'm sorry...please, fuck, let go!"

Nick let go of his fingers and I stifled a small laugh when I looked back at them. Patterson looked like he was about to piss his pants. He had blood running all over his face and into the gravel. I had never in my life been so happy to see someone bleed. My head throbbed at the spot where he pulled my hair and yanked me towards him.

"I...I didn't know you were her boyfriend, I wouldn't have touched her." He was still slurry, but his fear of Nick was obvious as he turned pale. Nick looked at him, confused by his statement about being my boyfriend, but didn't correct him. He grabbed Patterson by his blood-soaked shirt collar with both of his hands, pulling him right up off the ground to his knees as if he weighed nothing. He laughed an evil laugh, his disgust apparent.

"You shouldn't have touched her anyway, you sick fuck. Leave now before I change my mind and spill every one of your teeth onto the ground...just for fun." Patterson dropped to the earth with a thud as Nick let him go and turned to me. "Now!" he yelled over his shoulder, without looking back.

I could almost see the internal battle he was fighting. His words chilled me to the bone because I knew he really meant them. He looked like he would delight in ringing Patterson's neck. I had been scared two minutes before when that big dumb jock grabbed my hair, but seeing Nick angry, really angry, absolutely terrified me.

Nick's demeanor instantly changed as he approached me, with his hand out. *How could he do that? Go from one extreme to the next so easily?* His eyes were softer now, worried again.

"I shouldn't have left you, are you okay? I just happened to see him when I came around the corner." His eyes squeezed shut like he was remembering the scene in his mind.

"Fuck, Kate, I need to get out of here right now or I'm going to go back for him. What were you doing with him anyway? I told you to be safe." He helped me up, brushing the dusty earth off of my knees. The knuckles on his hand were busted open and bleeding. I reached to touch him, he pulled his hand back. "It's fine," he said quickly.

I looked to his eyes. "I didn't want to talk to him—" I was cut off by the rest of the group joining in on the commotion.

"Who brought him?" Nick asked. The chill in my spine returned with his tone.

Casey looked mortified and terrified all at the same time. "I'm so sorry Nick, I barely know him. He brought us some Jack. I didn't drink it, just some of the other guys did."

Patterson was scampering up off the ground, he looked scared. He stumbled up and ran away with his buddy in tow. I knew they were gone for good. Nick held onto me, and I felt his body relax a little.

"It's not your fault Case, I'm going to take Kate home now." He patted him on the shoulder with his free hand as he walked by, never letting mine go for a second. I said a quick goodbye to Lena, who also wouldn't stop apologizing for leaving me alone. I told them it was fine, I wasn't a child. I just wanted the safety of Nick's truck after the whole episode.

If Nick hadn't been there... I shuddered at the thought. There were plenty of spots Patterson could have pulled me to and done who knows what to me. With all the noise and commotion, would anyone have even noticed?

Nick gently let go of my hand and I hated myself for caring that he did. He pulled my wrap from my arms when we got far enough away from the group that we were alone and bent down to my face, lifting it up to his to look into my eyes. Searching them to see if I was really okay. He brought me to his chest, pulling me into a hug I instinctively remembered from being young. His arms wrapped around me. His hands gripping my shoulders through my hair. Covering me with safety.

"Are you alright?"

"I think so." I answered honestly. He backed up and placed my wrap around my shoulders tightly as we started walking again, keeping his grip on me all the way to his truck.

The truck was warm, but I was shivering when we got in.

"I think you might be in a bit of shock." Nick said to me. "Are you really okay? I'm so sorry. He's a real piece of shit, Kate. I should've never left you alone. I'm going to explain this to your father. If he's going to hear about it, it has to be from both of us. I should've been with you."

He was rambling at this point.

"I didn't want to talk to him, I was just about to scream. He just kept getting closer to me, he wouldn't let me by him or let me get away. I would never be interested in someone like that." I don't know why I felt the need to tell him that.

My voice was hoarse. It was the first time I had really tried to speak. Maybe he was right. Maybe I was in a bit of shock.

"My dad's not going to be upset with you. Lena was there, I wanted to see her and spend some time with her. You're not my babysitter," I said a little hotly.

I was so grateful to him but still not happy with him.

"Thank you, though," I added, realizing I hadn't thanked him yet. I didn't normally condone violence, but in this case, I welcomed it. "I don't know what he would've done if you didn't come just at that moment."

Nick closed his eyes at the implication. It touched me how much he cared about my dad's opinion of him. I could tell he really didn't want him to be disappointed in him for leaving me. I was a mess. My hair was falling loose from the barrette I'd pinned it back with. Nick's face softened as he looked at me. He touched my hand. Pulling it away quickly after only a second.

"It's okay, I'm just glad I didn't kill him. Jail isn't for me," he bit out.

We rode the rest of the way in silence, listening to his Tyler Childers playlist. I knew every time I heard *Lady May* for the rest of my life, I would remember that night. I gathered myself together and fixed my hair, rubbing the mascara off from under my eyes. I hadn't even realized I had been crying. I was warm finally by the time we pulled into the driveway, feeling clearer and more like myself. Nick got out of the truck and walked around to open my door.

"You don't have to walk me up the driveway," I said to him, wondering what he was doing.

"I'm making sure you get home safe," he stated firmly.

"My home is here." I laughed, but there was no arguing with him.

He walked me right into through the front door and into our large foyer facing the parlor. My dad's voice startled me.

"You two are back early." He sat in his chair in front of the fireplace.

I straightened up instantly. "Dad, what? How are you down here?"

"Roger and Frank helped me down. I have the wheelchair and I'm going to sleep in the den for a while. I like being on the main floor. I needed a change of scenery for a bit. I need to be in the action."

"Sir." Nick said it like hello, professionally, as he removed his hat.

"Hello son, how was the night?"

Nick skipped the small talk. "I feel the need to tell you, something happened. That's why we're back early." He told the whole story, claiming full responsibility for not being with me every second, to which I rolled my eyes and stepped in.

"For the record, I wanted to go with Lena. He isn't my handler. I'm almost twenty years old. Assholes are everywhere. He wouldn't have hurt me. I would have screamed or kicked him and screamed, there were people everywhere. He was just drunk and stupid."

Now that I had some time to think about it. I realized I probably wasn't in as grave a danger as I thought. There had been a lot of people around, if I had screamed loud enough someone would have turned to see what was happening and helped me. Nick continued on and finished the story ending it with him punching Patterson in the face to get him away from me, leaving out the tone in his voice or the look in his eyes that had sent a shiver up my spine.

"I hit him pretty hard, more than once, but it had to be done. I lost my temper. I understand if that disappoints you, but I don't regret it."

My dad looked ready to kill someone. He sat for a few minutes in silence. It was too quiet in the parlor. You could hear the crickets outside.

"Nicholas, I would get up naturally, but I am unable to. Can you please come here?"

"Of course." Nick quickly walked to him. He looked calm and ready for whatever my dad was going to do or say. Fire him? Hug him? Yell at him? Thank him? What? I was frozen.

"It's my experience with Katelyn, that when she makes her mind up people aren't really able to change it. I didn't expect you to babysit her tonight. I expected you to keep her safe and you did that. If she wanted to go with her friend, you did the right thing by giving her some space. This sort of thing could've happened even if I had taken her." He stuck out his hand for Nick to shake it. "Thank you for watching out for her...and I wouldn't normally say this but thank you for punching er...taking care of that kid. What was his name again?"

Nick dutifully shook my dad's hand.

"Brent Patterson, sir. He's not really from around here. I've only seen him a few times. He goes to school in Austin and works at the chicken feed supply in town."

Not anymore, he doesn't.

Knowing my dad, he would take care of that really quickly. You don't disrespect my dad in Hill Country. Sometimes it seemed silly, but today, I was glad my dad had the pull he did. I wanted Patterson as far away from here as possible.

"Good, thank you, I'll take care of that, and get some ice on that hand," my dad stated.

Nick nodded. "Well, if it's all the same to you both, I'm going to head back to the bunkhouse?" He said it more like a question.

"Of course, thank you again, son."

Nick turned to me. His eyes were soft and I could tell he was still feeling sorry for me. He rubbed my arm briefly. "Sorry you had to go through that, Kate. I'll see you tomorrow."

"Thank you again," I said awkwardly. I had decided maybe one more time to show him I appreciated him was warranted.

Nick returned his hat to his head, said goodnight to us both, and left us in the parlor. The door creaked shut behind him and he headed out to his truck.

I was fairly certain my dad was about to give me the third degree to make sure I was really okay.

Chapter 18 - Her addict
Nick

I failed. That job I had? To stay away from her? Failed it like a fifth grader taking a twelfth-grade trigonometry final. I was fucked.

It's been a long time since I felt that kind of anger rush through me. I took off for the short drive back to the bunkhouse and reminded myself of all the changes I had made in my life. Reminded myself that finding that motherfucker and kicking him in the face wasn't worth my life. Reminded myself the adrenaline I felt when I hit him was only a temporary high. I wanted to kill him. *Fuck. How had I let this happen? How had I let myself have these feelings for her?*

This was all because she sat on that goddamn hill beside me and smiled at me. One smile. It hit me like a fucking tsunami. It actually took my breath away. She has the most beautiful, life-changing smile. If I could wake up in the morning and inject those three seconds into my veins, I would do it every single day and happily become her addict. I felt completely out of control around her and kissing her in the barn hadn't helped. I didn't plan it. She just looked up at me, so fucking beautiful. The second I felt her tiny hand in mine it was like bringing the first shot of whiskey to my lips and letting it slide down my throat. Just enough to coat the fire but not enough to satisfy the craving. I wanted more. Needed more.

I felt crazed sliding my hands over her, feeling all that creamy skin, how helpless and pliable she was under my touch. She had no idea how much power she had over me and after her little stare fest at my naked top half in the field, I knew she wasn't as collected as she let on. Whatever this was between us, she felt it too.

I tried to rid my mind of the way her bare shoulders looked in that dress, the color of her eyes when I picked her up. The smallest move almost crumbled every bit of resolve I had. She had pulled her thick, silky hair over her shoulder, bringing it all to the front of her body while we drove. Just a standard habit she has I'm sure, but suddenly I could see it all from my seat beside her—her upper back, her neck, all that creamy skin, the scent of vanilla filling my truck. Her existence begged me to reach out and touch her, even just for a second.

She was the beginning of my demise on this ranch, I had no doubt. But the thing was, I wasn't ready to stop it even though I knew I should.

When I was younger, a school counsellor told me I had a habit of self-sabotaging, ruining the good things in my life. Was that what I was doing here? The ranch was the good thing I was ruining, wasn't it? Or was she the good thing I ruined by dismissing her all those years ago?

It didn't matter anyway.

Right when I had decided I was ready to tell her what I did was wrong when we were young. Right when I knew I had to have her. Right when I was ready to give her everything she deserved, hoping this time she'd stay and maybe give me another chance to show her the man I was now. I was flatly told I could not have her.

My brief hopes were fucking demolished when I had gone back to the bunkhouse to get ready that afternoon.

Chapter 19 - Warning
Nick

I went over the warning in my mind again. Just as I had already done a hundred times over the last six hours. I rushed so I could pick her up. I found myself desperate to get back to her. Feeling her lips on mine had ignited something in me. It was like a drug I didn't know I needed.

The bunkhouse was a gong show, it always is on nights where we all go out. Cowboys rotated through the showers getting ready for the fair, saturating the space with different kinds of cologne. A few guys were drinking beers, it was time to let loose and have fun. Some guys were cooking. It could get chaotic, but I loved it. Especially on the weekends when the cook wasn't there. I was used to it after almost three years. It wasn't very often we got through with our work early and had the whole night off. Frank understood that letting the guys go and have a little fun every once and a while was important. A happy cowboy worked harder.

Frank had lived this life for his entire forty-two years. His wife Sheila and their seven-year-old twin boys Oscar and Evan lived on site in the small "boss cabin" a half mile away. He had been the cow boss for six years and he liked me. We got along really well. He always told me I reminded him of himself when he was younger. He looked tired when I came in the front door of the bunkhouse, he was sitting at a large table drinking a big, steaming mug of coffee. He had probably been up since three am.

"Am I alright to go get ready or do you need anything else? I have to head to pick Kate up in an hour."

I knew we were done with work early, but out of respect, you always asked the boss one more time if there was anything else he needed before you left. It was just unspoken.

"About that…" Frank started.

"Can we chat for a minute?" He raised his mug toward the front porch.

"Sure." *What did I do?* The porch was *the place* to talk. If you looked outside and saw Frank on the porch with someone, you didn't go out until they were done. It was the spot Frank used to give you a heap of trouble, and I didn't like the look he wore. It was serious. Her eyes flashed through my mind, distracting me even then. I started wondering what she would wear when I picked her up. Would it sit just right on her the way her jeans did? Hugging every single curve?

"I'm going to get right to it." Frank broke me out of my thoughts, sounding like he was going to go on a rant. His drawl was thick.

"It's okay for you to pick Katie up, of course. I know Daniel asked you to. I want to make sure you understand the unspoken rule between a rancher, his daughter, and the cowboys that live here. You haven't had to deal with this er…situation before, but you've seen it," Frank said.

Not leaving time for me to answer, he continued his speech. "She is simply off limits to any cowboy on this land. In fact, any relationship between employees working on this ranch is off limits, you know that. I understand she's a pretty girl and you've been spending some time with her. I hear things. Some guys are saying you have a thing for her."

I made a mental note to find out who was running their mouth and deal with them later.

"I want to make sure we nip this situation in the bud. Things get messy and complicated when cowgirls are added into the mix. She is leaving in a few months when Daniel is well and the last thing we need is a depressed cowboy, or worse yet, drama between the two of you. If you break her heart Daniel will never look at you the same and that is just a fact. People like to say they can keep business life separate from personal life, but it is rarely the case."

I sat on one of the chairs, feeling like the wind had just been knocked out of me. I hadn't even thought of that yet. I knew the rule the same as everyone did, about no dating in the bunkhouse, but hadn't thought of it that way since Kate wasn't technically a cowgirl or living *in* the bunkhouse. I managed to nod in response. Still, Frank continued on.

"I see a long future for you here son, keep your nose clean and keep things between you and Katie friendly but professional. Just like you would any other bunky. She's not a girl when she's here. She's a cowgirl. An employee. Am I making myself clear?"

His look was stern, and I knew there was no arguing. The talk was short but a lot had been said. I knew what this meant. We weren't kids anymore and letting her back in was off limits.

Completely off limits. My job would more than likely depend on it. The problem was, I already had.

"Crystal," was the only word I was able to get out.

Frank nodded and dumped the rest of his coffee into the grass and headed for his horse. I realized then that he had waited on me just to have that little chat.

"Good. I may see you at the fair," Frank said before taking off for the barn.

Whatever I felt for Kate would never become anything. I couldn't risk my ranch life to be with her, especially since she was leaving in a few months anyway. If I let it go, the feelings would pass, or at least I hoped they would. I was nothing if I wasn't a cowboy here and I needed the stability and money for my dad and what little we had left since he wasn't able to work anymore.

So, I went with it. It was easier to tell myself all this when I wasn't with her. I picked her up, ignored her hair, her eyes, her legs in that fucking blue dress, the curve of her back under my hand, her voice that was enough it in itself to make me hard at the sound of it soft and almost husky as it coursed through me. The way her skin felt as I pulled her up from Patterson, how her body moulded to mine perfectly when I hugged her, the face she made when she intently listened to me in my truck. Everything about her that felt like it was made just perfectly for me.

I got into my bed and laid awake for hours, trying to formulate a plan. Figuring out how I was going to put her out of my head, and how I was going to forget about her this time. It was an impossible task because she was the fucking ocean I was drowning in.

Chapter 20 - Self Care Sunday
Katie

I woke to a cloudy and dark sky Sunday morning and instantly remembered what had happened the night before. *What a disaster.* My face crumpled up into a look of disgust, and I pulled the warm comforter up to my neck. The back of my head still hurt a bit where Brent had pulled at my hair. It was seven a.m. Sundays were the only days everyone around here relaxed a little.

    It was a day for recharge. These cowboys really worked hard all week and a day at their family home was important. Frank had it down to a science. It worked out that most of them only ended up being on rotation one Sunday a month and even that day most of the work was done around church and before dinner. Church was exactly where I figured I was supposed to go with my aunt and uncle. Yet at this particular moment, I felt like doing exactly what I *wasn't* supposed to do. I was tired of doing what everyone else wanted. Over the last week it had seemed to put me only in embarrassing and even dangerous situations.

I dozed off for a few more minutes and woke again to a light knock at the door.

"Katie, love..." Melia never missed a beat. She was the quiet weaver that kept this house of threads running smoothly, and she didn't want me to be rushed for church.

"I'm up, thank you Tia," I whispered.

I threw my blankets back as Melia closed the door and reached for my warm, fleece robe. I pushed my feet into my slippers and headed down to the kitchen. The light patter of rain filled the quiet by the time I got downstairs. The weather matched my mood and really made me feel like staying in my pjs and watching romcoms all day. My father was up, having wheeled himself from the den into the parlor. His wheelchair parked beside his favorite wingback and a stool with a pillow propped up under his leg.

"I'm surprised you're not up making breakfast," I joked.

He was really doing better by the day.

"Not quite." He rubbed his leg.

"I couldn't sleep. My knee was killing me. I've been up since five."

My dad is a tank. He hates pain medication. He would rather have a little pain than feel out of control or woozy. I admired him. He was unstoppable and my biggest hero.

I was still grateful to him for how he had handled the night before. He didn't flip out like I knew he wanted to. He was calm and great with Nick. Although I knew we would probably never talk about it, I was certain a call had already been made to the feed and supply about Brent and if he wasn't already, Brent would be fired. My dad told me after Nick left he was lucky he didn't charge him with assault. I pleaded with him. Making him promise not to. I didn't want my name dragged through the mud or his ranch. It had barely been a thing and Nick had handled it. Now it was over. Besides, Brent Patterson would probably never show his face around Reeds Canyon again. He looked genuinely very scared when he ran away.

My dad had agreed to my terms, but I knew for certain by the end of day Brent would be looking for a different job. It would be much more important for the owner to keep his relationship solid with my dad. Part-time workers were a dime a dozen.

"So, what's on your agenda for today?" he asked.

"I'm thinking coffee." I smiled at him, sleepily. "Want one?"

"Love one."

I trotted off into the kitchen.

I pulled out my favorite mug and added some sweet vanilla almond milk to it. The coffee was just finishing brewing when I walked in. I grabbed another large mug and added a good helping of cream for my dad. My aunt and uncle sat at the harvest table eating breakfast, already dressed for church.

"Morning Darlin'," my aunt said happily. "You coming to church today?"

"I'm not sure." I tightened my robe. "I'm so tired I might just stay with Dad and in my pjs today."

"We'll be back after lunch and football will be on tonight if you want to watch Dallas destroy Philly?" Uncle Roger smiled at me as he asked.

"Sounds great." I truly meant it. Football with Uncle Roger and my dad was my childhood in a nutshell. Aunt Tracey was always a good sport, sitting with them dutifully. Instead of watching the game, she mostly knitted her latest project or read a book, but the effort was there nonetheless. I smiled, I actually couldn't think of anything better.

I moved quickly back to the parlor and handed my dad the steaming mug.

He took a large sip and sighed. "Ah that's good, Melia makes the best coffee." I nodded in agreement.

"So, I'll ask again, what are you doing today?" His tone showed his worry. He was afraid I was traumatized. I knew it.

"I know, you're probably going to tell me to go to church, but I'm exhausted after last night and maybe it's this weather. But I just want to stay in my pjs and watch football with you and Uncle Roger."

"Actually, I was going to suggest that. I know you're brushing this off, but it was traumatic Katelyn, you need to relax today. We could play cards too, if you want?"

I smiled. "Love that idea. First I'm going to have a hot shower and change."

"It's a plan then."

We sat quietly after that, drinking our coffee, watching the rain run off the porch through the large front window. I felt at peace thinking of the lazy day that stretched out in front of me.

Chapter 21 - You talk in your sleep
Katie

True to my word, after a big plate of cinnamon pancakes that Melia graciously made us, I had the longest and hottest shower. I just stood there for a long time letting the previous night's events wash away.

I should probably be more upset about the whole thing, but I just wasn't. As soon as Nick was there, I knew I was safe. I knew he would take care of it. It was obvious at this point he wasn't interested in me the way I was interested in him, but he had been there when I needed him. It dawned on me slightly that maybe he was only doing what he would do for any other girl.

After changing into my coziest tights and a big, gray Cowboys hoodie, I went downstairs and found my dad wheeling around trying to get some exercise. We played a game of Uno, and then Gin after that, while we waited for my uncle to get home. My dad won every game of Gin, as he always did. He almost always wins at everything he does. No one can beat him.

My uncle came home as promised, just before one o'clock, and when he and my dad started talking work, I escaped to my room for a few hours with a late lunch and a good book. After a long call to Charlotte to tell her what had happened the night before, I settled in and drifted off in my book. When I woke up, it was just after four-thirty. I yawned and headed down to see if I could help my aunt with dinner.

My dad was dozing in his chair when I came down, so I crept by him into the kitchen. My aunt was working hard getting potatoes peeled for the roast beef dinner she was making for all of us. She just loved Elvis more than anything so it was no surprise when I entered the kitchen to hear him playing again in the background and saw her singing along to *Suspicious minds*. A smile broke across my face.

Another two days and then she and uncle would go home. I would miss having them. After that, it would be just my dad and I in the house. Although, my aunt did promise to come back on Sundays for the next little while to make dinner for us and check up on my dad.

"Need some help?" I grabbed an apron from the cupboard, knowing she would find a job for me.

"Yes, I'd love some. Can you peel the carrots over there and then chop them?"

"Sure." I began pulling carrots out of the bag and started peeling them just as I was instructed. "How was church? Did I miss anything?"

"Oh, you know, the usual. But lots of gossip about you being home."

She looked like she was trying to figure something out. "Nick was there—"

"Nick went to *church*?"

She looked at me. I knew she was thinking it was rude that I had interrupted her.

"Yes, he comes sometimes with his dad. He's trying to be a better man. He asked if you were coming and how you were feeling today. Were you not well last night? He also came by about an hour ago to check in on you. After he talked to your dad I sent him up, but he came back down and said you were sleeping."

Mortification washed over me. Nick had come up when I was sleeping? How long had he stood there watching me while I slept?

It was my own fault, I had left my door wide open. I wasn't expecting anyone to come up there. My dad was on the main floor for the time being and so were my aunt and uncle in the guest suite. The only one I would ever expect up there was Melia.

A thought occurred to me then. I stopped chopping.

"I'll be right back." I told her quickly.

I ran up the stairs to find my phone. It was still on my bed from my phone call with Charlotte.

Kryptonite: *Came to see if you were ok, didn't want to wake you up.*
Kryptonite: *You talk in your sleep and you snore.*

Shit. I sat on the edge of my bed and buried my face in my hands for just a minute before snapping out if it. My embarrassment wasn't going to invade my peaceful self-care day.

I would weather it the next day, when I knew he would not let me hear the end of it. It was inevitable, but today did not involve him. And I did *not* snore.

With that, I officially forced myself to ignore him and his bag of mixed signals. I spent the rest of the day helping Aunt Tracey prep dinner and when it was ready, we all dined together just before kickoff. I was glad to have my dad downstairs. It was weird with him always up in his bedroom. Downstairs, he could be a part of our day-to-day.

We all gathered in our main floor family room for the game. It was another wide space in our house with vaulted ceilings. There was a stone fireplace that reached the ceiling and a huge TV hung on the wall over the hearth. Two large, comfortable sectionals formed a giant U in front of it and bookshelves filled with books flanked the fireplace on either side. Behind the sofas was a pool table with a fully stocked billiard area for playing. I loved it in here, it was the coziest room in the house.

We had ice cream sundaes and watched the Cowboys beat the Eagles seventeen to three. By the time the day was done and I went up to sleep at ten o'clock, I was happy, full, and grateful for the restful day with my family.

I knew the next day I would have to play what-personality-will-Nick-have? The sweet, caring compliment giver with the soft green eyes that kissed me until I felt dizzy? Or the cold, allusive Nick with eyes of ice that made me feel like he was judging me every chance he got? I was certain of one thing though, his moods weren't going to dictate mine. He could be Jekyll and Hyde all he wanted, I wasn't going to walk on eggshells around him. It wasn't that difficult for us to get along, all he had to do was be straight with me. Did he dislike me? Fine. Did he like me? Fine. Either way. I just needed him to pick a damn path.

Chapter 22 - Thanks for letting me know Katie

I moved steadfast like a woman on a mission. It was five a.m. and I walked into the barn ready to turn over a new leaf. I had been up since four and I was ready to work. My day's break from Nick's eyes had given me some clarity. I would be friendly to him, I would keep my distance, I would treat him like Carter or Zac or anyone else on site. No more games.

    I headed toward the corridor Buttercup lived in through the night. As if he had heard my thoughts, Nick appeared from the stall with King. He smiled at me, a slow smile that almost brought me to my knees. Nice Nick today. *Perfect. Thanks for letting me know.*

    I forced myself to not get pulled in by those eyes.

    "Morning," was the only word I said as I breezed by him.

    "Morning." He said it like he saw right through my smoke and mirrors.

    I forced myself to keep walking.

    Frank was directing some of the guys when I walked out. I knew they had a bunch of cattle fencing to repair that day on the southeast pasture. I wanted to make sure I was helping with that. I had done it with my dad when I was young and best of all, I figured Nick wouldn't be doing it. It was a simple job not really meant for experienced cowboys.

"Morning Frank, do you mind if I jump on the fence repair crew today for a few hours?" I asked just as he finished up with a few of the other boys.

"Sure, you can. That'd be a big help actually. I had to have some of the guys go to the west. We're going to have to move that herd within the next few weeks for sure. I'm happy to see you offer. Fixing fences isn't really a fun job."

I knew it, he was right. It was tedious. No one liked to do it.

"Perfect. Should I go with them?" I asked, pointing to Zac, Jacob, and Trent.

"No, they're going to help Dr. Lopez vaccinate some calves." He looked around.

"Sam can go with you, and I already had Nick as point on it, and Caleb and Matthew are going too."

So much for my plan to elude Nick for the day.

The sun was bright and warm. All the rain from the day before was long gone. The Pine Warbler birds filled the air with their continuous song while I worked. I paused from knotting fence, giving myself a small break to watch a few monarchs flutter around the bushes, preparing for their migration through to Mexico.

I paired up with Sam Cortez with ease. He was a year younger than me. This was his first full year on the ranch. He had moved to Texas when he was two from Mexico with his mom and dad. They had been ranching since they got here on their cousin's land. He was always happy and smiling. Our conversation was constant while we worked the long stretch of fence. Sam wanted to hear everything I had to tell him about New York. He had never been east, so hearing it firsthand was exciting to him. I, in return, asked him all about his trips back to Mexico to stay with his grandmother, his "abbi" as he called her, every summer.

Hearing him talk about his family there desperately made me want to travel everywhere. I had never really been immersed in any other culture other than my distant Apache heritage that was taught to me by my grandmother. My Grandpa Charles, our family patriarch who started our ranch, was married to an Apache woman. My great great great grandmother. My family still had one photo of them. I heard stories about her as a child. Her name was Illari. My grandma said it meant "new dawn." She was beautiful and strong, a family legend who died very young from scarlet fever. My Grandpa had raised their boys alone and never remarried. Funny how history repeats itself.

It was ten minutes to twelve when Nick made his way over to us.

"Time to break for lunch kids."

Sam jumped up immediately. He was the typical always starving eighteen-year-old. Nick didn't have to say the word lunch twice to him.

I got up more slowly and walked back with Nick. It was a little awkward. I decided shop talk was best. It's what I would do with any of the rest of them. I still hadn't forgiven him for bruising my ego the other night, but the silence seemed worse than talking.

"We got most of that half of the fence done." I spoke. "Just have to get a cart loaded up with all the fencing that came down."

Nick smiled, amused by my demeanor.

"Great work, cowgirl."

I ignored his tone and continued. "Probably will be only an hour or two more I'm thinking."

"10/4." He said military style. I didn't laugh. My small legs walked faster than his longer ones, so I kept ahead of him.

"Katelyn." He grabbed my arm, I spun around to face him. "I came to check on you yesterday after church and I texted you, you never answered me. How are you doing? I've been...concerned."

"Why do you call me that?" He looked at me, confused.

"No one calls me Katelyn, only my dad."

He stood stunned for all of one second and then actually laughed out loud, rolling his eyes. "You can't possibly have a problem with that. I've called you Katelyn since I was old enough to talk, today it bothers you?" He let go of me, insinuating I was being childish. I was, I knew it.

He began walking again. "Look, whatever, just come and eat so you don't faint again like last week and maybe it will make you a little less sassy."

"I am not sassy, Nick. I am just sick of being on this roller coaster with you. One minute you're kind to me, the next minute you aren't, or you're annoyed with me and you're making fun of me. I had just started to see a hint of the old us the other day. Or, at least I had hoped it was possible. You asked me to go to the fair with you like you *actually* wanted to be the one to take me, you kiss me in the barn, I don't have a lot of experience but it felt like a really good kiss to me." I laughed, an uncontrolled, ridiculous sound.

"And then you ditched me as soon as we got there, like you could care less. It made no sense. Then you come in like a goddamn UFC fighter to save me from Brent, not that I don't appreciate that, because I do, but you, acting like you care about me or something, it's too much, Nick. I just don't want to be a part of your game anymore. You've just changed. You used to be sweet, you know? Kind? You just aren't the same person I knew. But whatever, we'll just be acquaintances if that's what you want. I'll make it really easy for you."

I couldn't care less what he thought. I called him out on it all. I stood there with my arms crossed in front of me, waiting for him to respond.

Chapter 23 - It was shitty, I'll admit it.
Nick

She was right but I couldn't let her know it. I did have a split personality when it came to her.

She was right about another thing too. I *did* want to be the one to take her, not just to the fair. I wanted to be the one to take her *everywhere*. I just couldn't tell her, and I certainly couldn't be with her, so what the fuck was I actually doing with her? Whatever it was, it wasn't fair to her. I had to make sure we kept our distance. I had to backtrack, remove my feelings from her mind. Stay cold with her, push her away…again. And fuck if I didn't feel like the world's biggest prick. But I needed space from her if there was a hope in hell that I wasn't going to cave. The last thing I needed was for her to keep looking at me the way she did two nights before. I was one hundred percent sure that I would get to the point where I lost control. I was so close. I was hanging on by a thread.

What I did next was really shitty, but she had it coming with that little speech. I half wanted to reach across the space between us in the field and kiss her right there. I had to be mean to her, and it would definitely do its job of keeping our relationship platonic.

"Katie." I embellished the IE as a point. "You're right, I'm not the same person you used to know at all. I didn't mean to give you the wrong impression about the other night. I told your dad I'd take you and that is that. I like you, of course, as a person, and we do have a history, but that's where it ends. I'm sorry. We are not the same you and I anymore. There may have been something...back then, when we were kids, but now we're *just* old friends, okay? I just had a moment of weakness in the barn. Yes, I wanted to kiss you in that moment, but I don't have some deep seated feelings for you that I'm not telling you about. It was just a kiss. I'm not insecure about anything. I'm just...indifferent."

She flinched at my words. I felt like such a fucking asshole, but I couldn't help myself, I just kept going.

"You're Daniel's daughter, and while you're here, you're just like any other ranch hand. I protected you from Brent because that was the right thing to do, I would've done it for a stranger. It's not my fault you misunderstood or made it out to be more than it was."

She looked at me and said nothing. She almost looked like she might cry. I could see her confusion, wondering how she had been so wrong about me. A moment of insanity crossed my mind.

Maybe I could leave the ranch for a while? Temporarily. I could make up a reason, just so I could let my feelings spread for her and see where it could go while she was here. Before the thoughts could fully clear my mind, she spoke, her lips hypnotizing me even with her words that followed.

"Okay then, Nick. I must have misinterpreted. We work together? That's it?"

She looked at me expectantly, waiting for a second to see if I had anything else to say. If I didn't know her so well, I wouldn't even know she was upset, but the fire behind her eyes said otherwise.

"Got it. How stupid of me. I should have known. I won't misunderstand again." She nodded and turned to walk away, leaving me standing there feeling like shit.

In just a week, she'd gotten back under my skin. I knew what I said to her would hurt her, insult her even. If she was having feelings for me before, she certainly wouldn't be now. This was for the best. Even if we could be together, I was still no good for her. That was obvious by how easy it was for me to hurt her with my words.

I started the walk back knowing we were probably not going to be speaking anytime soon. The worst part of it was I knew I had done it mostly for myself.

I was selfishly motivated to keep her angry at me. It was a lot easier to stop myself from grabbing her and crushing myself to her every time I saw her if she wasn't smiling at me and looking at me like I was the person she used to know. I sighed, thinking about all the fucked-up shit I did, telling myself I was doing it for the ranch and the ranch alone.

Chapter 24 - You can't fake that
Katie

I spent most of the rest of November helping my dad with physio outside of ranch hours and trying to keep myself busy with Lena when I could. We shopped, went to the movies and Casey's football games, we even went all the way to Austin to see the opening of the lights at Zilker Park. It was a beautiful sight I hadn't seen since I was little. Over seventy lighted tunnels and Christmas displays came to life shining in the night. It was the first time I had felt Christmas magic in a while.

Still, somehow, something was missing.

I hadn't spoken much to Nick other than work chat in the last few weeks, yet even though we weren't speaking really, when he was there, in the vicinity, I felt peace. That same familiar pull emerging when he walked into a room. I know that's messed up, but it was true.

We had reverted back to simple, awkward exchanges with each other, I think our emotions from the day in the field had long since dissipated. As infuriating as he was, the attraction I felt when I looked at him couldn't be pushed down. When I heard him talking to other people, his voice still made my stomach do flip flops. I knew at this point he didn't feel the same. I can't be sure, but I think that made me give in to my feelings for him even more. If it could never be, what difference did it make if I was watching him?

Lena thought I was nuts, although I hadn't told her, or anyone else, about our kiss. I was too embarrassed, but I told her everything else.

"There is not a chance in hell that he doesn't have feelings for you. I saw the way he looked at you, maybe you didn't. It was like you were *his*. When I watched him hit Brent, this is probably going to sound dramatic, but he *scared* me. You can't fake that kind of emotion. He didn't let you go from the moment he hit Brent until you left."

I nodded, I remembered thinking Brent looked scared too. "Yes, but he cares a lot about my dad's opinion, I think he was worried about letting him down."

She twirled her long braid between her fingers as she shook her head.

"No way, girl, his eyes followed you. I can't explain it, but I know it."

"Well, regardless, I can only go by what he says. It was like something in him snapped between the barn and the fair."

"Hmmm." She thought for a minute. "Maybe he cares about you more than you think and he is afraid you're just going to leave?"

I contemplated her words carefully. I hadn't thought of that and it made me feel a little better thinking I had been totally wrong to begin with.

The words "I'm indifferent" had hit me more than anything else. They had stung me to my core. In other words, he had meant *"I couldn't care less anymore"*. It had been loud and clear.

I delved into the other side of the ranch business with my dad. Learning the suppliers and buyers, taking a particular interest in the accounting side of things. My dad was happy to teach me so I could help him with it. I did ride out to tend to cattle when needed, and a few times a week I helped with the horses and other daily chores, so I still saw Nick for short times every day, but it was easier to not consume my thoughts with him when we weren't spending the whole day in the field together.

He said good morning to me like everyone else every day, and I always said it back. Another week would pass by and it would feel a little less awkward with every day. I never believed it before, but it's true that time passing does really make things easier. Even the other cowboys noticed something was up. Carter caught me listening to him talk to Zac from Buttercup's stall while I brushed him the week before and embarrassed me by whispering from behind me. "Take a picture, it lasts longer, yeah?"

I swatted him and tried to go back to working. I was such a creep and he caught me red handed.

"You know, you should talk to him." Carter smiled. He looked at me like he saw right through me.

"There's nothing to say, he can't decide whether or not we should be friends. I don't know what it is about me that offends him, but I'm not going to waste my time trying to be friends with someone who doesn't want to be friends with me. He's indifferent." I used his words that cut me to the quick. Carter smiled at me, shaking his head.

"Things aren't always what they seem. Someone who's 'indifferent' doesn't just change their physical being..." he stammered, stopping himself.

"What?" I asked, thoroughly confused at the statement.

"Nothing, just uh, give it time, bud." He patted my shoulder and left the barn, leaving me wondering what the hell he knew that I didn't.

Chapter 25 - Three weeks and five days
Nick

Those passing three weeks and five days were the worst and most alive I had ever felt on the ranch since she left for New York. I just knew it had to be this way. I tried to make it easier for her. I didn't talk to her unless I had to. I was what Frank would call "cowboy cordial."

I had long given up on letting go of my feelings for her. This wasn't going away and I knew it, but if I could just be nice to her, get her through her next few months, then maybe, once she was gone, I'd have a small shot at recovering. At least that's what I told myself. It was the only way I kept myself sane.

I learned so much about her second hand. The ten seconds we said hello in the morning was the best part of my day. I made sure I was there, keeping busy while I waited to see her perfect face. I actually found myself jealous of Sam, who's literally the nicest fucking guy in the world, only because she worked with him all the time. After spending a month with her, I was crazy about her, and it was irreversible. It was just the way it was.

I thought about her constantly. She invaded my head, no, *my soul*, in a way I can't explain. Seeing her so much brought back all the memories. All the conversations. All the things I confided in her and she in me. The way she made fun of my girlfriends—the ones I dated to keep myself from pursuing her—the jokes, the long rides at night that became almost a ritual for us back then. Looking up when I played football to see her with Lena's family in the stands. Her eyes the night I told her about my dad, right before everything changed. All of it.

I imagined myself running my hands down her neck, kissing the full lips that I was destined not to have. Like karma for all my years of different women. The one woman I wanted, needed, I couldn't have. I had no idea how to let go of her. For the time being I was just making it through my day knowing I would get those ten seconds again the next.

Chapter 26 - One step forward, two steps back
Katie

It was a frigid morning in early December when I came into the barn smiling at Nick, a real smile, when I said good morning to him. It was so cold. I had to dig out my big, plaid, flannel jacket lined with fleece to keep warm. My hair, which I had braided when it was still damp, almost felt frozen hanging down my back. It felt almost like New York weather outside the barn, and I was just trying to stay warm before an early ride to the creek beds on the west side pastures led by Frank. We were scoping the best spot to move the large herd we had been planning to move in November. There hadn't been a need yet. The weather had stayed nice, the grass had stayed thick, and the area had been good to them. Now it was time.

    It would take two full days and a handful of cowboys to move the herd. I originally asked to stay out of the move to try to keep my distance from Nick, but now that it had been a few more weeks I was feeling like if they needed me I would be okay to do it. I knew the land a lot better than some of the newer cowboys, so I would be a good help.

At some point, I realized I had to just continue on. I couldn't hide from him forever. Every day I was less embarrassed about it all. It was just taking me time to be civil with him again.

That particular morning, I was feeling festive. The air was crisp, it was beautiful and getting close to Christmas, and it was a special day. He smiled back at me, and my chest tightened. *One step forward, two steps back.*

Nick wandered into the stall behind me and Buttercup. "Happy birthday to your Mama today."

I looked up in surprise. He normally didn't seek me out like that, and I didn't expect him to know it was her birthday.

"Thanks…how did you—"

"Your dad reminds us every year." He began his best impression of my dad. "Vanessa was what got me through winters, weaknesses, and times of wanting to quit. A night for only her is warranted."

I just looked at him so he continued with his explanation.

"He's also always unavailable. Only night of the year we know he's off limits, unless something is on fire. It was a bit sad he would just be there alone." My face dropped, his comment made me feel like crap.

"Fuck, Katelyn, I'm sorry. I didn't mean…I was just talking without thinking."

"No, it's okay." I felt the need to be honest. "I should've been here. I could've been, easily. I always had the option to stay the week after Thanksgiving. We would talk or Facetime, but it's not the same. I'm starting to realize I have a responsibility here that I think I had mentally blocked out for a few years, you know?"

He nodded.

It was the longest conversation we had had in a month.

Before either of us could say anything else, Frank came in and broke up our conversation. "Let's move out, you two."

"Coming," I said back.

I looked to Nick then, he gave me an "after you" face.

At least we were being nicer now. It was better than the tension we had before. If that was all we had going forward, I would take it.

Chapter 27 - Bunkhouse Plague
Katie

"I reckon we're gonna have to move them fifteen to twenty miles east of the barn," Frank yelled over to us. We had been observing the cattle in the west. The sun was rising bright in the morning sky. He pulled his hat off and wiped his brow.

"Nick, Zac, Trent, Will, Caleb, and Matthew, and we'll get James and Sam also if they're feeling better."

Everyone nodded in response. Both James, a newer cowboy, and Sam had been very sick for almost two days with some type of stomach bug. At first, they thought it was something Sam had eaten until James came down with it too. Sicknesses through the bunkhouse happened from time to time. It was inevitable with everyone living so closely. It was important to try to keep it to a minimum. Ranches didn't run themselves and we couldn't afford to have cowboys sick in large numbers.

"We'll head out here again tomorrow morning. Katie would you be okay to come too if needed? I gotta plan for one of those boys not being able to make it."

I answered right away. "Of course."

I was ready for a little adventure. We'd for sure be gone for two days and one night moving them. We would camp and keep watch of the cattle, then continue to move them the next morning before riding back on a three-hour trek. All in all, we'd cross about twenty-five miles on horseback through the property. This time of year, the sun set early and it got cold at night. Sometimes freezing. This big valley we were moving them to would protect them from cold this winter.

We pushed on riding to the move location and stopped for lunch at the east pasture near the creek. The sun was high in the sky by then and it had warmed up enough for me to take off my fleece and flannel jacket. Fall was so weird in Texas. It was cold enough to turn your heated seats on but warm enough to still wear your sandals most of the time.

"You all set for this?" Frank asked me as we ate sandwiches from a cooler pack.

I shrugged. "I haven't gone along to do this in probably five years." I took a bite of my sandwich and thought for a minute. "But, it is kind of like riding a bike so I think I'll be fine."

He nodded. "It won't be too cold for you, we'll keep a fire going over night and—"

"Boss, I'm not feeling so well." Trent had appeared and he looked downright pale and clammy.

"You aren't looking so great son, you feel queasy?"

"Yeah I do, I think it would be best if I left. I hate to ask but do you mind if I go now? I can have someone meet me up the road a mile. I'll hold Rebel's reins out the window."

He was asking to be respectful, I'm sure but he must have known there was no way Frank would say no. He looked awful.

"Yeah, bud, go ahead, text us when you get back, okay?

Trent took off as fast as his horse's legs would take him in the direction of the barn. I saw him on the phone before he was out of sight. I'm sure that the last thing he wanted to do was be sick in the pasture in front of a girl. One more down and out.

After he left we all finished lunch in silence. Frank looked worried. His crew was dropping like flies.

Nick and Frank rode ahead of us on the way back, talking about a game plan I was pretty sure, probably about what would happen if those three boys weren't available in the morning.

We weren't halfway back to the barn when Will pulled off in the trees, feeling sick. Frank looked calm but I was sure he was starting to panic.

"That sounded pretty rough, Parker." Nick smiled, calling Will by his last name and patting him on the shoulder when he came out of the hedges. Will was not looking well when he returned, and we kept him in front to keep an eye on him.

"Ugh...laugh now if you want. You won't be fucking laughing when you get this," Will yelled back to Nick.

After a painful two more stops for poor Will, we finally made it back to the bunkhouse. Nick offered to handle his horse for him and to run to the silos office for some meds to help settle his stomach. Will did not waste a second arguing. He disappeared as quick as he could.

I followed Nick into the barn and settled Buttercup in for the night. I was truthfully a little worried about this flu going around. I made a mental note to do a good job washing my hands at every turn for the next couple days. I also didn't want to pass it to my dad.

I passed by Nick on my way out. I stopped at King's stall. "See you in the morning, unless you're next."

He looked up at me. Heart dropping eyes. Internal swoon. Kryptonite.

"Don't worry about me, I never get sick. I'm as heathy as… my horse."

He patted a happy King and smiled wide at me, momentarily rendering me speechless.

"You on the other hand…" He stood and started wrapping a rope around his arm in the stall and I drank in the site of him. How the veins in his hands became more pronounced when he moved. How he worked to ravel and tie it without even looking or thinking, his muscles contracting in his arms as he gripped it. I shamelessly wished I was the rope and then I moved on to feeling like the typical hopeless girl who always wanted the man that didn't want her.

"It could be you, you know?"

I looked up, aware that I had been staring and wondering if he read my thoughts.

"I'm sorry?"

He noticed my stare and chuckled, I'm sure my cheeks were giving away my guilt over daydreaming about him.

"It could be you," he repeated. "The next victim of this bunkhouse plague." He said it ominously, like I should be afraid.

"Ugh. I hope not. Fingers crossed."

He hung up the rope and shut the door to King's stall. He squeezed my shoulder quickly when he walked by me, turning me to cinder.

"I guess we'll see tomorrow. And also, have a good night celebrating your mom." He smiled at me and I melted all over again.

The house was lit up with a soft glow when I got home. It was twilight, and I smiled. An unpopular opinion maybe, but I love when the sun goes down early in the winter. It feels protective and cozy. I couldn't remember the last time I had felt so comfortable. I had really settled in over those five weeks and I couldn't even imagine being back in New York.

Thanksgiving with my dad the previous week had been so perfect. It was the first year I had been home for it since I left for school.

My aunt and uncle had come, and they had prepared a huge feast. I made pecan pie for my dad and helped Melia make fresh rolls. Her daughter Sofia and her two-year-old granddaughter Whitney joined us for the meal, and it all made me feel guilty after the great day. Charlotte, Tessa, and Remi had even come from school for dinner and we all stayed up playing cards and charades and laughing at my dad as he tried to act out everything from a mostly seated position. I had *missed* that for the last few years. For what? I could've come home six times over those years, but I didn't.

At the end of the night everyone left and Charlotte and I got to spend some one on one time together. She of course wanted the dish from me on what was going on with Nick.

"Nothing at all." I had answered honestly. "We're just 'work acquaintances.'" I said, using air quotes.

Charlotte listened intently to me vent about the different things that had happened, leaving out the kiss because I wasn't ready to share that yet. She analyzed my every word while sitting on my bed cross-legged in her pajamas. After I was done, she shook her head.

"Something is up. Mark my words. I mean, it makes no sense. He just ditched you at the door, then jumped out of the bushes to rescue you and knock some loser guy out that was harassing you? Uh-uh…no way…That's sooo hot though. Told you he'd anger fuck you. Yummy."

I rolled my eyes at her.

Her face suddenly lit up. "Maybe he just doesn't think he's good enough for you. He is *just* a cowboy after all and he used to be like, a criminal."

I rolled my eyes again and snorted back laughter. A couple bar fights didn't make him a criminal. "You're such a snob, Char."

I had never seen being a cowboy as anything but honorable and strong. That thought had never even crossed my mind. Charlotte pulled her long, chocolate colored hair into a messy bun as she spoke.

"Why? Because my future husband has to be super hot *and* a rich doctor?" she asked, feigning innocence. I smiled in response and shook my head.

We were as polar opposites personality wise as we were in looks.

The two of us stayed up late into the night talking about everything we had missed out on since our last visit in the summer. We snuck downstairs in the middle of the night to eat more pumpkin pie and ice cream on the porch. Our rustling in the kitchen woke my dad up. He said he could hear us from the den laughing in the dark, but he didn't look like he minded. He had looked happy.

I climbed the front porch and knocked my boots off, I was ready to make an new memory with my Dad. It didn't ease the guilt I felt completely, but it helped.

.

Chapter 28 - Happy Birthday Mama

Katie

Leaving my memories of the previous week behind, I stepped through the front door to the scent of angel food cake. My dad was up with his walker, moving in circles on a makeshift track in his mind around the parlor. He had to do it multiple times every day, as per his physio therapist. He looked up at me as he always did, with a smile on his face.

"Some angel food cake for my angel?" he asked.

I laughed. "Cheesy, but cute, Dad. It smells so good. Did Melia get the mac n cheese done or does she need help?"

"Actually, I made the mac n cheese." He smiled, looking proud. "With a little help from Melia, of course."

I figured as much anyway. Cooking had never really been my dad's strong suit.

"Look at you go, old fella." I patted him on the shoulder as I walked by.

He was improving so much.

I was proud of him. I excused myself quickly to run up and change, remembering to wash my hands extra well before throwing on my beloved tights and hoodie. This wasn't a dress up kind of meal.

We dined at six o'clock together, all alone in the parlor. Using old TV trays from the seventies that had been my grandpa's, we sat in the wingback chairs together talking about my mom. I loved hearing stories about her that I never knew. It hurt me still that I never got to know her. From how my dad spoke about her, she was the most magical woman in the world.

"I have a little surprise for you," he said when we were all done with our dinner. "Let's get some cake and go into the family room."

He had piqued my curiosity, so I obliged. Heading into the kitchen, I said hello to my tia who was already busy cleaning up. I cut three large slices of cake and topped them with more strawberries and whipped cream, sliding one to Tia before I carried the other two into the large family room while my dad hobbled behind me, as slow as a turtle.

He sat down on the comfortable sofa.

"I had Nick take these old video tapes to Pitman's Office Depot a few weeks ago. Gerry Pitman put them onto DVDs for me so we can watch some old home movies of Mom together tonight."

He pointed to the coffee table where there was a pile of ten or more DVDs. "I also had Nick buy a DVD player."

I laughed at his mention of purchasing completely dead technology. He'd probably never use this DVD player for anything else.

I felt myself tearing up a little. Unseen footage from my childhood? Of my mom? I had never seen any footage of her before. Until that moment, I didn't even know it existed. I did remember my dad recording us with an old-fashioned video camera when I was young. These must be those tapes. I didn't waste any time and popped the first one into the player. It was labeled "Katie's second birthday". There were many under it, all labelled in my dad's handwriting.

Charlotte 2 weeks old.
Katie's third birthday
Christmas morning 2007
Christmas morning 2009
And the list went on and on.

I looked at my dad, gentle tears falling from my eyes. "Have you seen these?" I asked.

"Not since they happened." He answered honestly. I think he was as excited to watch them as I was.

I got up and went to my dad to give him the biggest hug. "Thank you," I said.

We settled in and started the first DVD. A beautiful scene. A simple moment in time. The back yard under the tall live oaks. Me, running around the yard on a gorgeous sunny day in a pretty pink party dress. My mom wore a long yellow dress and my dad doted on her, joking with her. She was running around getting food for people. Her blonde hair tied back and blowing in the warm breeze. Relatives and friends talked, music played. Aunt Tracey looked so young, toting Remi around on her hip. She was a year younger than me, and I had to admit she had been a really cute baby. My Grandma and Grandpa. All the people I loved in one place. Even our dog Sunny, who had passed away when I was twelve.

There was a lot of activity, but my mom was what kept catching my eye. I saw it instantly, the resemblance between us. Not only in our looks but in our mannerisms. It was like looking in a mirror. We even sounded the same.

The movie continued on, me on a big tan blanket on the grass. My mom bringing a cake lit with candles and placing it in front of me while everyone sang happy birthday. They were mid song when a little boy, maybe four or five years old, came running up, plopping down beside me with a thud. We looked at each other and he smiled. Two-year-old me looked around while everyone finished singing and my mom helped me blow out the candles. A large cheer erupted from the crowd which startled baby me. The boy saw me start to cry and patted my hand. He stuck his fingers in the icing, pulling them out and putting the icing on his nose, then mine to make me laugh, which I did, instantly.

The moment was saved forever. I watched, crying. Of course, the little boy was Nick. The same familiar pull to him hit me in the pit of my stomach, but not for want.

I *missed* him. I missed that person he was back then. I wondered if there was any part of him that was still there.

The movies continued on well into the evening. I spent most of it crying happy tears and soaking in every second. What I would give to just jump into one of the videos. Even for five minutes. These were such a blessing.

My dad even got choked up a few times. He said he had forgotten how perfect and wonderful she was. Hearing her voice just brought her alive again and suddenly I felt like I knew her a little better. This small piece of her would be something I could keep and cherish forever. It was the best gift I had ever gotten from anyone. I couldn't wait to show Charlotte.

We finished the last of the DVDs just after ten o'clock. I knew I had to go pack still and go to bed, but I had felt the need to absorb every little bit of my mom on her birthday. I kissed my dad on the top of his head and went upstairs to get ready for a busy few days.

When I was all finished, I laid awake in bed that night, thinking about what a beautiful surprise it had all been. "Happy Birthday, Mama," I whispered before I drifted off to sleep.

The air was cold the next morning. So cold, I almost regretted agreeing to go with the crew on the trip. I bundled myself up in the warmest clothes I could find. It was overkill for this weather, but better to be safe than sorry. The weather always had a way of surprising us.

I gathered everything and headed to the barn just before five-thirty. I fully expected to see a bustle of activity, but what greeted me just seemed eerie and odd. Frank and Nick stood there chatting quietly. No one else in sight. The lights were low. Only three horses saddled, mine included. As I walked up to them, Nick walked toward me. He wore jeans, a white Texas Longhorns hooded sweatshirt, and his Hennessey Ranch baseball hat. I knew his cowboy hat wouldn't be far, somewhere in his saddles. He smiled a breathtaking smile and offered me a large, steaming travel mug. His fingers brushed mine as he passed it to me, sending a current through my whole body. I looked at him as I took it, confused by the gesture that was very simple and sweet.

"Double vanilla almond milk, right? You're going to need it."

I took a sip. It was literally perfect. I was surprised he had remembered that. I had only said it once as a joke on my first day.

"Thank you," I answered. I looked to Frank, then to Nick.

"Y'all, am I early?" I'm sure they could see my lack of understanding. "Where's the rest of the crew?"

Frank put his hands into his pockets, looking like he was carrying a heavy weight on his shoulders.

"Well, girl, you're looking at it."

Chapter 29 - Just you and me, Blondie
Katie

"I don't understand."

Frank shook his head. "Zac, Caleb, and Matthew all came down with the flu between last night and this morning. The rest of the guys are at that huge branding at Cedar Springs until Tuesday."

"I slept in my truck. I'm not getting this virus." Nick piped up as he pushed items into his saddles.

Frank was quick to respond to him. "Smart, but uncomfortable, I'm guessing." He seemed distracted. He cared about the cowboys and I'm sure he hated to see them sick.

"It might be uncomfortable, but it's worth it if I don't get sick." Nick's smile was almost contagious as he made the best out of this situation.

I had done a cattle push like this before with only three people, my dad, Uncle Roger, and another cowboy, when I was young.

I, of course, was just there to tag along at that age, but my dad always explained things to me as we went along, so I had a good understanding. I tried to remember how many cattle we had moved the times I was there, but my fuzzy memories of being young weren't giving me the number. All I could think of was it had seemed like was a lot.

We gathered up what we had and readied ourselves to head out. Nick didn't seem worried one bit about only having the three of us. It felt cold enough to snow and was still dark when we set out. The sun wouldn't be up for a couple of hours yet. I had one look back at the barn and got Buttercup moving, guiding her to the west pastures.

The sunrise was a spectacular sight over the valley that morning. A light frost had formed, and everything was dewy. Nick rode behind me, laughing at how I was bundled up. I had left my hair down for extra warmth and had a winter hat with a pompom on top.

It wasn't a morning for a cowboy hat, although I had mine with me for later to shield the sun. It wouldn't get worn until my ears didn't feel like they were freezing in the morning air. I also wore warm mittens on my hands and my thick, plaid flannel.

"You are bundled up like you're in Aspen," he said.

"Shut up, don't make fun, alright? I have to." I laughed. "I get so cold. Tiny person problems."

"I guess so," he agreed, chuckling.

"Hey, I wanted to thank you, by the way." I slowed to meet his pace and ride beside him. It had been on my mind since the night before. "It made my dad's day, and mine yesterday, to watch those home movies of my mom. I didn't remember her voice until last night. I had forgotten over the years and now I can hear it any time I want. It meant so much to us, so thank you for taking them when my dad couldn't." Tears sprung into my eyes, her beautiful voice still fresh in my ears.

He was shocked. "You've never seen any footage of your mom before? How is that possible? Did your dad not have a cell phone?"

"No." I laughed at my dad's old ways. "He had a video camera when I was little and all our movies were on Hi-8mm tapes. You can't buy anything to play them in and I honestly didn't even know he had them. I guess he must have kept them with him in his room. He just got his cell phone when I was in middle school."

We both started laughing.

"He hadn't seen the movies since they were made, or close to it. It meant the world to him too."

Nick understood, like everyone else, how much my dad had loved my mom. He said something then that surprised me.

"I always wondered why he never remarried, but I'm starting to understand. He just loved her the most, you know? No one else would ever be as good as her in his eyes, so what would be the point at settling for second best?"

"I never thought of it that way. I understand that I guess."

"Just my take on it." He shrugged and continued. "I had no idea it would be that special to you both. I really didn't do anything, just found the place to transfer them and take them there, so it's not that commendable really, but you are welcome nonetheless. I'm glad it was a good night for you both."

We paused the conversation as Frank came into our immediate sight.

He had stopped short a little ahead of us, waiting for us to catch up. He wanted to gauge Nick's perspective on the move.

He rode along beside Nick. I spoke when necessary, but for the most part ,I let them talk.

The air was already starting to warm up some and the sun felt good. I could feel my fingers starting to thaw out as the day progressed.

I spent the rest of the ride just falling a little behind the two of them, listening to their chatter. Nick, gave Frank ideas on where to push the cattle so they'd follow the river the best. Areas with pre-built shelters in case of storms. He knew the ranch's strengths and weaknesses and was logical and wise. He had never set foot inside a traditional college or university, but he was smart from just his own push to learn and from experience. He had learned extra parts of the ranching business in his own free time and Frank sounded genuinely impressed with what he had to say. Like they were equals.

We reached the cattle by late morning and took a break, sitting on a small hill in the sun and eating hot soup from Thermoses. Nick looked back at Frank, who was somewhat struggling to keep it together. He didn't look well. He ate a few crackers on the other side of the hill and kept his distance from us. About twenty minutes later when we were finishing up, he made his way over to us.

"Well, it's official, I believe the flu has got me," Frank started. As if his subconscious mind was now allowing it, he looked like he was rapidly beginning to feel worse. "If I were to leave you two to do this, would you manage or should we get some grain up here and do it next week?" I knew this wasn't the option he wanted. Grain was always a last resort.

"If you leave it with us, we'll get it done," Nick answered quickly.

Speak for yourself. All alone? Was he sure? What if one of us got sick?

I pushed myself to fake it, sighing deeply before I gave in. "Yeah, we got this. We'll get it done," I confirmed.

Nick smiled at me, happy for my support.

Frank nodded. "I'll send help if some of the boys are well enough. I texted Sam, he said he feels a lot better today," Frank added. "Okay, you two. Don't let me down."

He made a quick call on his cell and took off to meet his wife seven miles up the road. He texted Nick just before we started moving from his wife's truck. Sam and James were feeling much better, almost normal again, so they would make the ride out to help us keep watch through the night. He wished us well and told Nick to report to him at the end of the day with our progress. Suddenly, it was just us.

Nick put his phone away in his pocket. "Well, this shit just got real. It's just you and me, blondie, at least for the next few hours." He smiled at me, an almost mischievous grin, one I knew well, like the challenge excited him.

"What have you gotten us into?" I put my head in my hands and laughed, looking out at the stretch of field below us littered with cattle ready to be moved.

Chapter 30 - I felt myself fall
Katie

Moving cattle from one place to another was an art that took cowboys time to learn. Nick was highly experienced at it, although he had never done it by himself, he went with his instincts and spoke to me as we approached.

"We need to move slow and calm, okay? It's the fastest way to gather and move them."

I nodded, paying close attention, moving as he moved.

He continued with ease and I followed, knowing from my early lessons with my dad that fast movements or making loud noises would ultimately initiate a flight response with the cattle. That was the last thing we wanted.

This was a tame herd, so we were already lucky in that way.

"It's important to use the natural instincts of them..." Nick continued, pulling his hoodie off and pushing it into his saddle. I'd never really been a Longhorns fan before, but that sweatshirt on him had almost single-handedly made me one. "But they also need to feel like we're in control. We're the predator that moves them in the right direction, understand?"

I nodded and took it in. I watched him, again noticing how gorgeous he was, his confidence as he worked. His green eyes were so intense, focused. His body moved easily with King, like they were one. His t-shirt strained against his upper arms as he managed the reins. His shoulders wide and strong. What the hell did Charlotte know? This cowboy was turning my insides to lava as I watched him.

Everything he did was *beyond* attractive. I was having trouble focusing on anything else, especially the harsh words that passed between us weeks before.

"You're going to go to the back behind them and zigzag," he said, snapping me out of my daydream.

"They need to feel stalked by us, they'll naturally begin to bunch up. After they've done that, we can apply more pressure from behind to initiate more movement. I'll lead them from the front. We want them to follow us but we don't want them to feel threatened and begin to run away. Got it?"

"Clear as mud," I stated, only half joking.

We gathered the heard together, and I did as he said, riding in a zigzag pattern behind the cattle while Nick came up through the middle. It took some time but eventually, slowly, the cattle began to bunch and follow Nick. He rode carefully up the side of them, keeping the water to their right. I pushed them forward in the most nonthreatening way possible.

This was cattle driving.

We continued on this pattern for a long while. A few hours passed before we decided to stop for the night to water the horses, set up our camp, and eat. Nick was pleased with the time we were making and the day had grown warm and beautiful. It was almost four and the sun would soon be setting behind us.

Nick had been in touch with Frank over text. Most of the guys were over the worst of it, so he knew he had about another twenty-four hours of it himself and he was feeling awful. Sam and James were in the best shape, but unfortunately, they were the least experienced with cattle driving. They had just left the bunkhouse and were heading toward us, hoping to meet up by around eight o'clock. They would take an early night shift watching the cattle so Nick and I could sleep. By two or three, we would wake and he and I would take over for the two boys.

Sam was feeling almost like himself. He texted Nick and told him he was looking forward to the fresh air after almost three days in his bed at the bunkhouse.

I wore a huge smile when we stopped. I couldn't shake the feeling, I felt alive.

"Why the world's biggest grin?" He chuckled at me. "You look like the cat that ate the canary."

The sun was golden in the sky. I could feel the warmth of it on my face. I turned to face Nick, but he quickly looked away from me, gathering things from his saddles.

"I feel so...so proud." I stumbled on the words. It took me a few seconds to find the right ones.

He smiled and spoke without looking up from what he was doing. "Exhilarating, isn't it? Makes you forget there is anyone else on this earth but you and God."

I smiled, taking in the rare moment of him speaking from his heart. "Yes," I agreed, thinking his description fit my feelings perfectly. He looked up then and his eyes held an understanding. I couldn't help but feel the familiarity again, of us from another life.

We chose a spot on a hill that overlooked the cattle while they grazed on new to them pastures. I sat there in awe of the beauty that was the valley below me. How had this been here all these years and I never appreciated it like this? For tonight, this beautiful spot was our home.

Nick paced the area looking for kindling. He easily found some and pulled dry firewood from his packs. He started a fire, and I pulled up a thermal sleeping bag to place under us. He set up a tent to sleep in but said it would just be for me, claiming he always slept under the sky if he could. I began placing us a makeshift dinner of meats, cheeses, fruit, and seasoned potatoes that had been wrapped in tinfoil for heating over the fire. I smiled when I saw that the cook had even put in the makings of s'mores for us. He had thought of everything, as always.

We sat down to eat as the sun started setting. We talked about my school and what I was missing this semester. I found myself easily talking about my dreams of starting my own home décor line, maybe my own studio.

"My inspiration is this place..." I rambled on as he listened. He was easy to talk to when we were alone with no distractions. It was almost like old times.

"There are so many pieces in our home that have been here for over a hundred years that my ancestors bought or even made themselves. They're old, but they're still beautiful and timeless. And this..." I waved my hand out over the valley. "I want the fabrics to be as organic as this valley. Neutral and natural colors. But this is all a pipe dream. Right now, this is where I am and I'm really starting to be okay with that. I'm not sure I even want to go back to New York."

In my heart, I knew I was staying. I couldn't even imagine going back. I realized then that I had been talking for a while and I turned to him to see him sitting and listening intently, like he was even intrigued by what I had said.

"Sorry, all this home décor talk is probably fairly uninteresting for you." An awkward laugh escaped me.

"Not at all." He sounded honest. "I've never had any desire to do anything else other than this, so it's interesting to me to hear your thoughts. This is my place though. You can't beat this kind of peace." He gestured to the sky as he leaned back into the grass.

"I'm starting to agree with you," I said back quickly. We stared at each other for a few seconds in silence. I looked him dead in the eyes, as much as it tore at my soul.

"Look at us, you'd think we were friends." I smiled at him in a way that told him maybe we actually could be now.

He pinched my t-shirt. "Yep. Could fool anyone, couldn't we?"

When his eyes met mine and he smiled, I felt the familiar flip flops start in my stomach. I did my best to ignore the feeling he gave me, averting my eyes to watch the fire spark into the sky. Our talking continued with ease, like we could go on forever. I shivered from the cool night air. He noticed right away and added more wood to keep me warm, then reached behind him and grabbed his Longhorns sweatshirt off the blanket and handed it to me.

"Here, you can wear this."

I reached out my hand to take it but he pulled it back slightly and grinned.

"Be gentle, it's my favorite."

I took it from him immediately, probably too eagerly, and pulled it over my head, breathing in the deliciousness that I can only describe as the scent of Nick. It was huge on me, but it was so warm. I looked at him to find his eyes raking over me in a way I hadn't seen before, his bottom lip between his teeth.

"It looks better on you." His voice was calm but sure.

He looked away from me. I said nothing in response, and we settled back in as it became his turn to talk. He told me about the programs he was taking online through A.U that I had no idea about. Business management, leadership, and human resource courses to help lead the large crew we had here. It was inevitable he would take over one day for Frank, and he wanted to be ready. He was insanely smart, as if I needed another thing to find attractive about my Kryptonite.

We decided to make the s'mores for dessert when it got dark. The sky was bright with stars and the moon shone intently down on us. I knew I should be cold but I was surprisingly warm, wearing his sweater, sitting beside him and the fire.

While he roasted marshmallows on a stick for me, he talked about my mom. He said he always wondered if I had the better end of our deal. His mother had turned into a walking nightmare over the last six years, but he had her still. Mine was an angel, but only a memory.

"Sorry if that sounds mean, but I just don't feel the same about my mom anymore. I sort of became her for a while. I was so angry at her. I was so worried about my dad, and it was just easier for me to drink a lot and forget about all of it. I'm not proud of the things I did back then, but I guess it helped me to become who I am today and I'm okay with that person, with my place here on this ranch." He half smiled for one second and then his face dropped. "I haven't said that out loud before."

"That's okay, it was honest," I answered. I wanted him to feel like he could speak freely to me. "I just have no experience to compare to yours. I'm sorry I'm no help. I think my dad has always tried to make up for us losing her in so many ways. He over compensates."

He thought for a minute. "Your dad is a great man. I admire him. So much that I would never want to purposely do anything to offend him."

He looked even deeper in thought for a minute. We'd finished with the marshmallows and he began peeling apart a blade of grass. I felt like I was missing something there but didn't pry. We had been talking for hours.

"Oh I see how it is..." I smiled at him. "But offending *me* is totally fine, you know, spilling dinner on me and laughing about it." I began making a list and pretended as if I were counting the things on my hand. "Leaving me mud pies outside the back door."

He looked truly shocked that I remembered that from when we were young and started laughing, laying right back in the grass.

"I can't believe you remember that." His body shook with laughter, his dimples on full display as he said that I had pulled something from the depths of his childhood memories.

I continued. "Or, you know, leaving me to fend for myself with Lena and her boyfriend. I was the third wheel; do you know how painful and awkward that is? Oh, and we can't forget leaving me to fight off random drunk jerks."

Clearly, we were past all the tension now about that night, but what I said must have struck a nerve with him. He sat up, looking a little more serious.

"Truthfully, about that night, I shouldn't have left you. I didn't want to. I regret it every day. I just feel the need to tell you. Again."

I shook my head. "You couldn't have foreseen it, Nick, and my dad wasn't even disappointed about it."

He looked at me, confused. He pushed his hair back off his forehead. "No, I was never worried about your dad's disappointment. He's been disappointed in me many times and he will be again, I'm sure. I was disappointed in myself. When I turned that corner and saw him grab your hair, I almost lost control. If I would've been alone with him I might have killed him." He looked serious.

"You know I get...angry. If he had really hurt you-" He stopped himself, shaking his head and closing his eyes to scratch the memory from his mind. "I wouldn't have been able to live with myself. All I kept thinking was I should've been there with you."

I looked down at my hands sitting in my cross-legged lap. Suddenly a light conversation was becoming much more open and raw. I asked the question I had wanted the answer to for over a month.

"Why did you? Leave me that night?"

He took a moment and then sighed deeply. His eyes met mine, and he startled me by reaching over and running his fingers gently over my open hand in my lap. I didn't dare move for fear of him pulling it away as the familiar electricity shot through me. I have no idea how simply tracing tiny circles on the palm of my hand could cause my body to turn to fire, but it did. In fact, I was pretty sure it was disintegrating into ash. I was on a tipping point, at the top of a cliff, and I swear, my heart felt like it had stopped beating.

I looked back up at his green eyes and I felt myself fall right off the edge as he spoke.

"Choice is a crazy thing. One split decision and everything changes." He was deep in thought. "I could've went down a very different path...you know that. I was already on it. If it wasn't for this place, for your dad, I don't know what would've happened. I owe him everything for the choice he gave me here." He thought for a second longer. "But I don't know *why* I let you go. Every day I wish I had made a different choice." He looked at me then, his normally dark eyes lighter and honest. "One where I decide to stay with you and win you some stupid stuffed animal, make you smile all night long, and tell you how insanely beautiful you always are, inside and out."

My mouth fell open slightly as my eyes looked down. He noticed and cupped my chin, tilting my face up to him. "Don't look away. Own those words. I really fucking mean them."

He dipped his head down to meet my gaze. "It's indescribable how beautiful you are, Kate."

My heart was hammering in my chest, so much so that I was sure he could hear it. I reminded myself to breathe while he traced between my fingers and my wrist, back and forth, blazing a trail as he went.

"I've kissed a lot of different women, too many probably—"

"Nick, I don't need to hear—"

"Katelyn, please, I don't always say things the right way maybe, but I want to tell you this."

I sat quietly and let him go on.

"I have kissed a lot of women, that's part of my past. I can't change that, but I've always searched for the feeling I got here ," he patted his chest, "when I kissed you. The truth is, I've never been able to find it again. Not even fucking close."

I stared at him, entirely speechless. I had only kissed three guys ever. Him, my sort of boyfriend Blake from our church that I dated in high school for a few weeks, and the gross guy that kissed me at a club in New York uninvited. But Nick didn't know any of this, so I said the words to show him I understood. I had never had that feeling again either.

"I still remember too," I stammered so quietly.

He pulled his hand away to run it through his hair as he often did when he was stressing about something. I loved that I knew him well enough again to know that about him. A few seconds went by, and when his hand returned to mine, a small sigh of relief that I couldn't prevent if I tried left my lips.

He looked at me when he heard it, but when his eyes met mine, the look he gave me surprised me. He looked like he was at *my* mercy.

"Sometimes, we want something so badly but the repercussions of it can alter our life forever, or even someone else's. I'm just...I'm having trouble fighting this, Kate. I can't do it anymore."

My pulse raged under my skin. I moved my other hand to trace over the base of his tattoos that met his wrist, giving in and touching him like I had wanted to for forever. Sitting so close to him, I realized that the words pouring down his arm were all song lyrics. I recognized the ones I knew, not realizing that my fingers were moving part way up his arm, tracing there too.

He sat quietly, just watching me for a few minutes, appearing totally calm. His breathing sounded shallow. I let my fingers run back down to the base of his wrist. That small action brought his eyes back to mine. He slid his hand up my arm to trace the base of my collarbone as he pushed my hair off my shoulder. His skin was warm on mine, and he smelled *so incredible*. His hand moved to the side of my face, his thumb tracing my cheek bone softly, as if he was analyzing my reaction to his touch. I turned my face into his palm to show him I approved. I was electrified.

He spoke, almost in a whisper. "I've lived through some pretty fucked up situations and probably a thousand different experiences where I should've been afraid, but I never really have been." My breathing quickened. "Aside from now..."

He moved both of his hands to the back of my neck, through my hair, holding my head gently in place. Coming closer, dangerously close to my lips. "It's just you, Kate. I've always been afraid of how I feel about you." Before I could stop myself, I leaned in, closing the short distance between us, and crashed my lips to his.

After one tiny second of bliss he pulled away from me and the feeling of him doing that before came rushing back to me. I scrambled for my words, feeling flustered.

"I'm sorry...I...I didn't...I don't know."

He shook his head as I panicked, a slow smile spreading across his face. He moved even closer, and I settled instantly because the look he wore said he *wanted* me. His hands were still firmly in place on the back of my head. "Shhh, Katelyn. Just be still."

I did as he said. He was controlled where I was not. My breathing was erratic, uneven, like I couldn't remember how to bring in air properly. I knew what his kiss felt like, and the anticipation of it was quite literally killing me. He moved slowly and intentionally. Pressing his lips to mine, then pulling his perfect face back to look into my eyes, stroking my cheeks with his thumbs. His pupils were blown out, his green eyes intense, pulling me down deeper every second.

"We're not going to rush this, baby. Let me take my time."

I tried to be calm, but my body was betraying me. I was ready to combust. His kiss and his words completely consumed me.

Soft. Warm. Full.

His lips parted and I reveled in the most delicious feeling of his tongue sweeping against mine in a perfect, torturously slow rhythm. I had no thoughts as I let him completely flood my senses. The expert way he kissed me told me that he knew, without a doubt, how to play my body like an instrument. I went weak and my chest filled with pure fire as I felt him smile into my lips.

"This...this is the feeling," he whispered.

I pulled him to me with all my strength. Inviting him in. Offering more. Pushing my fingers through his wavy hair, then down the back of his neck as a tiny moan escaped me. He groaned in response and I felt it pulsate throughout my entire body as he let go. His mouth claimed me with an unyielding passion.

It felt like he was losing some sort of internal battle, giving in to the moment completely as his hands moved over me, through my hair, up and down my shoulders, to my back, under my shirt. His hands felt just like I imagined on my skin, pulling me to him until our bodies were pressed together in the grass and he hovered over me, freely exploring the electricity that flowed between us. I never wanted it to end.

There was no going back after this. Nothing would ever be the same. It was inevitable that he would change my life. He'd either flood it with pure joy or he would ruin me. I was ready to accept either fate because, in truth, I didn't stand a chance to fight it.

Chapter 31 - Why pretend?
Katie

"I guess it's okay if you call me Katelyn now." I pulled away from him when I whispered it.

He smiled at me. "Katelyn."

The butterflies resurfaced.

"You look fucking adorable in my sweatshirt." His thumb was still stroking my face as he looked down at me, holding himself up on his side. He began tracing my lips as he spoke. "I dream about kissing these full, perfect lips every night."

I blushed fiercely, not used to the words so open, honest. He continued to trace my bottom lip with his thumb before pulling it into his own lips. He was killing me. Dulling and heightening the fire in me all at the same time.

"It's okay because I feel the exact same way," I said breathlessly. I let my hand graze his upper arm. I had wanted to touch his arms for two months. They were my favorite part of him, so far. I squeezed my thighs together as heat washed over me. The feeling he was giving me was like nothing I had ever known was even possible.

He looked down, away from my eyes. He was harboring something in his. "That's the thing...It's not *really* okay for us to do this."

As if on cue, at the worst possible time, familiar voices and shadows appeared in our line of sight off in the distance, breaking our gaze and bringing us back to reality.

Riding towards us fast were Sam and James. Nick gently pulled me up with a last look, getting up to grab some more wood. Our moments of privacy were over as the two boys bounded into camp laughing. Sam yelling, "You owe me fifteen bucks!" to James. They obviously had been racing the last little stretch.

The four of us sat around the fire for a little while. Nick and I made sure to keep far enough away from each other. Nothing would indicate we had been any closer before. I sat quietly, listening to them joke around and pick on each other, almost the way brothers do. Every so often I would feel his eyes on me, and the longing I felt for him would take over. My mind was clouded, all I could think about was how it felt to kiss him. I decided to get up to just go into the tent, saying good night to them and wishing he could come with me.

None of it made sense. If he wanted me the whole time, why pretend he didn't?

Chapter 32 - Two reasons
Nick

Status? Definitely failed, but definitely don't give a fuck anymore. Would I get fired for this? Probably, yes. Did I want to keep her anyway, even though it seemed impossible? Still yes.

I stretched out in my sleeping bag, set up beside the tent and under the stars. I stared up at the sky. I had really gotten myself into an impossible, fucked up position. She was so close, only ten feet away from me. There was no way I was going in that tent no matter how fucking badly I wanted to. For two reasons.

Reason one, I knew I would start kissing her again and there was no way I'd be able to stop myself. The way her lips felt on mine was enough to break me. I fought it all day, every time she looked at me, I fought it. I was doing just fine until her face was glowing beside the fire, her hair was all around her in my sweatshirt. I had no choice. I had to have her. The way I wanted her wasn't normal. At least not for me. It had taken every fiber of strength I had in me to not tear all of her clothing off and make her mine right there in the field, and she would've let me. The newest and most surprising number one on my running Kate fantasy list was her, wearing only my favorite sweater, with my face rightly buried between her legs. She was a test of my will. If she knew all the things I was thinking it would make her pretty head spin. I was sure that she was still a virgin and the responsibility of being the first of her experiences made things even more complicated...and enticing as fuck. She *could* be mine, *only mine.* But at what cost? Could I be who she needed? I didn't regret kissing her, not for even one second. I just didn't know how I would ever stop because I couldn't be near her without wanting to be closer to her.

Reason two, Sam or James could come back to camp at any moment, for any reason, and this was not something I wanted to be spread as gossip around the bunkhouse. The guys knew me. Well, they knew the old me, and they would probably assume I was just trying to hook up with her for fun. She was too important for that assumption. In truth, I had no idea what my feelings were for her. But they were powerful. Overwhelming.

I tried my best to fall asleep, knowing I didn't have long to rest, but sleep just wouldn't come. All my thoughts were consumed with her.

When two-thirty came I woke up, I think I slept, I can't be sure. I looked in on her. Hearing her breathing softly looking like an angel, I let her sleep while I tended to the fire and managed the horses. Sam and James were already getting ready to snooze around it. I took off into the field as quietly as I could in search of the wildflowers that reminded me of her.

A little while later there was no sound in the air besides the slight groans of the cattle and crickets while I rode back and forth keeping them all honed in. The animals could always sense the weather. The sky was immanent to produce some much-needed rain.

We had a few hours of riding once the sun came up before heading back to the barn. I was trying to do the job of two people, but my mind was flooded with Kate from the moment I left camp. I just couldn't bring myself to wake her at two and answer to her questioning eyes that early. With a few more hours to think, I knew now that this was inevitable since the moment she got into my truck, even long before that.

I couldn't think clearly, and I truthfully thought maybe I was going fucking crazy. I had worked so hard to be where I was, and if she was leaving in a few months, was it fair to have her just while she was here? Could we just keep it quiet and then move on after? Could I survive again after she left? Thoughts of her face, the warmth of her lips, her body, her quiet little moans while I touched her, how her skin felt under my hands, flooded my mind. I felt myself beginning to crave her, like I used to crave whiskey.

"You're fucking losing it," I muttered to myself just as the rain started coming down.

"Sorry?" Her voice sounded from behind me.

Chapter 33 – You think I wanted this?
Katie

"I'm just talking to myself apparently." He turned to smile at me and sighed deeply. "God, woman, you're like a breath of fresh air this morning. How did you sleep?"

He moved a little closer with a look I was starting to recognize. The same look from the night before that said, *"I want to kiss you and run away from you all at the same time"*.

I answered him. "Longer than I should've. You didn't wake me. Why?"

"You looked so peaceful. I knew I'd be okay for a few hours alone."

"That's a suitable answer, I was wondering if you were avoiding me after last night." I said it cautiously, but I had to say it. He was so hot and cold it was hard to know if I would wake up to him telling me it was a mistake again. There was no point in pretending anymore about what was happening. He escaped it once, but he couldn't now. I wouldn't let him. If he was having doubts, I was done playing games and I wanted to know.

"Thank you for the daisies, they're beautiful." He smiled and nodded.

I found them tucked in my reins the moment I approached Buttercup. I now had the three stems tucked into my braid. It seemed like the perfect place to put them. The gesture had given me hope he hadn't changed his mind, but his eyes were tormented as he spoke. "Kate, about that kiss last night—"

"Several kisses actually." I corrected him.

"Yes, several, I just…" He struggled for the words. "I care about you so much Kate, but…"

"But what?" I prompted, pissed off already.

"But you're *Daniel's daughter* and you're leaving in a few months, are you not? This isn't about you. It's not you at all—"

"It's not you, it's me?" I interrupted again, as calm as could be, surprising myself with my fiery tone.

He wasn't getting off that easy. I knew one thing. The way he looked at me told me that I was more in control here than he let on. I had felt his eyes rake over me every time he saw me for weeks. I told myself I was nuts, that I wasn't seeing it, but now I knew I had been seeing it right the whole time.

I raised an eyebrow. "That's all you got Stratton?" I was starting to realize why he was fighting this.

He ran his hand through his hair. "You think I *wanted* this, Kate? To feel this way about you?" he started. "You think this hasn't been a struggle? I was finally settled. I felt good. This ranch is what I'm good at. Suddenly, here you are again, grating on my last nerve and looking so goddamn beautiful all the time. Invading my head every fucking second. If I let this continue with us and you go back to New York, that would be…difficult for me and my state of mind. For everything I've worked toward. I'm not playing games with you, Katelyn. I'm being honest. As honest as I can be."

I just sat there, taking it all in. The rain was coming down harder. He continued without giving me the chance to speak.

"Besides, you, Princess, are untouchable. It's forbidden. It's the nail in my coffin. Frank reminded me of the rules the night of the fair. I fucking listened to him when I shouldn't have and pretended I didn't care about you going off with Lena. That piece of shit Patterson almost really hurt you because of that. It was my fault." I listened to him ramble on. "I don't have a minute in any day where I don't think about that."

He was releasing all the feelings that he had been keeping in, and after two months of wondering, I was ready for it. I didn't dare interrupt him.

"It killed me to act like I didn't care about you that day in the field when I said all those hurtful things to you."

"I'm indifferent."

He looked at me, surprised I remembered I suppose. "Yes, but I am not indifferent. I want you just as badly as you think I do."

I let out a dense breath. I didn't expect all of it, but it all made sense finally. He hadn't wanted to leave me that night. *I wasn't crazy.* He was told he wasn't allowed to date me. *Who the hell do these goddamn men think they are? Like it's their decision what I do?*

It was all hitting me at once and I felt a strange sense of calm wash over me. He had been holding this back from me for a long time.

He got down off his horse and came to me, as if he was reading the thoughts racing through my mind. He held his hands out to help me down as the rain slowed.

He lifted my hat off my face and looked into my eyes in a way that made my knees weak.

"Last night, Kate... I argue it can't be and then, when I kiss you, I forget why. I'm exactly the kind of guy every dad hates, and your dad knows my past better than anyone. All of it. He knows who I was and who I am now. This isn't a normal situation with me working here, having my whole life wrapped up in one place."

I smiled wide and burst into laughter. He was being dramatic. My dad could never hate him. Sometimes I thought he loved Nick as much as he loved me.

Nick pulled me closer. "That, right there, that smile..." His thumb traced my bottom lip, sending shivers down my spine. "It gives me no choice, because the alternative is living every day without that smile that makes me feel like I'm home. It's my new purpose."

I could feel my heart beating rapidly as he kissed me lightly on my lips, his words giving me some courage to speak freely.

"You struggle with this decision as if you think you're making it *without* me. I let you go once. I pretended I didn't care when you hurt me." He flinched. "I spent years trying to figure out why you didn't want me or what I did wrong. I spent years running from those ghosts, mourning our friendship, and I missed you so much."

"I know, I'm sorry, baby." He grazed his lips against mine again, igniting me. Every time he called me baby my heart felt like it might explode. It was quickly becoming my favorite word.

My voice was a whisper. "This time, Nick, *I'm not giving you up*. That's the end of the conversation-"

He silenced me with his lips and I instantly relaxed, realizing his internal fight with some crazy part of his conscience seemed over.

The rain started again, coming down on us in a mist as we stood there in the dark, giving in to everything between us. I wasn't going to let his ego or self-loathing over his past mistakes dictate this. I had made my mind up and when I did that, not much could stop me. Not that he was *trying* to stop me.

He kissed me like it was quickly becoming his preferred thing to do.

"And by the way, you think *I* wanted this all these years?" I whispered. "Why do you have to be so goddamn frustrating and gorgeous?" I asked, my voice was no louder than a whisper.

"I don't know, why do you have to be so untouchable *and* beautiful?" he retorted.

I shrugged. "Maybe that just means we're perfect for each other."

His eyes grew serious as he answered. "I just don't know how to give you back if you leave again." He ran his hands down my back and rested them on my hips.

"I'm not leaving, Nick. Like I said last night, I have other dreams. I've decided I'm going to take a break over the summer, maybe finish my studies online out of Austin, maybe not. I don't know yet. But I'm going to stay on the ranch, my dad needs me here, and I never knew it until I came back, but this is where I belong. I belong here on this ranch and I belong with you. I decided before any of this happened with us. This is where I need to be. New York is over."

He looked at me, his hands still running the length of my back, not knowing what to say, so I continued.

"I didn't like it there, but I was fully determined to finish because it was the right thing to do, or so I thought. Coming home, I realize I just don't want to. Not because of you and I, but because I went there for all the wrong reasons to begin with. Seeing my dad injured scared me and feeling this...this freedom, feeling this land in me again for the first time in a long time, I realize it's just where I'm supposed to be. I can study design anywhere if I choose to, or even open my studio in town. I'm not sure but, I'm staying so you're stuck with me...for now." I pushed myself up onto my tippy toes and kissed him on his chin because it was the only place I could reach when he wasn't bent down to me.

"Well...that changes things entirely, and just so we're clear, there's no 'for now' with me. You're mine, Katelyn. You've always been mine."

I knew he was right, I always had been in some way, at least I had always wanted to be.

"You need to know that I don't give a fuck what anyone thinks. I'll tell anyone who will listen that you're mine all day long, I don't need permission from Frank or your dad under normal circumstances. It's not my intention to keep whatever is happening with us a secret, in fact, it might be the hardest thing I do, but your dad needs me here until he's healed. His cowboy pride aside, if he's going to fire me, I want him to be well enough to be back in the field when it happens."

"Well, I'm going to alternatively choose to have faith that it will be fine. But I agree we should wait to tell him." Archaic rule or not, there was always room for negotiation. He grinned at me, the slow, intentional smile he only gave to me as he leaned in to kiss me again.

"We'll see. I am going to be very selfish with you until that day comes. I want to learn everything about you again, take advantage of it, and like I said, take my time."

I smiled back as his lips came crashing down.

My God. If I had to choose, I would've been happy to stay in that moment him forever. Rain and all.

Chapter 34 - We were now the secret
Katie

Time seemed to move way too quickly while we kissed. We could hear the clomping of hooves in the distance. The two boys were up and coming toward us to finish moving the cattle.

Nick groaned insatiably as he pulled himself away from me. A sound that was quickly becoming one I would seek to earn as much as humanly possible.

"You're making me slack off from my job this morning with those lips, miss." His voice was quiet and raspy.

I laughed, regretfully pulling away from him too. I got to Buttercup and assumed the position of dutiful cowgirl just before the two boys came into our sight line.

The rain didn't return through our morning. Sam and James had packed up the rest of our camp and with four of us, the rest of the cattle push was easy. The air warmed up and the sun shone down on us and the land, drying up the earth.

I took off my thick flannel jacket and let the sun warm me up. No one said a word about me wearing Nick's sweater. Sam and James were definitely feeling better and were more themselves, racing and joking with each other at every turn.

They were fun to be with. Sam was hilarious and spent most of the ride making us all laugh. We arrived at the new pasture just before lunch and sat together in the sun eating and talking. I truly understood the pull Nick felt to this life. This wasn't easy, but it sure didn't feel much like work. It felt *natural*.

The herd was settled and happy when we left to head back to the barn. Nick texted Frank to let him know we were on our way back and the job was done.

I watched him as we rode. He was an excellent leader. The other guys really respected him. Hearing his words the night before, I realized what this life meant to him. I couldn't help but look at him differently now. The honesty that had passed between us that morning had changed everything. There were no longer any secrets between us. We were now the secret.

I had no idea how this was going to work with watchful eyes around us all the time, but I would do whatever it took and I got the feeling he would too. I looked at him again. As he looked back at me from his spot in the field, he smiled at me. I couldn't believe he could possibly be mine.

We reached the barn just after two o'clock. I was dirty, tired, and excited to use an actual bathroom instead of bushes. Deep in my thoughts of a hot tea and shower, I heard Nick and James enter the barn while talking about the next day's work. I finished tending to Buttercup and heard James yell back "Later" to Nick, who was still in the stall with King in the next row.

I headed over to him. Being careful to keep a friendly distance. I knew there were cameras pointing at this particular section of barn but thankfully, no audio.

"Well done today, cowboy." I smiled at him from the front of King's stall. He took his hat off and pushed his hair off his forehead. His eyes raked over me, setting something off in me without even touching me. The intense, raw masculinity he possessed rolled off of him in waves. It sucked the life from me.

He was perfect.

He sighed. He seemed relieved the cattle drive was done. I realized why. It made him more valuable and I think he hoped that would mean something after all this came out. None of that was my concern while he looked at me. The only thing that mattered in that moment was us.

"We make a good team, I'm thinking." He stood up and leaned against the wall in the stall. What a difference a day made. We had left barely as friends and returned connected to each other in a way that would make it almost impossible to come between us. I smiled at him.

He continued, "I have to say though, it makes me wish we had had more cattle to move just so we could have had more time alone in the field. Or alone anywhere." Just hearing him say the words brought me back to the night before, kissing him by the fire. It turned my insides to mush.

His green eyes lit up. "Plans tonight, or can I steal you for a bit?"

I looked up as if I was deep in thought about my non-existent social life. "Let's see. First the world's longest shower, food, and then I'm going to check in with my dad..."

"As much as I'd like to stand here and imagine you having that long, hot shower, I can't because I need to go out there and face a group of cowboys level-headed right now, not hard and distracted." He smiled and heat gathered in me with his words.

"Listen, how about you do all those things but don't eat dinner and meet me instead? I want to show you something."

"Where?"

He smiled at me in response. "Just meet me in the east pastures where we had trouble with the calf that morning." I remembered the morning that seemed so long ago, although it was only six weeks prior.

I was so tired, and the last thing I felt like was riding a horse, but I answered on instinct, not thought. "Okay, I'll be there by four."

"Perfect." He smiled and said nothing else as he finished with King. As he walked by me on the way out of the stall, he squeezed my hand. "See you soon then, Princess."

Chapter 35 - Just trying to keep your hands off me
Katie

The bottom of my white marble shower was covered in a fine layer of mud and grit while I stood in it, letting the water wash the pastures off of me. Being in my house, thinking about the night before seemed surreal to me. He set my body on fire. I couldn't imagine ever getting used to his touch. He made me think things I never thought possible, like how much I wanted him to be in that shower with me.

This was a complicated situation, I was willing to admit that. Cowgirls worked here from time to time and romantic relationships complicated things. There was no time for drama here. Too much work had to be done daily to fit in love quarrels. It hadn't even crossed my mind that that was part of what was holding him back. Frank had pissed me off, but he wasn't about to get in the way of Nick and I, Nick had been clear about that. But it really bothered me that he had threatened Nick's future here. I understand that his heart was in the right place, protecting my dad's business and all of that, but he was pushing the boundaries as far as I was concerned. I could be his boss one day. He needed to remember that.

I went down the stairs to the den to see my dad but he was sleeping when I peeked through the door. I was happy to see him resting. I knew Frank would've been filling him in throughout our day and I had talked to him through text when we had returned to the barn.

He had been with his physiotherapist then. His physio had been grueling. He was healing very well but getting himself back to normal at fifty-five was harder than it would've been at thirty. He was pushing it to heal, I knew it. It made him sleepier than he normally would've been. I was okay with it for today. I would see him when I got back. Adult or not, I wasn't in the habit of lying to my dad. Telling him I was going for a ride with Nick would've been the extent of our conversation.

The sun was still high in the sky when I saddled Buttercup and left for the east pastures. I noticed King was already gone and wondered how much earlier Nick had left.

The ride to the east pasture was quick and simple. The air had a summer feeling to it even though it was early December. The sun shone down on me and I felt excited, among other things. My body was so sore from riding already and I wondered why I had agreed to ride again. Could we not have walked?

That thought left my mind the moment I rode into the pasture and saw him standing there beside his horse. He was devastating. It wasn't anything in particular he was doing that got to me. He just stood there, wearing a black t-shirt and fixing something on his saddle. His body was so strong and powerful, I had to resist the urge to walk right up to him and push him to the ground right there in the field. The ruggedness that radiated from him almost brought me to my knees.

"Well, aren't you a sight for sore eyes," he called as I rode up to greet him. I handed him his Longhorns sweater back, folded neatly.

"I'll get you back into this soon enough." He kissed my cheek. "Just in time to get you out of it." The look in his eyes when he took it from me stunned me. I still wasn't used to how beautiful he was.

"Don't try to distract me with those eyes and that charm. Where are we going?"

"Charm?" he asked, intrigued, hopping up onto King. "I charm you, do I?"

"Yes, all the time...so much," I admitted.

He smiled a mischievous grin. "Come on, baby, let's see if you can keep up." He laughed, taking off into the fields.

We rode along for a short while. It was easy terrain almost to the end of our journey when we began an uphill trek. The horses slowed a little, and we talked while we rode along.

"I am not sure I've been up here before. If I have it's been a long time, I can't even picture where we'd be going. We don't move any cattle up here." I was intrigued with his intent direction. It was obvious he had a precise place he was taking me.

"This is a treat for you then. But you can't tell another soul about it. It's my place. You have to promise."

"Should I be flattered you're sharing it with me then?"

He looked me dead in the eyes. "Extremely."

I glanced around trying to see what could possibly be coming. I always thought this area was rocky and barren. I was wrong. As we climbed, the surrounding area revealed thick grasses and fields of wild winter pansies. It was beautiful. Just as I thought it couldn't get any prettier, we reached the top and the whole valley opened up below us. Eastern cedars lined the hills and the sun was just beginning to think about setting. Right on the flattest part of the wide hill under a giant live oak laid a thick, quilted blanket and two sealed containers. I realized instantly he had set up a picnic for us. He even had some wood placed for a small fire when the sun set. My breath caught. I hopped down off of Buttercup, holding his reins.

Nick tied up King and came up beside me as he heard me gasp.

"I know, right?" He spoke in barely more than a whisper.

"How have I never been up here?" I asked, shocked my father's land held so much beauty I hadn't even seen yet. Another thought occurred to me. "And how did you do this?" I waved to his picnic, realizing the amount of work that must have gone into it. I was touched.

He gave me a big, perfect smile. "I smuggled the food. No one noticed. If Frank was around it wouldn't have been as easy." He pulled Buttercup's reins from me. We walked to tie him on the other side of the hill.

"As far as this place, no one comes here but me. I've never seen another living soul up here. Except you, now."

"Well, thank you for sharing it with me. I probably never would've come up here otherwise. I would've figured it was rocky and rough because that's what it's like at the base. I didn't expect lush and green and these wildflowers."

"Yep," he said. "Just nature protecting itself. Doesn't show its beauty until you get close to it."

He pulled me in and kissed my forehead.

We looked at each other for the smallest moment, but with all the feelings of the last two days…the last weeks…the last ten years. It seemed endless.

Nick lifted one hand and ran it from my neck down across my collarbone to my shoulder, sending my stomach into butterflies.

"I'm going to kiss you right now but you have to promise to stop me long enough for us to eat, okay?"

I nodded, unsure of my will as he bent down and kissed me on the lips, griping my face with his hand, his thumb on my cheek. He kissed me just enough to make me want to kiss him more. Forever. He pulled away and I opened my eyes, half expecting him to be standing there, but he was already walking to the picnic spot, smiling over his shoulder while I stood there with my eyes closed, not even realizing he had left me there, stunned.

"Come on, let's eat before the sun goes down."

I let myself breathe and realized he had done it again. "There! See! Charming me…that's what I'm talking about!"

"I have no idea what you mean." He feigned innocence. "I'm just trying to keep your hands off me long enough to give you a nice dinner after a long day. This is a first date, you know? Control yourself, Katelyn."

He turned away from me, shaking his head in mock shock, and headed over the hill to eat. I smiled, loving my view from behind him.

Chapter 36 - The Little Things
Katie

The spread he had set out for me was well thought out and set up beautifully. There was an assortment of meats, cheeses, scones with butter and homemade jellies, crackers, and in season fruit—strawberries, watermelon, grapes, and orange slices. All of it was covered with fastening lids and sitting on the ice packs to keep it cold.

He had even brought up glass mason jars of sweet tea with lids, made by the cook earlier in the day. It was perfect. The sun was beginning to sink down into the valley in front of us and the air was cooling off. He even had blankets for us to keep warm. He put some kindling in the fire and lit it up.

I sat watching him work, wondering how I got so lucky. Most people didn't see this side of Nick, I knew it was special to witness it.

"Who taught you to be this romantic?" I asked him as he assembled a plate of goodies and handed it to me.

"For you, Princess," he said, presenting me with a small feast. When he called me Princess on my first day it seemed condescending, but at that moment, it felt only like a form of praise. Like I was *his* princess, that made it more than okay with me.

He shrugged. "I don't really believe in traditional romance." He looked me in the eyes. "I just feel the need to please you."

I pushed my insane hormones for him down long enough to eat while he explained.

"My parents always genuinely liked each other, I think, when I was young. At least from what I can remember before my dad got sick. I can remember him bringing my mom flowers from the fields. Whatever was in season, it was such a small gesture, but it gave her so much joy." His eyes were focused, lost in a distant memory.

"They laughed a lot back then, Then he got sick and it all went to shit. They stopped taking the time to care. My mom started drinking a lot more." He broke out of his stare into the fields and looked at me again. "Small gestures mean everything. Seems cliché, but maybe it really is all the little things that count. I'm convinced if they had handled their adversity better or differently, maybe my dad would've healed even faster."

I loved hearing his thoughts but it hurt my heart to hear how his home life had gotten so bad. I realized how hard it must have been for him to watch everything just slip away and not be able to do a damn thing about it.

I spoke quietly, trying to remember what I could from my very early years. "I think my parents were really happy too, although I don't know how much of their own adversity they faced to test that love, they weren't really married all that long. I do remember them together a little bit, not much. I always remember them being with me and together."

"Your dad loved her so much. I still remember her, your mom. I think I was nine when she died?"

I nodded, he was.

"I still remembered hearing my parents talk about it at the kitchen table. My mom was crying and asking my dad 'what will Daniel do now'?"

I looked down. "I worry about him. It's a big part of why I'm staying, he needs family around. I know he misses both Charlotte and I. Charlotte will never settle back here. I know she'll end up somewhere like LA or New York. She isn't built for ranch life or even small-town life. Truthfully, though, I didn't realize how much I actually disliked living in the city until I had the chance to leave. I was relieved."

It felt good to talk freely about changing my mind. I was slowly learning that it was okay to do that, to admit maybe I had absolutely no idea what I really wanted to do. As hard as that was for me, not everything had to be planned out and I was starting to be okay with that.

He pulled me from my thoughts, pushing on one part of what I had said.

"So, it's only *part* of why you're staying? What are the other parts?" he asked, running his hand up my arm. I smiled at him then, the mood shifting rapidly.

"Well, I mean, there's this nice weather of course. This sure beats the snow and cold." I gestured to the sky. "And I really missed Buttercup while I was away."

"Mhmm, I see." He leaned in and kissed me on the cheek first, then the lips. "Those are some pretty strong reasons...any others?"

"Lena, I hadn't seen her in so long." I persisted, but as he ran his tongue from my collarbone to my jaw, I forgot what I was even talking about.

"See...so charming..." I said in between kisses to prove my point.

"You're pretty charming yourself, it's the most lethal combination because," he stopped to kiss my neck, "you just don't even realize how fucking incredible you are. It's honestly infuriating." But he didn't seem the slightest bit mad as he started kissing me again. The fire that was becoming very familiar started burning in me.

My phone buzzed in the grass. I groaned. It was my dad, awake and wondering where I was. He had expected me to be home after he saw my message that I had gone for a ride before dinner. I texted him and told him that I had lost track of time. I said I'd be home within the hour. It would only be believable to be out riding for so long. He seemed satisfied with my answer. He knew if I was out on our property I was safe.

"I think I have to go." I said sadly.

"*Ugh.* I don't want to give you back but it's for the best. I'm a little worried you might try to take advantage of me. I'll remind you again, this is only the first date." He kissed me in a way that made me want to do anything but leave.

I laughed and swatted him. "I'm sorry, I'll do my best to control *myself.*"

He tackled me to the earth from his sitting position as I laughed and kissed me once more before we begrudgingly packed up our makeshift picnic and sanded the fire. He had thought of everything. It was the best first date I had ever had and I hadn't even left my home. I told him as much as we started heading back. We rode slowly, talking along the way.

"And just how many dates have you been on?" he asked.

I looked at him, it was a sad roster.

He raised his hands. "Purely research baby, I just need to know what my competition is."

I laughed out loud. "You need to know *your* competition?" The sound echoed and filled the space around us. "Trust me, you have none. I've only been on a few and they were terrible. New York didn't have any men that appealed to me."

"It took a Texas cowboy to do it for you?" He chuckled at me.

"Yep. Who knew that was my favorite kind of man?"

He smiled at me before he spoke again. "I can't even imagine myself in a city like that. It would feel like a jail to me. I actually couldn't even picture you there now."

"I don't know why we're talking about me, I'm the one who should be worrying about *my* competition. I can't even imagine the girls you have had."

He looked ahead in the field, quietly answering me. "I see why you'd say that, but I didn't care about any of them, Kate."

I said nothing in response. There was something to be said for hearing that I was the only girl he had ever really had these feelings for. The darkness in his eyes from mentioning his past lightened as I shifted to talking about the future.

I told him about my plans to let my apartment's lease expire. I was prepared to fill my dad in as soon as I had time to sit and talk with him. I hoped he would be happy I was staying, and I was excited to tell him.

We stopped at the barn, and Nick waited patiently while I settled Buttercup.

I rode with him on King back to the house, his arms around me as we rode together. Feeling him kiss my neck from behind me was enough to make me want to pull off into the brush and do things to him I had never even thought about before. He left me on the back porch. My dad would be in the den on the other side of the house. This way he knew I got home home safe, he'd said.

"I'll text you in a bit." He kissed me before he left me in the dark. I couldn't help but realize we had come full circle, only this time he was leaving me much happier on that back porch than the first time, five years before.

Chapter 37 - The Problem with Small Town Life
Nick

I rode back thinking about her every damn word, every gesture, every face she made. I couldn't believe this was me. I had never called a woman baby in my life, I always thought nicknames were ridiculous, but there was no other way to describe her. She was mine. She *was* my baby. The word girlfriend even seemed too trivial when she was starting to feel like so much more.

Everything she did just consumed me entirely. Admitting it now wasn't easy. It meant trusting myself to give her what she needed, but I wanted to be the best man I could, for her. I reached the bunkhouse in no time, lost in my thoughts. In my almost twenty-two years, I had never felt this kind of pull to any woman before. All I could think about was consuming her entire body and driving her fucking crazy, but that couldn't be rushed with her, I knew that. That time would come and until then, it was a good thing I was a very patient man.

She looked up at me with those innocent blue eyes every time I touched her, propelling me to believe what I already assumed to be true. I was the *only* one who had ever touched her. That idea almost sent me over the edge when I let myself think about it. I wasn't just obsessed with her physical beauty. It was also what I knew about her, entirely. She was brilliant still, as she always had been, sweet and just pure *good*.

I could only imagine the face I wore coming up to the porch. I had been mid-memory of her taste and the scent of her long thick hair, like sunshine and vanilla.

"Hey son, how was that ride?" Frank asked casually, setting his empty mug up on the porch rail and leaning forward into it.

I nearly jumped out of my skin. I hadn't even been paying attention and I didn't expect anyone outside.

"Shit, boss, what are you doing sitting out here in the dark?"

"Getting some fresh air, just checkin' in on the boys. Everyone seems better. Hopefully that's behind us." It had been the worst flu that had gone through the bunkhouse in two years. At least it had been quick. Frank waited quietly for me to realize he was still expecting an answer.

"Yeah, uh, ride was good." I stumbled over my words. "I just needed to clear my head after that push, you know?"

"Yeah, I bet." Frank raised his chin up like he was analyzing my answer. "You got it clear now?" The look Frank wore when he asked told me he knew something was up.

"Nothing a ride into the hills couldn't fix, but uh, I'm bushed. I gotta sleep. I'll see you in the morning unless there's something else?"

Frank was silent for a moment. "Nope, nothing, just wanted to make sure everyone was good. Oh and Nick, good job last night. I appreciate you handling it all so well when I couldn't be there and for keeping everyone going."

"Sure thing, glad you're feeling better. Night." I turned quickly to head inside so I didn't have to look Frank in the eye anymore. Although this was complicated, it really was no one's fucking business until Kate and I thought it was. That was one problem with small town life. Everyone knew everyone else's private life. Especially on this ranch. I was in deep with this girl and I had the most important job of all, and that was to protect it with everything in me. I would never give her up. She may not have truly known it just yet, but she was mine. It was non-negotiable.

I could see her in my memory when she was young, playing in the mud, never afraid of bugs or snakes like the other girls would be. I could see her now, wild and free on the back of her horse, hair flying, eyes alive with the sun. What excited me, shocked me for thinking it, and scared the living shit out of me all at the same time, was the image of a future her. One with long braids and flip-flops chasing my babies in the sunny fields of the ranch. I knew she was my past, for now she was my present, but I had no idea if I'd be lucky enough for her to be my future.

Chapter 38 - She's You
Katie

The parlor was dark when I came in through the foyer. I could hear the inkling of a TV on the main floor and followed it to the family room where dad lay snoozing on the couch with his knee elevated.

"Night, Dad." It was a whisper. I didn't want to disturb him, only let him know I was home now.

He smiled, half asleep, glad to see me back. "Good ride?" He stretched, waking himself up a little. I should've known he wouldn't sleep through this conversation, he hadn't seen me in two days.

"Yes, I just needed it after the last two days. The stars were so beautiful tonight and it was so peaceful. I ran into some of the guys and we all were talking. Sorry I didn't text you."

He smiled. I had never been sneaky my entire childhood, and he would never think I'd have a reason to start now. "You and Nick are the dream team I hear." He was more awake now.

"We did well." I laughed at the label. "We got it done. The push was exhilarating. I had my doubts but we did it and it went perfectly." I changed the subject from Nick to work.

"Of course, it was a lot easier when the other guys got there, but I felt so proud afterwards. Sam and James are so nice and hardworking, Dad, you have a really good group of cowboys. Everyone really enjoys working here. Even the younger guys." I was rambling nervously.

"Well, we'll see how happy they are in the next couple of weeks." He chuckled. "There's a record cold coming in here and I hate being stuck like this for it." He gestured to his current state on the couch. "I should be out there. The animals are going to need a little extra help if it goes down below freezing like they're saying it may. We're going to need to get some extra hay to stock it in case of frost too. May even need to get the coats out for the horses."

He was working in his mind. The pins were getting removed from his previously shattered knee that coming week and things were moving just the way the doctor wanted, just not fast enough for him.

"Freezing isn't that cold." I joked. "That's a warm January day in New York."

He knew it, of course, but wasn't accustomed to it the way I was after living there.

He turned to me. "Are you happy here right now, Katie?"

His question surprised me. Here he was, supposed to be focused on healing, and instead he was worrying about my happiness. Typical.

I felt the need to be as honest as I possibly could.

"Right now, Dad, I really am. I didn't realize what went into this place, or maybe I had forgotten, but I feel at peace here." I proceeded, now was as good a time as any to talk to him about staying longer. "In fact, I'm having a hard time picturing myself going back to New York anytime soon. Would it be okay if I stayed a little longer? At least through the summer? If I still don't want to go back, I can pull the rest of my courses from Austin online. I haven't really felt like I fit in since the start and coming home made me realize how much I actually dislike it."

"I had a feeling you weren't enjoying your time there, but I knew not to push you. You are nothing if not stubborn." He looked at me like I had just handed him the world. "Katelyn, you can stay here for forever and a day and I would be the happiest dad on earth."

I sighed, relieved to hear the answer I knew he'd give me. I told him all about my ideas for a mercantile and my décor line, he listened intently, loving the idea.

"I've wanted to make more ranch merchandise with our logo for a while, maybe sweaters and t-shirts too. That would be a great thing to put in your store, you could help me design them?"

I loved the idea. I told him about wanting to contact local artisans too, to pull items in from all over central and west Texas.

"I'm enjoying the work so much too, more than I ever expected." I felt myself getting re-attached to the ranch rapidly. I was weaving myself back into the threads of it daily.

"And Nicholas? I know you two got off to a tricky start those first few days."

"Yes, we're okay. I thought he was still frustrating, like he was when we were younger, and don't get me wrong, sometimes he is." I said honestly. "But I realize he is just so dedicated to you and this ranch. He'd do anything for you." I figured a plug for him couldn't hurt. Maybe he'd remember it when he found out about us.

"Good, I'm glad. He's really turned his life around. He's a good man. I'm hard pressed to find a better cowboy. I'm really glad you're happy Katie."

"Thanks, Dad, I am. I feel home." I kissed him on the top of the head. "You need help up?"

"No, I'm still pretty tough for an old man." Although he was hardly old. "I may sleep here tonight, I'm pretty comfortable. You go ahead, don't worry about me. The morning comes early."

"Okay, love you," I said before heading upstairs.

When I got to my room I washed my face and changed out of my clothes, except my t-shirt that still smelled like Nick. I could hear my phone buzzing from the back pocket of jeans.

Kryptonite: *"Did you get a third degree?"*
Me: No. He trusts me so much, I actually feel guilty for not being honest with him.
Kryptonite: Frank was here when I got back. I think he saw the look on my face and knew I was with a woman tonight. I didn't realize he was there and I wasn't being careful. I must have looked pretty happy.
Me: She must be pretty special then.

It had only been an hour since I had seen him and I missed him already. His warmth, his face, his perfect slow smile, his strong arms. I craved it all, like a drug. I couldn't wait to see him in the morning.

He cut off my daydream about him with his answer.

Kryptonite: *She is, very.*
Me: *What is it you like about her?*

Who the hell was I?

Kryptonite: *She is the most beautiful woman. So beautiful, I question if she's even real every time I look at her. She has the biggest heart. She sees the good in everybody. She is shy and sweet but I just know she has a side no one else will get to see but me.*

I wondered if he had these ready and waiting as he continued with more.

Kryptonite: *She thinks I don't notice how often she looks at me, but I notice every damn time. She makes me question how I ever lived without her. She makes me crazy, and she makes me miss her all at the same time.*

Warmth and yearning filled my chest. He couldn't see it, but I was blushing hot fire reading his messages. He wasn't afraid to tell me how he felt and I loved that about him. He was confident and strong and quite literally sweeping me off of my feet.

Me: *Well... aren't you observant.*

Pathetic answer, but I couldn't get much else out.

Kryptonite: *She's absolutely perfect for me, and you know what else?*
Me: *What?*
Kryptonite: *She's you. Now go to sleep so I can see you early, princess.*
Me: *Goodnight Nick.*

I was in deep, deep trouble with this man because my heart was his and I was never getting it back.

Chapter 39 – Water's edge
Katie

The following few days were both idyllic and torturous.

We always had to assume someone was watching. It was such a busy time on the ranch which made all of the cowboys distracted. Busy times did create some small opportunities for kissing behind the barns whenever we could be alone, but the problem was, we never got more than five minutes. We hadn't had even had one night to go back to Nick's space in the hills. Frank had him working fourteen-hour days with the cold coming in. A week or so after the cattle push, we took off from the group alone to move a small herd to the shelters ahead of the cooler weather. When we got them to their destination we decided to take a small break at the edge of the water to eat. There was no one around for miles. I didn't even have the chance to finish tying Buttercup up before Nick was to me, his body pressed against mine.

"We're not eating lunch, are we?" I questioned, giggling.

"Nope," he said, popping the P. He smiled, then kissed me again. "Fuck it, I'll starve," he mumbled into my lips. He began pulling the ponytail from the bottom of my long braid, separating each pleat carefully, never breaking the kiss. When my hair was free he lost his hands in it, kissing me so powerfully it made me dizzy to the point that I think he may have been actually holding me up. He pulled away from me, staring into my eyes, his large hands gripping my face.

"You're so stunning right now, you're not making this easy on me." He devoured me, kissing and nipping down my neck to the most perfect spot over my collarbone. He lost his hands even further to my hair. Every part of me buzzed under his touch. I could feel him hard and pressing against my stomach through his jeans as our bodies molded together. A moan escaped me and it must have fueled him. "I need to get you somewhere more private, now."

He pulled me by my wrist to a tree right down at the edge of the water, an area hidden by grasses. His flannel came off in record time and he laid it in the grass. He picked me up as he kissed me, then placed me down on top of it, pausing to hover over me, as if in a pushup position. He looked down on me, stunning me with how gorgeous he was as he studied my face.

His lips moved to my neck as he whispered, his voice full of gravel, "You're going to be the death of me, woman."

My eyes narrowed. "Woman?"

"Yes, *my* woman."

"I can live with that." In fact, I could live with anything if he kept kissing me.

His lips found my neck again and I reached my hands up to run them through his hair, kissing him slowly, savoring every single second. He groaned the magnificent sound I hoped he would as I tightened my grip on his thick locks. I loved that after all the women he had in his life, I could make *him* groan like that with desire for *me*.

"You're much better at this than you know." He smiled into my neck as he kissed me, tracing his fingers down to the valley of my breasts over my shirt.

"So are you," I stammered as he slid his hand down. I struggled for every breath when he reached under, his hand was warm on my skin. I had no idea what he was planning next, but I knew I was ready for it and I wanted it *all*.

Chapter 40 - I needed to know
Nick

Fuck, if I wasn't desperate for her before, I was now. Seeing her there, laying in the sun, looking up at me with those incredible eyes...

My fingers traced along her satin skin, working my way under the rim of her shirt, then up her rib cage to cup her full breasts. Her chest to rose and fell with heavy pants. I had been so good, so fucking good, trying not to take anything too far until she was ready, but that moment, in the grass, I saw nothing else. There was only her.

It was easier to resist when time was constrained or we knew people were around. It was also easier when she wasn't wearing those fucking jeans that hugged every inch of her perfect apple-shaped ass in just the right ways that had me daydreaming about bending her over any available hay bale. If we were getting thirty minutes alone, I was fucking taking every second offered to devour her. The irony wasn't lost on me that the only woman I had ever really wanted in this insatiable, out-of-control way, I had to wait for. No matter what I did, I never really felt like I could get close enough to her.

It honestly baffled me how in the fuck she was still untouched to begin with. She kissed me back so intensely that I could feel her pulse quickening under my hands, see the flush in her cheeks. Without even trying, she was driving me crazy, teasing me and showing me that she knew way more than she let on. Either that or she was just naturally incredible. Her hands moved under my shirt, and I felt my boxers tighten around me to the point of being uncomfortable. The way she squeezed her thighs together and looked at me almost took me out. It was like she *needed* me.

"You're so fucking sexy, Kate."

She smiled, and I groaned as I sat her up and began pulling her shirt off over her head. That simple, white, lacy bra and her hair, still wavy from the braid I had just pulled out, was all mixed up with the look in her eyes that told me everything was brand new to her. *Fuck.* It was enough to break me.

I gave in and crashed my mouth to hers, laying her back down in the long grass. I kissed her slowly, trying to maintain some form of control as I ran my hands over her, cupping her perfect tits. The silkiness of her skin was unfamiliar still, such a stark contrast to my rough, labored hands.

Her nipples reacted to me before I even touched them, pebbled under her bra as I ran a thumb over them first, then my tongue in small, torturous movements. Her breathing was out of control as I sucked and pinched her nipples through the lace.

"Why?" she moaned through her uneven breaths. "Why does that...feel...so good?" Her whimpers punctuated the words.

"Katelyn?" I whispered. I needed to know for certain.

"Yes?"

"Has anyone else ever touched you like this before?"

She looked at me, slowly understanding what I was asking. The innocent eyes I knew I couldn't live without challenged me to show her what I meant. I shifted my body to lie beside her and ran the edge of my fingers under the top of her jeans, feeling the lace and cotton underneath. She moaned again, her body pressing up to encourage me. I carefully undid the button, sliding my hand under. She shivered as the warmth of my hand met her skin, and she let out the most fucking exquisite sound as my fingers reached into her panties.

"No...never."

I sucked in a sharp breath when I felt how wet she was already. My dick strained against my zipper, begging to be freed. Fucking beautiful torture.

"I didn't think so." I looked into her eyes. "I'm going to give you what you want baby." I kissed her lips. "What you need, to help you soothe this ache okay? "I pinched her swollen clit lightly between my fingers and she let out the sweetest moan. Fuck she was perfect. "But You have to tell me what you want and if anything that I do is too much, okay?"

She nodded, looking at me much more like *please fuck me now* than *stop*.

"I do...I want it...I want you to do whatever you think." She breathed the words quickly, rushed.

I laughed, but fuck, if I didn't love it.

"Okay, baby, I know you do." I was going to take care of her. So well that it would ruin her for any other man. *Ever.*

A tiny whimper left her as my fingers pinched and circled her clit.

"Mmmm, feels good?" My voice was low and quiet under her ear. The sweet vanilla sugar of her skin overwhelmed me.

She nodded to me while shorter little pants and moans escaped her. She was erratic. "Yes...Nick?"

"Yes, Princess?"

"Don't destroy my heart again. I wouldn't survive it this time."

I smiled down at her. That's what she was worried about? "Breathe baby. I've got you. The only thing I'm going to destroy is the chance for any other man to have you."

I kissed her lips as I slid my fingers over her. Learning her center completely. I pushed one digit into her gently as she bit her bottom lip at the foreign sensation. A perfect replicated vision beneath me bringing to life in the many moments I spent with my cock in my own hand, picturing her, since she came home.

She was so fucking soft, so tight, so untouched. She moaned and grinded against me greedily as I darted in and out of her while my thumb stayed over her clit, bidding her to climb higher toward her release. This wasn't going to take long, and I wanted to enjoy every moment. I watched her, knowing how badly she wanted it, how badly she wanted me. I slowed my fingers down to an agonizing pace, letting my mouth travel down her neck, to her waist, taking all of her in. She moaned louder with every passing moment until her body trembled below me.

"Good girl," I whispered. "Give in for me now, baby."

"Mmmhmmm," she managed. She was a goner. "I'm going to..."

Fuck, yes.

"Kate?"

"Hmmm?" she mumbled between moans.

"Open your eyes. Look at me while you come."

She whined at my words but did as I commanded. Her eyes opened, wild and ferociously blue, burning into mine until she couldn't keep them open any longer. They closed and her head fell backwards as her pussy tightened around me. Her hands gripped the earth below her while she shamelessly fucked my fingers. Her back curved into a perfect arch as I held her there.

"Oh...my...God...Nick." She moaned breathlessly, then repeated my name. I smiled at her, loving every single second, cupping her pussy and kissing her waist until her breathing slowed a little. I moved back up to her lips while she came down. I was fucking dying to tear her clothes off and bury myself in her but I knew I had to be patient. And I *could* be a very patient man, so long as I had these moments while I waited. Hell, I could live off these moments forever if I had to.

This was my new reason for waking up every day. Her.

I pulled my hand from her jeans and rested it on her stomach, leaving a trail of wetness, giving her a moment to catch her breath. I fought it for so long. I had resisted her. She was worried about me destroying her heart? She *owned* mine. There was no turning back. I would never forget the way she just looked at me. *Never*

Chapter 41 - Conversations in the grass
Katie

I had never felt so energized and so calm at the same time.

The way he touched me, it was like he knew every single spot that would drive me crazy. I laid there looking at the open blue sky as my breathing returned to normal and realized how turned on he must be. I had no idea what I was doing. I knew I had to be straight with him.

"I don't know what to do...for you now."

He smiled at me, watching me recover. He raised an eyebrow. "You don't have to do anything for me today, okay? I want you to feel comfortable. I wanted to make *you* feel good. You can worry about me another time. I have enough up here," he tapped his head, "to get me through until later."

His eyes were intense in a way I had never seen them, almost carnal but still calm. Like he was a master of self-control. I blushed, not used to such open talk, and now I was picturing him getting himself off, and I *liked* it.

"Nick, I want to do everything right. I mean, there's nothing more that I want in the world than to be with you but, I mean, I don't, I mean...I haven't had or done anything like this with anyone yet. Obviously." I followed my garbled speech with an awkward, embarrassed smile. I wanted to be with him. In fact, there were times I was desperate for him, like five minutes earlier. I just wanted it to be right. I figured I would know when that was, I would feel sure.

He lowered his head down to kiss me again. "I know, Kate, that's a good thing." He instantly made me feel better. "I'm not going to try to have sex with you."

I looked down, but he pulled my gaze back to his eyes, tilting my face up at him.

"Yet," he clarified. "Trust me, I really fucking want to. What I mean is that I would never expect anything from you until you're ready. We have all the time in the world. This is going to go very organically. I've waited years for you, forever, actually. I can be very patient."

He sat up and handed me my shirt. It was weird feeling shy after what had just happened, but now that I was clear-headed again, I took it from him. It was like he knew how I would feel. That I might be shy. Then it hit me, of course, he did. He did these sorts of things with women all the time before me. My gaze fell.

He cupped my face with his hand.

"Are you sorry? Was that too much for you?"

"No, it was...amazing...so good. It's just, I realize that for me this is new, but for you it isn't. At all."

He wrapped his arms around me, shaking his head. "You're wrong. This is new to me too."

I looked at him confused. I knew he had been with other girls, I didn't want to even think about how many. None of this was new to him.

He continued, "Yes, there were others. I don't even remember them all."

I flinched. Sometimes he was too honest.

"But I just used them, Kate."

I flinched again.

"Fuck, I'm not helping, am I?"

I laughed at the way he had just read my mind.

"Let me start over. They were fully willing. Let's start with that. They used me, but I used them too, to distract myself from the anger I felt. It never helped though, only temporarily. I told you that I searched for *this* feeling, the one I have with you. I never found it. And all that sleeping around was a long time ago. I haven't been with anyone in so long, by choice. There's been no one that I have *ever* felt like this with, so this *is* all new to me." He looked at me with pleading eyes. Was he worried I thought badly of him?

He added, "Let me explain. I just enjoyed myself more now, just watching you come than anything I've ever done...with anyone."

I smiled, embarrassed he was watching me so intently.

He lifted my chin so my eyes would meet his and he could read my mind. "Don't be shy. There is *nothing* more mesmerizing than watching you come. I'm officially addicted to it after just one hit."

I laughed and nodded. He changed the subject. "Listen, I got a fresh start when I came here. I wasn't perfect at first, but the more time I spent here, around other men who were good, like really fucking good, the better I wanted to be. I went to the doctor and got a clean bill of health after my previous ways. I knew I was always safe, but I wanted to know for sure. I didn't ever want to be with those women, not the way I want to be with you." He shook his head. "I can't explain it to you with words, how I feel." He ran his hand through his hair.

I silenced him with a kiss. "You don't have to. I understand. And also, I'm on birth control, so you know, even though this or anything like it," I waved to us lying in the grass, "was never even an option for me before now."

He looked confused. I shrugged in response.

"I plan everything, even that. I can't help it."

"I'll wait as long as it takes for you to feel comfortable. In case you didn't notice, I have been spending a lot of time on your ranch pining for you for these last few years."

I laughed, that seemed true.

"Besides, there are so many other things I want to do with you first." His hands roamed my body. I sucked in a breath. He was already getting to me again, the fire resurfacing under my skin.

"I already can't stop thinking about you, now that you've given me this, it's going to be so much worse," I blurted out. I looked to him, my own personal Adonis at my side. I laughed then and added, "They say men think about it a lot, I think that I might think about it more than you do."

His green eyes, full of want, took my admission in. "You're thinking about us a lot, are you?" He looked happier than I had ever seen him, flushed almost.

"Only all day." I beamed as my breathing increased at the feeling of his hands on me.

"Good to know." His fingers traced below my belly button, coming dangerously close to my underwear again.

"Okay, Nick, that's not helping," I said, snapping myself out of it and burying my face in his chest. I knew we had to head back soon or the crew would wonder where we were. He laughed at me then and whispered into my lips as he kissed me.

"I'm going to spend as much time as I can just pleasing you so that when you're ready, you'll be begging me to fuck you." My body went limp at his words and as he moved to kiss me under my ear and splayed his large hand across my waist, gripping me tight, I seriously questioned why in the hell I was waiting at all.

Chapter 42 - According to Frank
Katie

The promised cold front came through over the next few days and everyone but me acted like they were in the Antarctica. Extra hay was brought in, as my dad had suggested, not only for food but also for comfort to the animals. Some of the calves were still so young and they couldn't handle the cold. Frank and Nick had gone with Trent and Will to break ice off the ponds to access water for the animals and equipment. Sadly, six older cows were lost in a two-week period. The stress of the cold was just too much for them.

It finally started warming up a little just before Christmas to give us all a much-needed break, although another cold front was expected to pass through soon enough. The ranch hands were exhausted. It hadn't been this cold in ten winters, my dad said, it was just rotten luck that he wasn't able to be out working with his men.

He was walking much better now, though. His pins had been removed and almost two months had passed since his surgery. He walked often and the effort was paying off. He made the ten-minute walk out to the barn very early one morning, two days before Christmas, just to visit his horse, aptly named Chief. He wasn't ready to ride yet, not for another two months at least, but just getting out in the fresh morning air was helpful. Sam had been riding Chief for him every day to keep the horse happy and healthy. But it was obvious Chief had missed my dad. I found them there together when I arrived in to saddle Buttercup.

"Well, this is a long journey for you this morning," I commented as I entered the stall. "Did you walk here?"

"I did." He said proudly. "Although I think I will cart back. My knee is a bit tight now."

"One step at a time, Dad." I reminded him of his physio therapists words.

We talked briefly about the day's work ahead before I left him with Chief to head to Buttercup across the row. I saddled him expertly and headed for the open field to meet the crew when Frank startled me.

"Morning, you got a minute?"

"Sure, I do." I followed him into the open barn entryway.

"I just want to check in with you. It's been almost two months since you've been home and your dad says you're thinking of staying on over the spring into the summer. Is that right?"

"Yes, I am." I answered him cautiously, this was an odd conversation for five in the morning. "I am feeling very at home here. I didn't realize how much I missed it."

I was comfortable. I was happy, in fact, I had never been so happy. I was curious as to where this conversation was heading. Nick thought Frank had noticed something was off. He wasn't exactly hiding it the best. He said the other guys teased him mercifully about having "some girl in town" because he was always headed to bed early with his phone. None of them could quite figure it out, but Frank must have had an idea.

"I can *see* that you're happy here," he stated. "You seem connected. You're working well with the crew?" he asked?

"Yes, they're all great." I answered.

Then he braced the subject. Right to the point. "Nick has been having a hard time keeping your name off his tongue lately, saying you're doing a good job. In fact, he talks very highly of you most of the time. You two have gotten closer now?"

Thoughts of Nick keeping *me* on his tongue went through my mind briefly. I snapped out of it.

"Yes, we get along very well. We work well together."

"I'm glad, I just want to have you understand the type of future Nick could have here on this ranch. Sometimes in life, when you're young, it feels like it may be worth it to risk a career for one reason or another. I look out for my crew, and you're part of that crew now. When the crew isn't cohesive problems arise, so we all must make sure we're in sync and that we all get along. Not just now, but in the future too. Do you know what I mean?"

He was worried about Nick taking the fall with my dad if this didn't work out. He was the best cowboy he had. People didn't take jobs in farming or ranching anymore. Finding someone as hardworking and reliable as Nick, who was young with a long future ahead of him, wasn't easy these days. Frank didn't want to see my dad let him go if he hurt me, but this was *my* father's ranch. I may be young, but I wasn't about to let Frank act like he knew more than I did about what was best. I thought for long moment before answering him. Aside from knowing his heart was in the right place, I was a little annoyed. I chose my words carefully, trying to avoid going off half-cocked as I tended to do normally.

"I'm not sure *exactly* what you mean but I want you to know, my *only* desire on this ranch is helping to look out for it while my father heals, and I'm doing the best I can for it."
I put on my riding gloves while I continued. "This is *my* family's ranch after all and ultimately mine. I, just as much as anyone, know how important this place is and how important it is that it runs smoothly. I wouldn't do anything to jeopardize that. Now, if you'll excuse me..."

I turned to leave Frank just as my dad peered around the corner. Fucking Frank. Massive overstep.

"Everything alright, Frank? What are you two chatting about?" he asked. I smiled smugly, knowing Frank would need to think of something to tell my dad, something other than "*I was low key talking to your daughter about her love life.*"

Chapter 43 - Are we going to go inside?
Katie

I ran out the front door on Christmas Eve to hug Charlotte, who was being delivered home by Uncle Roger. She had just arrived from Dallas for the holidays. This would be the first time my dad had both of us girls home in the house for more than a day since I left for New York, and he was so happy to have an old-fashioned family Christmas.

My aunt and uncle would arrive with their girls for dinner the following day, and any cowboys that couldn't travel home would join us as well. A feast was already underway and Melia had been cooking for two days. Her daughter and granddaughter were coming again for dinner.

I was actually beyond happy to see Charlotte's face. We had plans to shop sales after Christmas together, have movie marathons, and eat all the Christmas food.

"I have a list of all the movies we can watch Boxing Day," she prattled on as she helped our uncle unload her bags from the back of his truck. "*Legally Blond, Mean Girls, Princess Diaries, She's the Man,* oh and all *the Hunger Games* of course." Charlotte had had a Liam Hemsworth obsession for years.

I laughed. "Can we watch some oldies too? I was thinking *Ten Things I hate About You, Clueless.*"

"I swear sometimes you're really thirty." She laughed. "But yes, we can compromise." And then, as a second thought. "How's Daddy really?"

"He's good," I answered.

She looked at me with her I-don't-believe-you face.

"He really is. Going a little stir crazy, but he's good. I spent Mom's birthday with him. You really have to see these home movies. It's so amazing to see her, to hear her voice."

"Yeah, we'll see if we have time."

I got the feeling she didn't even want to watch them. To Charlotte, my mom was always a fairy tale figure. She didn't remember her at all. I had vented to Nick about it the week before.

His advice was smart, and he said that maybe watching the videos would make my mom more real to her and she'd have to actually attach some emotion to her. Right now, it was easy to avoid emotion over a woman who only existed in photos and stories. I hadn't thought of it that way and it made sense to me.

"Aren't you curious to see what she was like at all, Char?"

Charlotte sighed. She hated this conversation. "Not really. I don't remember her at all. It would be like me asking you if you want to watch boring home movies of our great grandpa, you know?"

Sometimes I was surprised at how self-centered she could be. I wondered where she got that from. My dad wasn't like that at all, and from what everyone told me, neither was my mom.

Our dad interrupted us then, coming to the porch and welcoming us inside. Charlotte chatted his ear off for over an hour about school and her teachers she didn't like and how unfair they were. Then she shared all the extracurricular activities she was involved with.

I smiled while listening. Not once did she ask him what was going on here. Typical.

By four-thirty I had heard enough and decided it might be a good time to excuse myself. I had plans anyway. I used the excuse of finishing my last-minute Christmas shopping in town and maybe stop at Lena's to say Merry Christmas. Nick was already home for Christmas Eve. Almost all of the ranch hands were gone home to be with their families until at least Boxing Day, some for a little longer. In truth, Nick's parents were gone to his grandparents in Wimberley since they were too old and frail to leave their retirement home. They were taking them to a Christmas Eve service at the chapel and having a big dinner after in the main hall with all the residents and their families.

We would have his whole house to ourselves for a few hours. I was excited to see his family home with a fresh view. I had been in it multiple times as a small child, but only the front entry or back kitchen off their yard. I didn't remember much from it at all. It had been years, and as we got older, he mostly came to me.

His home was only a ten-minute drive from mine and now technically smack in the middle of our property.

The lights glowed softly from inside the house when I pulled up the driveway in my dad's Silverado. The acre their home was set on was a truly beautiful property. My dad had purchased the rest of their land years before to help with medical bills. Their original six hundred acres now belonged to us.

The house was surrounded by trees and set back far enough off the road that it was not visible through the trees until you pulled right up to the front of the house and rounded the circular driveway. It was a two story, with white siding that was worn and fading. It was a cape cod style with a covered front porch that ran the whole distance of the house. The large, forest green front door was flanked by windows on either side.

Nick came out onto the front porch. He didn't look like a cowboy, he looked more like a GQ model in jeans and a black cable-knit sweater that made him look even more tanned than normal. His dark wavy hair looked like it may have still been a bit wet from the shower. I felt my heart do the same familiar flip flop it always did when I saw him. I jumped out of the truck.

I had chosen a black skirt, shorter than I normally wore, it was Christmas after all, and went with a deep scarlet peasant blouse that hung off my shoulders with loose billowy sleeves that cuffed at my wrists. I left my hair loose in beachy waves and it was blowing around in the warm breeze. He didn't look disappointed as I walked up the steps to him.

"You are extra beautiful today, Princess," he whispered as he kissed me. "Fuck. Is this my Christmas present?" He grazed my shoulders with both hands from my neck out. No one could see us on his property. It still overwhelmed me every time he kissed me. Just once was all it took to set fire to my insides.

"You're very distracting. How am I supposed to keep away from you long enough to give you your present when you're looking like *this*?" he asked.

"Pretend we're in the field and I'm up to my knees in mud?" I teased.

He stood there and stared at me for a few moments as if trying to picture it. "Nope, not working. In fact, it's making me want you more." He pulled me easily into him to kiss me again then moved down, kissing my shoulder in a soft little line.

"Mmmmm, I remember the first time I saw your shoulders in that dress at the fair. How badly I wanted to touch you then but didn't." He bent down to kiss across the other shoulder, but he didn't stop there. He kissed all the way up to my neck, like he was just lost to the enjoyment of being able to kiss me now. The familiar feeling in my stomach was tightening into a coil as heat gathered between my legs and my nipples went rigid under my bra. I hadn't even made it in the damn door yet.

"Are we going to go inside?" I whispered. "You're killing me."

"If we must." He rolled his eyes dramatically at me. "Now, this isn't your magnificent manor," he pushed the front door open, waving me inside before him, "but come inside."

Chapter 44 - I had a task
Katie

I stepped into the little foyer and looked around, taking in the feel and space of their home. Immediately to my right was a large, gray living room with a white fireplace and white built-in bookshelves flanking each side.

Comfortable furniture filled the room. A large overstuffed sofa faced the fireplace and two gray wingbacked chairs sat on either side of a big picture window. In the far corner sat a TV on a rustic stand that looked to be quite a few years old. Throw blankets were available in every sitting spot and accent cushions in every corner of the sofa. Nick had a fire going in the fireplace. It was adding a little warmth to the room. Two table lamps glowed beside the chairs and a large square coffee table sat in the middle, strewn with fishing magazines and crochet patterns and how-to books. It was cozy and clean and homey. The whole house smelled like cedar and orange. The scent was warm and inviting. Just like Nick.

"Your house just feels like you," I said to him as I entered.

He laughed. "It does now. What you didn't see was two hours ago, cleaning everything and getting rid of the empty booze bottles from the kitchen counter. I'm my mother's parent when I'm here." He looked down. "But you know what though? You being here gives it a totally different vibe. A really, really good one."

He kissed me on the top of my head as he frequently did and my heart went out to him.

"Let's go, I'll give you the grand tour," he said, showing me the way while holding my hand.

The maple wood floors continued all throughout the house. A dining room with a large table was just beyond their living room and it led into a small kitchen with white cabinets and a center island cluttered with a low-hanging pot rack filled with pots. The kitchen was the one room I had been in before. A tiny family room with another fireplace and a small den filled out the left side of the house. The back of the house was all windows, looking out into a big square yard. A tumbled stone patio with an in-laid fire pit and built in seating was just outside patio doors off the kitchen. The yard was flanked with trees still for privacy. Bird feeders and flowers sprinkled the yard on shepherd's hooks. It was like a little private paradise.

"My dad likes to garden now." He shrugged. "It's therapeutic for him and keeps him busy."

"This is still my favorite part of the house." It was beautiful, like I always remembered it being, but even more so now after his dad's hard work.

He led me upstairs to three bedrooms. Nick's still looked like he could be living there. Like nothing had changed since he'd moved to the ranch.

His floors were wood, like the rest of the house, but a large soft area rug filled most of the floor. A double bed that looked like it would be way too small for him was in the middle of the room. A small desk and the filled bookshelf beside it rounded out the room.

I gravitated to the bookshelf to check out the titles on it. His book collection was eclectic and well rounded. *The Log of A Cowboy* by Andy Adams, *Butcher's Crossing* by John Williams, and a handful of other important western themed novels. There was no doubt where his interests lied from a young age. *War and Peace*, Shakespeare's *Hamlet*, a large collection of Tennyson's poetry, all marked with little sticky notes inside of them. *Wuthering Heights*, a vast number of early edition *Hardy Boys* with simple beige covers from what I could only imagine to be at least the 1950s.

"Impressive collection," I said to him.

"I used to read a lot," he replied sheepishly. "Some were my dad's, he used to read me the *Hardy Boys* when I was young. I just collect them now."

"I remember you reading when we'd ride out in the fields, we have that in common." He was such a deep soul and no one would guess it.

"I know." He walked over to look out his window, deep in some memory of his own. "I remember the summer I was maybe fourteen or fifteen, the first summer I worked on the ranch, you were in that old swing that used to be on your front porch reading every day. Every day I'd come back to the bunkhouse and there you were, on the porch, reading in the shade. I always wondered what you were thinking. Your face always looked so concentrated and pretty." He turned to face me.

"That was the summer I started reading Sylvia Plath. Her poetry. I remember. Charlotte thought I was so dull but I couldn't put her works down." I couldn't believe he had noticed me. I remembered seeing him walk by every day too. I just forgot about it until now. I hadn't even realized he had seen me.

He came toward me and wrapped his large hands around my waist, his thumbs resting just under the rim of my top, where it met my skirt. He pulled me to him easily.

"I think you're the least dull person I know, just for the record."

I was pretty much helpless like that under his grasp, he was so much stronger than me. I felt my body respond to him instantly. I squeezed my thighs together, I could feel every place where my clothing touched my skin. My nipples instantly hardened under the soft linen of my blouse as he ran his thumbs back and forth over my waist. He kissed me longer and more powerfully than he had before, it was chaotic and slow all at the same time.

Fire flowed through my veins. His mouth searched mine and I melted from my head to my toes. Suddenly I was very aware we were alone in his dark bedroom. This was different than being outside in nature. It was safe and warm and very inviting, plus it had what nature didn't. A real bed. I couldn't help myself, I ran my hands up his shirt onto his back, feeling the strength and warmth of it. He was a work of art; his sculpted body was complete and utter proof of that.

I kissed him back more intensely. He stopped and pulled back from me. Trying to keep himself controlled, I imagine. I closed in on the space he created, reaching up to kiss him again. I let go, roving my hands over his back and waist. I had no idea what I was doing really but I knew I wanted to make *him* feel good. As good as he made me feel. I felt brave, there was no one around and we had hours.

I used every single possible ounce of willpower I had to pull away from him. Looking at him slowly, I backed up toward his bed and sat on it, motioning for him to come to me, leaning against his headboard with the pillows behind me. He groaned, approaching me, joining me on the bed, kissing me as he ran his fingers up my arm, stopping to trace my shoulder, then my neck.

"Kate...I'm hanging on by a thread here. If you want me to control myself at all, you can't look at me like that." He kissed slowly across my collarbone, making me incoherent.

"Like what?" I pulled away from him, looking up at him to question him.

"Like *that*." He elaborated as he peppered kisses down my neck. "Innocently, like you have no idea what you're doing to me. Like you're an angel right before you kiss me like you've been doing it forever. I can't take it and be expected to control myself." His voice was deep and raspy, just how I liked it.

If I didn't take what I wanted very soon I would be at *his* will on *his* bed letting him do whatever he wanted to me. I sat up, startling him out of the kiss and pushing him flat onto the bed.

"I want to do something, okay?" I said quietly. Slowly, I straddled him but hovered, keeping a distance between us that he wasn't about to let me have.

"If you're going to do it, do it right, baby."

His hands slid under my skirt and up my thighs. He grasped my hips, pulling me down onto him forcefully and making me very aware that I was doing a pretty good job of getting to him. I could feel him pressing against me between my legs with what seemed like a very impressive package.

He groaned, kissing me more intensely than he ever had, claiming my mouth as his hands pressed into my hips with such force I feared they would leave marks in their wake. I could physically feel him letting go. His body losing control. I pulled at his sweater. He realized what I wanted and sat up slightly, gripping it with one hand behind his neck, then pulling it off along with the t-shirt under it.

Hold it together. I took the sight of him in. My body was dying for him to touch me, and he was so beautiful in the dim light of his room. I reached my hands down over his jeans, undoing them much easier than I thought I'd be able to.

"What are you doing?" he asked slowly, smiling at me.

I looked up at him again. "Trying to make you feel as good as you make me feel. Can I try?"

He bit back a groan as he took his bottom lip between his teeth and nodded.

"Of course," he said calmly. This was the first time I had seen him without his shirt on since the quick twenty second tease in the field weeks before and it was so much better than the first time because I was on top of him and he was looking at me like I held his world in my hands. When he reached up to pull my shirt off I could see every single muscle in his arms contract and the sight of it alone was almost enough to make me forget my own name. His hands held me at my ribs, guiding me, showing me what he wanted from me.

I couldn't believe this was me. I told myself not to overthink it. Here I was, in my bra, on top of this unbelievably gorgeous man in his bed, and the only thing I wanted to do was make him come. I just wasn't one hundred percent sure *what* to do.

I let my body take over. I tugged at the waist of his jeans, he pulled them off from under me without even really jostling me, throwing them to the floor. I was so much closer to him like this, with my skirt around my waist. Only two layers of flimsy fabric acted as barriers between us.

I pressed down on him again, desperately searching for friction against the ache between my legs.

He smirked. "I love how ready you are for me, always so wet, aren't you, baby?" He reached down and touched me over my panties.

"Yes. A-always," I stammered.

His fingers applying pressure through the lace was too much for me. My head fell backward and my eyes rolled as he expertly circled my clit. "Your sweet little cunt only gets this wet for *me*, Kate. It's mine, isn't that right, baby?"

Can you come from words and words alone? Because I was shockingly close. I reminded myself to get it together. I leaned forward into his neck. I had a task.

"Yes...all yours," I whispered, trying to take control of his attention. I was rewarded with a nearly animalistic growl. I moved my hand slowly, the bravery returning as he kissed me, and began touching him through his boxers. The moment my hand connected with him I heard him suck in a sharp breath. I could feel nothing but his size and how badly he wanted me. All I could think was *how on earth is he going to fit inside me?* I had no other experience, but he felt too big.

I moved my hand slowly, pressing against him and feeling him under my fingers, rubbing up and down the length of him while I kissed him. I don't know how my body knew what to do, it just did. I traced the band of his boxers, completely losing every inhibition I had.

I slid my hand inside them and he helped by pulling them off completely. I repeated the same action as before. Pressing my palm to him, pumping softly. His groans and his hands gripping the flesh at my hips told me he liked it.

"I knew your hands would feel so fucking good wrapped around my cock." He ran his tongue along my bottom lip and pulled it between his own, kissing me roughly.

"I want to feel these perfect lips now, Kate," he whispered, encouraging me to do what I already wanted without making me ask. I pulled back and looked at him, moving my hand with a little more confidence, his words pushing me to earn more of his praise.

"I'll show you what to do baby, don't worry." He assured me as he traced my cheek with his thumb. I leaned into him, pressing my body against him, and began kissing his neck. Slowly, carefully, moving downward over him, I kissed and licked a hot trail from his collarbone to his waist. His skin had the best taste to it and I became almost lost in it. I shifted onto my knees between his legs, gripping his length, taking the first couple of inches of him into my mouth, lapping up little beads of pre-cum with my tongue. I looked up at him through my lashes, his chest heavy as he looked back at me. God, the site of him like this was making my mouth water.

"*Fuck.*" Escaped his lips when I took him in deeper. His skin was soft but he was so hard, so long, so thick, so *solid*. His groans from above me were like a shot straight to my core, proving him right, my pussy was only this wet for him. I imagined what it would feel like with him inside me and it made me clench my thighs even tighter. I was desperate for some sort of friction. He gathered my hair into his hand as I hovered over him. I let him guide my mouth for me. I continued running my tongue the length of him as I took him in as far as I could. When he hit the back of my throat, I reached my limit and my eyes started to water. I used my hands over the rest of him to compensate, still not covering him. He had no business being this big or this perfect.

"That's it Kate...*fuck*...you feel so good. You're doing so fucking good, Princess." His hand held my hair, guiding my head up and down. I had no control over my own actions as he took over, moving in and out of my mouth at what I can only imagine would be a slow, torturous rhythm for him.

"You can take more now, just relax for me." He pushed his hips upward, plunging himself deeper as he filled my throat with so much more of his cock. It caused me to gag and sputter as his hand still firmly gripped my hair. I somehow was able to adjust to what he gave me though and I moaned around him. A single tear escaped as he continued to hit the back of my throat and he caught it as it trailed down my cheek, licking it off of his thumb before moving his hand back into my hair. Such a simple gesture seemed so erotic in the moment because I realized that he was still watching me so intently from above. Giving him this pleasure was the biggest natural turn on I had ever felt. His words were driving me crazy. I was sure I was on actual fire between my legs.

"Good girl baby, see? That's it. Just. Like. That." His praise was a deep, raspy whisper. I moved my mouth up and down the length of him, hollowing my cheeks out, inching him closer and closer. Letting him maintain all control as his hand held my head, losing myself in him and my movements with every swipe of my tongue over him. Minutes passed and his breathing grew heavy, ragged. His words brought me back to the moment. They sounded breathless and surprised. His voice was gravel.

"*Fuck*, I'm gonna come."

I moaned over him again when he said it and felt it vibrate down his length. He groaned the most beautiful sound. I slowed down, pushing against the strength of his hand in my hair to take back the control, savoring him. He let me. I felt his legs tense under me and heat spilled into my throat. "Katelyn..." He growled before muttering inaudible cuss words and then breathing out "*Fuck*." It was a long, drawn out version of the word as I watched him through my lashes, his chest moving up and down, his breathing heavy. It was the most out of control I had ever seen him, and I loved it. I wanted more. I swallowed his release down, pulling every last drop in as best as I could, feeling some escape down my chin. Before I could register what was happening his thumb was there, dragging it up and swiping it into my mouth, pressing it into my tongue. I licked it off and he groaned. "Every last drop, baby." He scolded as his head fell back onto the pillows. He still gripped my hair so tightly it hurt in the best possible way.

I moved up and rested on his chest.

"Was that right?" I asked him, looking up at him. I didn't fully know what a good blow job entailed, but I thought that must be close. He looked down at me and groaned uncontrollably. Then pulled me up to him, into his arms.

"Well, seeing as no one has ever made me come before in all of five minutes, I'd say it was fucking unreal. You are incredible." He smiled.

"I loved it," I confessed, but it sounded more like a moan as I squeezed my thighs together, the heat between my legs getting the better of me.

He sighed into me and chuckled quietly.

"What?" I asked. Again, it was more like a moan than a question.

"Mmmmm...you just have a side to you that I can't fucking wait to unravel." The words spoken into my neck vibrated through my whole body. He kissed me at my breasts and started offering me light little flicks of my nipples under his thumbs, laughing quietly in the dark.

"You didn't think I was going to forget you, did you?"

"Nick...please?"

He smiled at me and kissed my lips.

"I'll take care of you now, baby," he whispered, high still off of his own release and focused intensely on me.

I only nodded to him, little moans escaping me as he began kissing my neck. He looked at me like I was in for it.

Chapter 45 - I had nothing but time
Nick

I lifted her off of me, laying her like a flaming hot little package down on my bed under me. She was more animated this time than last and I loved what was ahead of me. Just thinking about it was enough to keep me hard for the rest of the night, no, the rest of my life. I pulled her skirt and her soaking panties off, tossing them who knows where. The second I touched her, her back moved to an arch and the most exquisite little moan came from her that I knew she had absolutely no control over. I spread her legs, getting comfortable between them, I had nothing but time. I wanted to soak in every single expression she made. She looked like she was about to go crazy, but I wasn't going to rush it. I moved my finger over her, between her two perfect, bare lips, sliding it downward and into her. I could almost taste her sweetness. She was driving me half mad with the need I felt for her. Slowly and not-so gently, I grazed the inside of her thighs with my lips and teeth as I pumped my fingers in and out of her, kissing her from her knees all the way up, hearing her moaning my name and pushing her fingers into my hair. Her body knew instinctively that she wanted my tongue but she'd never ask for it. Not yet. I moved back up to her face, running a finger that was soaked from her pussy over my bottom lip. Sliding my hand to her throat, then kissing her, I whispered, "See how good you taste baby?"

She surprised the absolute fuck out of me by licking her lips and nodding at me. I felt her swallow under my hand. The look she wore just begged me to make her come. *Fuck.* My every fantasy of her come to life. I pushed my fingers back into her as her eyes rolled back, then closed.

"I'm going to devour your sweet pussy now, Kate, is that what you need?"

"Yes...please," she mumbled between moans like she was asking.

I moved back down between her legs, kissing every square inch of her along the way, planting one singular kiss to her clit first, taking just a second to acquaint myself with my new home. She moaned at the simple feeling as I fanned over her and then I fucking ravaged her, getting to work like it was my job, the only job I'd ever worked. My mouth covered her entirely as I let her fill my senses, circling her clit and fucking my tongue in and out of her, taking up every last drop of her like a starved man at his last meal. I felt her body writhing under me. Her hands moved through my hair as she whimpered and moaned like a caged little animal. She was everything and everywhere all at once.

"Your pussy is my fucking utopia baby."

I was aware of her thrashing and gripping the sheets, but I was so utterly lost in her. Overcome. She was so sweet, so warm and tight. Everything I could ever want and so much more.

I snaked my arm under her lower back and around her waist to hold her in place as her nails dug into my shoulders. I continued this torturous teasing until she couldn't take it anymore. Her legs began shaking.

"Nick…please…" she begged. I chuckled from my place between her legs. My girl didn't like to be teased when she wanted to come. Noted.

"Okay, Princess, you want to come now? You can come…" I slung her legs over my shoulders and added my fingers back into her, hitting that perfect spot inside her, the spot that I have no idea how other men have trouble finding, the one I knew would drive her crazy as I kept my tongue on her, sucking her clit and timing my movements to her bucking hips, sending her over the edge.

The orgasm consumed her entire body. She pushed her hips into my face with not a care in the world while she called out my name breathlessly into the silence of my room. She was naturally wild, she just didn't know it yet, and that created a need in me that was unlike anything I had ever known. I kept my fingers inside her and my mouth and tongue licking and sucking vigorously while she rode out her high for what seemed like minutes. When her cries finally stopped, she was trembling and dripping down my hand. I kissed her once more at the apex of her thighs, before rejoining her in the middle of my bed, resting my head on her stomach, looking up at her. Her hands moved through my hair while her breathing slowly returned to normal. There was nothing as natural and as all-consuming as the fucking primal need I had for her. I would never, ever get enough of her or tire of her. My tiny little goddess with the golden hair and sky-blue eyes. The perfect blend of innocence and indecency.

Chapter 46 - I bet
Katie

A few minutes later when I regained my thought process back, I leaned down to his head at my waist and kissed him in his hair. The smile he wore was contagious. New discovery, Nick was apparently the king of eating pussy. I don't even remember anything but a white, hot haze of pleasure washing over me and the feeling of my entire body shattering like glass under his touch. This was something I would never stop wanting.

"I can't imagine anything better," I whispered. He moved up to me, laying on his side, kissing me. I could still taste myself on his lips.

"Do you want your dinner first, or your Christmas present?" His smile was mesmerizing.

"Dinner. I'm starving."

"I bet." He sat up, pulling me up from my elbows.

"Come on then, I made Christmas Eve Alfredo." He smiled a huge, proud of himself smile, then shrugged.

"My mom used to watch the same Christmas movie every year and that's what they do, so I figured, why not?"

"I know the one." I laughed at him mentioning *The Holiday*, it was one of my favorite Christmas moves too. "Alfredo sounds amazing."

He led me down to the small kitchen. We decided to eat out by the fire because the night was so beautiful. He left me with a hot chocolate and ventured into the backyard to light a fire. The back patio was covered, just like the front, and lit with multi-coloured old-fashioned-style Christmas lights. He turned them on. Besides the fire, they were the only lights on the entire property.

The oven was already on low and when he returned, he pulled a large foil tray out that was covered with aluminum foil.

"Can I help?" I asked.

"You could make us a salad?" He answered like it was a question. I started by opening the fridge and pulling out ingredients easily found for a simple garden salad. He pulled two plates out of the cabinet.

"I think that's what we need, I just kind of picked up what I thought would work for a garden salad." He shrugged, hoping he was right.

I nodded. "It's perfect."

I couldn't help but smile to myself while I worked, picturing him at the grocery store with a list, shopping to make me dinner. Was there anything he did that wasn't attractive? I made the salad and he got plates ready for us. I had never felt as comfortable with another living soul as I did right then in that kitchen making dinner with Nick.

His Alfredo was amazing, another discovery. Nick could really cook. I was touched by his effort when he told me he had followed a recipe online, making the sauce from scratch.

We sat out at the fire, he brought me out a blanket and wrapped me in it. The sky was bright, littered with stars. There were no streetlights to stop their glory, no industry. In fact, all the surrounding land for miles was my Dad's. It was peaceful and romantic and the most perfect Christmas Eve ever.

He brought out red velvet cake afterward that he had ordered earlier in the afternoon from Vignette's Bakery in Reeds Canyon. It was delicious.

"You are spoiling me," I said to him after we were finished. "This is the best Christmas Eve I've ever had."

He got up from his chair and came over to me on his knees, wrapping his arms around me and the blanket and kissing me again as if he could never tire of it. "I can't wait to spoil you in every way. You have no idea baby."

My body went limp as he planted a string of kisses down my collarbone. He smiled at me then and got up, disappearing into the house. He returned a few minutes later holding a small, perfectly wrapped box tied with ribbon.

"Your Christmas present, Beautiful." He presented it to me as if it were Cinderella's glass slipper. I laughed and nervously took it from him.

I opened it at once, pulling away the delicate ribbon and opening the box. Inside was a rose gold chain with a monogram circle at the bottom. Where an initial would normally be, there was just a single daisy flower carved into it. It was perfect. The notecard read, "A daisy for every moment she crosses my mind, means I would walk in my garden forever."

"Tennyson?" I asked, recognizing his twist on the famous line. His eyes lit up in surprise.

"Yes, and to remind you of me, but in a way that no one else can see. The wild daisies remind me of you, they always have. After you left, every time I saw one, I thought about you. I'm partial to Tennyson, his words...they stick with me," he said quietly as I pulled it out of the box.

I understood then that was why he always left them for me over the years. To show me he was thinking about me. My heart felt like it might explode. To anyone else it was just a necklace with a simple flower on it.

I flipped it over to the back to reveal the other side of the circular charm. Simply, "My Princess" carved into the back that would sit on my skin.

He had thought of a way to give me a special gift that meant everything but said nothing to another living soul.

"It's so perfect. That story is the gift. I didn't know you thought of me that much after I left," I said, feeling tears in my eyes. He lifted me up, sitting down in my chair and pulling me onto his lap. He kissed me at the base of my ear. I ran my hand down his arm, over his tattoos.

"Kate, I've been thinking about you since I was twelve years old. Now you'll always have me with you. Even when we have to be apart, I'm right there," he said, putting it on me with ease. It fit perfectly and hung just to the crevices of my collarbone. He kissed me there then, slowly moving down my chest.

"You're not doing a very good job keeping me out of your bedroom with kisses like that."

"Baby, the last thing I'm trying to do is keep you out of my bedroom." He smiled.

"Okay, but I just want to give you your gift now." I couldn't top his, but I was still exited to give it to him.

"If you must." He sighed dramatically, as if I was forcing him. I got up.

"Kate?"

"Yes?" I turned back to look at him.

"Hurry." He smiled at me and I laughed, heading into the kitchen to grab my purse. I reached into it, pulling out a box wrapped in festive paper. I came back into the yard and dutifully took my spot in his lap.

He opened it carefully while I watched with anticipation. He lifted out the small, Apache made, bull cutter pocket knife, hand forged with the finest steel. It was covered in a handmade leather sheath with the coordinates 29.8752° N, 98.2625° W engraved on the underside.

"What are these coordinates? This is incredible, Kate." He ran his hand along the engravings.

"My cousin hand made it, the coordinates are to the hill." I shrugged. "Our secret place."

He kissed me then with so much passion. "No one has ever given me such an incredible, thoughtful gift." He smiled against my lips and I felt something stir in me again.

"I'll never understand how do you that, make me want you in one second flat." I laid my head on his chest, still tracing his arm. I studied the intricate drawings on his skin, recognizing some of the lyrics. I lifted his t-shirt sleeve to get the full view.

"What do these all mean?"

"Which ones?"

"All of them."

"Well, my arm was the last thing I had done. It's a work in progress. It's mostly lyrics and images of songs that are important to me or helped me through some period of time in my life that I remember. Reminding me that the past is the past."

He pointed to each one, telling me what they were as he went. "*Whiskey River; Willie Nelson, Country Roads; John Denver, Feeling Whitney; Post Malone. Walk the Line; Johnny Cash, Mama Tried; Merle Haggard...*"

"Tell me more..."

"*Only God can judge me; Tupac.*" He pointed to the skeleton figures I had noticed in the field. "*If we were vampires; Jason Isbell.* I had a local artist sketch me this one..."

I had never seen him so light, so sweet. He spent time telling me about all the songs, the angel from *Nirvana's Heart Shaped Box*, an intricate clock he said was from a *Led Zeppelin* song. It was a very eclectic and well thought out list and there was still room to spare to add more as he fell in love with new music.

"What about these others?" I patted his other side where the writing ran down his ribs. It was my favorite.

"Well, first, this one here," he reached for his back. "is a Sicilian cross. My mother has one from her family that came from Italy. I always loved the look of it. It's so gothic and intricate. The bones and leaves that sit within it are a symbol of the bones in this land, it reminds me that this world was here long before me and will still be here long after me. It keeps me humble."

"And this writing? Is it Italian too?" I touched his side.

"No, that's Gaelic, you know my dad is from Scotland, it's the language my great grandparents spoke."

"It is something special about them or your family?"

"Not exactly, but it is special. The most—"

My phone buzzed loudly on the table and Charlotte's face was smiling at me when I looked at it. I tried to ignore it, but she just called again.

"I'm sorry. I have to answer it, she'll just keep calling." He kissed my neck as I answered.

"Where are you? I've been waiting for an hour to bake with you?" her tone was impatient, not even saying hello.

"I'm coming soon," I answered, which made Nick chuckle as he reached under my skirt between my thighs, making my words sound more like a moan.

"Okay, hurry up. How much shopping did you have to do anyway?"

His fingers pushing my panties to the side and sliding into me was too much, and I knew I had to get off the phone with her immediately.

"I'll be there like…in uh…a half an hour, Char." I hung up on her, and Nick laughed while he kissed me so powerfully it consumed all of me. As I kissed him back and fell completely apart under his expert fingers one more time, I didn't care if I ever came up for air again.

Chapter 47 - Busted
Katie

I left him reluctantly just after nine-thirty. Thoughts of his body, mouth and hands on me fresh in my mind the whole way home. I had to make my shopping and visit length believable to my own family. We made plans to meet up on the day after Christmas at the nest. We would see each other at church on Christmas Day but of course, we would have to just behave like work acquaintances in front of everyone. I loved Christmas but was dreading not seeing him for the whole day. *Thank God for cell phones.*

    I pulled into the driveway and parked the truck in its usual spot. The lights were bright in my house and Christmas lights glowed all around. Our giant ten-foot tree shone through the front windows and I wondered why it was so bright inside until I noticed the familiar truck at the other end of the driveway.

    When I came into the front door I was greeted by my father, Frank, and his wife, Sheila, sitting in the parlor near the

Christmas tree, their two small boys ran in circles around the room with excitement, hopped up on sugar more than likely.

"There she is!" my dad boomed. "We were just talking about you."

"You were?" I asked nervously.

"Yes, I was telling your dad I ran into Lena's parents tonight at Kroger's, they must not have known you were stopping by," Frank said. "They told me the whole family was going to Christmas Eve service tonight, your dad thought you may have stopped there?" Frank said to me.

BUSTED.

I thought quick on my feet. Frank was becoming a pain in the ass.

"It wasn't a solid plan, I ended up shopping till the stores closed and then I thought I'd go for a drive in Wimberley to see the Christmas lights, remember like we used to, Dad?"

"Sure do, we should do that together before the New Year." He smiled at me. *Done. Butt out, Frank.*

I turned to see Charlotte standing in the kitchen entryway, her reindeer jammies were covered in flour and her hair was in two space buns on the top of her head.

"You're home, finally. Come and bake cookies with me for Dad," she said, trying to pull me by my arm into the kitchen. "I'm just about to start rolling them out."

"Okay, let me just change." I said to Charlotte, pulling my arm back. "I'll be right down."

"Wait, you look pretty nice to have been out shopping, you got a boy in town we don't know about?" Charlotte joked. The three other adults in the room laughed. Frank stood up to get going home. It was late and his kids needed to go to bed so Santa could make an appearance.

"Merry Christmas y'all," he said before he gathered up the kids and headed out the door, tittering with the kind of laughter and noises only Christmas Eve could bring.

I ran upstairs quickly to change and check my phone.

Three texts from Nick.

Kryptonite: *Tonight was amazing, the best night I've ever had so far.*
Kryptonite: *Have fun with your sister and we'll talk later if you can.*
Kryptonite: *Also, wear that skirt more often.*

I would remember this night always. I knew at this point I loved him, but it was so much, so quickly, it actually scared me.

Me: *Wait up for me. Next time I'll wear it with no panties under it.*
Kryptonite: *Fuck.*

I smiled at his words, or lack thereof, and slid my phone away in my nightstand.

A vision of other Christmases where he could be here with my family went through my mind. I daydreamed about it as I changed into my pajamas. I piled my hair high on my head and ventured down to find Charlotte in the kitchen listening to Christmas music and creating the world's biggest cookie making mess I had ever seen.

"You're later than I thought you'd be, where'd you go?" she asked. I gave her the same story I gave my dad, but Charlotte was more skeptical than him.

"You just drove around after alone? That sounds boring, why would you—?"

Her eyes got wide like a new reality had just dawned on her. "You WERE with a guy!" she yelled so loud, even over the Christmas music I was sure my dad would hear.

"Shhhhhhhhhhhh." I ran over to her to hush her. "No, I wasn't."

Charlotte laughed. "Bullshit, you were so, otherwise why would you hush me?"

Crap.

"Okay, but it's new, Char, you can't say anything. You have to promise."

"Who is it? You were in Wimberley? Do I know him?" She squinted suspiciously at me.

"I'm not telling you yet," I stated. "It's too new, I want to keep it to myself."

She stared at me intensely, as if looking at me would make the name appear on my forehead.

"Wait, is it serious?" She seemed beyond intrigued. I had never really had a boyfriend.

"I think so, I mean, he's so amazing, Char."

"Have you guys done it yet?"

"No, not yet," I said to her quickly.

"But you want to." She laughed. "I can tell by the look on your face."

"Yes. But it's...I think it's kind of...special." No point in lying to her. I did want to.

"Is he hot?" No fear in asking the direct questions, as always.

This time I gave in. Even if his identity was a secret, it actually felt good to tell someone how amazing he was.

"He is *so* gorgeous, honestly, and he is just incredible."

Charlotte looked at me skeptically with a little smirk. "I'll find out who it is before I leave here. You have to tell me at some point. In the meantime, start rolling these out with me? I'm bored with doing it."

Typical for her. Starting something and then expecting someone else to finish it for her. Today, I didn't mind. I had just had the most amazing night of my life. Nothing was going to ruin my mood, not even cleaning up Charlotte's mess.

We made a total of three dozen sugar cookies and sat in the family room with our dad eating them and talking. We placed our gifts out to each other. Even my dad was well enough now to be getting up and down to place his gifts.

It felt like the Christmas Eves when I was younger, with all of us there. When we went up to sleep I was glad my sister was home. She grated on me sometimes, but I still missed her fiercely when she was gone.

"Night, Bug." I whispered through the adjoining bathroom to her.

"Night, Pug." Charlotte whispered back. I smiled at our silly childhood nicknames. The best part of my night was closing my door to my room. I couldn't wait to talk to Nick. When I finally got to my phone he was there, like he said he would be, waiting to talk to me. I got under the covers and dialed his number to FaceTime him.

"Merry Christmas," I said as he answered, shirtless in his bed and making me wish I could reach out and touch him just as my clock struck twelve.

"Merry Christmas, baby," he said back.

Chapter 48 - Time and place, Charlotte. Katie

I entered into the second oldest church in town, which my family had attended for one hundred years, on Christmas Day with my dad and Charlotte. It was packed, as it usually was at Christmas, and we navigated our way through the crowd of people. It seemed like the whole town of Reeds Canyon was there. Even in a crowd, I spotted him instantly. Nick stood with Pastor Benson and his family in a dark suit. His tie perfectly tied into a full Windsor knot. I had never seen him look so incredible.

"Good God, Nick Stratton got *HOT*!" Charlotte blurted out louder than she should've.

"Time and place Charlotte..." our dad said in a quiet, monotone voice, reminding her to have social awareness. He was used to her behaviors being off the cuff.

"Sorry, Dad, cover your ears. Katie, is it just me or is he even hotter than he used to be? I just saw him in the summer. *How do you work with him?*"

"Charlotte!" my dad reminded her in his angry whisper.

"Well, I'm a mature person is how, and I doubt he wants to be ogled by a seventeen-year-old," I snapped back. I turned to look at him again to see what Charlotte was seeing. I sighed. I couldn't argue. He *was* so hot.

"Well, aren't you grumpy." She pretended to be hurt and then started laughing. "Oh crap, of course he's coming over here." She turned away from his direction and started fixing her hair.

"Hello Sir, Kate, Charlotte." Nick reached his hand out to shake my dad's. "Merry Christmas to you all."

"Merry Christmas to you too, son. Deacon, Amber-Lee, how've you been?"

They were a striking couple, looks wise. Deacon Stratton was a very handsome man. He was big like Nick but blond and viking-like. It was like Nick inherited his father's size and striking features with his mother's dark hair and green eyes. Whatever way the combination came together, Nick was a perfect blend of the two of them. Deacon and my dad started chatting right away, they had been friends for a long time. Amber-Lee was already a little slurry with her words, and I felt like Deacon wasn't just gripping her arm to be a gentleman. It appeared he was actually holding her up. We moved to the side to let them talk.

"Your dad looks well," I said to Nick, and I meant it. I hadn't seen him since he was sick and he looked a lot healthier. He had put weight back on and was moving around with ease.

"He is doing so much better. How has your Christmas been?" he asked, trying to make our conversation appear casual. His eyes bored into mine. All I wanted to do was pull him into the church hallway and make out with him.

"It's been good. Yours?"

"Yesterday was pretty good." He lingered and smiled at me, the smile I loved.

I smiled back slowly, letting the vision of his face buried between my legs and the secret between us vibrate on its own frequency.

"Today we have dinner with my parent's friends in town," he added.

Silence took over while we stood in a suspended state, just sort of staring at each other while simultaneously listening to our parents talk. We weren't very good at this pretending.

My dad spoke as the opening music began to play. "Well, we better take our seats."

"See you next week." I said to Nick. "Merry Christmas Mr. & Mrs. Stratton," I added, turning to them.

"Merry Christmas dear," Amber-Lee slurred, patting my arm a little too sloppily. In her already fuzzy head, she remembered me at least.

We left them then, my dad taking his usual spot on the left side of the room and the Stratton's taking their usual spot closer to the back.

The service was what you would expect on Christmas Day. A beautiful sermon and music, finished off with prayers for the year ahead. We prepared to leave immediately afterward. My dad's knee was bothering him after a busy couple of days.

When we got into my dad's Chrysler Pacifica, I glanced at Charlotte, who was staring at me. She joined me in the front row so Dad could stretch his knee out a little in the middle. We waited patiently for him to get into the car. He had been stopped by one of his cowboy's fathers and they were talking about the cold weather coming in from what I could hear through the window. I tapped my fingers on the steering wheel to the radio. I could feel Charlotte's eyes on me still. I turned to her.

"What?" I asked her.

Charlotte wore a smug look on her face. "You think you're *so* smart." She giggled.

"Excuse me?"

"I should've known. How could I not?" Charlotte continued half talking to herself. She whispered the next words slowly. "It's *h i m*."

"Who?"

"Nick Stratton. Holy shit, Katelyn Danielle Hennessey, you bad girl, you. You said nothing was happening with him!"

I turned my face so Charlotte wouldn't see me blush. My cheeks always gave it away.

"I don't know what you're talking about." I said quickly.

"Lies! Anyone with half a brain could feel the connection you two have. I swear, the older people maybe didn't notice it but, W O W." She annunciated every letter. "I thought he was gonna jump you on the spot. The way he looked at you? How long has this been going on? Dad's going to be pissed." She started laughing. She loved a good scandal. "I gotta say, I'm impressed. God, he's so fricken gorgeous. How have you *NOT* done it yet?" she continued on.

I wondered the same thing myself sometimes.

There was no point in lying, I realized. I knew my secret was safe with her. Besides, I hadn't told her, she had simply figured it out. It might be nice to have someone to confide in, even it was Charlotte.

"I can't believe you figured it out and oh my God, Char, I want to. He's amazing." I said quietly.

She let out a mini scream. "I knew it!"

My dad turned to us from in front of the van.

"Shhhhh you have to promise me on your life you won't say anything. For the exact reason that you said. It's new, we are figuring it out, and Dad might be mad. Nick is worried he may get fired."

"Well, ya. 'Cause of the rule."

I pursed my lips. How did everyone automatically think of "the rule" but me? Had I really been that disconnected from the ranch for that long?

"Yes, the rule. But there has to be room for negotiation, everything can't be so cut and dry. if this turns out to be serious, that's what we're hoping at least. That Dad can find a way to accept it somehow and we can make it work.

"Don't you remember last summer? Britney Cates was here from Rockham working for a month and her and Steve Whitmore did it in the bunkhouse? Frank caught them. Dad let them both go. You two better know what you're doing. Be careful."

"Well that's the difference. We won't be doing it in the bunkhouse or anywhere for right now. But certainly not the bunkhouse."

"I don't know why you wouldn't. You have way more willpower than I do."

She sped up her words, my dad was heading toward the back seat, his conversation over. "And P.S. you *have* to tell me *everything*!"

We both stopped talking immediately as the back door slid open. "You girls ready?" Dad asked.

We looked at each other and smiled in response.

"Yep," I said.

We pulled out of the parking lot and headed for home. Out of the corner of my eye I could see Nick standing at his parent's truck, talking to another family. I pretended not to notice as Charlotte snickered from the passenger seat.

Chapter 49 – First Things First
Katie

My aunt and uncle brought the girls for our family dinner and they seemed to have fun, even taking a time out from their social media to enjoy themselves. At the end of the night we all sat outside around a warm fire roasting marshmallows and drinking homemade hot cocoa. My dad excused himself early to meet with Frank, they had to talk.

Christmas or not, we knew that a storm was coming within the next twenty-four hours and it would stay for two or three days at least. We had to be ready. They were predicting snow but there was a possibility it could end up being ice. Below freezing temperatures were coming with it and high winds. I could hear the tension in my dad's voice as I listened to him talk to Frank from the hallway. With the winds, it could be closer to minus fifteen. I heard Frank say he would send Nick and Sam to keep an eye if needed.

Most of the other cowboys were still with their families. Caleb, Matthew, Sam, and Nick would be back later that night or the next day, with the others returning slowly over the following few days. They would have to ready the horse's coats and extra hay.

The cattle were the main concern though. Most of them hadn't seen this kind of weather much before. They were made for it in the north where their coats grew thicker, but not in Texas. The next day would be spent checking on their pre-built storm structures in the fields that we used for warming. They were at least twenty years old and rarely ever used. They were huge, and crucial for stopping the wind. The guys would add heavy duty tarps to form a layer on the huts if needed, and they would add lots of hay inside on the floor. They would feed the cattle up really good to help keep their energy up to handle the cold. It was all they could do.

My dad had been through storms before where power was lost and he knew the key was that we had to be ready for anything. Generators had to be ready to go and filled with gasoline. Extra fuel had to be brought in so there was no worry of losing power. Even if mother nature intended it, we had to do our best to keep things running. It was close to nine o'clock when Nick messaged me.

Kryptonite: *I'm back. Dinner was a fucking disaster. My mom was a mess.*
Kryptonite: *I need to see you, it just might save my day. Besides, I couldn't stay there and listen to her. I just wish I could've brought my dad with me.*

I understood.

Kryptonite: *Can you sneak away? Meet me at near the barn for even an hour? It's all I have. Frank and I are starting prep at three. He's going home to be with his family after he sees your dad so there should be no one else in the barn and I have a little work to do there anyway.*

Our plan to spend the evening at the nest the next night would have to wait. The ranch came first, of course.

Me: *Yep, he's wrapping up with my dad now. I'll wait twenty, then come.*

I went up to change into jeans and a warm, thick sweater. As disappointed as I was to not spend another night with him, the rancher that was blooming in me knew what was most important. Keep the cattle safe and protect the ranch.

I pulled my hair down from the high, messy bun I had it in all day, then went to find Charlotte for an alibi. I found her in the kitchen sneaking sips of champagne with Remi and Tessa when my aunt wasn't looking.

So much for that. I didn't trust her to cover for me if she was drinking. I just would have to go for it and answer questions later if my dad was looking for me. It wouldn't be unreasonable for me to say I felt like a ride before the storm. Frank was gone, so I snuck out into the side yard and grabbed a golf cart.

The ride took all of five minutes and I had a text waiting from Nick when I got there.

Kryptonite: *On the mezz, come up the back stairs.*

The mezzanine in the barn was a large loft we used for storage. It had a back set of stairs from behind the barn that didn't have camera coverage. I looked around to make sure I was good to go. Not a soul anywhere.

He was inside pulling out large red jerry cans to move down to the first level. They would need to be filled with gasoline and be ready to fuel the generators.

"Already working, I see," I said, leaning against a wall, watching him. My twang was thick when I said it like I'd never left Texas.

He breathed a heavy sigh of relief, raking his eyes over my figure like he always did. At first it made me self-conscious, now, I loved it. He looked at me like he couldn't wait to touch me.

"Always working," he answered, coming toward me. "But first things first." He scooped me into his arms and kissed me like I wished he could have earlier in the day at church.

"Did you wear that dress today to torture me?" He kissed my neck as he said it gruffly.

Goosebumps instantly covered my body.

"I have no idea what you mean." I answered with the sweetest sounding voice. I had worn a simple hunter green A-line dress with long sleeves. I had piled my hair into a loose bun with little wisps at my face. At my neck was his gift to me. I didn't get dressed up very often and had had fun with it. I even put on mascara and red lip gloss.

I was having a hard time collecting my thoughts with him kissing me.

"Well, you did. I've never seen you look so beautiful. That dress with your hair up like that. Your neck, I've been thinking about it all day long. It was fucking killing me standing in the church foyer."

"You're doing a pretty good job killing me right now." I finally got some coherent words out. "Did you want to see me about anything specific, cowboy?" I asked, laughing.

"I can't remember."

I felt him smile into my neck. Another chill ran up my spine. He smiled bigger when he realized the effect it had on me. He moved back to my lips and kissed me there. He stepped back a little to regain his composure and ran his hand through his hair. I moved closer. I wasn't quite done kissing him yet.

"This is our only time together, we might as well enjoy it. Tomorrow sounds like it's going to be a lot," I said it as best I could, trying not to sound too disappointed.

He answered me seriously. "It is. I haven't seen this kind of weather since I was young. There's a lot to do, I'm sure your dad will need your help, even just to distract him. He isn't good at sitting around. It's just so crazy that it's right over Christmas. It doesn't help being short most of the cowboys for a few days. Too bad your sister has no idea how to work." He laughed when he said it, knowing she would be useless as help on the ranch. She might chip her nail polish.

A thought occurred to me.

"Charlotte knows about us," I blurted. I wanted him to know.

"How? Kate, we weren't going to say any—"

I interrupted him. "I didn't tell her, she just knew. She said...she said it was how you looked at me today at the church."

He softened. "Well… that's your fault for being so enticing." He kissed me on the head and smiled at me, and then he went back to sorting the cans for the next day.

I was just relieved he wasn't upset.

"We can trust her, Nick, I know we can." I started helping him.

"Are you sure?" he asked.

"Trust me, she owes me tenfold for all the times I covered for her ass over her life. She won't say a word."

He nodded. He had no choice. He had to believe me at this point.

"Plus, I actually think Charlotte's happy for me. She seemed to be anyway. She's been telling me to get a boyfriend for years."

"So you just rolled up to the ranch and took the first cowboy that came along?" He threw the last three jerry cans the six feet off the mezz—they landed down below, each one with a small thud in the hay on the barn floor.

"Something like that," I said to him, tilting my head to the side.

He looked around satisfied that he was done, at least with work. With me, he looked like he was just getting started.

He moved closer. The way he was looking at me made me feel like prey he was hunting. There wasn't any feeling in the world I loved more. It told me all good things were coming to me.

I felt my body welcome him, like gravity I couldn't fight. Even if I could, I wouldn't want to.

I smiled up at him slightly and put my arms up around his neck, reaching up on my tippy toes to kiss him. He moved his hands from my face as he kissed me, then down, losing them in my hair, down again to my waist and under the back of my heavy sweater. His hands were so warm, and he kissed me like he couldn't ever get close enough to me. He ran his fingers from the middle of my back to the sides of my waist. The slightest touch that almost brought me to my knees. I tilted my head back and sighed quietly, letting the molten fire I felt for him swallow me. He pulled me closer, pressing me against him.

Suddenly it was like sunlight exploded in the room. Sixteen incandescent overhead lights caused us both to squint blindly and pulled us out of our delightful entanglement.

"What in the…?" a loud booming voice that I recognized immediately echoed from the front of the barn.

Chapter 50 - Worst Timing Ever.
Katie

We straightened up instantly. I looked to Nick, then back to my dad. I regretted that he came in and interrupted us, and of course I felt a little embarrassed. However, that's where the regret ended.

A small part of me maybe even felt relief. My life had been shrouded in secrecy for the last couple of months. We stood frozen as my dad began to speak.

"Of all the people that I expected to find in here you two were the last."

Charlotte's words of Britney and Steve doing it in the bunkhouse rang in my mind. I didn't realize what this looked like to my dad until that second.

Worst timing ever.

"Dad, what are you even doing out—" I began, but he interrupted me with an authoritative tone.

"I wanted to stretch my legs. There's a lot to think about tonight. Too much to deal with this." He gestured to us. It was quite a sight I'm sure, seeing us entangled with each other, my hair a mess.

"I heard banging in here, I thought a raccoon may have gotten in, I did not expect this!" His voice filled the barn, getting louder as the reality of our secrecy and betrayal of his trust hit him fully. The memory of Nick throwing the cans down flashed through my mind. He had thought it was an animal, probably unable to see the mezz light on from the front of the barn.

He rubbed his forehead back and forth for a moment to collect his thoughts.

"You two are an issue I'm just frankly not prepared to handle today." He looked to the floor to see that the jerry cans had been pulled out and were ready to be filled. He turned to Nick then.

"I trust you're finished with your work here?" he asked calmly.

Nick answered, never wavering. "Yes, I am."

My dad sighed, looking down. "Son, you're a hell of a cowboy, but you leave me in a very difficult place right now. I hope you understand that. I want you to go home now and get yourself some sleep and get cleaned up. With only four of you here for the next few days I need you out there, clear-headed, in the field." There was no room for argument.

Nick nodded, knowing what he meant. In other words, if there wasn't a massive storm coming he may be gone right now, but until it was over, my dad still needed him. "Understood, sir," Nick said.

"We will talk after the storm then." My dad looked to me. "When I say we, I mean all of us. I will say Katelyn, I'm very disappointed in the position you are putting me in too. I trust you two the most. I'd expect this from Charlotte maybe, but not you."

"Daniel—" Nick began to defend the situation, but my dad wasn't having it tonight.

"We won't talk about it now. I trust you both will go home and keep the rest of this night professional."

With one more look to me, he turned and left the barn, leaving us only to obey his orders. We shared a look then hurried to leave the barn, knowing my dad would be waiting the see how fast we followed. Nick quickly kissed me before we parted ways. He had pushed my dad far enough today and he knew it.

"It's going to be okay, I promise. Don't worry, okay?" he whispered to me. "We'll talk later." He squeezed my hand one more time and kissed my forehead before letting me go in the opposite direction, only ten feet behind my dad. He probably had no idea *how* it was going to be okay, but if anyone could keep that promise, it was him.

Chapter 51 - Ready, Set, Storm.
Katie

By the time the sun set the day after Christmas, we were as ready as we'd ever be on this ranch for what weather forecasters were calling "the storm of the decade."

Over the course of a day the temperature dropped over twenty degrees and it was expected to continue to drop into the night to just above freezing. The snow and ice were due to start falling within the next twelve hours and high winds were already beginning to blow.

Forecasters kept repeating to residents to be prepared and to have a backup power source. Hydro lines would be pressed and roads would be a mess. I heard my dad say it only took a half inch of ice to add five hundred pounds of pressure to lines and trees. Police were telling everyone to stay off the roads once it started.

The ranch bustled with activity. Charlotte and I had spent the day with Melia preparing easy to eat meals that didn't have to be heated up. We watched our rom-coms while we worked, appreciating the technology while we had it. We had one large generator for the house that would run a few heaters, the refrigerators and freezers, and the internet if the lines weren't down, but that was it. Basic necessities. All the rest of the generators were needed for the ranch itself, so any meals that could be pulled from the fridge and not have to be heated were best. We made potato salads and baked beans, we sliced up left-over turkey and ham for sandwiches, made fresh bread and cookies. It was all about ease while we worked. My dad rushed around as best he could to help Frank get prepared but after a few hours he needed to rest his knee. I took over for him, driving to the gas station to fill up the jerry cans with gas. Frank sent Sam with me so he could help me lift them. Nick and Sam had been out in the pastures earlier tarping the simple structures for the cows. Hay had been brought in, tractors were ready in case, axes readily available for chopping ice. All we could do now was wait.

    We had a quiet dinner together that night. My father hadn't spoken much to me since the night before. He had been back and forth with Frank and seemed to be throwing himself into the preparation work. It was an odd feeling, having a parent be disappointed in me. I had never felt it before, and it was awful. A million thoughts raced through my head. A million emotions came and went but not one of them was regret. I wouldn't have changed a thing, other than how we were caught, of course. The feeling Nick gave me when he looked at me or touched me was worth the disappointment, silent treatment, and anything else my dad could throw at me. Bring it. I would take it with ease. There was one thing I wouldn't give up under any circumstances, and that was Nick.

    The day flew by with work but also felt painfully long at the same time. The awkward silence in the house, the waiting helplessly for the storm. It was like dread had encased the house in a dome, affecting all of us. I took a long, hot shower while I still could and stood in the steaming water thinking about Nick and what had happened the night before.

    He had been working since three a.m. and hadn't really slept. He had told me earlier in the day over text that he was already exhausted and would probably not get a break until the storm was over. It had only been a day but I was already missing him. With nothing left to do to prepare, I said goodnight to Nick, knowing he probably wouldn't be able to answer me, and went to sleep, awaiting the unpredictability of mother nature the next day.

The next morning dawned as angry as I had ever seen it. Snow and ice pellets sounded like glass droplets hammering onto the metal roof and windows. I wandered down to the kitchen in my pajamas, exhausted and in search of coffee. I hadn't slept all night, heading the wind shake through the house, knowing Nick was out minding the cattle in the rough weather. He had texted with me at two, after he had checked the pressure pumps at the wells to make sure they were thawed out for the barn animals.

    It was minus ten degrees with the chill of the wind and the animals were anxious. Everyone could tell this storm was going to be vicious. My dad was on the phone with Frank, who had moved some of the older, weaker cattle into the barns. They weren't happy there, but they were warm and safe. We still had almost a thousand cattle out in the pastures and Nick, Sam, Frank were already tired. All they had to do was get through the next day until more cowboys were due to be back on property.

"Well, let him sleep for a couple of hours at least," my dad said to Frank. I knew instantly he must be talking about Nick. I knew he would've been up most of the night before.

"Yep, it's going to be a long night," was the last thing he said to Frank before he hung up the phone and rubbed his forehead again.

I disappeared into the kitchen for hot coffee and Tylenol. The lack of sleep was weighing on me and all I wanted to do was curl up in Nick's arms and forget the rest of the world existed, even for just a minute.

Kryptonite: *I'm gonna need a fucking vacation after this. Somewhere far away, and hot, with a beach and you.*

It was just before noon. The weather was so bad I couldn't even see the live oaks out the back doors. Ice was just starting to build up in the branches of the trees.

Me: *Good morning sunshine. Did you sleep at all?*
Kryptonite: *A little. Just wanted to tell you I was thinking about you. I will message later. Just know that whenever I have a minute, it belongs to you.*

No sooner did his message come through than the entire house went dead quiet.

I looked around. The power was clearly out.

"Shit." I muttered under my breath. I had been hoping we would avoid that part.

Me: *We have no power.*

A few minutes passed before he answered me.

Kryptonite: *Yep, we're out too. Your dad is here, he hasn't killed me yet by the way so I'm taking that as a win. He wants Frank and I to come and hook up the generator at your house while he teaches Sam how to start the pumps at the well.*
Kryptonite: *We'll come over and get them going.*
Kryptonite: *Be there in ten.*

Regardless of the situation, I was happy to see him for even a few minutes. I brushed my hair and washed my face. As far as I knew, my dad hadn't spoken a word about us to anyone. Nick said Frank was still as normal as could be with him. He had no idea that in a few short days Nick could possibly be let go.

I ventured to the parlor to start a fire in the hearth. I wasn't surprised my dad had gone to the bunkhouse. He'd want to talk to the guys before they headed out into the pastures. They had to mind the trails for the horses. The snow wasn't deep. It was the icy, crunchy snow you ended up with when the ground wasn't frozen under it. The horses knew the property well but they had to be careful. A simple broken leg meant the horse would have to be put down, and no one wanted that.

I knew the closer east pastures was where some of the cattle would be checked first, the guys had their arctic tents and Frank was thinking they'd maybe camp out to be able to keep a close eye for the night if they had to. Frank thanked his lucky stars Nick and I had moved the rest of the cattle from the west when we did. It was so much windier on that side. At least in the east the valleys protected them naturally.

Nick said my dad hadn't tried to kill him. I hoped he hadn't been rude to him either. The more I thought about it the angrier it made me. Nick loved this ranch as much, if not more, than even I did. All he wanted was to do his job, which he was spectacular at, all the time. He couldn't help it any more than I could that we felt this way. All I could hope was that when this was over in a few days, my dad would see that keeping him here would be more important than some ancient rule from the sixties.

Nick and Frank arrived as promised, within ten minutes. I just wanted to hug him, he looked exhausted and disheveled. He smiled when he saw me.

"Two fucking tired genny techs at your service."

Frank smacked him for cursing in front of me, which made me smile. I'd heard a lot worse come out of his mouth.

"Perfect, come on in. I'll show you where to run the cords. My dad took them out already."

He had the cords run within a few minutes. Frank ran them back to the large generator outside one of the garage doors. We decided to place two space heaters on the main floor. One in the kitchen and one in the family room. The parlor was already being heated by wood.

"Daniel wants us to run a cord up to Katie's room, or even the hallway with a space heater." Frank told him.

At least he didn't want me to freeze to death. That was a good sign.

"Sure thing," Nick answered.

Charlotte's room didn't need one. She had my uncle pick her up the night before. It was just as well, I hadn't been able to bring myself to tell her my dad had caught Nick and me on

Christmas night. I didn't want her to feign doom and gloom to me and be all dramatic, and I certainly didn't feel like receiving advice or I told you so's.

She had warned me to be careful, and I wasn't. At least it was easy to avoid conversation with her. She wouldn't even notice I was upset. She was too busy worrying about herself, knowing a storm was coming. When Tessa asked her to come, she jumped at the chance. I had been a little bothered she hadn't offered to stay and help, but I wasn't surprised she chose to go somewhere that had less of a chance of losing power. Typical Charlotte, everything was about her.

Frank spoke, pulling me out of my tired thoughts. "Katie, can you please show him where you want the heaters up there?"

I looked at Nick and seized my opportunity. "Yep, sorry guys, I'm tired," I muttered.

We ran up those stairs as quickly as our legs would carry us. I shut the door behind him quietly and he enveloped me instantly. I knew we had maybe five minutes if we were lucky.

"*Ughhh.*" The slightest sound escaped him. Exhaustion, stress, worry, it all radiated off of him. He bent down to kiss me with both hands on either side of my face.

"You alright?" I asked him.

"I am now."

Still gorgeous as always, but he looked very tired. Five hours of sleep in two days does that to a person.

"Please be careful out there tonight," I said.

"Yes, Princess. I need to live for your dad to fire me, you know."

I swatted him. "I'm serious, have faith."

He ignored my authority and kissed me behind my ear. "*Mmmm*, you smell so fucking good," he said, burying his face in my hair. "Just let me enjoy this. For just five minutes, all I want to think about is you. Not the ranch, or the storm, or your dad relying on me. Let me have it, baby."

I said nothing, giving into his request.

"I'd rather just stay here with you anyway. Can we just live in your room?" He kissed me from the base of my ear all the way to my collarbone in small, soft kisses that felt like hot feathers down my neck.

I remembered those kisses between my legs and I shivered. "You are delirious from no sleep." I smiled at him.

He chuckled. "Maybe, you know how you can help me feel better?"

He didn't wait for me to answer, he kissed me long and slow on the mouth, picking up right where we left off the night before. I felt relieved, among other things. Nothing had changed. He wasn't regretting anything. He was just as crazy about me now as he was the day before.

He seemed so tired and it was like he needed me so badly. He let go. Taking every second to feel my lips on his. I kissed him back more intensely; he was driving me crazy. My hands moved down his back slowly and underneath his t-shirt. His back was so warm and strong. I knew our time was limited.

He smiled at me between kisses. "You know, if Frank or your dad caught us like this, it would probably result in my murder, but if this is the way I have to die, it's a pretty close to perfect way to go."

I ran my hands up and down his back. Slowly dying from how good his body felt under them. I pulled them forward around the sides of his waist, running my fingers over every muscle he had. God, he was so hot.

"You have no idea what you're doing to me." His voice was raspy and barely more than a whisper. It sounded starved. Desperate. I knew exactly what I was doing. I was reminding him why he had to fight to be with me and stay here.

"Well, you better come home safe then," I whispered back, kissing him. He stopped, pulling my hands out from under his shirt and made a groaning sound when he did.

"I want you to know, just so you can plan ahead…" He kissed me on my cheek, his voice still strained in my ear. "The first time we are together and alone, and you let me fuck this sweet pussy, *my* pussy—" His hand drifted down between my legs, my knees went weak. "You better make sure you have nothing to do and nowhere to go for quite a while. Like maybe two days." He kissed my other cheek.

"Noted." I breathed out erratically.

There had never been a time in my life where I wanted someone, or anything, so badly. It was all consuming. He ran his hands through his hair to sober himself up. He had to go downstairs and face Frank.

He brushed my hair from my face, his tone getting serious.

"I might not see you or even be able to talk much for a couple of days now. We're going to be so busy with the herd in the southeast. If it starts to freeze we may have to ride out to the far east too."

I nodded, taking him seriously, I understood their worry over the newly placed herd. I prayed the ice would stay light and they wouldn't have to go.

The far east was such a remote area. Most herds could be reached by truck if necessary, but this one was only accessible by horse. I knew the cell service anywhere in the pastures wouldn't be the best. I also knew if he could talk to me and update me, he would.

"I promise I will make it up to you when this is over. A whole night for us, okay?"

The thoughts that entered my mind as I thought about what he proposed startled even me.

I put my forehead to his chest, wanting so badly to tell him that I loved him.

He kissed me one more time to show me he meant what he said. I could sense the urgency in it. I knew whether or not he admitted it, this storm and his impending fate on the ranch was rattling him.

Our time was up and so, to not raise any suspicion with Frank, we separated. The last thing he needed was to listen to Frank bitch at him for the next two days. We hooked up the cords and heater and hurried downstairs.

My dad had come back in the meantime and was surprised to see us coming down the stairs together. He looked at me like he was compartmentalizing it for a later time. He spoke with Frank for a few minutes about what was next for the day and the possibility of having to travel over by horse to the far east.

He turned to Nick, and I saw him brace himself, but what my dad said next surprised him. "Good job checking on the shelters. Frank said they're all set?"

"Yes, sir, and we'll check on the far east if we end up having to go out there."

"Let's hope it doesn't come to that," he said to Nick. He wished them a safe night before heading back into the parlor.

Nick turned to me. He looked like he was as dying to kiss me, as I was him, but not daring enough to try with Frank there and my dad in the next room.

"I guess I'll see ya soon, Kate," was all he could say, but his eyes said so much more. He smiled at me, my favorite smile, before heading out the door. I stood in the window watching him ride away until he and Frank disappeared into the snow and ice.

Chapter 52 - My wait continued
Katie

The storm howled all afternoon against the house, causing creaks and cracking noises in places I didn't even know existed. A fire was going in the parlor fireplace and heaters were pumping out adequate warmth everywhere else. The internet was still working for the time being which allowed me to watch movies while we waited for updates from Frank about the cattle.

Nick and Sam had ridden out to guide them to shelters in the southeast pastures. The ice and wind were quickly becoming a problem. What was supposed to be snow was coming down as ice and fast. Six main hydro lines were now on the ground that fed most of the valley. If it kept coming down like this, with these temperatures, everyone's fears would be directed toward the far east pastures.

Our barn tryst from two nights before was all but forgotten as the storm consumed my dad's thoughts. He was going stir crazy, pacing around in a limp while waiting for news. Nick took the time to text me around seven o'clock to tell me all was well and that he would be heading down to the creek in the pasture closest to the barn to scrape ice if this cold kept up. So far, the need to go to the far east didn't exist, though the water was quickly freezing.

Be safe, please, was my only response. I didn't want to take time away from his work. I wanted it to be done and have him back here. I just wanted it to be over.

My dad and I ate sandwiches in silence and I heated up soup for us on a hotplate like we were camping. He could be mad at me if he wanted, but he still had to eat. I was not going to let him make me feel like a badly behaved child. I had done nothing wrong but fall in love. It happened to be with one of his cowboys, yes, but I was determined to say my piece to him when I had the chance. For now, I was doing anything and everything I could to not focus on worrying.

The horse's footings in the ice were my first worry. Keeping the cowboys on them was my second.

Everything was covered in an icy layer of white and the creek at the bottom of the valley was freezing over. It would take expert skill to chip it out right and out of the small number of cowboys that were here, only Nick and Frank had done it before. The worst part was not knowing what was happening out there. I wanted to go check on the animals in the barn but my dad was adamant I should wait until the ice stopped.

So, I sat and waited. Reading, scrolling through my social media that I never kept up with anymore. I stopped at my last posted photo. Me, out for dinner with two sort-of-friends from F.I.T in September before seeing Moulin Rouge. How different my life was back then. I looked at the seemingly happy girl staring back at me. She had no idea what she had been missing in Reeds Canyon, Texas.

I let my mind wander to Nick. Wondering what he what doing at precisely that moment and aching to be covered by his strong arms. I had heard nothing from him since seven o'clock, and I thought I would've heard *something* before I fell asleep.

My wait continued.

Chapter 53 - Cold, Ice, Coffee
Nick

Frigid wind blew against my face. The tiny ice pellets stung like needles. I pulled my thick flannel coat up around my neck.
So far, so good. The cattle seemed okay. I heard an older heifer groan when a wind gust hit her.
"I know how you feel." I said to her under my breath. It was as cold as balls. Colder than I remembered it being for a long time. The ice was expected to last into the night.
"Nick?" Frank called through the wind. I turned to see him riding up from about fifty feet away.
"How's your side?"
"Okay, they're fucking freezing, but they're okay," I yelled back. "Yours?"
"I have to get more hay for them from the main, going to try to add some bed to the shelters over there. Can you send Sam to help?"
I nodded and called over to Sam, who came immediately to help Frank.
Suddenly I was alone again with the cattle. It was seven o'clock. I took a second to text Kate with frozen fingers.

Me: *Just checking in, it's a mess out here but we're all okay. Heading to the creek to scrape if this keeps up. Can't wait for a hot shower and my bed when this is over. I'll message as soon as I can.*

A minute passed. She replied.

Goddess: *Be safe, please.*

I put my phone into my pocket and rode down to the river to check the ice layer. It was sealing over the water quickly. My mind went to the far east, knowing it, too, would be freezing over. It was constantly in the back of my mind. Cows were down trying to drink out of the iced over mud. I knew there would be a time very soon where myself or Frank would have to start chopping ice here.

One lonely well was up at the main barn that could pump water out for the horses and cows there, provided it didn't freeze. Caleb and Matthew remained there tending to the barn animals and checking the many generator fuel levels as needed. We had gathered enough fuel to get us through another three days.

Frank and Sam were gone a long time. I decided I would stop and eat, climbing into the arctic tent I had set up.

The wind was gone the moment I stepped inside. It made all the difference in the world. I pulled out a sort-of-warm thermos of hearty stew and ate some with cold bread. Exhaustion almost knocked me on my ass. It was ten-thirty, and I hadn't slept in so long.

I heard something rustle outside. My tent unzipped from the outside and Frank was there, back from adding the hay to as many shelters as he could. Sam was just beyond on his horse.

"Fuck, it's cold. How are you, kid? Just getting some food in?" He looked beat too, I realized. It had been a long couple of days for all of us.

"Yeah, what's up next?"

Frank smiled at me and patted me on the shoulder. "You're the best cowboy I have 'round here."

He had said this to me before, but it was bittersweet to hear it now, knowing I might not still be around after the storm let up.

"What's up for you is some sleep, at least for a few hours, then I'll switch you out. You look wrecked."

I answered him honestly. "Yeah, I could use a little."

"No sense in trying to be a hero. I'll move King under the shelter with the other horses. Sleep, kid, tomorrow will be shitty."

I laughed. It hurt my lips. Everything was cold and dry. "Thanks, can't wait."

Frank left me then. The cattle were settled and fed, the barn had power for the night. I leaned back, thinking about Kate. I was so fucking in love with her and I hadn't even told her yet. I almost did, I almost told her everything right before Charlotte called on Christmas Eve. *What was I waiting for?* Now that Daniel knew, I had no reason to fight this anymore. There was no going back now. As far as she was concerned, I was a fucking goner.

That woman would be my wife one day. I had never been so sure of anything, especially right then as I listened to the wind and ice blowing outside, thinking of the warmth of her small arms wrapped around me. It soothed me. *Just a few hours sleep,* was my last thought before I passed out cold.

The next "morning" started at two a.m. Frank woke me to take over the watching of the herd. In three hours, we would start chopping ice. Frank just needed a power nap, he said. I really admired him. He was getting older but he was a fucking beast of a man still and as strong as any twenty-five-year-old.

I let him sleep. He was going to need it. It was inevitable at this point we would be moving to the far east pastures by dawn. Worse news came when I talked with Caleb by text. No cowboys were getting in or out. He had heard the valley was closed to vehicle traffic. No one else would be coming to the ranch to help. The county was at a standstill.

I woke Frank at five.

"It's me, you, and Sam," I said, giving him the bad news.

"Shit," Frank muttered. "I was afraid of that."

He took a sip of half-cold coffee from a thermos. It was better than nothing. He looked like he felt his full forty-two years and then some that morning.

"You up to chopping?" he asked. He knew I was. When it came to this stuff, I went into autopilot and was like a machine.

"Yep. I'm going to drink some of this nice, half-cold coffee you have here, then I'll be at your service on the ice." I raised my thermos in the air. "Let's get this shit over with." I said under my breath, Frank chuckled in response.

I was ready to do whatever was needed for everything and everyone to be safe on this land. After, I was going to kiss my girl, sleep for a week, then probably reassess my life.

I bundled back up and unzipped the tent, stepping into the cold. It felt like a punch in the face. The familiar ice needles hammered my skin. They had been coming down for hours. I could hear and see broken tree branches falling and the ones that had already dropped were scattered in the dark. The weight was too much for them.

I called for Sam to come with me and mounted King. We rode the short two miles to the first creek. It was brutal. I knew the land better than anyone, as did King. I wasn't worried about his footings, more so about the ice. King was tired. These animals weren't used to this weather either. I patted him on the neck, talking to him on the way down to the valley floor. I would've preferred to do this chopping in the daylight, but it needed to be done.

Sam and I went to town on the base of the creek, I showed him how to form holes in the ice until a good base of water flowed out in multiple places for the cows to drink from. I could see the cattle coming down the hill in the dark. Frank had added extra feed for them again that morning to keep their strength up. It was all we could do to help them. We left the creek, our arms tired and heavy. The longest part of our day was ahead of us.

I breathed a heavy sigh and headed back up the hill, picturing only her beautiful face under me as I began to prepare for a long, cold ride east.

Chapter 54 - Winter Not So Wonderland
Nick

We packed up the tents and tools. Frank had been to the barn and bunkhouse to gather up food and fresh water for us. It wasn't even six a.m. yet. He wasn't about to bother Daniel.

He filled Caleb in on where we were heading and the job we had to do. Frank knew his cell service may be dicey on the trip. The internet had finally gone out all over the county, almost all the way to Austin. There wasn't a power line in the vicinity that wasn't affected by this storm.

The ice was thick and heavy, Frank had measured over half of an inch on either side of a branch near the barn. Meaning well over an inch of ice had fallen in less than twenty-four hours. It was unheard of.

Literally crippling.

Tree branches were down all over the ranch and falling by the minute, the ominous crackling sounds they made as they gave way to the weight filled the air.

The trip to the far east was long and grueling. We moved at a snail's pace in silence, stopping often to water the horses and allow them to feed. They were just as tired as we were riding them. In Sam's words, "This weather was some bullshit."

All the while, ice and wind whipped against us. I was certain I was starting to fight some sort of frostbite on my fingers. I just kept pulling up my neck warmer and coat collar to keep only my eyes exposed. The amount of tree branches down as we entered the clearing to the far east pasture was staggering. The structures we had put tarps over just two days before were doing their job. Cattle were scattered around and gathered under them. Many were down around the creek bed, drinking from any tiny stream of water that eked out—two or three cattle at a time competing for a drink. We had gotten there just in time. They still had feed, but it was freezing quickly and what wasn't frozen was wet in most places.

It was daylight, just before eleven a.m. The trip had taken us longer than expected, almost five hours in total. The ice was finally starting to let up but it was still so cold. I had never been happier to see a storm come to an end. My face got a break from the tiny ice needles hitting it. I allowed a thought to enter my mind and almost felt giddy thinking it. By that night I would possibly be able to sleep in my bed, eat hot food, maybe see Kate, or at least talk to her. I hadn't since the day before and I knew she'd be worried, but Caleb knew where we were. We had no cell service out here.

We had enough food for the rest of the day and even the next day if need be, part of being a cowboy meant always being prepared. We spent a lot of time breaking ice up and pushing it off the tarps over the shelters. All the while hundreds of loud, moaning, cracking tree branches rained down around us and into the valley. The live oaks especially couldn't bear the weight of the ice. They all still carried their leaves through the winter into spring, the added weight was crushing. I knew in the back of my mind the amount of work it was going to take to clean this all up after. Maybe they would keep me on to help with that and I could buy myself another week or two. I shook it off. I couldn't let my mind go there yet.

We broke to eat at just after three o'clock. Starved and exhausted. We still had to tend to the other creek bed at the opposite end of the valley. We'd have to work fast to free some water from it for the cattle before dark. Ice poured down again, like mother nature couldn't make up her mind.

We huddled at the backside of the shelter, letting it shield us from the wind, sitting on hay beds and eating sandwiches Frank had carried in for us. No risk of them going spoiled out here with the cold. I pulled my gloves off and pulled my last dry pair from my pockets and put my last palm warmers inside them.

The warmth was soothing to my hands, which felt like they'd never be able to get warm again.

"Seems like a limb down every ten seconds," Sam noted as the creaks intensified. He had never witnessed anything like this and looked so exhausted and nearly ready to cry. He wouldn't admit it to his boss or to me, but he was scared, I could sense it.

I reassured him while we ate, referencing the forecast. By this time the next day it could be close to sixty degrees and the ice could be long on its way to melting. It seemed impossible to imagine now as we looked around to an apocalyptic winter-not-so-wonderland.

"You boys have done a hell of a job." Frank looked at us. Tired. He was fucking done for.

"I couldn't have done this without both of you. All we have to do now is break up the creek bed. We'll head home, and as long as it stops icing, we'll be back in the bunkhouse by maybe midnight. We'll maybe even start cleanup in a couple days."

Sam let out an audible sigh of relief. I am sure I even looked relieved. I hadn't really slept since Christmas Eve, and it was now the twenty-eighth of December. Four days almost, and I had probably only slept a total of fifteen hours. *One more small stretch of time,* I told myself as I climbed out from behind the shelter.

We got to work chopping ice. The cattle gathered to drink from the holes almost as soon as we made them, as they had in the southeast. It took us three more hours to get everything done, but by six o'clock we were fairly close to being ready to pack up for the long ride back to the barn, We would have to quickly check on the southeast pasture along the way.

We were just getting ready to leave when Sam headed over about a hundred feet or so from where we were working. There was a group of cattle huddled near a massive live oak with heavy, large limbs that fanned out tall and wide to create an umbrella. The heavy limbs had been rattling for the last hour. Something in him must have told him to head over and try to guide them out.

He rode quickly to the trees just as a huge gust of wind blew through the valley. His horse knew it was coming before he did and bucked him high and hard as the sound of the wind ripped through the valley. It was so loud that I didn't even notice he had left our tool zone until the ominous crackling sound of a huge limb breaking in the air was followed by the hideous scream that came from Sam.

Chapter 55 - Discovery
Katie

I paced the same figure eight I had followed for the last three hours. Up through the parlor and into the den and back out to the front window.

It was five o'clock and I hadn't heard from Nick in twenty-three hours. We had no internet and no cell service, and to make matters worse, my dad hadn't even heard from Frank since the day before. Caleb had ridden up to re-fuel our generators just after breakfast and told my dad he was heading back to the bunkhouse to sleep. He passed the message that the three men headed to the far east at five a.m. but he hadn't heard anything since.

My dad had to admit it had been the right call to head out there. There was just so much ice and the temperatures had frozen everything. Our entire immediate property was littered with tree limbs and branches. The live oaks in that pasture would be taking a beating.

I paced and did the calculations in my head to keep busy. Even if it took them six hours to get there and six hours back, with a few hours to chop and re-feed in between, they should be back by nine or ten o'clock. I told myself to stay calm, but it looked like the end of the world outside. Beautiful but sinister.

Everything was just silent.

I had tried to text Nick but everything just kept bouncing back, telling me to try again.

Caleb returned to refuel the generators at dinner time to get us through the night. My dad had managed to plug in a radio to the generator to listen to the local station. The county was contemplating declaring a state of emergency. Widespread power outages. Accidents all over the roads. They continued to urge people to stay home.

We shared a small dinner but I could barely eat. I just wasn't hungry. I waited while the time ticked by.

Seven thirty.

Ten thirty.

Midnight.

Two o'clock.

I opened my eyes and looked around the room. I had passed out for a short time on the couch. I checked my phone automatically but knew there would be nothing. It was three-fifteen. I could still hear the silence of no power. I could hear our clock ticking in the parlor and the hint of the generator running from outside the front of the house.

I looked out. It almost seemed to be raining. The weather had changed. I made a split decision. I felt it was no better time than any and my dad was sleeping so he couldn't say no. I bundled up quietly and threw on my heavy rain boots, heading outside. The four golf carts that sat at the side of our property were wearing their covers and a layer of ice sat on top, welding the cover to the metal, so I started walking. Moving as careful as possible so I wouldn't slip. The walk to the barn took me twenty minutes instead of ten. It was dark when I arrived. I couldn't go to the bunkhouse, Caleb or Matthew would surely be in there sleeping, but what I could do was check the stalls. If I could just see King, I'd know Nick was home safe and sound, and then maybe I could actually get some sleep too.

I pulled the door back, using all my might. It was wet and muddy and heavy. I was sopping wet and my boots were caked with mud. I frantically made my way to the stall to see if he was there, settled, comfortable. Praying silently all the way.

Please let him be back. Please... I turned the corner to spot Buttercup, well and warm. From my immediate view, I could already see across the row to his stall. It was empty. I was ready to turn back to go home, helpless, until something caught my eye out the back window. A shiver ran through me from my head to my toes. Outside the barn near the horse pen was

Frank's horse, Cash, Sam's horse, Dusty, and King. Loose and free of their riders.

Chapter 56 - Adrenaline
Nick

I dropped everything to the ground the moment I heard Sam scream. I shouted for Frank as I ran. I couldn't get there fast enough. The ice wouldn't allow me cross the short distance as quickly as I wanted to.

A massive fallen limb pinned him to the ground. Those screams. I'll never forget them. Echoing clear across the valley.

Frank arrived almost at the same time as me. I assessed the situation. Who knows how heavy this thing was. It pinned Sam down by his arm, which was clearly badly broken. It also laid partially across his torso. He was face down in the snow, screaming.

"Get it off…Pleeeeaase."

I worked as quickly as my shaking hands would allow, pulling off my thick coat and ripping myself free of my long sleeve flannel shirt, leaving me in a t-shirt. There was no blood anywhere on Sam, but I had to wrap his arm in something and create a tourniquet before we lifted the tree limb off of him to stop the sudden release of toxins from pushing into his system.

Sam vomited in the snow. He was in shock. Frank and I shared a look, we had no idea how badly his insides were mashed up. We could only treat what we saw.

"Okay, bud." I spoke as calmly as I could. "You're alright, okay? We have to tie this shirt around your arm to pull the limb off of you and it's going to hurt. I'm so sorry." I tore a long strip off of it and gently slid it under his arm as gently as I could, wincing the whole time. As quickly as possible, I got it around his bicep, tying it around as tightly as I could.

The sound Sam made when I did it would haunt me. I looked up at Frank, who was trying to hold his cell phone up towards the sky to get any service from anywhere while gathering items we might need into his bag. If we could get a call out to emergency, we may be able to get a helicopter in to air lift Sam out. If his cell service wasn't working he would still be able to get a call out, but if the towers themselves were all out, he wouldn't.

When I said it was like the apocalypse, that is exactly what it felt like. Quiet darkness everywhere.

"It's done, let's get this thing off him," I called to Frank.

I moved to the top of Sam to lift the broad, heavy end of the branch that lay across his body.

"I just wanted to get her out." Sam was crying. The cattle had moved out of the way when the cracking began. Animals seemed to have faster instincts than humans, and in this case the cows were fine, but Sam was a mess.

"I know buddy, it's okay. She's safe. We're going to get this off you now. Can you feel your legs? Your feet?" I asked him, trying to get a gauge on whether or not his back was injured, not only from the limb but the fall off his horse.

Sam wiggled his toes in his agony, a good sign. My brain processed it while another part thought about how I was going to remove the tree limb.

I had to lift it straight up. It couldn't be rolled. This was a quick job on a normal day, when I wasn't soaked to the bone and the tree limb wasn't a sheet of ice. If we dropped it and it landed on Sam again, it could be catastrophic. I already didn't know what damage it had done and normally I wouldn't ever try to move him. But if we didn't, it was possible he'd die there. We had no choice.

At that moment, it hit me. We had no cell service and it was nineteen miles to the barn. We had to get him to a hospital, and I had no idea how we were going to do it.

First, we had to remove the log.

"Ready?" Frank asked.

"Yep, let's count it down."

Frank began. Both of us gripped the trunk with all the strength we could muster and raised it up a couple inches from Sam's body while he groaned and howled under us.

Adrenaline must have kicked in, taking us all of two seconds after that to cast the log aside. It rolled slightly downhill with a loud thud. Once he was free, Sam rolled himself over, writhing in pain. I pulled open his shirt to check for internal bleeding. Frank also assessed. We looked at each other. Frank said nothing. He wouldn't want to scare Sam.

"We've got to get him out of here."

My mind worked while Sam cried.

"I want to go home...I want my Mom. I can't breathe."

I felt so bad for the kid. My heart went out to him. He turned to the side and threw up again. He was definitely in shock.

Frank rode as quickly as he could to the shelters and used his knife to cut down a huge piece of the tarp from the top. Ice fell in pieces to the ground with ease. It was raining now and the ice was sliding off of everything. There was no other option, we couldn't put him on a horse. One person couldn't carry him. We had to work together and get to a spot where we could call an air ambulance.

"Help me!" Frank called. "We need some fair sized branches!"

I and ran to help him scavenge for large enough branches to create a makeshift stretcher. That was one good thing, there were no shortage of branches or tree limbs in the pasture. They were everywhere.

Frank laid the large tarp flat and I came running with two long limbs that were sturdy and at least seven feet long.

I placed one large branch in the middle, Frank folded the tarp over it to touch the other end.

"He's got a ton of broken ribs. No internal bleeding, I don't think." Frank spoke to me quickly while we worked.

"I thought so too, no redness that I could see."

I placed the second branch in the fold and we overlapped the remaining piece into the middle. We had done enough safety and survival training to know that Sam's weight should hold the tarp in place.

We looked at each other for a split second when it was done. Time to move him.

I moved quickly to let our horses free. They were trained to go back to the barn. Sam's was already free and would follow. Someone would notice they were there. It was an alert to anyone who saw it—Something bad happened, call for help.

We carried our tarp stretcher over to Sam and got ready to roll him over so we could slide the tarp as close as possible under him.

There was no time to waste. As gently as possible, we rolled Sam onto his good arm. He yelled out in pain, ribs on that side of his body appeared to be broken too. There was no way we could move him without causing pain. We just had to get it done.

We quickly got him flat and lifted him up. He was whimpering in the stretcher. Half out of it. Delusional and in shock.

Frank led the way and we began the nineteen mile walk back to the barn, praying we'd hit an area where a phone call could be made and help could come in for Sam. If we could hit an active tower the call would go through.

"Sometimes you can ping off the neighbor's Starlink tower." Frank yelled back to me.

Something had to give.

It was an hour before we stopped. We needed to drink. Sam wasn't a big kid, but it was taking all my strength to carry him. He was groaning still from the pain. The rain had stopped when we began walking again, but we were frozen and sweating all at the same time. We only stopped for six minutes. My arms were on fire but I knew how precious the time was and we had no idea of Sam's internal injuries. Frank pulled out his cell phone searching for bars. None. And his phone was at twelve percent.

"Shit," he muttered under his breath.

"Keep moving," he called to me. I did what he said. We were only about a quarter of the way back. It was ten o'clock.

We continued. Another hour. Another check of the phone. Nothing, and less battery. Sam's groaning was a whimper now. His body was somewhat used to the pain and he was completely out of it. I was pretty sure he might have concussion as well. There were few moments where I was afraid he might die right there on that stretcher. I didn't even feel that my own fingers were frost bitten. My toes were numb. My body was cold. But I didn't feel any of it. *Get Sam to safety* was the only thing I could think of.

Another hour. Midnight. My chest and throat burned from panting through the field. Frank turned back to me with the look he had given me twice before. Time to stop. The ground was slushy now so we were moving faster, our feet pushing through the ice with every step and landing in wet, muddy grasses. We set Sam down for a minute. I bent down to listen to his labored breathing. It was his ribs, I assumed, that were causing him to breathe so shallow. He was crying softly and groaning under his muffled breaths.

"We're almost there, man, you're doing so great. Just a little while longer."

"I got it! I got it!" Frank yelled with intense relief from twenty feet away. He dialed emergency. He didn't dare move and risk losing the signal. I could hear him connect to the operator.

I pulled out my phone to see if I could use maps to pin our coordinates. It was dead. I wasn't surprised. Frank described our exact location as best he could to the other end of the line. They were sending a helicopter immediately from Austin. It would be to us in twenty-five minutes. Frank had two flares that he had taken out of his saddles. He would light them when we heard and saw any inkling of the copter. The operator hung up, leaving us with directions not to move until help arrived. I put my head down to Sam. They didn't have to tell me twice. I couldn't move if I wanted to.

Relief over me. They were coming. My body gave out and I fell to the ground beside Sam.

"They're coming, bud. They're coming. It's gonna be okay."

Twenty-four minutes to go.

Chapter 57 - Out of Body Experience
Nick

Thirty-three minutes later, the sound of the emergency chopper was like music to my fucking ears. Frank lit his first flare, which did its job. The helicopter landed expertly in the field.

Everything happened very quickly then. Emergency personnel ran toward us, first tending to Sam, loading him onto a proper stretcher, and carting him away.

They took one look at us and were adamant that we were going to come to get checked out as well. We protested, insisting we were fine, but it didn't help. There was no arguing with the first responders. We were going to the hospital too. No question. I just wanted to get back to the ranch.

They loaded Sam and allowed us to come on board ourselves. Sam was stable for the time being. I listened to them converse with the hospital over the radio. They were prepping an operating room in case they needed it for him. They would have to check for internal injuries, but it was obvious he was suffering from all three major bones in his arm being broken and several broken ribs. He had frost bite and possible hypothermia and a concussion, probably from the fall from his horse. The "two other males were stable," they said, but "both suffering from frostbite and possible low-grade hypothermia and dehydration."

I felt like I was having an out of body experience. Were they talking about me? I didn't feel like I had hypothermia. I looked down at my hands for the first time. They didn't look like my hands. My fingers were red, bright red. I knew by looking at them they were frostbitten. Stage one.

I leaned my head back and almost passed out cold as we flew toward Austin. Nausea washed over me. I thought about Kate. My baby. I knew she would be so worried when she saw my horse without me, but I couldn't think anymore. I let my mind go and the adrenaline of those last five hours left my body. Everything went black as I dozed in and out of consciousness.

I opened my eyes as we landed on the helipad at Dell Seton. The noise startled me. I forgot where I was. Commotion was everywhere all at once. More nausea came.

We moved through emergency very fast. I didn't even see Sam before they carted him away in a hurry to X-ray and give him a hefty dose of pain medication.

Frank and I were taken in slower, our situation not as urgent. Our vitals were checked. My fingers were still beet red. Just as I had assumed, I had stage one frostbite on my fingers and toes. My body was warmer now, and I was no longer shivering. I listened intently as the doctor told me the adrenaline may have stopped both of us from ending up with hypothermia. We were both suffering from extreme exhaustion and dehydration, but we were very lucky and we could go home the next day if we got some sleep and were feeling well.

We were admitted and given IV rehydration. No sedative was needed because we were both dead on our feet. In the quiet of my room, my mind was full of only Kate, allowing myself the privilege of thinking about her for the first time in too long.

I understood in that moment what Daniel meant about Vanessa getting him through the hard times. Throughout the entire ordeal, it was Kate's face or some formed thought of her that got me through. I could see her when I closed my eyes. Riding her horse in front of me through the warm pastures, her hair flying out from behind her. The sun hitting it just right, like it does sometimes.

She looked back at me and smiled that fucking earth-shattering smile. Then I was kissing her, feeling my mouth on hers. The silk of her hair. I could even feel the heat from the sun on my face as I slid out of consciousness into a sleep deeper than the dead.

Chapter 58 - We go way back
Nick

The sound of a cart coming through the doorway woke me from a dead sleep. My eyes opened. Daylight. *What time was it?* I looked around for my phone. I couldn't see it anywhere, or any of my things. I wore a hospital gown.

I focused groggily on the small clock on the wall. Twelve-thirty. *In the afternoon? What day was it? How long had I been asleep?* I felt fucked up and foreign in my own body.

I looked down at my hands. My fingers were still slightly red and a bandage covered the space an IV had been placed the night before.

Now I remembered.

I remembered a nurse I couldn't put a face to removing it. It had stung, but I hadn't fully woken up. I was hydrated well enough, she had said to another nurse in the room. She mentioned that I just needed to sleep a little more. I slipped back into the dark abyss. The last time I remembered even seeing a clock it had said three a.m. I think.

"Time for some lunch for you," said the voice pushing the cart.

I woke up a little more and looked around. I was in a semi-private room. It was beige and plain. Consistent beeping carried from machines in the room next to me. I looked instinctively to the window, the blinds were closed so I couldn't see outside. I was alone in the room. I was grateful for that.

I had walked fifteen miles in the freezing rain. I remembered that. My body was screaming it. Suddenly I became very aware of how hungry I was. *When had I eaten last?* I strived to remember. *Sam. Where was Sam?*

"Excuse me?" I addressed cart pusher. "Could you ask a nurse to come?" My voice was so hoarse. It sounded off.

"Yes," answered the small, frail woman who had delivered my lunch.

I pulled open the tray. Lasagna, soup, bread, cookie, grapes. Typical hospital food. I didn't care. I would eat it all. I was ravenous. I started by chugging the apple juice on the tray like it was the first drink I'd had in weeks.

I had just finished the last bite when a nurse came in. She looked to be in her mid-fifties with shorter dark hair and glasses. Her name tag said Rhonda.

"Well, you're looking worlds better." She spoke like she knew me. "We go way back." She winked, sensing that I wasn't remembering her the way she remembered me. "We've been together since seven when I removed your IV, maybe you don't remember, you barely woke up."

I felt awkward knowing she had cared for me and I had basically slept right through it.

"Thanks for everything," I managed. My voice was still raspy and my lips stung. "I don't remember much, but can you tell me where my friend is we brought in? Sam Cortez? And my boss? Frank Gibson?"

"Frank has been down here to check on you, a lot. I wouldn't let him wake you, he's okay. And your friend Sam is in recovery."

Of course. Of course I had slept longer than Frank. He was such a fucking beast, he probably snoozed for twenty minutes in a fucking chair in the hall and then sauntered on down to see me. I'll never fucking hear the end of that.

"They did surgery on your friend's arm last night. It was broken in four places. He's going to be fine, but his recovery will take some time. You two are heroes. You saved him. He was lucky. No internal bleeding or major organ damage, though one of his ribs made a small puncture in his lung."

She smiled a motherly smile. "Would you like me to tell Frank you're awake? He's right down the hall and champing at the bit."

"Yes please. And…my phone?" I asked.

She walked to a small cabinet on the wall and pulled my phone out. "I'm afraid it's dead, hun. You guys will be out of here in no time. You can use the desk phone if you think you can get through to anyone. You and your boss are both doing just fine. We think you were suffering mostly from exhaustion. Are you feeling okay?"

"Yes thanks, stronger every minute." It was the truth.

My mind went to Kate. She must be worried sick. There had been no connection to the ranch as far as I knew other than our horses arriving back without riders.

"Excuse me, Rhonda, one more thing?"

"No problem, I am here to help." She looked like she meant it, smiling so sweet to me.

"Do you know what is going on with the storm?" I looked to the window. "I mean, have you heard if the power is back on in West Hays or anywhere surrounding it?"

Rhonda shrugged.

"Far as I know it's done icing but the whole valley is without power still, there is one open road in and out of some of the smaller towns and no phone or internet last time I checked. My brother lives in Chesterville, I was trying to get him last night and couldn't. I've also been trying my wife's mom in Rockham all morning and can't get her either."

She mentioned the towns closest to the ranch. That meant they were still without any hydro or internet.

"Thank you," I said quickly, lost in my own thoughts. No point in trying to call them. I wouldn't get through anyway. "Do you think I could maybe take a shower before I go home?"

"Of course, hun." She peered her head into the bathroom that joined my semi-private room with another. "It's free now. Are you okay to stand up?"

I gave it a try, moving to the edge of my bed and getting onto my feet. I stood still for a minute, letting the earth settle under me. My legs were sore. To say my back and forearms were sore was an understatement. They were on fire. Carrying a person through the ice that far took its toll on my body. I don't even know how I did it. I have no idea how Frank did it, twenty years older than me.

I looked at her to let her know I was fine. "I'm okay." She seemed satisfied.

"Okay." She turned then to yet another cabinet in the room and grabbed a large white towel and a washcloth, both of which said "Property of D.S." on them.

"There's soap and shampoo in the dispenser on the shower wall. Don't take too long, okay?. I'm going to let the doctor know you can be checked on one last time and then I think they'll release you if you feel ready to head home. Do you have someone who can pick you up?"

My mind wandered. We couldn't reach the ranch. I could try Roger.

"I think so, I'll talk to my boss after my shower. Thank you, Rhonda."

"No problem. Again, it's why I'm here." She smiled warmly at me and left the room to go tell Frank and the doctor I was awake.

I stood in the shower, letting the steaming water run down my aching body. My fingers burned. My muscles ached. The full weight of what had happened hit me like a ton of bricks. I stood there for a few minutes soaking it in.

Emotions overwhelmed me now that it was over. We could've lost Sam, I should've been watching him better. He is so new and so young. What had he been thinking to ride over there? What would Daniel think? What was Kate thinking? Had someone been able to reach Sam's mom? A million thoughts raced through my mind. As upset as Daniel was with me, I was sure he would be worried about all of us too.

I got out of the water and wrapped the towel around me. It seemed insane to think in this day and age that communication could be completely lost. My dad always says we're just insignificant as humans in comparison to mother nature. I realized now just how right he was.

An inch of ice and phone lines, power lines, and cell towers were all rendered worthless. I stood in the mirror, wiping the steam away with my hand. I looked rough.

I dried my face and glanced around to see where to put my towel and washcloth. Individually wrapped, disposable toothbrushes and tiny tubes of toothpaste sat on the shelf by the sink. I brushed my teeth and felt almost half human. I had no choice but to put back on the clothes I arrived in, which were tattered and now dry, but really dirty. I couldn't wait to get home. Burning this fucking outfit would definitely be in order.

Frank sat in the chair in my room, wearing his own tattered clothes, waiting for me.

"You okay, kid?" he asked. "Good to see ya."

I looked at Frank and laughed out loud. "You fucking look like shit."

Frank laughed with me. "I didn't get as much of a beauty sleep as you did, but back at ya."

I knew it.

I chuckled, absorbing his not-so-subtle dig.

We exchanged a look between us. What an experience it had been. We had worked so quickly and in-sync during our unrelenting push to get Sam to safety.

There wasn't another man I would've wanted to be stuck with in that moment. I knew Frank felt the same.

"Never want to go through that again, but glad we got through it. You really impressed me, kid."

I nodded in response. "Ditto," I said, and then, "Has anyone talked to the ranch?"

I was so worried about Kate.

"We can't get anyone. I tried Caleb, Matthew, Daniel, Katie, even the old land line is out. I couldn't even get Roger. I ended up getting a hold of Shelia's brother Chris here in Austin. He drives a big truck and has a towing company. He's going to take us home when the doctor lets us leave. From what I can tell, they're going to start cleanup tomorrow on the smaller county roads. All of West Hays is a mess."

The doctor popped her head in the room, knocking lightly as she entered.

"Good, you're both here. In case you don't remember me, I'm Doctor Hill. I saw you both last night, but you were a little worse for the wear. Good to see you two up and moving again. Which one of you would like your vitals done first? I'd like to get you on your way home. I see no reason to keep you and I'm sure you're both ready."

Frank and I nodded simultaneously.

I volunteered to go first, and Frank excused himself to go to his own room, where the doctor would follow up with him next.

The doctor was happy with my vitals.
"Can I see my friend we brought in, Sam Cortez?"

I asked, when she was all done with her check.

"Yes, sure you can. He's in and out. They have him on a lot of pain meds right now but he's in room three-oh-eight. Rhonda can take you, it's just down the hall."

"Thanks Doctor." I shook her hand, still feeling my fingers sting from the frostbite.

Sam's room was dark when I popped my head in. The curtains were slightly closed and he was hooked up to an IV and monitoring machine. They had to put pins in his arm in two places. It was elevated in a sling.

I moved to the side of his bed and squeezed his good arm. "Hey, bud, I just wanted to check on you. I'm so glad you're okay. You had us worried for a minute," I whispered quietly.

Sam opened his eyes groggily upon hearing my voice and looked at me, clearly exhausted from his ordeal and the medication. Tears gathered in his eyes. Poor kid.

"Thank you…Thank you so much," was all he said before he fell back asleep.

I patted his arm. "Anytime, brother," I said quietly.

I put my head in my hands for a minute. It had been such a long and worrisome few days, but for the time being, all was well. I breathed a heavy sigh of relief. Sam actually seemed okay. Better than I had expected.

I left him after a few more minutes to let him sleep. I had just wanted him to know I had been there.

The doctor said he would be in the hospital for at least a few more days. They wanted to monitor his lung and make sure he was able to move around before they released him. They had miraculously managed to reach his mom. She was staying in Georgetown and they hadn't lost power. She was coming up to the hospital with her brother and his wife later that day to be with Sam.

Frank returned to my room after his follow up with the doctor. "Ready to blow this pop stand?" He had called his brother-in-law, and we would be leaving within twenty minutes.

"Fuck, yes," I answered. I was dreaming of getting home and just seeing her face. We gathered up our few belongings and signed our release papers before saying thank you and goodbye to the nursing staff and Dr. Hill. We headed down the elevator and out the door to Chris's truck parked in the pick-up zone.

    I rested my head against the back seat. It was finally over. An hour or less to those beautiful blue eyes and to saying the words I had held in for so long to the woman who had always been my lifeline. My basis of comparison against all the others. The one who lit my otherwise doomed soul on fire.

    I thought of nothing else as we left the hospital parking lot and headed down the highway for Reeds Canyon.

Chapter 59 - They're watching us
Katie

I paced my figure eight again and again. Eleven agonizing hours since I had found King, Cash, and Jasper at the barn with nearly all the men's personal belongings.

Almost forty-eight hours since I had spoken to Nick. It has been silent. Not even a word from Frank to my dad. No news to the bunkhouse. Their phones had to be dead by now. And it didn't matter since I couldn't even make a phone call out. I wore the same thing I had on when I had gone to the barn at three-thirty in the morning, hair piled high onto my head in a messy bun. I hadn't even thought of changing.

I hadn't even eaten or sat down once since I came running back from the barn that morning and woke my dad frantically to tell him. He had scolded me for being out in the freezing rain, but in truth, he was glad I went and noticed that the three men were missing. My mind had been in a panic all day and I was afraid to even breathe. God only knew what had happened to them. It had been too long.

The scenarios in my mind were running wild by this point. Had someone gone through the ice while chopping? Nothing made sense. There wasn't a space on this property that Nick couldn't get home from.

The radio said power crews were working tirelessly all over the valley and half-way to Austin to try to restore power to overhead lines and cell towers. They were making progress, but it was slow going. They were hoping to have some power restored by that evening.

Trent and Will came back to the ranch that morning to help with cleanup, not knowing what waited for them when they arrived. The trees had been cleaned up enough on the main roads for them to make their way through finally.

All four available cowboys rode out to check the pastures they could get to and nothing. Not a trace of them, other than remnants from a fire in the far east pasture and lots of foot tracks. They returned two hours prior to fill us in.

The after math of the ice was apparent. The property was a mess. The fallen limbs impaired the cowboy's ability to search. They were definitely missing but they had done their job, Trent told my dad. All the herds were doing well now, with the ice starting to melt and the grass poking back through the fine layer of snow. Nick, Frank, and Sam had kept them safe, warm and fed through the storm. But with everything melting, the foot tracks were disappearing quickly, so it seemed like they just ended. It was just like they had vanished into thin air.

My dad sent Trent to drive into town to get more fuel for the generators and visit to Sherriff's office to notify them that the three men were officially missing.

I felt utterly trapped on the ranch.

I had never been so worried or felt so helpless in all my life. All the memories of the past two months with him flooded my mind. Thinking about them kept me sane. His touch, his kiss, the hours we spent just talking to each other. I poured over the conversations in my mind.

The way he smiled at me in a way he didn't smile at anyone else. The sounds he made when I kissed him. His strong arms around me that made me feel as safe and warm and happy.

Sherriff Bill Watson pulled into our driveway and stopped just short of the house—the fallen tree limbs blocked his path. He walked the rest of the way and I watched him through the large picture window in the parlor. I called for my dad, who went to greet him at the door.

I wiped my eyes. They were red and puffy from my tears. I sniffled and tried to straighten myself up. My dad looked at me before he answered the door, startled to see me crying so hard.

"Pixie, are you okay, love? We're going to find them." He hated seeing me cry. He always had. He walked over and wrapped me in his arms.

"We're going to find them love," he said again.

Fresh tears fell from my aching eyes.

"I'm just tired, Dad, and so worried." I blew my nose and sat down, facing away from the door as he let the Sherriff in. They talked in the foyer for quite some time about the circumstances surrounding everything. He was going to send officers and the K-9 unit out to start search and rescue right away. The Sherriff did a good job at calming us all down. It was a vast property, but he reminded us that these men were trained in survival. Despite that, wasn't taking it lightly and was getting the search started right away. He agreed it was troubling that they had been seemingly out there for two nights and most of this day in wet clothing with no shelter. While the ice had stopped, the rain was still coming down in a misty fog. It had warmed up but still was cold and damp out.

It made no sense why they hadn't returned. The storm had mostly moved on. Even *walking* back, they would be here by now. If anything happened to him and I hadn't told him I loved him I would never forgive myself. But that wouldn't happen, I reminded myself. He would find a way back.

I looked out the window and had a sip of water. I sat and watched the rain fall as the Sherriff shook my dad's hand and let himself out. Rain pelted off his had as he walked back to his car. I watched him climb into the driver's seat and enter notes on his car tablet. The rain and fog blurred my view, but something caught my eye further down the property.

. I stood to get a closer look, the blanket I had been sitting under fell to the floor. An old, beat-up tow truck ambled down the long dirt road that led to the driveway. I stood, frozen, trying to get a glimpse of the driver. I didn't recognize them through the tinted windows.

The truck pulled up beside the Sherriff and I watched with wide eyes as the face I was dying to see emerged from the backseat and shut the door behind him. His clothes were filthy, and he looked utterly exhausted, but it was Nick.

Suddenly, I was running. I had been so worried something terrible had happened to him. This became one of those moments in life where your brain doesn't push the thought to your body, it's the other way around. I ran as fast as I could out the front door and down the steps, racing into the driveway in my socks and pajamas, which were now soaked. I ran the hundred feet to him with ease. He saw me coming and beamed, moving to meet me as fast as he could.

I slammed into him with all the force my tiny body could produce. He didn't even move an inch. He sheltered me in his arms, burying his face into my hair. Tears of relief streamed down my face. He was back and safe and okay.

I threw my arms up around his neck and kissed him like it was the last kiss I would ever give him. He kissed me back without a care in the world. His hands grasped my face, slid down my shoulders, squeezing me like I was his anchor.

"Oh my GOD, Nick, what happened? Where have you been? Are you okay?" I placed my hands on either side of his face to look at him. His answers didn't matter, he was here, in one piece and safe and mine. He pressed his forehead to mine and stroked my hair down my back. It was starting to dampen from the rain.

He whispered between kisses, his voice hoarse and dry, "I'm okay. I love you, Katelyn. I'm sorry I didn't tell you before but I'm telling you now. Saying I love you isn't enough. I exist for you. Every part of me belongs to you. In some way, I always have,"

"I love you so much, Nick. I always have too, *always*."

We continued this way, in our own little world where no one mattered for a two-minute-eternity, until somewhere in the back of his subconscious he remembered that we weren't alone.

Nick sobered up and pulled back just a fraction of an inch.

"They're watching us, Kate," he whispered. I hadn't thought. I had just acted.

I turned to see my dad and Frank standing on the porch, and the Sherriff from his car, watching us kiss each other in the pouring rain like the end scene of a rom-com.

Chapter 60 - I'm going to make this quick.
Katie

We separated from each other as my dad spoke, but Nick didn't for one second let go of my hand.

"I think we had better talk inside," he called out to us.

The Sherriff approached, realizing his services probably weren't needed anymore, and shook my dad's hand before he headed out.

As the police car left the driveway my dad glanced at us, before silently walking into the house.

Frank, exhausted and pissed off, came quickly to Nick's side.

"I told you about this kid, it isn't gonna end well. I get it, young love and all that shit but Jesus, Nick, of all the days."

Nick gripped my hand even tighter, as if to say to me, *"We're in this together."*

"It is what it is now. I don't regret it. I love her too much," Nick said firmly.

I felt my heart turn to mush. Defending us confidently made me love him more and saddened me that it had to be this way.

Frank laughed and put his head down.

"Let's go, Romeo. I want to get this over with and go home," he said, patting Nick on the back and leading the way into the house.

My dad was sitting at the large harvest table when the three of us walked into the house. We stood so as to not soak the fabric chairs. Melia was there instantly with towels for us. I took off my wet socks and dried myself as best as I could.

"I'm going to make this quick," he began, his voice firm and authoritative. "I'm sure you both want to get home. You look like you've been through hell and back and you've both got some good frost bite."

He turned to Nick and me. "We will discuss the matter of both of you tomorrow, after I have had time to think of a solution that best fits this ranch." He continued on, "Now that the storm is on its way to being over I will be carefully considering how we'll move forward. I've already explained to you the position this puts me in, but I need to deal with what is most important and what is at hand. Where is Sam?"

Frank looked at my dad, then at Nick. Surprised, obviously, that my dad knew about us.

Until that moment, I had been so wrapped up in my bliss over Nick's return that I hadn't even made the connection that Sam wasn't with them.

Nick began, "There was an accident yesterday in the far east pasture—"

Frank turned to him and put his hand to stop him from talking. "I got it from here, kid."

Nick knew when to shut up. For the time being, Frank was still his boss. He let Frank explain every detail to my dad and me.

It all finally made sense. Why it had seemed that they disappeared into thin air, because effectively, they had. Why we couldn't reach them, why the horses had returned. All of it.

As Frank finished out the story, telling my dad about Sam's hospital stay and his prognosis, I felt a wave of relief wash over me.

They were so lucky. Nick was a hero. I was so relieved he was okay. My eyes welled up with even more tears. Poor Sam. I genuinely liked him so much and couldn't even imagine how scared he must have been. But after spending almost two days worrying about Nick's safety, thinking he could even be dead, I didn't care what my dad said.

I was unconditionally and inescapably in love with him and I was so glad I had told him. I couldn't and wouldn't live without him. Sensing how upset I was, Nick instinctively put his arm around my shoulders, rubbing me gently to make me feel safe.

He leaned down and whispered to me. "It's okay, we're okay." There was no point in pretending now.

My dad paused from speaking with Frank and watched the two of us interact. Likely realizing that this had been going on for a while. We were too comfortable, too familiar. He focused back on the situation at hand, turning to both men, he cleared his throat and spoke.

"I want to thank you both for being so brave and going well above and beyond what was required of you to help a brother. I couldn't be more grateful for that, nor can I express to you how much it means to me to have such good men in my presence when it comes to the work you both do for this ranch."

He looked at Frank. "I'll need you here at seven a.m. tomorrow morning. In the meantime, go home, Sheila's been here four times today. She is absolutely worried sick. We will talk tomorrow, and Frank, sure glad you're okay." He shook his hand and patted him on the shoulder with the other one. My dad had known Frank his whole life, he was only seven years older than him. They grew up together, he thought of him like a brother.

Frank didn't argue, saying goodbye to us all and taking a moment to hug Nick. It was the type of awkward hug two men have when they can't quite express their feelings to each other. "That was a roller coaster. You did good, kid. Get some sleep."

He looked at my dad then, with a look that said, *"have mercy on him."*

Frank headed out the door while Nick and I stood frozen, waiting for my dad to speak to us. He glanced between us. His face was tense like he was trying not to say something he would regret later.

He turned to Nick. "Son, I'm very glad you're okay. I'll say it again, you're a hell of a cowboy."

"Daniel, I just want to say, the only thing I'm sorry for is the way you had to find out about us. I was planning on telling you about Kate and me as soon as you were healed up and ready to come back out into the field. I know your rules and I always follow them, aside from this." His gaze focused on me. "It was never meant to be sneaky. We aren't afraid or ashamed to explain our feelings for each other."

"Well good, you'll have the chance then. Frank will be here at seven o'clock tomorrow morning to discuss the need for replacing Sam for a few months while he heals. After that I'd like you here by nine. We'll figure out what is next then."

"Yes, sir," was Nick's only response before hugging me and heading out the door.

Chapter 61 - It was all just a dream
Katie

I turned to my dad, not sure if I should speak. I had never seen him like this. Not angry, just very let down. Disappointed in me.

"Katelyn, for the first time in my life, I haven't anything to say to you. My knee is sore and I'm exhausted. I need to sleep on this. We'll talk tomorrow, okay?"

He turned away to head into the den. I felt the walls closing in. He would fire Nick and nothing would ever be the same.

Sometimes, it takes feeling the hand over your mouth to give you the courage to scream.

I let myself say the words I had been keeping inside of me since Christmas day.

"Dad." I spoke, barely over a whisper. "It's okay if you don't want to talk. I know you're disappointed and I hate it, but I have to say something."

He paused to look at me, so I continued.

"I just need you to understand that I *love* him and I'm a grown woman, capable of making my own decisions without your approval. Although I always want your blessing, I don't *need* it. The only thing I need your blessing on is him staying here. He deserves it."

Slow tears tracked down my cheeks. I had never cried so much in my whole life, my emotions from the day, and the shock of everything getting the better of me.

"I didn't mean for this to happen, there's always been something between us that we didn't understand. Maybe even since we were young. He's such a good man, Dad, and he respects you and this ranch so much. I've wanted to tell you so many times but I didn't want him to lose his job. It was easier to keep it between us for a while."

I wiped my eyes as I spoke, determined to sound strong. "He clearly would do anything for you, even risk his own well-being. Please consider an alternative to letting him go. I'll do anything you ask except give him up. I just love him so much." I was a mess, totally sobbing now.

He approached and wrapped me in his arms.

Sensing I was finished, he spoke. "We'll talk tomorrow. I just need some time to think about how to handle this properly." I nodded and he left the room.

I sat by the front window of the parlor for the next hour, letting all my emotions out. I knew my father couldn't hear me and I was so exhausted and heartbroken over the way he had looked at me. I felt a little woozy and decided I needed to eat something. I had barely touched any food in two days and finally felt like I could eat.

I stood up to walk into the kitchen. Sounds of appliances beeping and lights turning on startled me. I looked around and realized what was happening. The power was back on after two and a half days.

I grabbed some strawberries, yogurt, and granola and placed it all on a plate.

I returned to my haven of blankets and my chair in the parlor, wondering how I was going to make this work to keep both the men in my life happy.

My phone buzzed the familiar sound of a text message. Apparently, at least one cell phone tower near us was working again too.

Kryptonite: *Well that was fucking brutal.*

I laughed through my tears.

Me: *That's an understatement.*
Kryptonite: *I have to see you, when can we meet?*
Me: *You are crazy. You have to sleep and eat.*
Kryptonite: *I'll be crazy if I don't see you. I did eat, lots, and showered and even have clean, dry clothes on. I started packing some stuff up. I'll sleep when I'm unemployed. I need to see you.*

I felt sad reading the words he wrote about losing his job. I wanted to see him too. In fact, *needed* to see him was a better way to describe it. I knew *exactly* how he felt.

Me: *Ok, I need to get a couple hours sleep. I'm dead on my feet. Let's meet at the nest. Eleven?*

His answer was instant.

Kryptonite: *Yes*

I finished eating, realizing how hungry I had actually been, and then headed upstairs for a long, hot shower, my first one in three days. I could hardly wait.

The shower felt seriously heavenly. I hadn't been truly warm in three days, with only a few space heaters going in the entire house. I could hear the furnace running before I even entered the bathroom and was grateful for a much warmer night's sleep.

My mind went to Nick and Frank and Sam while I conditioned my hair and thought about where they had been just twenty-four hours before. No matter how mad my dad was, he had to admit that no one else that worked for him would have had the strength or perseverance to get Sam to the hospital the way Nick had. If it had been anyone else out there with Frank, who knows what may have happened.

I shut the water off and wrapped myself in fresh towels. Exhaustion washed over me like a tidal wave. Four long hours I had to wait to see him still. I wanted Nick to sleep too. He needed it for the next day and I was exhausted. I would curl up in my bed for a nap when I was done. A few hours would do me wonders. The stress of everything had been so physically draining I could feel the tension from it in my shoulders. My puffy eyes needed a break from the light.

I dried my thick hair then pulled on my tights and a t-shirt. Getting into my bed, I set my phone alarm for ten fifteen, then fell asleep faster than my head could hit the pillow.

The rising sun coated the sky in orange and pink fire. The tops of the trees in the distance cut into it like a painting. I stood on my wide front porch, leaning against the railing and drinking coffee, the heat of a Texas July morning warming my skin already.

I put down my cup to push the sleeves of my robe up to my elbows when I felt him behind me, pulling the tie open and sliding his hands around my waist. I smiled, feeling the warmth of his body around mine. I turned my head to the side. He bent down and kissed me. He was dressed in a t-shirt, his cowboy hat, and worn boots. Heading down to the barn, no doubt, to start his day.

"I'll see you tonight," he whispered to me quietly. I smiled, feeling the warmth of his lips.

My eyes opened and suddenly I was seeing a different view. My bedroom ceiling in the ranch house. My phone buzzed its wake up call to me. Ten-thirty. I hadn't moved an inch from the position I fell asleep in.

I closed my eyes and tried to remember the sweetness of my dream. It had seemed so real. The porch was covered and wide, railed with wood spindles, the Edison lights hung from the ceiling of it, but the thing that most stuck out was the view. I had been looking out right from our nest.

It was a perfect dream, but it wasn't real. I squeezed my eyes shut and rubbed them, wishing I could go back.

I forced myself to sit up. I was so tired, but I had to see him. Even if it was just for an hour.

Chapter 62 - Part 1 - Not a moment before
Katie

The house was dark and quiet when I crept out the back-sliding door. It was the furthest away from the den and would be the quietest. I made it out with ease, knowing my dad was probably out cold. He was asleep before ten almost nightly, that or deep into an episode of something on the History channel. After the last few days, he should be asleep for sure.

I thought about the dream my alarm interrupted just a few minutes before. It gave me peace to imagine myself like that with Nick in the morning hours of any random day and with a lifetime stretched out before us.

Nick waited at our space in the hills already. He had set up a tent with a removable roof—it had a screen for star gazing—and he had a fire going for us. It was almost warm. As if mother nature was apologizing, trying to make up for the carnage she'd caused. Nick seemed unfazed as he greeted me. He helped me tie Buttercup up on the opposite side of the hill with King, far enough away from us that the fire wouldn't bother them or cause them stress.

"If this is my last night here it's going to be outside under this sky."

I had to admit, he looked much better than he had that afternoon. He turned to me, relaxing into my arms as they tried to accommodate his much larger size. I kissed him, reminding him what we were fighting for. We moved together to the fire. He held my hand, like he just couldn't stop himself from touching me, not even for a second.

He had quite literally created us a giant nest, with waterproof thermal pads, pillows, sleeping bags, and blankets. He always thought of everything. We sat together and he wrapped the blanket around me.

"I was so worried about you." I spoke without a filter. "That fear I felt, it's a feeling I never want to live through again, the unknown. It was awful."

"I know, baby, I felt so bad not being able to tell you I was okay, especially once I knew Sam was fine and I was coming home. I wish I could've warned you, I'm sorry to put you through that."

I shook my head. "It's not your fault. I just hope you're not upset with me for today, for outing us to Frank like that and putting you in that position in front of my dad. I didn't think, I just saw you and ran."

His voice was calm and reserved. He ran his hand back and forth over my arm. He gave me a warm smile as he snuggled in close.

"I've thought a lot over the last few days. I had lots of time to." He repositioned the wood in the fire while he spoke. "I'm done hiding anything I feel for you. I'm worth a lot to your dad here and if he doesn't know that by now, or can't accept us, then I can't control that. I hope it will work out, but if it doesn't, there are other ways. To some extent, I've been in love with you my whole life, Kate." His eyes met mine and what I saw was raw, honest, and full of love. "You asked me Christmas Eve what this tattoo says." He rubbed his side where the Gaelic writing trailed down his torso. I looked at him, not understanding the correlation.

"It's the same saying I wrote to you with your gift."

A daisy for every moment she crosses my mind means I would walk in my garden forever.

If there was a proverbial rug that lived under me, I assure you the very moment that sentence left his mouth it was no longer there. I just stared at him in disbelief while his eyes were light on mine, enjoying the fact that he had just fully blown my mind.

"Tennyson?"

"Yes, baby." He kissed my lips as I sat there, stunned. "You're the daisy that crosses my mind so fucking much, that if there was a garden of my thoughts of you, I could walk in it forever. It was fitting."

"How did you? When did you?" I stammered in disbelief. The words just wouldn't come. He grabbed my hand.

"I got it the summer you left, not long after I started here. I saw your face everywhere I looked, it followed me. Putting these words on my skin helped me take control of that reminder, but they also remind me every day in some way to be good. Good like *you*. You were part of me even though you were gone. I know now that I can be the man you need, finally. I also know that even before I knew what love really was, I felt it for you."

Thoughts of Carter and his words, *"you don't just change your physical being for someone,"* made sense to me now. He knew.

Nick's voice remained quiet and deep as he spoke. "Now you know everything. My last secret. It's always been you, Kate. Every good memory I have has you in it. I just had to convince myself I deserved you. I'm actually *relieved* it's all out in the open. Whatever happens now, happens. As long as I have you, I'm a very happy man."

His lips met mine, and I thought that my heart might explode. I couldn't even be upset that he didn't tell me sooner how he felt, because *now* was our time and not a moment before.

Somehow, this man who was once so broken found his way back to me and was giving himself to me entirely. He was risking everything he had worked for his whole adult life for me. For us.

"The thought of leaving this place kills me." He grinned then and pulled my hand to his lips, kissing it in multiple places. "But, it will be okay. This is me having faith."

I knew one thing for certain, I was done letting people decide for me what was right and wrong. I was not a child. I would *make* my father keep him employed.

He shifted closer, wrapping me up in his arms.

"We're in this together," he whispered.

I turned myself more toward him then, kissing him with all the love I felt for him. What was *I* waiting for? Twenty-four hours before I didn't even know where he was. Every minute was precious. I wanted to give myself to him, the way he gave himself to me. Wholly and entirely.

I crushed my body to his, differently than I ever had before. I reached down over his broad shoulders, then to his waist and under his shirt, over the ink in his skin that now held so much meaning to me. The heat from his body transferred to mine and radiated over my hands. I ran them up his sides and then onto his back, my body taking over. He gave in to me, backing away from my face a fraction of an inch, letting me pull his shirt off. He said nothing, kissing me, pulling my jacket off, then undoing my hair clip, letting my hair fall down around me. His hands ran under my shirt, his thumbs grazing over my rib cage, under my breasts. They gripped my t-shirt with force, pulling it off, tossing it into our growing pile of clothes in the grass. He added my bra to it with a quick pull of the clasp. As I sat in front of him, topless, I heard his breath catch in his throat.

"So fucking beautiful." The words were almost a growl, fueling the fire low in my stomach that ebbed down between my legs. He stopped wasting time and buried his face in my breasts, running his expert tongue over my nipples, carefully focusing on each one equally, heightening my fire. Nipping and sucking as he raked his large hands down my back, digging his fingers into my flesh.

His arms wrapped around me in a crushing hold, I could feel my bare chest on his and the heat of his body on mine. The orange glow from the fire shone between us and was our only light. He smiled at me as he spoke, his voice a gruff and pleading whisper.

"You have no idea how fucking badly I want you right now, but baby, if you don't want our first time to be in the grass on this hill, we have to find the strength to stop taking all of our clothes off or I'm not going to be very good at stopping…

Chapter 62 - part 2 - Otherworldly Nick

"I don't want to stop…"
 Those five little words held so much power. They pulled all the available air from my lungs. She kissed me as she said it, trying to show me she meant it. I clutched her hair in my fist, using it to pull her head back gently, her face still close to mine. The look she wore said she was serious. She wanted this to happen. Now. I smiled at her,
 "Be sure, baby, because with the way I'm feeling right now…by the time I'm done with you every single creature in this valley will know your body is mine."
 A coy little grin took over her face. "Didn't you say I would beg, cowboy? I want you. Here. Now."
 I had never heard any words sound so fucking sexy, ever.
 She used her small hands to push me to the ground and I groaned as I let her, her legs straddling either side of me. I rushed my hands over her full hips, down her thighs, then back up, squeezing her pert ass through her tights while I kissed her. Always trying so hard to get closer to her. She sat up and just stared at me lying under her in the grass for a minute, tracing

the crevices of my chest with her fingers. The sheer beauty of her crippled me as I watched her. Just the *sight* of her. Her hair covering the naked top half of her body and her nipples while the rest of her perfect tits and curves were in plain view as her skin glowed by the fire. She looked like a work of art as she bit her bottom lip and began moving back and forth, rolling her hips over me, searching for friction to satisfy the aching bud of nerves between her legs. I breathed out an uncontrolled groan of raw desperation and fucking *need* for her. I sat up easily with the weight of her on me, crushing her body to mine as I kissed her. "You know what you're doing to me, don't you?"

"Maybe…" she breathed. It was a rhetorical question. We both knew. I had never been so hard in my life, pressing between her legs. Her hands slid down my chest to reach for my belt.

I grasped for my bag beside us in the grass before things went too much further, but as I pulled the condom out of it, she reached her hand out to stop me, shaking her head.

"No, Nick, I don't want anything between us, ever."

Fuck me, this woman…

I had definitely had a lot of sex in my life, but I had never once had sex without a condom. The idea of truly feeling her around my cock…her proposal caused the purest form of adrenaline to rush through my body. I filled with white heat as all control left me, turning me into more of a beast than a man. I ran my tongue over her pebbled nipples, working them to pull forward the sweet little moans and pants from her lips that I knew would come. She shivered when I pulled back from her and I swear to fucking God, she pouted at me.

I paused to ask her, "What do you want?"

Her eyes hypnotized me through her lashes as she answered. Her voice smooth and husky. "Just you, baby."

Hearing her call me baby for the first time ever filled my entire soul with fire. "Katelyn, you were fucking made for me." I breathed.

But she wasn't just made for me. She was *it*. She was everything.

Her lips curled up in a small smile like she was some sort of all-knowing sex goddess as she placed both of my hands under hers onto her hips while she continued to roll her body over me in the most enticing way. She was driving me fucking crazy, testing all of my willpower.

I struggled to stop myself from flipping her over and just fucking her ten different ways from Sunday. She leaned back in to kiss me, her heart beating rapidly against mine. I lifted her off of me then and laid her down in the blankets in the grass, pulling off her tights and squeezing her thick, silky thighs on my way down.

I removed my own clothes from my body as she motioned for me to come to her, opening her legs from their closed position, welcoming me between them. Her eyes grew as wide as saucers at the vision of my cock, as hard as it's ever been and pointing straight at her. Just that look alone almost undid me entirely, and she wasn't even trying. I pulled her panties off, almost tearing them as I did, and threw them into the grass as she pressed her palm to me, pumping my length in desperation. I sucked in a breath and muttered some words I couldn't remember if I tried.

As I hovered over her, I pushed her hair from her face and watched her chest rise and fall heavily with her breaths. I kissed her slow on the mouth, one moment to take her in, to burn this image of her below me into my memory forever. I gently pressed my fingers to her soaking pussy. She was always so ready for me, but I didn't want to hurt her, even though I knew it was inevitable that I would.

"I'm going to try two now, okay, baby? It might…help."

She nodded, understanding me immediately. She looked equal parts desperate for me and afraid. I kissed her lips and pushed two fingers into her. She moaned. She was so tight around them. The anticipation of knowing in the very near future that would be my dick was killing me and forced another groan from my throat. I gently moved my fingers in and out of her, encouraging the part of her brain that was desperate for me to take over the part that was scared.

She reached her arms up around my back, digging her nails into my skin so deeply while I reveled in the incredible fucking pleasure of her coming over my fingers with her naked, warm skin pressed against mine.

I took in the sight of this woman I loved more than my own life coming completely undone under me. I memorized every second. Every little moan, every pant, her mouth in a perfect O. All of it.

"I'm going to spend my life giving you nights like this, Kate," I whispered to her. I built her fire back up gradually. Consuming her for what seemed like an eternity with my fingers, my lips, and my tongue. Readying her for me. Slowly? Quickly? Who the fuck could tell? There was no sense of space or time, everything was hazy around us, and I couldn't wait to bury myself inside her.

"Please, Nick?" she begged into my lips. I swallowed the beautiful sound of her whine.

"I want you, please...be inside me now," she moaned.

This fucking woman.

I parted her legs and moved between them, hovering above her just a few inches. "Are you sure?"

Her eyes were soft, her pupils blown out, her cheeks flushed as my hands stroked her face on either side. I traced the beautiful lines of it as I kissed her. She nodded to me, stoic and sure, but I needed more.

"Say the words, Kate."

She moaned. "Yes, I'm sure."

I relished the moment, pushing myself into her just a little bit, getting her used to it. Heat and the sweetest warmth I have ever felt in my life engulfed me with every dip into her, just enough to render me fucking speechless with the feeling. I was trying so hard not to hurt her, but my last thread of willpower quickly evaporated as she clenched in anticipation, practically strangling my cock in the best way possible. So wet. So fucking *tight*.

"You're doing so good, baby," I encouraged softly, cradling her face. "Are you okay? Do you need me to stop?"

"No, don't stop." She moaned breathlessly. "I just...is that all the way?" Her eyes were wide.

I smiled down at her. She was shaky, lucid. It was so overwhelming, my love for her.

"No baby, not yet." I was maybe giving her half.

"Okay," she managed, her voice trembling. I kissed her.

"You're going to tell me when you're ready for all of me, okay? You're the boss."

She smiled the most crushing smile and nodded. She was like looking at the sun. I cupped her breast, taking her nipple between my fingers, bringing it to my mouth as she moaned. I pushed a little further into her again, taking advantage of her desire. I thought carefully about every single player's name on the Dallas Stars roster and the most unsexy, random thoughts that I could as heat and pressure built in my spine. It was almost impossible to control. Her pussy was the brass fucking ring of pussies, I had never felt anything like it. The feeling of her wrapped around my cock was indescribable. She molded to me in a way I couldn't explain if I tried.

It was fucking otherworldly.

I moved my fingers down to her clit, circling over her, encouraging her to stretch and adjust to my size, offering pleasure with her pain because for me, being inside of her was the be all and end all of every single nerve in my body. She began moaning again and pressing up closer to me, her body taking more as I did my best to be slow and careful with her small frame.

"Nick…" she moaned quietly. "I want…all of you now…please?"

The vision of her below me, begging me for more of my cock, was almost pornographic. I lost all control and let myself go, sinking into her entirely. She was so wet and ready for me, there was no friction but *holy fuck* with nothing between us I could feel *everything*.

Goddamn, fucking utopia.

She gasped, her eyes wide and her breathing ragged, but she took all of me like a fucking warrior. Every cell in my body was alive, dopamine flowed through my veins with this feeling, it literally overpowered me. Every single piece of my soul, every shred of who I was, shifted in one second flat. Everything I was as a man became hers. I was born again in her. For the first time ever, I finally felt like I was close enough to her.

Chapter 62 - part 3 - I might need more than one
Katie

The moment he pushed into me my breath caught in my throat. It hurt just like I feared. A lot. Even with how desperately I wanted him, the fire of adjusting to him burned. He was much too big, but the closeness I felt to him outweighed the pain. He began slowly, like he knew exactly what my body could handle. Filling me a little more with each gentle thrust until I could no longer tell where one of us ended and the other began. Leather and spice mixed with the scent of the wild pansies from the field washed over me like a sweet, intoxicating fog. His fingers moved to my breasts, then to my slick core, making my body shift from pain to desire once again. I was ready. I began pushing my hips up further to him, without even thinking, my body completely took over. Begging him to fill me.

"Nick…I want…all of you now…please?" I could see him dying to give me more and I was as ready as I'd ever be.

He kissed me with a low growl but he did what I asked. A loud gasp escaped as he pushed into me fully. His mouth instantly covered mine to absorb the sound.

His breathing was uneven, heavy, and he groaned into me with the pleasure. I felt it wash over his entire body with a shudder. The intensity in those seconds is something I'll never forget.

"God, you feel…unbelievable, so fucking good, Kate. The best." He kissed me softly, moving to my neck, my shoulders, dotting my skin with his lips. "My fucking utopia."

The words he spoke made me feel entirely savoured. Worshipped.

His deep, raspy voice alone brought my desire back to the forefront. He was so intentional and so careful. I gripped the muscles of his arms as he moved in and out of me like it was an art form while he kissed me. That's when things changed. That's when it started to feel *good*. With every full thrust into me he hit a place inside me that almost made me pass out with pleasure.

I closed my eyes as I moved my body up to meet him. He squeezed the flesh of my hip under him in a heavy hold with one hand while he held himself up with the other, guiding me, lifting me to him exactly how and where he wanted me. Tiny beads of sweat covered us both.

It was like he was testing himself, pushing deeply into me, then slowly, tortuously dragging himself out, only to push into me again, hitting that spot inside me every damn time he bottomed out.

For a brief moment, I was grateful for all the experience he had before me, bringing him to this point of mastering everything my body could ever want or need. The feeling of being connected like this was way too much for either of us. He moaned with me, feeling my body completely swallow him up. I was filled entirely of him. I wrapped my arms around him, pulling him in, closer and closer to the edge.

Letting his sounds of desire pull me down into the abyss with him, an intense orgasm coiled low in my stomach. Surprising control flowed through me while I waited for him to let go with me. I spoke the words that shocked even me.

"Nick. Look at me while you come, baby."

He sucked his breath in sharply.

"*Holy fuck, Katelyn.*" He growled, his green eyes wild and carnal looking into mine. I had never seen him look more gorgeous or more out of control. My vision was lost as the orgasm racked through me so powerfully that I could've honestly died right there in his arms. Pleasure and pain blended together in perfect harmony, completely shattering my soul into a million pieces from the inside out as the never-ending current between us exploded. The sounds of this intense love we share echoed through the night sky in the valley as he spilled into me. Changing me forever. Making me only his as he kissed me, whispering his praise and eternal love for me.

It was fucking beautiful.

When it was over I felt dizzy and my legs shook. I let my head rest in the blankets on the grass.

"I need a minute," I said to him.

He laughed breathlessly. "Fuck, I might need more than one."

Ten minutes later I was wrapped in blankets beside him.

I turned up onto my elbow. Never feeling so comfortable in my naked skin.

He looked at me differently. So calm, so open, so satiated.

"Did I hurt you too much, baby?" His thumb traced my cheek. I shook my head no, but holy shit, I was lying. I could feel the dull ache throbbing between my legs, but I didn't want to take away from the look he was wearing. I didn't want him to worry. He looked at me skeptically. He saw right through me. I shrugged.

"It aches because, well, to put it plainly, you're huge. But it was…incredible. Is it normally like that? For everyone?" He smiled at me, then kissed my lips, looking at me seriously, moving his hand to begin tracing the outline of my shoulder with his fingers.

"No. It's never been like that for me. *Ever.* Not even close. You surprised me. Telling me to look at you…"

I looked down, slightly embarrassed.

"Don't do that, Kate." He tilted my chin up to look at him. "Don't ever be ashamed of anything you say. Everything we do is between us and for us, only."

I nodded. Trying to be bold.

"Well…thank you for at least for making sure I was ready, but my mind was made up." I patted him on his arm. He grinned, so much love showing through his eyes it warmed me.

"I fought a good fight? Is that it?" he asked, laughing.

"Yep, basically." I laughed back at him.

"I'll remind you, I am older than you. It makes sense that I would have more willpower and be more responsible…"

I raised an eyebrow. "Is that a challenge?"

He pulled me close and hugged me. "No, baby, I'd surely lose."

Our laughter was the only sound echoing through the field.

Chapter 63 - I'm gonna miss this place
Nick

I arrived somber, promptly at eight forty-five am. I had everything packed and ready to go home. I knew what was coming. Kidding myself would be a waste of time. I had been trying to get in touch with the Rockham Horseshoe Ranch for a half hour but couldn't make it through. I gave up, deciding their power there must still be down. I would have to go home anyway and explain this entire thing to my parents.

My father had finally gotten through to me the night before and I had had to explain to him everything that had happened. I must have assured him ten times that I was fine and let him go, telling him I'd be home in a few days to visit both of them. Maybe for a while, although I didn't say that. I kept trying to have a little faith, just like Kate told me to. I didn't have much of it, but what I did have in me came from her.

I had gone over the scenarios in my mind. What would I say to Daniel? *"Thank you for this opportunity? Sorry I let you down? Sorry but I can't live without your daughter?"*

I hadn't slept much, I just laid there holding her, not wanting to let her go and thinking about the future. I was exhausted but it was the most amazing kind of exhausted.

When I slid into her my whole world shifted, she became my only center. There was nothing now that would keep me from her. If all the shit I went through in my life was to bring me to this, to her, I was going to fight for it with everything I had. I could still feel my body in hers, taste the sweetness of her, and there was nothing that would ever compare to that. Nothing was worth giving that up. I would fucking die first.

I knocked at the door. Melia answered, telling me to come in. I was dressed in regular clothes. I wasn't going to assume that Daniel would send me out into the field after the meeting. Trent, Will, and the other cowboys that were here were already out there starting the cleanup. They were probably wondering why I wasn't with them.

I had gotten up by six even and had my area in the bunkhouse cleaned and ready to go. Everyone was gone so they would never even know what happened until they got back from their day. The rest of the cowboys were due back by dinner from their Christmas destinations and the ranch would be in full swing cleanup mode by New Year's Eve. They would have a lot of work ahead of them, but the weather looked warmer and sunny for the next week. I was really gonna miss this place.

Melia directed me to the den, the door was closed over. I knocked at nine a.m. I shut my phone off and waited.

"Come in." Daniel's voice was firm and serious. I entered the room, completely calm and ready for my fate. Whatever Daniel had decided, I was ready. As long as it didn't involve giving up Kate, I would agree.

Chapter 64 - The Gray Area
Katie

My morning before the meetings was a blur. I had been up for hours. I laid down in my bed at four thirty, after I got home from being with Nick on the hill, dreaming of the night. Waking in his arms after a brief sleep was best rest I had had in weeks. I felt more alive. I know it seems cliché, but I felt like a woman. Nick's words ran through my mind. *Fucking utopia.* Heaven. Having him inside me was like heaven or as close to it on earth as we could get, I was sure.

I was downstairs by five-thirty making coffee. I grabbed a large mug and headed into the parlor figuring I was alone, but I wasn't. My father was sitting in his chair.

"Couldn't sleep?" I asked him quietly startled by his presence.

"No, I have a lot on my mind," he answered. "I want to say something to you, Katelyn, so you understand where I'm coming from today. Leading this ranch means doing the right thing for everyone. As we've grown over the last few years with distribution, I've been out in the field and neglecting paperwork, invoicing, accounting. I know we have talked about this in the past, when you first arrived. I wanted to get you more involved on the business side. I don't *need* you to be out there in the field. I have many capable people for that. I needed you paying more attention to the business side for me, but I always want you to be happy. I let you venture into the field these last months because I thought you had it in you to be on the land. You telling me that you were going to stay here longer, I thought it was because you had reconnected with this place. Seeing you with Nick in the barn," He paused to find the words, "affected me. Not because it was Nick you chose. I know his past, I know he's not perfect, but he is a good man. It was because I felt like it was all a lie and the real reason you were here was because of your…" He waved a hand around, again searching for the words. "Hormones," he blurted out.

"I never expected that from you," he continued. "I was sad because I thought maybe, just maybe, you felt this land in your blood and were making a choice based on that, not a man. Just disappointed I was wrong, I guess."

"Dad, I do love this ranch. It was not a lie. It was and still is about the land, and you, and being home in general, but it is also about him. This thing with Nick and me, it isn't a fling. I *love* him and he loves me. I have felt more connected and alive here the last two months because of this land *and* Nick. I love it all and it's where I need to be right now. My dreams have just changed, I guess." I shrugged, letting everything out to him. I had nothing to lose.

"We know that because of this longstanding rule you may feel you have to let him go or maybe I will have to figure something else out, but we *will* still be together. If there was a way it could work where he stays that would be a miracle to us both. You are the only one who can decide. There always has to be a gray area. We aren't two temporary workers making out in the bunkhouse. There is no man I could ever see myself being in love with like this. He is it for me. For the first time in my life, when I'm with him, I feel like I can breathe, like I'm at peace. It may be here, or Rockham, or wherever Nick can work, but we will be together. The choice is yours and if you let him go, you know it will be a devastating loss for you."

He listened intently, watching me, Then he sighed and nodded. "I am realizing you are no longer a child. You are a wonderful young woman. Strong, honest, and clearly in love. What more could I want for you?"

He put his head down. "Leave this with me, Kate, but I'd like to see you earlier than Nick. At eight in the den."

I nodded, knowing our conversation was over. We sat for a while together like that, drinking our coffee in silence and waiting for the sun to rise.

I showered and got dressed for day. I had already decided that no matter what happened, I was going for a long ride in the fields after this to clear my head. I dressed plain in jeans and a white t-shirt, French braided my hair, and grabbed my boots on the way downstairs.

It was seven forty-five when I entered the den to sit with my father. I looked around, slightly confused at the scene. I expected Frank, who was there, but he was deep in discussion with other people around the large coffee table. I observed the energy in the rest of the room. My dad and Frank were talking quietly about our invoicing system, with them was Amanda

Beckett from Beckett Grain Supply, whom I had only met once before, other than during early childhood, and another man I had never seen. He was maybe mid-twenties, blond hair, longer and wavy. He looked like a Californian Thor and entirely out of place for the Hill Country. Dressed in jeans and a white cable-knit sweater, he was fresh and clean cut. His shoes looked like they cost more than a vacation. The expression he wore was one of sheer boredom, like he was being forced against his will to sit there with them.

I proceeded to sit at the side of the room in one of the wingback chairs beside the window. The room was large, the thick sofa bed my dad had been sleeping on for the last few months was folded up and the room was meeting ready. The coffee station on the wall was stocked by Melia and a platter of donuts, muffins, orange juice, and teas was set out. Meetings were often held here, it was easy to prepare.

Frank was the first one to speak before I could reach my chair. "Good morning, Katie."

"Good morning, Frank," I answered quietly.

"Amanda, you remember my daughter Katie?" my dad asked her.

"Yes, of course," she said, standing up to shake my hand. "How do you do today, Katie?"

She wore jeans and cowboy boots, her short hair held her glasses on top of her head, as if they had all been in deep discussion before I arrived.

"And this is Amanda's oldest son, Beau. Beau has just moved back here from Stanford after finishing his MBA in business and accounting."

Sounds about right, he looked like sunshine and the beach.

"Hello, Katie," Beau said quickly, standing up to greet me, extending a large hand and reaching well over six feet in height. His voice was deep and smooth. His face etched in a permanent scowl like it pained him just being there.

"Nice to meet you." I answered as I shook his hand. He kept eye contact with me the entire time, but shook my hand quickly. His expression radiated misery.

"Nothing like coming home to Texas, is there?" My eyes were kind and warm. They matched his in color, but that was where the similarities ended. His were cold, fierce. His face never wavered. A sullen Scandinavian god.

"Yeah." He half scoffed at me. "Feels like I never left."

I turned my attention to my dad, confused and done trying to make nice with the morose creature.

"Have a seat, Katie," my dad directed. "Let me explain what I'm thinking for the new year."

Chapter 65 - Solutions
Katie

"Now that we're all here, let's get started," he began. "Katie, as I've said to you, this morning, and over the last few months, I've wanted to be able to focus on the day-to-day of the ranch with you home, while I continue to heal at my own pace. Beau is going to begin working here at the ranch part time. He has a lot of accounting experience and has been telling me how he's able to transform our ancient invoicing system and make our entire business model run more efficiently. His ideas are excellent and modern. He even wants to create social media accounts for us and possibly ranch merchandise as promotional items to generate more income, just like you and I discussed. I would like it very much for you to work with him to learn the ins and outs of the business side. You will still be able to assist with ranching when needed, but I would like you to focus where I need it most."

He turned to Beau. "Katie went to school in New York at F.I.T for the last year and a half, she minored in business marketing. I think you two will work well together."

I sat there. Afraid to move, not really knowing what to say or what was happening. My dad could tell by my face, I'm sure, that I was confused.

"You see, Katie, by you focusing on the accounting and business end of things more, I will be able to work with Frank, Nick, and the other cowboys as I heal and even after I'm better, if you'll still stay on that is. I can spend less time worrying about the business side of things. Let's face it, it's not my strong suit." He smiled sheepishly.

He continued, "I can focus on training them the way I would like. Especially Nick, now that he's moved up. Frank won't be here forever, someday he'll want to retire and Nick will need to be ready for that. I'd like to train him while I'm still young enough to do it. If everyone agrees, I'd like to start this right away in the new year."

What was he saying? Nick could stay? I felt like I couldn't breathe. All I had to do was work with California here and Nick could stay?

I looked at Beau, who was staring at me, waiting for my reaction with a blank look on his face. He would've been very good-looking if he didn't look so pissed off. Charlotte would be drooling over him. I wasn't impressed, but I could work with confident and crusty Mr. California if I had to, for Nick. It would be a cakewalk.

"That sounds excellent, Dad." We exchanged a look of understanding. I knew what he was doing, and I was grateful. He created a special position for me outside the ranch day-to-day that I could focus on. Nick and I would no longer would be in direct connection, removing us as the comparison in the future for any other bunkhouse relationships.

He could stay. Those were the most important words I had heard. He could stay on the land he loved, land he had poured his heart and soul into. Daydreams of spending every single night with him flooded my mind. Waking up and knowing he was here. Sunset rides, dates. Real dates! We wouldn't have to hide anything. I could barely hold back my tears as my dad spoke more with Beau and Amanda. He had come through for me after all. My mind raced. I couldn't wait for my dad to tell Nick.

"Well, that wraps us up, I think." My dad stood to signal the meeting was over. "I have Nick coming next. Frank, you can go if you like to meet the boys. I'll send Nick after we're through. Beau, Amanda, good to see you both. I think this will work out just perfectly." He shook Beau's hand firmly and gave Amanda a hug. Amanda said her goodbyes to us, and Beau turned to me again. He was polished, I sensed he was the brainy type but something in his eyes when he looked at me made me feel like there was a side of him that wasn't about business.

"I guess I'll see you in the New Year then," I said as I reached out my hand, trying to seem very grown up and professional.

"Guess so," he replied, shaking my hand again gently.

The five of us turned to the sound of Nick entering the room. My heart leapt in my chest. Now *that* was the epitome of a man. He was dressed in his jeans, boots, and a gray and white flannel shirt. He was freshly showered and looked prepared for anything. Strong. Calm. Confident. Flashes of the night before rolled through my head. I pushed them away, saving them for later.

He looked from me, to my dad, to Beau, not understanding what was happening. He said hello to Amanda, removing his hat. She must have felt the safest.

"Hello, sweetie," she replied, hugging him. He hit Beau with a look I didn't understand.

"Beau," he said, extending his hand for shaking.

"Nick," Beau replied, grasping Nick's hand. I got the feeling they not only knew each other, but didn't really like each other too much.

"It's been a while. You home for good?" Nick asked.

"Yeah, for now. Guess I'll be seeing you a little more often." For one second, Beau's furrowed brow turned to pleasure. He seemed delighted to fill Nick in. "I'm going to be handling some of Daniels's business for him." He looked right at me over Nick's shoulder when he said it.

"I see, well, good to have you aboard," Nick responded, always confident, always stoic, but glancing between me and Beau.

The two men were so contrasting standing side by side.

They were almost the same height and size but where Nick was strong, rugged, and dark. Beau was a polished, glossy, and blond. You could tell by looking at Nick that he was a cowboy through and through. Beau looked like he had been born with a silver spoon in his mouth and had never known even one day of hard physical work in his life.

My dad spoke. "I'll walk you all out." He gestured to Amanda, Beau, and Frank.

Suddenly, Nick and I were alone in the den.

"What the *hell* is happening?" he asked.

"He'll explain everything," I informed. I wasn't wasting one second. I kissed him quickly, multiple times.

"It's good, trust me, it's going to be okay," I whispered. His expression brightened, like he was letting some hope sink in as my dad re-entered the room and the three of us took our seats.

"Nicholas, this has been a difficult journey for me for the last few days," my dad began. "I struggled with my feelings about you hiding your relationship with Kate and my feelings for you as a young man. I have known you for a long time. You and your family. I know the man you are, inside and out. I know you pride yourself on honesty and loyalty and your work ethic. This is why I found it so upsetting that you felt the need to keep this relationship from me. Both of you, I expected better of you."

He looked at us both, then turned back to Nick. "There are no other people on this earth more important to me than my girls. I don't have to explain that to you. You already know it."

"I do, sir," Nick answered.

"At first, I thought this was something frivolous between you two, but now I can see there are real feelings here."

"Sir, if I may say so, we were trying to figure out what our feelings were for each other before we told anyone else and we knew this would be frowned upon because we were working together. Your rules are well known about that. We love each other and this ranch equally, and I selfishly didn't want to lose my place here or Kate. I also wanted to give you the chance to heal up first, but I want you to know, we would've told you soon enough. Kate says she loves me, and well, I love her too. Very much. More than I can explain with words." He looked at me beside him. "Aside from you and Frank, no one knows."

"And have you? Fully figured out your feelings and intentions with my daughter going forward?" my dad asked directly, sounding very old-fashioned and very southern.

"Yes, somewhere in me I've known what they were since we were kids."

My dad sat back and crossed his arms.

Nick sat quietly for a few moments, gathering his thoughts. He looked at me as he spoke his answer, not my dad. He grabbed my hand.

"I wonder how someone like her can love someone like me, but she accepts me. All the stupid mistakes I've made, my imperfections, my past. She sees me for who I am and who I want to be. To put it as plain as I can, if I had to choose between her and breathing, I'd tell her I loved her with my last breath. I'll love her as long as she lets me."

A moment passed. Nick looked back at my dad. I squeezed his hand.

Always the tough exterior, my dad was rendered speechless. The answer Nick gave him, the honesty, more than satisfied his concerns about his feelings for me.

"Well...that tells me what I need to know then." He cleared his throat. "To fill you in on what Kate already knows after this morning, I have decided to create a position for her that allows her to work here for me separately from your types of duties. She's not part of Frank's staff any longer, she'll work directly with me and now Beau. Although sometimes we will all need to work together, like the next week or so to clean up, she won't be part of the day-to-day work in the fields. This will allow her to finish her studies in design also if she chooses. There are also vacant spots downtown that would be perfect for your mercantile, Kate. I've already looked into it if that is truly something you want to pursue."

He looked to Nick again. "I did this to keep you here, Nick, because truth be told, I really *need* you here and I love my daughter with all my heart. I just want her to be happy. What you did for this ranch, for my cattle and for Sam, in the last two days, has shown me your level of dedication and loyalty to this ranch and this family. I'm sure you assumed you would've been let go, yet you still gave me your all and then some. I respect that."

Nick nodded and my dad continued.

"I also respect why you didn't tell me and the fact that you never waver an inch when it comes to Katelyn. Now, I can't give you my permission to be with her. She doesn't need that, she's a grown, beautiful, and amazing young woman and the man she chooses is her choice alone. But if you are him then I welcome you, son. You aren't the only lucky one. Kate is lucky also to have you. I've made this decision to keep you here, that is, if you'll stay on, based on these special circumstances. It's not a black and white situation. I'm finding the gray area."

He used my words from that morning, which made me smile.

"I would like it very much if you would continue the excellent work you're doing for me here on this ranch. This is your home, as long as you'd like it to be, and you both have my blessing. Just don't fuck it up, either of you." He chuckled.

Tears of happiness ran down my face as I laughed at his words. This was the absolute best-case scenario I had been hoping for.

I stood and went to my father to hug him.

"This ranch means more to me than anything, Daniel, if you had wanted me to, I would've left but I would've never given Kate up. The fact that you're allowing me the opportunity to stay means so much to me. I won't let you down on either account."

He stood to shake my dad's hand.

"Then it's settled." My Dad stood to meet him and let a large sigh escape.

"Now, that's enough drama for me for the year."

Laughter filled the room. I think we all felt the same way.

"You may continue to the field now, son. If you're feeling rested enough and up to it, Frank is waiting for you. It's going to be a long week or two getting this place cleaned up."

"Will do, sir, thank you again." He turned and smiled at me. "I'll see you later then."

I smiled back. Yes, yes he would.

Chapter 66 - If you think we didn't know Nick

Cleanup on the ranch from the storm meant a long day after our morning meetings. Everyone who could help, helped. Frank and I used tractors to haul away large fallen limbs and the chipper was set up to dispose of them, turning them into mulch to use around the ranch. The damage was devastating.

The day was warm and sunny, which put everyone in good spirits while we worked. Sam would be released from the hospital the following day and we were all going to sign a card and send a basket with his favorite foods to come home to. He would be away from the ranch for two months. Daniel figured we would be able to get along without him. The winter was a slower time and he'd be back for spring.

The workday ended before dusk. Frank didn't want to overwork us and he knew we would be going non-stop for the foreseeable future. Even Daniel had been out helping where he could. On top of the cleanup, all of the regular ranch tasks had to be completed. I stopped on the front porch to call Sam on the phone and talked to him for a few minutes. I felt a brotherly connection to him after what we had gone through together. He was doing well. His arm had no pain after three days in a cast, only his ribs were still bothering him and would for a couple of weeks.

"I have said it to Frank too, but bro, I would've died. I'll never be able to thank you enough. The pain...I can't even remember what happened. I think I blacked out."

"You would've done the same for me. It was just what had to be done. You don't have to thank me. I'm just glad you're okay." We hung up with me promising to come and visit him the following week.

The bunkhouse was alive once again when I went in that night. The guys were happy to be back after the holidays and glad that storm was behind us. Some were cooking food and eating. There was a game of beer pong happening on the harvest table. I walked by to head to one of the showers as a loud roar came from the table when someone sunk an impossible shot.

I showered as quickly as I could. Hot water was a commodity around there, especially after a long day.

I changed into jeans and my favorite hoodie and grabbed a water from the fridge before going out to the porch.

Me: *Drive?"*

The feeling of being able to pick her up and take her somewhere was exhilarating.

Goddess: *What do you have in mind?"*
Me: *I think you know. But first, let's do something normal and go for ice cream in town.*

The memory of the night before ran through me. I fucking loved how she looked under me, her hair all around her, her lips, her hands, our bodies moving together. I closed my eyes to hold it together. My thoughts quickly got out of control. She consumed my mind.

First things first, I had ulterior motives tonight. I wanted to talk to her about something, but I also wanted to just see her and kiss her and breathe her in. She had been working in the fields with the rest of us, but I hadn't had any time to see her since that morning.

Goddess: *I'll be ready in ten.*

I went back inside to grab my flannel jacket and my hat.

Carter called to me from the table. "Where ya heading, bud?"

I had already filled him in and this was his way of nonchalantly letting the bunkhouse in on it.

"Just heading out for a bit, into town."

Carter snickered. It started a chain reaction of snickering around the table.

I turned to look at them.

"Alone?" Carter egged me on.

I smiled at them all, glad they were back. "Yeah, myself and Katelyn." A chorus of laughter erupted from the room.

"About damn time," Carter said. "If you think we all didn't know…shit, dude, you must be nuts."

"Plus, bud, she's fucking *hot!*" Will yelled from another corner. More laughter.

Hearing anyone, even Will, saying she was hot boiled my blood.

"I'm an inch from cracking your skull if you say she's hot again," I said back, only half joking, as I left the bunkhouse.

Echoes of laughter rang out as the door shut behind me.

Chapter 67 - Whole
Katie

My dad was sitting in the family room watching football when I found him after my shower.

"Dad?"

"Yes, Pixie?"

He had missed me too. He hated fighting with me, I knew it and I felt for him. Everyone wanted a piece of him constantly and sometimes some things had to give. Even temporarily. I could tell he felt comfortable with his decision. He could make the rules and he would do anything for only three things in this world: myself, Charlotte, and the ranch.

"I want to thank you for today and for Nick. I can't tell you how much this will mean to him to be able to stay here. I saw it in his eyes. He would hate to leave."

"Nick has proven himself here, now he just needs to prove to me that he's worthy of you. I always knew he liked you." He chuckled.

I laughed and remembered something Carter had said to me almost two months prior about Nick picking on me as a kid because he liked me.

"Well, he is coming now to get me, we're going into town for ice cream. I'll be home in a couple of hours."

Being honest was new and odd, but it felt much better than lying and sneaking around. I kissed him on the head and left him there, watching the game. He was my first hero and he never let me down. God may have taken my mom, but the father He left me with was exceptional.

The doorbell rang. This time, I didn't make him wait. There were no games, just us, honest, open, us. I closed the door behind me and jumped into his arms. I kissed him like the day had been painful without him, and trust me, it had been. I took a moment to breathe him in.

"God, I dream about how you smell when I'm not with you." I said to him. "It's delicious."

"Well, I dream about a lot of things too," he whispered. He seemed elated. Free. Like he was truly happy.

He kissed me one more time, slowly and softly on my lips.

"I dream about how your lips feel." He kissed me again. "And how they taste."

He groaned in pleasure and it vibrated against my lips. My whole body went weak.

"I can't stop thinking about you. You're like a drug I'm addicted to. The best kind."

I smiled at him, he was describing exactly how I felt. When we were together I felt...whole.

We had been through a lot in the last week and neither of us ever thought at the end of this day we'd be having a normal date. The things other people took for granted we were basking in.

"So, this is what a normal night out feels like." I laughed as we pulled into Mable's Homemade Ice Creamery. It was a Reeds Canyon staple, located on the corner of Main and Fifth Street. An old brick building that stood three stories high with a covered patio at the back where tables were set up. Twinkle lights hung in soft swoops from one corner to the other and a jukebox from the 1960s played old music and new if you had a quarter. People came from outlying counties just to try the unique flavors and specialty shakes. On the weekends, the owner would greet customers and take their photos at the side of their shop.

A large hand-painted mural graced the brick that had become a photo wall in recent years. The photos were taken on customer's phones with the hopes of it being shared to their social media accounts. The idea had grown their business and made them a small-town famous spot, especially in the summer months when a lineup was near constant during opening hours.

Two enormous cones in our chosen flavors were handed over to us. We sat at the outdoor tables under the lights, eating and talking about the weeks to come. There was a lot to do on the ranch, yet I had never seen Nick so relaxed. When we were finished, I stood to head back to the truck.

"Wait," Nick said, stopping me in my tracks. "Let's do a photo." He motioned to Barbara, who was over at the mural snapping a couple's photo.

I loved the idea. It would be the first picture we were in together since I was a child. "Okay," I answered. It still felt odd that we could just be together.

Barbara was a sweet lady, second generation owner. Mable had been her mother.

"Hello, kids, whose phone am I using tonight?"

I handed the cute little woman my cell and the two of us went over to the wall. Nick stood behind me and wrapped his arms around me, pinching my waist. I laughed and the photo was taken as he kissed me on her cheek.

"Adorable!" Barbara handed us the phone. Nick gave her a tip and shook her hand. I reached up to kiss him. The picture was perfect.

"Twice in one day. Lucky me." A dark voice spoke from behind us.

I turned to see Beau Beckett heading up the steps to the ice cream shop with a pretty blonde girl I had seen before but couldn't place. She was tall and her hair framed her face in a smooth bob.

Nick's face hardened instantly. I realized Beau must have seen us kissing.

"Beau," Nick said. "Following us?"

Beau laughed. "Hardly. Better things to do than give a shit what you're doing, just getting ice cream for Carleigh."

Carleigh Beckett, I remembered where I knew her from. She was Amanda's daughter and two years younger than me. Charlotte used to play with her when we were younger. They were in the same class.

"I didn't realize you two were a happy couple." Beau smirked a devilish grin. I instantly got the feeling he had been drinking.

Nick put his arm around my waist and clasped my hand. Carleigh was bored and decided to roll her eyes and start into the store. Beau turned to follow her, chuckling.

"We'll see how long *that* lasts, won't we, Stratton? You don't have the best track record for keeping a girlfriend." He turned then, laughing to himself all the way into the store.

"Entitled asshole," Nick mumbled. He couldn't stand him. I was right.

We left Mable's then, hopping into the truck.

"How do you even know him? He has to be twenty-five," I said. "I remember his sister. I guess I knew she had a brother, but he was so much older. Charlotte hung around her for a bit in middle school."

"He's twenty-four. He worked for my dad for a summer when we still had farmable land. He was always hitting on Kristin Kessel when we dated. We weren't serious and stayed friends afterwards. She kind of fell for him, possibly when we were still together. I don't know exactly what happened, but they went out a couple of times and then he just ditched her. She was really upset. We got into a fight over it one day on my front lawn. He said she was crazy and called her a bitch, so I punched him in the face a few times. My Dad grounded me for two weeks." Nick laughed at the memory.

"What?" I asked on a laugh. "You fought him?"

"Yeah, it wasn't much of a fight. He talked a lot but it only took one punch to knock him down. He never even told his parents. I think he was embarrassed. He told them he fell off his horse, or so I heard. It must be true because Amanda still loves me. It probably really pisses him off." Now we were both laughing hysterically in the silence of the truck as he drove to Eagles Perch, which looked down on Reeds Canyon.

"I learn something new about you every day." I said to him.

"Last I had heard he was living in Stanford with some girl, partying a lot. There were rumours he got into some trouble out there, but I don't know."

He parked the truck, turned the radio on, and opened the back window.

"I have a surprise for you," he said, changing the subject.

He hopped out of the truck, folding back his hard top cover to reveal a cozy little haven of blankets. "I thought we could just lie here together. The stars are amazing tonight."

We hopped into the back and laid down on our backs, looking up at the sky. He had created a perfect little tailgate bed for us.

There was no one around for miles.

I rolled over onto him and kissed him. No matter how many times I kissed him, it was like I could never get enough.

"I've never seen you dislike someone like that. That was kind of funny."

"Ugh...I hate that he saw us like that. I think he's going to try to hit on you now. One, because you're the epitome of beauty itself, and two, just to get to me. I wanted to warn you about him anyway tonight. He's a snake. Smart maybe when it comes to school, but entitled and sneaky."

He propped himself up on one elbow. "Amanda and Gary have worked their whole lives to have what they have, and they spoiled both those kids beyond measure. When he worked for my dad all he did was complain. I couldn't stand him."

I laughed into the night sky.

"First off, he seems annoyed with life itself, and I can't imagine him hitting on anyone, but on the off chance he wanted to, he has absolutely *no* shot."

Nick kissed me. "Yeah, there's that, and that I'd fucking break him if he tried."

"Touchy," I teased quietly, kissing his neck, secretly loving his protectiveness.

"When it comes to you, always, yes. I can't explain the level of protection I feel for you. Especially now. If anyone ever hurt you..." He closed his eyes, remembering. "Patterson would've been dead if that happened today."

"Well, good thing it was then and not now." I kissed him slowly in between words. "We couldn't do this if you were in jail."

"True. Seriously though, watch him. He is a self-serving asshole. I hate the thought of you having to work with him, but it's worth it."

I silenced him with a kiss. I didn't want to talk about Beau anymore. I lifted his shirt and ran my hands down his sides. I could feel the warmth of his body and see the bottom of my tattoo on his side.

"It will be fine. You are it for me, Nick, there isn't another man alive I could want to be with. I love you so much. Always. Nothing will ever change that."

I kissed him in the dark, squeezing my eyes shut, never before in my life feeling the kind of emotion that was running through me. Suddenly ,I needed him. His kisses and his touch sent my body into a flurry of want.

He pushed my hair over my shoulder, behind my back, grazing my neck all the way down to my waist. Goosebumps covered my body.

He smiled at me the slow, lazy smile he reserved only for me.

I pulled myself up, my eyes open, drinking every part of him in. I'm not sure at what point this incredible man went from being my kryptonite to my own personal superman, but he had weaved his way into the threads of my heart and I was never letting him go.

"Got plans for the rest of your night?" I asked.

He laughed. All his short-term worries about Beau and me seemed to be forgotten, at least for now. We knew, in that moment, under the light of a thousand Texas stars, I was his.

The End...For now.

CONTINUE FOR A SNEAK PEEK OF BOOK TWO COMING OCTOBER 25th 2023

-XO Maddy

Acknowledgements

I am beyond grateful for the support system I have in my life. The one that read my chapters over and over, offering critique and encouragement. The one that make me smile and is the guiding light to my words on the page. The one that delivers me chai tea when I have been writing for hours. The one that brings me joy. I wouldn't have the muse I do if you didn't exist.

Something In The Texas Sun

SOMETHING ABOUT OKLAHOMA

BOOK TWO
HENNESSEY RIDGE RANCH

Chapter 1 - Thoughts in Starbucks
Katie

-Sometimes fate is like going to Starbucks and having the barista hand you all sorts of odd little drinks you don't like and never asked for in the first place.

The line crept along slowly while I waited for my order. Grande chai latte for me and the most boring coffee they had, a Grande Pike Place with double cream, no sugar, for my dad.

I glanced out the window into the spring sunshine, a million things running through my mind as I watched the people ahead of me order.

Am I going to be late? Will the space be what I hope? Can I even sell anything if I get it?

Imposter ran through my mind as I ordered.

I came home six months ago and was no closer to a solid answer about my future now than I was when I left New York. Sure, I had ideas, but that was all they were. I had looked at six spaces and none of them were right. My father was beyond supportive, as always, coming to every single appointment, checking the structure, the storage, the location. He was my biggest champion besides Nick and finally back to his old self. His recovery from a flipped tractor accident which had shattered his knee, his wrist and some ribs had been slow and steady, but he was stubborn and strong and had the body of a thirty-five-year-old, according to his doctor.

I stepped out into the May sunshine, the town bustling around me. *This* was a nice block. *This* was where I kept hoping a space would open up for me. It was perfect, but patience wasn't my strong suit.

Quaint little mom and pop stores littered the street: a boutique-style nail salon, a tiny bookstore, Mable's Creamery on the corner. It was the ideal place for my store, "Homespun Mercantile". The idea had been the easiest part. A little luxury boutique-style store that held my own home décor designs. I had been working on them for months: handmade pillows, drapes, blankets, and laser-cut wood signs. Even some local artisan and indigenous pieces, plus my family's ranch merchandise. A catch all for everything handmade and local. Finding a place for it, though, that wasn't easy.

I smiled as I passed Mable's and entered the passenger side of my dad's Silverado. This block wasn't just aesthetically perfect, it also held a place in my heart. Mable's was the first place Nick had taken me last winter, back when my dad had decided his "no relationships on the ranch" rule could make an exception for ours. We've been together every day since.

We didn't mean to fall in love. We had no choice. It was fate. Drawn out by the universe since we were born, I was sure of it. We were inseparable. When the workday was done, where I was, Nick was, and vice versa. There was never a doubt in my mind. The more I got to know Nick, the more I loved him.

"Sounds like a doozy," my dad said as I climbed in and shut the door. "It's been a bad spring for it, that's for sure."

He spoke on the phone with someone as he pulled out of his parking spot and started the short drive to our destination. Three blocks south onto Edward Street. The store front we were looking at was a "diamond in the rough" with online photos.

An unideal location, but the rent seemed right. I was up for anything if it inspired me and could be fixed up.

My dad would foot the bill for the first year. He said, compared to New York, rent in Reeds Canyon was a drop in the bucket. After the first year I hoped to be able to cover it myself with my booming business.

"Okay, well, keep me posted. We've all had our share of bad weather this year, haven't we?"

I didn't know who he was talking to, but I knew what he was talking about. The ice storm we had seen on our ranch in December crippled the entire valley for almost a week. Leaving Nick and Frank, our cow boss, to help Sam, a fellow cowboy, to safety and for me to have no connection with them for almost forty-eight hours. Cleaning up tree limbs and debris had taken my father's crew two full weeks of long hours.

In the end, we lost seven big, live oaks and nine cattle. So far, we had been lucky enough to make it through the rest of the winter and spring unscathed. My dad liked to remind me one big storm like that every few years was more than enough.

He parked in front of the address the realtor had given us, and I looked around. Disappointment filled me before I even got out of the truck. The space was rough, even from the outside. Plain and boxy with ugly brown vinyl siding. Nothing like what I pictured for my store. Next to it sat a pawn shop and on the other side, a laundromat. I was out before I even went in.

"Okay, take care Stella, talk soon." My dad hung up the phone. It made sense why he sounded so concerned. Stella had been a rancher in the area for twenty years. My parents and Nick's parents grew up with her and her husband, Tom Harris. My mom helped them with their accounting on their ranch. It was where she was coming from the night she died. I hadn't heard their names in ages, but I knew they had moved north about ten years ago. They owned a good-sized cattle ranch in southern Oklahoma called Six Sheers.

"Everything okay?" I queried.

"Yes, Stella's asking if we can have Beau forward her our ID software link. They've had a hard time with rains this spring. They just want to be prepared is all. Looks like a bad few weeks of storms coming for them."

I nodded. At least that would be a conversation for my dad to have with Beau. Although I had to work with him three days a week, I liked to keep my conversations with him as limited as possible. To call Beau Beckett downright miserable most of the time would be a massive understatement.

"Ready to go in? Or should I just drive away?" My dad chuckled, looking at the sad building out his window.

I groaned. "No, we came all the way here, and there is Stephanie, let's get it over with."

I grabbed my latte and hopped out of the truck.

Chapter 2 - Hungry?
Katie

The interior was worse than I could have imagined. Exposed lathe and plaster, mouse traps everywhere, and I got the feeling someone had squatted there.

"I'm sorry you guys, we just can't find us a winner, can we?" Stephanie McLaughlin smiled apologetically. She was a very pretty woman of about thirty, with fairy-like features and shiny, raven colored hair. She always sported deep red lipstick that suited her perfectly. She had been looking with us for a space for three months. This one obviously wasn't it.

As I opened my mouth to respond something dark swooped over my head. I ducked and screamed accordingly. It was clearly a bat. That was it. I was out.

Stephanie was right behind me, and the two of us laughed hysterically, yelling manically and thoroughly freaking out once we reached the safety of the outside.

My dad ventured out a few minutes later. He wasn't about to run away from a bat.

He chuckled when he reached us. "I suppose this visit is over."

I could handle a lot of things after growing up in the country—snakes, bugs, mice, you name it. Bats were the only thing I didn't like. It was an omen, as if I even needed one, but this just solidified it. This wasn't the spot.

"I'll call you both as soon as anything comes up!" Stephanie waved to us both getting into her black SUV.

I looked at my dad. "Sorry you had to come all the way out here."

"It's all good, honey. I got a coffee, some sun, and a drive with my best girl." He smiled at me. "The right spot is out there. These things take time. Patience, Pix."

"Yep."

I sighed and sipped my latte, leaning my head on the seat for the short drive back to our ranch.

By the time we pulled into the long, circular driveway, it was almost lunch time. I could see activity in the distance at the barn. My boots hit the dirt with a small thud, my size not making much of an impact on the earth.

"Thanks, Dad."

"My pleasure darling, what do you have this aft?"

"I'm going to lunch with Nick, then consulting with Beau on the website and maybe getting some sewing in."

"Enchiladas for dinner." He smiled at me. "Don't be late, six o'clock. Will Nick be coming?"

"Probably," I answered, it was a rare day when he didn't.

I made the short walk to the barn, feeling the warm spring sun shining on my face. He came into sight before anyone else, just as he always did, working in the large, round pen training a new mare. I watched him silently from the side of the barn. My heart beat faster just looking at him, as it always did. I took a minute to enjoy watching him while he didn't know I was there.

His gray t-shirt gripped tightly around his strong arms, and his worn cowboy hat shaded his perfect face from the sun. Dust and dirt covered him from a day of hard work. He had overcome so much in his last three and a half years.

He wasn't perfect. He was rough around the edges sometimes. He struggled with his demons daily, and he cursed way too much and said the dirtiest things to me, but he ignited something in me I couldn't describe if I tried. There wasn't a moment when he wasn't downright desperate for me, and he made me feel like the only woman on earth every single time he looked at me.

There was a hypnotizing magic to watching him work. First, gently taking the halter off the new horse. Not driving her to run, not scaring her, but carefully patting her, then walking with her, showing her it was okay to trust him. Using his body to guide her to the other side of the pen. Showing her that he was her best option, and that they were going to be great friends.

No one did this like Nick. No one else had the empathy or the kindness mixed with his level of assertiveness and calm demeanor. Even the animals didn't question him. He was the alpha. Most would rush the horse while training, scaring them around the pen. Nick equated that to making the horse your slave. He didn't want a slave. He wanted a partnership.

Sensing my presence, he looked up. Our eyes locked and he smiled that perfect smile, the one that sent my stomach into butterflies every damn time. He winked and motioned to me, *five minutes*. I smiled and nodded from the sidelines, breathless from just one look.

Five minutes later, he stood at my side.

"Hungry?" I asked.

He looked me over, taking in all the curves my body had to offer. "Always," he responded, his deep voice smooth.

He leaned over and kissed me on the cheek. Activity continued around us. Everyone was used to seeing us together. What was once a secret was no surprise to anyone now.

We made our way to the bunkhouse where they set up a spread for the twelve-thirty lunch break. I went in to greet the cook, who was laying out pinwheels, fruit, and three different kinds of salad. I smiled at him. He was a large, but quiet man. His hair and beard were shiny copper, and freckles covered his face. His eyes were round and kind. He smiled when he saw me. He knew what I wanted. I did this nearly every day. He reached behind his work station into the cooler and pulled out a thermos bag packed with a lunch for two and handed it to me.

"Warm out there, isn't it? Have a good afternoon, Katie."

"Yes, it is. Thank you, you too, chef." I smiled as I left him behind and headed out to Nick.

I hopped up onto my horse, Buttercup, with ease. In my six months of being home, my riding had improved greatly. I didn't ride quite as well as Nick, but I was getting faster and loved to remind him every chance I could.

"Care to race on this fine afternoon?" I asked him with one eyebrow raised. He looked up, his gorgeous green eyes momentarily stunning me and filling with excitement at the tempting challenge I proposed. He loved to compete.

"Oh, Princess, why you gotta be such a sucker for punishment?" He laughed, fixing his hat. Before I could even answer, he was on his horse, King, and taking off into the pasture.

"Shit." I chased after him.

We rode fast and continuous to our daily lunch spot just east of the barn, about one and a half miles out. Our favorite live oak always provided us shelter from the sun there. I almost thought I was going to catch him but he turned quickly, cutting across the corner of the blue bonnet field, kicking his reins to increase King's speed.

"You cheated! You took off before we counted out!" I yelled to him over his victorious laughter.

He lifted me off my horse and swallowed me in his arms while I feigned protest all the way down.

"No, I'm mad. I'm not kissing a cheater!" I was actually slightly annoyed. I may have beat him if it had been a fair start. He'd arrived only seconds before me.

"Okay, fair enough. You can stay angry but listen, baby, can I just kiss you while you get over it?" He kissed my neck, making me forget why I was upset. "'Cause I've been thinking about nothing else but these lips all fucking morning."

His voice was gravel, and he didn't wait for me to answer. The moment his lips touched mine my protests ended. The warmth of his mouth rushing into mine still almost brought me to my knees.

I wrapped my arms up around his neck, feeling the little beads of sweat on the back of it, and traveled down to his wide shoulders. The feel of him under my hands was a shot straight to my core. Visions of peeling his shirt off and pressing my whole body against his in the grass went through my mind, consuming me.

He brought me in closer, deepening the kiss, and my body molded to his. I clenched my thighs together, letting him take over my entire being. I turned to putty in his arms.

Just as I felt his large, warm hands on my waist, he pulled away from me abruptly, harshly startling me out of my daydream. I remembered to breathe, and I'm pretty sure I may have pouted at him for breaking the kiss.

His green eyes looked into mine for a brief moment. He chuckled, loving the effect he had on me. "Later, baby. I know that look, get your mind out of the gutter. We don't have *that* kind of time. I have to meet Frank."

I stood there stunned while he grabbed our lunch out of my saddlebag and continued walking, knowing he'd called me out perfectly on my thoughts.

I pushed them aside for now, mentally calculating the hours I needed to wait to be alone with him as I followed him under the tree for lunch.

Something In The Texas Sun

Maddy C. James

Printed in Great Britain
by Amazon